rld

the North

WESTERN WALL OF THE FOREST

Unskara
THE ICE MOUNTAIN

Mountains of
Menace

EXECUTION RIVER

Fflorl

Pantheera

Nicobar

Entellus

Gyre

Janagua

Manaslangua

RS
98

The Freezing Fire
by
Andrew Bill

October 2000

Copyrights

This book is fully copyrighted.

All rights reserved.

Author's Note

Well, here we go again folks! Enchantica Book Four. There has been some debate in the product development department as to what one calls a set of four books. If three novels are a trilogy, what are four novels? (Answers on a post card to.....)

Those of you who are in the habit of sneaking a look at the back page just to see if those three little words, followed by a string of dots, are there (I know that some of you do!) will probably be amazed to find that this time the last of the three words is different. For the sake of those who do not sneak a look at the last page, I will say no more!

I would like to thank everyone at the factory who has helped in whichever way to make Enchantica the highly successful fantasy range that it is. This novel is jam packed full of new characters and new dragons, enough to keep us all busy for a long time!

I simply must give special thanks to the extraordinarily talented Miss Caroline Briggs, for her superb work on the colour origination of new Enchantica figurines. Where would we be without her?

I would especially like to thank Theresa, my wife, who has suffered the isolation caused by the writing of this novel with patience and grace. She would have liked to have expressed for herself her joy at the completion of this book but is too busy dancing in the street!

1998 is the tenth anniversary year for Enchantica. I can hardly believe it. Who would have thought back in July of 1988 when we launched twelve pieces featuring only Rattajack, Jonquil and Snappa, that the range would build into a collection of 180 pieces.

Incidentally, the tenth anniversary piece: The Adventure Begins, featuring those two well-seasoned heroes Jonquil and Rattajack, is the hundredth piece that I have personally sculpted. Believe it or not this is purely accidental!

When I was given the job of writing the first of the four novels: Wrath of the Ice Sorcerer, I had no idea whether or not I could do it. Well, two novels later, here I am introducing Book Four. Tolkien I ain't! I know that. But I hope these novels have done the job which I intended: which is to add enjoyment and colour to our range of figurines, and convey some of the enthusiasm and excitement that I have felt for this ground breaking range over the years I have had the privilege to work on it.

I still remember the original brief given to me over lunch at the Swan Hotel in Stafford, Easter of 1988. "We want a fantasy range which must include dragons, wizards and crystals!" So, for those of you who have expressed a preference - here is another tale which includes dragons, wizards and crystals!

If you enjoy this book, please tell your friends.
If you do not enjoy this book, this has been Terry Pratchett on a bad day!

Rush! Where are you?

A.B.

This book is dedicated to:

Starman, Rubber Woman, Mad Midnight Biker, Curly Kev, Star Wars Junkie, The Knutty Professor, Still Waters, Randy Bull

and most of all to
Mrs. Ottard

Acknowledgements

Colour Illustrations –   Craig Davison, Colin Paterson, Rob
                                       Simpson

Black and White Illustrations – Colin Paterson, Brian Bill, David Mayer,
                                       Helen Machin, Rob Simpson, James
                                       Brierley

Initial Character Concepts –   Andrew Bill

Enchantica Creative Team –   Andrew Bill, Rob Simpson, Caroline Briggs,
                                       Helen Machin, James Brierley, Andrew
                                       Hull, David Mayer, Colin Paterson, Craig
                                       Davison

Contents

A Deal with Demons

A cruel wind lashed its stinging cargo against the hunched profile of an uskyat and rider. The figure, thickly cocooned with furs and woollen wraps urged the muscular beast along the shallow, snow-lined valley which led to the footslopes of Unskara, the Ice Mountain. The uskyat let out one of its occasional plaintive bellows as if this would in some way appease the wrath of the tempest; but its assault upon them remained unassuaged as they slowly progressed towards the gateway of the mountain. The horizontal snow tore across their sight as an angry white veil, half obscuring the twin pillars of rock that rose out of the snowy dale marking the entrance to Unskara and the threshold of great danger.

The wizard drew his steed into a slight hollow to take a brief respite from the relentless blizzard. The powerful bi-ped lowered itself into the crust of snow, its legs neatly folded beneath it like an incubating bird. Its fur-clad rider stepped around to the lee side of the recumbent beast and nestled down against its flank, head bowed to escape the constant groaning of the wind in his ears. The uskyat extended its long neck until its chin was resting lightly upon the yielding skin of the snow blanket; and thus, for a short while they rested, whilst the fury of the blizzard raged all about them.

The uskyat was not averse to hardship. Indeed the Scoffees, the ice-nomads of the far north, bred the uskyats specifically to cope with conditions that would best most other beasts of burden. Although slightly bizarre in appearance - having a body that bore a greater resemblance to a large, naked, flightless bird than an animal (its strong forelimbs held folded against the body whilst in motion almost like wings), these resilient beasts were capable of feats of great endurance. They were also fast; their muscular legs able to cover even the most difficult ground with long, graceful strides; their thick, powerful tails beating a steady counter rhythm behind them. The uskyat's hide was thick and heavily textured, in places the hard leather moulding itself into calluses or plates giving the creature a rugged, armoured appearance. The head of the beast, which looked as if it might once have belonged to an emaciated, badly formed horse, was an elongated, bowed affair with two long nostrils at its tip, an indication of the animal's renowned sense of smell.

Whilst he had the benefit of a little shelter, the rider eased off one of his thick gauntlets and reached inside the layers of fur and hide wrapped about him to pull out a shiny object on a chain about his neck. He stared at it for a long time, lost in thought. It was a large, flat pendant made of silver; a wolf's head set in the centre of a delicately portrayed snowflake crystal. He had ordered it made by the craftsmen in Anconeus, shortly before he embarked upon what many would have considered a hopeless quest - if not suicide. He had no idea what the talisman signified, he had never come across the symbol anywhere before. He only knew that it had appeared to him in one of a proliferation of vivid dreams, and that a voice, or what had seemed to be a voice, or perhaps a directed thought, had communicated itself to him in relation to a journey, a journey upon which he was now engaged. Although the dreams had imparted no clear message to his unconscious mind, simply a kaleidoscope of cryptic images, somehow he knew that the wolf on crystal motif was imperative to the success of his quest; a quest which itself had been described in the glut of nocturnal illuminations that for a short, emphatic period had plagued his sleep. The imposing face of Unskara had been shown to him, frowning down with unveiled malevolence from the sullen clouds; and he knew that he had to go there, to seek out the King of the Mountain, that this awesome task was the first link in a long chain that connected him to his destiny.

He lifted the pendant and pushed it inside his layers of clothing and then let his head fall back into the soft fur of the uskyat's saddle. His eyes stared idly up into the rugged face of the hollow in which they sheltered. The crumbling bay of dark rock, probably the remnants of a small, collapsed cave, was trimmed with growing mounds and ledges of gleaming snow, interrupting the smooth incline of the valley walls like an exposed crescent of alabaster. The snowstorm still roared with anger, the blizzard slicing the air like a freezing sabre. He would have to continue, if there was to be any hope of ascending the mountain before the snow obliterated all signs of the paths they would need to take. He roused his steed and led him out into the stinging onslaught, raising his free gloved hand to spare his eyes from the worst of the blinding snow. The silent sentinels loomed ahead; and the rider searched through the sweeping screen masking his view for the shape of a figure, or a riding beast, waiting for him in the shadow of one of the lonely pinnacles. He approached the twin giants and saw nothing but a smooth covering of snow about the rocks' feet, no sign that another living being had come there before him. He looked around him, scanning the surrounding desolation for any trace of the one who had agreed to meet him in that fearful place: his confederate, his guide for the near impossible journey he was intending up the fearsome flanks of the great mountain. The name of the anticipated individual hissed through the wizard's teeth in the company of a curse; and his dark eyes damned the empty, snow-lined slopes for withholding his ally. Where was the old goblin? The time for their appointed rendezvous had long passed. The smooth lie of the ground around the rocks seemed to mock him in its blatant, inviolate state. It was clear that no-one had visited that place recently. Despite his frustrations, he just had to accept that the old goblin was yet to arrive; and if he didn't want to abandon his quest at its very beginning, the wizard would simply have to camp down and wait for him.

The rider pulled the uskyat into what little shelter from the storm one of the towering spikes of rock could afford, and tugged the carefully wrapped tent from the bundle of provisions on its back. With a last, venomous glance at the pale horizon, he set to work on erecting his crude shelter.

The tent, given to him by the Scoffees, at the same time as his indomitable steed - along with his present garb and a wealth of other survival necessities - possessed the finest qualities for life in the frozen wastes, despite its apparent frailty. It was so light as to be almost weightless, constructed as it was from the wingbones and membranes of a nalzarg, a species of small ice dragon. The cured skin of the animal was completely impervious to wind and driving snow, and its widely splayed, domed shape offered little resistance to the howling gales that were the permanent inhabitants of the vast snow deserts of Vrorst's old realm.

The wizard lay in the shadowy gloom of his low shelter, the fierce breath of the mountain groaning its threats outside and testing the fortitude of the bowed frame beneath the stretched sheet with petulant shakes. His Scoffee-made snowsuit kept him warm and dry, the skilfully joined lengths of tuthra's hide - a species of aquatic ice mammal - allowing none of the dampness from his frozen bed to seep through to his skin.

As he rested quietly, listening to the complaining wind, and the occasional whine from his uskyat - who was more troubled by being out of sight of its master, than being left without shelter - the wizard began to ruminate upon his situation.

The wizard shivered as an uncomfortable thought burned in his mind: What if the old goblin wasn't coming? After all, was treachery so unthinkable in a goblin? The wizard had chosen the elder denizen of the Mountains of Menace as an ally because of his past links with the King of the Ice Mountain from his former ambassadorial days, and his generous offer to act as guide and translator for the wizard. The meeting place had been arranged and also a time, a time that had now passed. The old goblin had promised faithfully to be there to guide him onwards from the gates; but somehow the wizard felt in the pit of his stomach that to wait for the goblin would be to wait in vain.

What to do now? Turn his back on his destiny? Or face the terrors of Unskara alone? What hope could there be without a guide? On the other hand, what life was there waiting for him back in Anconeus? To continue to play the fool for a fool of a king?

The wizard scrambled out of the tent and regarded the mountain, vague in its majesty behind a seething veil of snow. The sweep of the valley still yielded no lone traveller to his eyes, just an endless, white landscape, hardly discernible from the pearl-grey sky. He was alone. The uskyat roused itself out of the snow when it saw him emerge from the tent; but after withdrawing a little food and a blanket from the saddle pack, he urged the beast back down into the snow, to resume its restful attitude, for the day was almost over and they would not journey again until the morning. He spoke aloud, as if to the uskyat, and said that he would make his decision whether to go on or turn back on the morrow; but in his heart he knew that the decision had been made long ago, before he left the safety of the city walls and made the long trek across the snow plains to the peaks of the ice mountains, from whence rises Unskara the Great.

When the wizard burrowed his way out into the first tentative glow of dawn, he found that the blizzard had ceased. Before its passing it had relinquished a heavy burden of snow upon the footslopes of the mountain. The domed tent was half swallowed by a surging drift that had crept along the valley floor like a ravenous, white beast, devouring every small thing in its path. The uskyat, no stranger to the cruel elements of such extreme landscapes had calmly risen from its low-lying resting place and found a higher refuge. It trotted back through the new swell of snow towards the wizard, kicking clouds of white powder before it as though it splashed through a milky surf.

After repacking the bundle behind the uskyat's saddle, the wizard stared for a moment into the beast's eyes. 'This faithful mount would carry me anywhere,' he thought. 'Even into the jaws of death!' The uskyat blinked and gave a little bleat of impatience. The wizard fed it a handful of food and then climbed into the saddle. He turned the beast until they were facing the menacing rise of the mountain. This was the picture he had seen in his dreams; and he could hear once more the insistent voice that haunted his sleep. It urged him to go on, to climb the forbidden slopes. It told him to leave behind his old life, his old self. No more should he be a pike in a pool of minnows; his was a greater calling. 'At the summit of yonder peak lies the rainbow's end!' the voice continued. 'The means to reach your greatest goal!' The wizard could no more turn his back on his destiny as cut his own throat. Even though to proceed upon his intended path might bring him to a similar end.

The route beyond the stout gate posts of the Ice Mountain was a slow winding climb that traversed treacherous snow-clad slopes and rose upon precarious ridges of wind-lashed rock, that pierced the frozen skin of the mountain like the dark vertebrae of some giant buried dragon. The faithful beast bore its passenger over these hazards with a steadfast pace and a sure-footed tread; never once balking from its task no matter how daunting the path may have appeared. The uskyat only resorting to the use of its powerful forelimbs, which it normally preferred to keep tucked away, when the need for a firmer grip on the terrain became essential. Eventually the tireless creature brought its master to a wide lip of glazed rock which led to a narrow gully of ice rising gently towards the central thrust of the mountain.

The wizard blessed the Scoffees yet again; for his steed, which they had trained, seemed to have an instinct for seeking out the right paths - a gift which had enabled them to make good time on their ascent. The wizard even found himself beginning to feel a measure of confidence as they started along the ice valley. Then his mood darkened when he thought he saw a movement at the very edge of his sight: a shape darting back across the top of the ridge to his left. He turned quickly in his saddle to look back along the crest of the valley; there was nothing to be seen. Nothing, that is, apart from a few tiny globes of snow carving threadlike trenches in the smooth crust as they rolled down the sheer lip of the white wall. The snow balls gathered size as they fell until their weight finally defeated them and they sank into the soft powder. They may have been dislodged by the wind, but a tingling of his senses and a sudden agitation in the uskyat suggested a different cause. The ridge above offered no more clues to the nature of the disturbance, so he spurred his beast onwards, the feeling of eyes at his back - watching, following - clung to the wizard like a second skin.

Somehow the wizard had been able, so far, to shrug off the sense of danger and foreboding that should have been his constant companion on what most would have considered a fool's errand; but the vast emptiness of the landscape in which he found himself, brought a great sense of isolation and loneliness, as if he was the only creature alive in that frozen desert. The brief glimpse of life he had just seen served as a startling reminder of where he was, and the sheer enormity of the enterprise he had undertaken.

Suddenly he was all too sensible of his extreme vulnerability: abroad on the mountain's merciless flanks, naked of weapons or protection. He had no more justification for making this insane trespass into the realm of the Ice King, than the irresistible compulsion that forced him to do so. Neither could he rely on his sorcery to aid him against an adversary, for although he had always described himself as a wizard, his entitlement to do so was small. His greatest power was his skill in word weaving; a great asset in the court of an impressionable king, but little protection against the fangs of a mad snow beast or a swooping dragon. He was there in that dreadful place because of strange dreams; and what faith remained that he would survive such a journey, he placed in their vague promise.

As they progressed, the floor of the trench began to rise until the walls either side were reduced to a shallow ridge of sculpted snow drifts. The feeling of being watched weighed heavier with every step the uskyat took, and the wizard's charged imagination began to see poised assailants in the columns of bizarre shapes that overlooked them. The snow underfoot grew deeper as the full legacy of the previous day's blizzard began to reveal itself. The uskyat, however, seemed hardly even to notice, plodding steadily onward with barely a loss of pace. The sun finally hauled itself above the distant peaks behind them flooding Unskara's eastward face with its unbridled brilliance. A patchwork of violet shadow and glistening white was thrown across their path; the wind-carved waves of snow to their left, casting their dull profiles before them like the tortured trunks of a petrified forest. The wizard and his steed found themselves painted in sombre animation against the general gleam of the opposing wall, the uskyat's legs stretched to mere wafting straws beneath their combined, undulating mass. The wizard's eyes were suddenly drawn back to the pattern of shade beneath the east wall of the vale. He watched in mesmerised horror as the dazzling segments of sunlight between the shadows were gradually extinguished in a slow, liquid movement. The melding shapes eventually converged into a terrible moving profile, keeping pace with them, devouring the taut mosaic of light and shade as it progressed.

The wizard reined the uskyat to an abrupt halt. He felt as if a boulder of granite had just plunged into his stomach; and for a few terrible moments he could not tear his eyes from the great pool of shadow that had also ceased its movement. The wizard shook with hot tremors and tried to swallow a hard lump in his throat. Then, summoning every ounce of his will, he slowly turned in his saddle to look upon the author of the monstrous shadow.

Rising from the crest of wind-chiselled snow, its terrible profile silhouetted against the blazing orb of the sun, was the fearsome form of a wolvine. Pale yellow eyes, gleaming with hostility, shone forth from its dark mass, its powerful outline framed with an aura of burning gold. The giant wolf tensed its great bulk and leapt out from the ridge; its huge front paws, splayed wide with billhook claws, punched through the air leading its massive length in a flying arc towards the floor of the valley. The monster

plunged into the soft ground with an explosion of snow, a mighty cloud of debris hurled in all directions. The rising mountain of animal shook the shower of snow clods from its fur, and then lifted an enormous snarling face to the wizard and his steed, fixing them with a murderous stare. Its eyes were narrowed to evil half moons, its long snout drawn back in deep furrows to reveal drooling, cavernous jaws armed with curved, ochre-stained sabres of ivory. A deep growl, like the drumming of approaching thunder rumbled in its throat, as it very slowly began to creep towards the wizard and the uskyat. The two of them were mesmerised with terror. The giant wolf was holding them in a stalking spell, the overpowering intensity of its gaze freezing their limbs. Suddenly, its mighty jaws snapped furiously at the air, and its dread voice erupted into a screaming roar. The wizard and the uskyat jolted back to awareness as the huge beast sprang at them. The agile steed responded with a screech of terror and explosive reflexes, launching itself backwards with its powerful legs. The wizard was thrown out of his saddle to land some distance away. The nimble creature landed on all fours, and dodged past the lunging fangs of the wolvine to gallop on through the valley, great plumes of snow powder thrown up in its wake. Luckily for the wizard the monster was attracted by the uskyat's flight and chose to give chase to that quarry. This gave the wizard time to get to his feet and scramble up the bank of frost-hardened snow rising from the shallow vale. The wizard's feet were driven by panic as he heaved himself up through the bizarre formations shaped from the driven snow. On reaching the summit of the ridge, the wizard looked down over a vast plain of dazzling white dunes, which sloped in a gentle incline towards the distant frown of a line of cliffs, like the majestic sweep of a giant ermine cloak. The roar of the wolvine, dulled by distance, lifted out of the valley behind him. This dreadful noise served as a spur to start him moving again, and without further delay the wizard began to negotiate the descent to the snow plain below. The ground beneath his feet was treacherous, and several times his boots slipped and skidded as he tried to find a safe footing. Then suddenly the scattering of light powder snow gave way to a solid sheet of ice and the wizard's feet shot from under him. With a wail of surprise, he crashed on to his backside and began to slide uncontrollably down a steep, winding gully that wove through a succession of mounds and wind-shaped banks to reach the floor of the plain. The wizard's downward progress threw up a fury of snow dust which hung in the still air as a billowing trail of cloud. He hurtled along on his back, tossed and buffeted by the dips and bumps that rushed to meet him, the curved walls of the twisting channel catching and releasing him like giant hands playing with a ball. Eventually he was deposited, with a final shove, on to the edge of the great sweep of snow: a sea of gentle undulations rolling away into the shimmering distance.

The wizard found himself at the rear of a modest hollow, two steep arms of the ice ridge down which he had just been hurled, reaching out either side of him to form an elongated bay of open space. For a few moments he could do nothing but just sit where he had been so rudely dumped and gather his senses. His head still spun from his violent gyrations, and he tentatively examined his body and limbs for any sharp pains or numbness that might indicate something broken. After discovering that his injuries consisted of nothing more sinister than a few bumps and bruises, he decided that it was safe to thank providence for his deliverance. He was cautiously attempting to stand when he heard a slow, rhythmic crunching of the snowcrust. Faint at first but steadily growing louder, as what he thought to be the languorous gait of a four-legged animal drew nearer. The wizard stared at the edge of the headland to his left, as he perceived this to be the direction of the sound. Whatever manner of creature it was, it was moving with a determined, if somewhat relaxed pace; and from the noise of its tread it was clearly an animal of some size and weight. And why shouldn't its pace be relaxed? He was trapped; and both hunter and prey knew it. The creature was too close for escape, even if the wizard had the strength for such an exertion. Once again the wizard became paralysed with fear, his legs suddenly losing every ounce of vigour and threatening to collapse beneath him at any moment. His eyes, wide circles of terror, were glued to the point where the shadowy edge of the left promontory met the brightness of the open snowplain, waiting for the approaching creature to saunter into view. Even before the terrible shape appeared, starkly outlined by the dazzling backdrop, the wizard had guessed the owner of the heavy footfalls; and as the shaggy bulk of the giant wolf passed into view the wizard's legs finally surrendered and he dropped to his knees like a condemned prisoner. The devilish, yellow eyes locked on to the wizard's defeated stare, and the snout which shrank back to expose its armoury of elongated fangs narrowed the wolvine's slanted gaze to piercing crescents of evil. Its ghastly face was framed by a thick, bristling mane, erect hackles of steely grey rising as stiff plumes from its swollen neck. The wizard forced his eyes closed and prayed for a swift end; and the snarling of the wolvine throbbed in his ears.

Suddenly, a sharp bark reverberated off the walls about him, higher pitched than the voice of the wolf. The wizard's eyes snapped open to see the huge animal standing before him with its head turned back towards the opening of the bay. Something had entered the gap and was approaching slowly. The wizard could not see who or what it was because of the sheer bulk of the monster wolf filling his vision. Eventually, a pale form came into view from behind the wolvine, cautiously creeping forward, its blood red eyes glaring at the wizard with a fierce curiosity. The eyes of the wolf followed the figure as it passed by, its grisly countenance now a picture of alert deference.

The wizard's fearful eyes saw it was an ice demon. A squat body, about two thirds of his height, covered from head to foot by a thick coat of creamy fur slowly drew nearer. Its face was a dark mask of grey buried within a wild bush of pale fur. A flat nose sat on top of a bulbous mouth, the bearded lower jaw punctured by long, yellow tusks. Two tall, pointed ears, not unwolf-like, feathered with tufts of hair, rose like wings either side of a silver helm.

A barbed sword, a traditional weapon of the ice warriors, hung from a belt of silver mail, and a long wristband, covering most of the forearm, glittered on one of the creature's muscular arms. It may have been a trick of the light, or the fear-fuelled fever that burned the wizard's body, but he fancied he could see tiny blue stars hovering over the shiny surface of the wristband, like midges over water. The wizard's attention was drawn back to the two fiery orbs which burned like the eyes of a demonic cat. The hostility that radiated from that dreadful stare was equal to that of the wolvine, although the giant wolf was now standing in strained obeisance, like a hunting hound waiting for the signal to despatch the quarry. The ice demon continued to appraise the crumpled figure before him and then took a determined step forward. Although its savage face betrayed little expression, a decision seemed to have been reached. Its jaws parted in a jagged snarl, and the silver-banded arm rose swiftly into the air. A hand as dark as its face fanned its five digits, and a rash of blue stars began to sparkle at the claw tips. The hand then balled into a tight fist, and in an instant, with a flash like the glance of sunlight across steel, the sleek shaft of an ice javelin grew out of its grasp.

The wizard's breath caught in his throat. The ice demons' facility for conjuring spears of ice from the air was well known amongst their allies and enemies in Enchantica, but this was the first time the wizard had witnessed it with his own eyes. The warrior's arm reached back to throw, and suddenly the wizard's dread fascination was overwhelmed by a sense of imminent peril, and a surge of adrenaline forced him to his feet. As he did so, a bright patch of light played across the grimacing face of the ice demon, causing it to squint and avert its gaze. The light shard seemed attracted to the creature's ugly visage and hovered there, weaving back and forth across its fierce expression. The ice demon stepped to one side as if to avoid the source of the irritation, but then paused as if stricken by curiosity. The wizard breathed a small sigh of relief as he saw the raised spear-arm lower a little. The ice warrior was staring intently at the wizard's chest, almost trance-like. The wizard then became aware of other approaching figures in the gap, some of them bearing ice spears also, all of them waiting for the first ice demon to act. The wizard looked down at his chest, and almost cried out in wonder. The silver talisman hung outside his clothing, glinting against the rusty brown tuthras hide of his coat. The wizard guessed that it must have tumbled out from inside his warm wrappings during his violent descent of the ice ridge. He flinched as a hairy, clawed hand drifted into view. The ice demon, who had now moved very close to the wizard, gently lifted the shiny pendant on its wrinkled palm, its eyes narrowing in examination. Once again the sunlight caught the polished metal and reflected into the creature's face. The sharp blades of light seemed to galvanise its thoughts, and it turned to the rest of its party with a loud, assertive bark, the talisman still resting against its palm. A flurry of rough, staccato growls, that the wizard assumed was language, passed between the first ice demon and certain individuals of their number; the talisman seemed to hold equal significance for all the assembled ice warriors. The wizard could not tell the nature of the conversation; but a thrill of excitement shot through him. The wolf symbol that his strange dreams had linked with the Ice Mountain, and which had been crafted into a silver pendant in the hope that it might bring him good fortune on his quest, had already proved its worth at the very first test. The wolf's head on snowflake crystal was clearly a passport to favour amongst the feared warriors of the ice kingdom, though as yet the wizard had no idea why; and although he was still a long way from achieving his first goal, the undeniable power of the talisman began to fill the wizard with new hope.

The wizard snagged the toe of a boot in an ice hole and stumbled awkwardly, almost losing his footing. A rough, white-furred hand plunged under his armpit and hauled him upright. A loud, ferocious bark of incomprehensible abuse bellowed into his ear as a reward for his misfortune. The same hand shoved him forward when he began to drop behind the vigorous pace the party of ice demons maintained as they moved swiftly across the wide sweep of the snowfield. They were heading for the dark frown of cliffs that marked the beginning of the steeper climbs. The creature at the head of what the wizard gathered to be a hunting pack, judging by the quantity of game slung over the shoulders of some of the group, was the same individual who had first approached him in the ice gap, and appeared to be their leader. His barks and growls seemed to carry the most authority with the rest of the group, and even the three enormous wolvines that strolled contentedly alongside the pack, seemed to show this individual the most respect.

The wizard was amazed by the apparent docility of these huge animals. All of his previous encounters with the giant wolves of the frozen wastes, had taught him that they were insatiably murderous beasts that were possessed of only one thought: to kill. It had long been averred that the giant wolves were untameable, and therefore of no domestic value whatsoever. They were placed alongside the snowdragons and gluttungs on the list of scourges of the wild. With the Scoffees, it was a right of passage for a youth of their race to hunt and kill a wolvine; only then could he pass into recognised manhood and take a wife - first having presented the cleaned skin of the beast to her father. Yet even the Scoffees, who knew more than any other humans of life on the ice, did not consider the giant wolves that terrorised their beasts capable of being tamed. The wizard wondered what the great and the wise would make of the three subservient monsters currently padding through the crisp powder snow, carriers strapped to their backs, burdening the stacked corpses of the hunted. The wizard tried to surreptitiously glance at the collection of carcasses carried by the three wolves, to see if his trusty uskyat lay amongst the slain. He could only hope that the wily beast had found sanctuary somewhere, beyond the reach of wolves' fangs or demons' spears.

The ice demon hunting party reached the line of cliffs, and without pause began to ascend the vertical rock face by means of a roughly hewn ledge, that wriggled in a steep, climbing weave until it crawled to the summit and joined with a new, loftier path. It was an easy climb for the ice warriors whose roughly textured soles and strong, clawed toes made light work of the difficulties. The wizard found it a punishing task, and yet had cause to bless the Scoffees yet again. This time for the shark skin soles of his boots which practically glued his feet to the slippery rock, giving him far more confidence than he would normally have had on such a precarious path.

Some distance along the new trail, at a brief overhang of rock which looked well chewed by the teeth of the merciless climate, the creatures allowed him a short rest; the first concession they had made to his human frailty. The leader of the hunters - that the wizard would later learn was called Graquat - gave him a sip of a strange, yet fortifying cordial which melted into his chilled bones, wrapping him in a sleeve of warmth and injecting his moaning muscles with renewed vigour. Barely had the efficacious draught begun to infiltrate his weary body when Graquat dragged him roughly to his feet to commence the next thrust of their upward trek. The wizard noted wryly that his talisman may have contained sufficient potency to save his life, but clearly did not override the ice demons' innate hatred of humans and entitle him to courteous treatment; if such behaviour was even possible from an ice demon. The wizard also speculated on their destination; the hunting trip had been an obvious success, the ice demons and the wolves seemed endowed with a more than sufficient haul of meat. Therefore, the hunting expedition over, the only possible path for the hunters now was the one which led back to their high stronghold, wherein dwelled the mighty King of the Mountain. The wizard prayed that the mysterious power of the talisman would not fail when he came to present his case to the great Golitha - the aforementioned monarch.

The overhang of rock retreated from the path to rise a short distance higher up the white slope as a black crescent of low cliffs. The wizard's idle gaze rested on what he first thought to be a large, curious, wind-sculpted dune of snow piled across the cliff top, almost indiscernible from the white slope behind. Suddenly, Graquat gave a sharp bark of alarm, and the whole party froze. The wizard glanced about him and saw that all eyes, including those of the wolvines, were focused on the crown of black rocks; the hackles of the giant wolves rising in stiff crests from their tangled manes. The wizard looked again. There was something strange about the scene, but his mind was simply too numb with the cold to comprehend it. Graquat lowered to a crouch and crawled back towards the wizard, his movements slow and smooth, as if there was something he was trying not to disturb. Eventually, his blood red eyes were staring into the wizard's. There was clearly something important he wished to communicate. He made a hissing noise, which might have been a word, and scowled when the wizard failed to respond to it. Then, in the quietest tones he could manage, Graquat emitted strange calling noises, which sounded remotely like an eagle's cries to the wizard, and he followed these with vague flapping actions with his hands. The wizard looked over at the black cliffs once more, this time determined to see what it was that had so alarmed the group. There was definitely something odd about that carved and wrinkled snowdrift, that so melted into the brightness of the backdrop that the eye had to fight to stay focused on it; he knew that if he only stared long enough the hidden image would eventually reveal itself. When his eyes finally found their mark, a long gasp of astonishment poured from his gaping mouth.

Perched closely together on the top of the cliff, in an attitude of restful disdain, was a line of snowhawks. The dozen or so white dragons were crammed so close to one another that it was barely possible to distinguish one scaly individual from the next. Folded cloaks of white skin were wrapped about their stooped forms like crinkled shawls. Their sleek, pickaxe heads were tucked into their shoulders, powerful hatchet jaws resting upon the pouted fold of their necks. So slight was their movement that they might well have been carved from the snow; their colouration so perfectly harmonised with their environment that they were almost invisible. The rugged cluster of dark cliffs was obviously the dragons' roost, for there were no signs to suggest that the creatures had stirred from that place for some time. They seemed almost as inanimate as the stone. The ice demons, however, seemed in no mind to be casual with this rookery of killers for each one of them was tensed in readiness. Their trail, the wizard surmised, would pass right in front of the dragons. There was no possibility of traversing that open vista unseen. Graquat's keen sight saw that the dragons' eyes were not entirely closed. Each of them had one eye open to a black crescent, enough to keep track of any comings or goings that might be of interest to them. For these were the guarddogs of the mountain. Golitha kept them fed with game or enemies, and in return they used their keen senses and unmatchable speed to defend the upper reaches of the high kingdom. No armies would ever dare to launch an assault on the Ice Mountain now these consummate killers were at liberty. They struck like lightning out of the high mists - death swifter than sight. Between the snowhawks, the wolvines, the gluttungs and the ice demons, Unskara's deadly reputation seemed more than justified.

Graquat broke from a spell of deep thought, and dragged the wizard, by his collar, over to the nearest of the load-bearing wolvines. A low growl came from the huge beast at the wizard's approach, but a sharp hiss from the head ice demon was enough to silence it. After quietly summoning a few more of his warriors, Graquat ordered that the wizard be pushed into the blood-drenched pile of carcasses; the fresh wounds still oozing steaming trickles of red. At first the wizard resisted. Naturally he had no wish to be buried in a mound of corpses. Despite having to stay deathly quiet, Graquat managed to convey some powerful threats with the aid of his barbed knife and explicit sign language. The wizard did not realise it at the time, but the ice demons were not engaging in some depraved entertainment or ritual at the wizard's expense, they were actually saving his life. They heaved him into the pile of damp corpses; the slime of coagulated blood lubricating his body as it was eased inside. The ice demons then turned to one of the other wolvines and loosened a handful of meaty carcasses. They then carried these forward before the rest of the party into full view of the roosting dragons. The dead game was tossed into the snow. The bearers then sprinted back to the waiting group, to crouch down with the others and look on expectantly. They did not have to wait long. One of the dragons on the end of the hideous row threw open its huge wing membranes in readiness to swoop down from its perch. However, so tightly packed were the huddled creatures that the precipitous action caused the impatient snowhawk and its immediate neighbours to tumble down from their resting place in a furious tangle of thrashing wings. A cacophony of ear-piercing shrieks erupted from the ugly scrummage, and soon spread to the rest of the line, who began fighting to free their folded wings. Somehow the falling snowhawks managed to separate and skilfully twist themselves aright before crashing on to the slope, and, stretching wide their great sails of skin, captured the icy breeze to swoop gracefully down on to the strewn bodies. The first dragons thrust down with their legs and scooped up the dead prizes. The slower dragons had to chase the first to try and snatch a portion of their meals; and for a while the air was filled with wheeling, grappling snowhawks; squealing and cursing at each other as the air-borne carcasses were gradually torn to pieces. A few creatures that had been left out of the feast, dropped out of the fray and dived at the hunting group to try and snatch some meat from the wolvines' backs. The loose snow powder hissed and swirled beneath the frantic beating of the dragons' wings, as the great beasts hovered over the party of ice demons. Suddenly Graquat, who had been lying flat in the snow along with all the others, sprang to his feet, wrenched two stout snow boars from their bonds and swung them up into the air. With a burst of speed almost too fast to comprehend, the hawks seized the hurled quarry and surged back into the sky. Finally, the dragons chased each other out of sight over the brow of the slope, and when the last of the white wings had disappeared from the open sky, Graquat called the hunting party to order, retrieved the wizard from his foul hiding place, and set forth once again. The wizard was to learn more of the symbiotic relationship the ice demons shared with the snowhawks; and why the sight of a human, the hated enemy of both, would have sent the dragons into an uncontrollable killing frenzy that would have endangered the whole group. If he had known these things at that time, he might have appreciated the ice demons' actions more, instead of cursing them under his breath as he wiped the glutinous blood smears from his hood and clothing.

The wizard spent a further two nights on the mountainside, in the company of wolves and demons. The ice warriors built a kind of igloo to provide him with shelter from the bitter cold when the temperatures plummeted after sunset. They fed him with strips of raw, bloody meat, torn from the bodies of their catch, which, after he began to suffer painful stomach cramps due to hunger, he finally forced himself to eat.

At last they reached their destination; the mighty river of ice known as Glanhangel. The city of the ice demons was hidden deep within the body of the great glacier; a honeycomb of tunnels and caverns that accommodated the largest gathering of Vrorst's most feared allies. The wizard stopped in his tracks, overwhelmed by the spectacular vista that opened out before him. The hunting party had now climbed so high that the very summit of the mountain could be seen in the misty distance. Unskara's crown was cleft into twin peaks, reaching up to gore the sky like the white tipped horns of some giant snow devil. Descending from between these two ghostly spires was a broad swathe of white that fell like a snaking mane from a giant horned helmet. The ice flow finally came to rest in the yawning gape of a wide valley, its ancient face rising from the curved floor like a massive tidal wave, frozen in time. The soaring cliff of ice was cracked and crumbling like an old, decaying corpse, its brow a crest of clustered spikes that pointed like a splintered crown at the canopy of sky, once again bruised with clouds. Ice demon sentries were secreted in various holes and nooks along the steep climb up the slope of tumbled ice. They snarled their challenges at the party as each of them was approached, and Graquat barked the same reply which seemed to satisfy them. Eventually they reached the jagged mouth of a small cave just below the eaves of the glacier's spiny roof; a fringe of glistening tines hanging from the edge, each one bejewelled with a sparkling droplet. As the afternoon slowly surrendered to the dark threat of the evening, the wizard followed Graquat into the dark hole; and a long journey into the very heart of Glanhangel began.

Secrecy would have been superfluous beneath the thorny crust of the great glacier. Every tunnel or burrow that the wizard was led through looked and felt exactly the same; the light level along the way gradually fell to an inky gloom as they wound deeper into the labyrinth of the city, so the wizard was obliged to use his hands as much as his eyes to guide his movements. One tunnel, indistinguishable from a hundred of its predecessors, ended in a smooth sheet of ice. Graquat halted before this glassy barrier, and lifting his arm with the sparkling silver sheath, spread his palm across its surface. There was a brief flowering of blue fire from the tips of his claws, like the flicker of distant lightning, and the wizard saw in the short lived illumination that the skin of the wall was covered in a dramatic mosaic of crystalline daggers. Then a hole appeared around the ice demon's hand, the delicate pieces gradually disappearing as the wall shrank away until it was only a jagged frame protruding from the body of the tunnel. The procession continued; and unseen by the wizard, the last of the hunters used his special powers to restore the ice door, thus resealing the tunnel behind them.

The next stage of the journey offered little to distinguish it from the previous hike; tunnel after tunnel, burrow after burrow. The wizard found himself inventing new words to describe his weariness, as the old familiar ones didn't seem to do justice to his crippling fatigue. Deprived of daylight, he had lost track of time. He only knew that it had been a very long walk since his last rest. They did begin to climb a little, which hardly surprised the wizard after their long descent from the high cave, but then to the wizard's dismay embarked upon another endless succession of meandering passageways. The wizard noticed the mouths of a number of secondary tunnels open up along their way; and wondered if any of these anonymous routes might lead to the inhabited parts of the city, as, so far, he had seen hardly any evidence of life in that vast, honeycombed slab of ice.

Graquat stopped beside another patterned door, this time standing as a flat plane in the curved wall of the tunnel. He opened it as before, and, seizing the wizard by the arm, pushed him through the aperture. The wizard found himself inside a small chamber, barely large enough to accommodate his height, either standing or lying down. A fur blanket was thrown in after him; and a waterskin and small bundle oozing the rank smell of raw food was left just inside the threshold before the door was remade. The wizard assumed that he was to spend the night in the cell, which considering it was made entirely of ice was not as cold and uncomfortable as he thought it should be. In fact, that was something he had noticed on entering the glacier, and before that when sheltering inside the igloos the ice demons had built for him: the temperature inside these ice structures was actually warmer than it was outside, when simple logic dictated that the reverse should be true. However, the wizard was wise enough to know that the world and all its mysteries paid little heed to simple logic; and a person who wished to succeed in life had to learn a greater understanding. The wizard wasted no more energy on idle thought. He drank from the waterskin and again forced himself to eat the chunks of wet meat that left his beard dripping with blood. He longed for the comfort of a warm room, and the intoxicating smell of cooking food: of bread, cakes, broth and roasting meat. He had never smoked, but suddenly the company of a pipe and weed pouch seemed very attractive. Indeed, his thoughts began to stray towards anything he had ever known that was associated with warmth and the homely light of a flame. The despair of living in a world of ice; a world without the focus of fire, began to weigh heavily upon him. Then he thought of his destiny; his dreams; the promise of a higher existence; and suddenly he was able to bear the prospect of another morning in the chill world of the ice demons. This was but a minor sufferance in the cause of his ambitions. He would endure the cold, endure the loneliness and the fear, they were a small price to pay for the prize which awaited him. Moreover, he reminded himself that he would have to acquire a fondness for such conditions, for as the new Lord of Ice, this frozen world would form the basis of his new realm.

He wrapped himself up in the thick blanket and lay down to sleep; but before his eyes closed on that day he couldn't stop his rebellious mind conjuring up the image of a strong brew of spearherb tea, served in a clay bowl, a swirling cloud of steam rising in twisting plumes from its hot liquid. He could almost smell the aroma, almost taste the exquisite flavour, almost feel the heat of its wetness against his lips. He closed his eyes tight and banished these treacherous distractions from his head. He would focus on his purpose, and it was with that thought that sleep took him.

The enormous figure of the King issued a peremptory bark at Graquat, and the wizard was brought forward to kneel before the great body. The powerful ice demon was cradled, cross-legged in a wide basin of ice, surrounded by a flourish of angled spikes, so that the King's translucent throne resembled half of a vicious flower.

The wizard was dumbfounded at the sight of Golitha. He was a huge creature, almost twice as large as Graquat, who himself was clearly a fine specimen. He had a large, angular head, much deeper in profile than those of his subjects, which broadened out to a great, bulbous crown of fur. His thick roll of brow protruded over his eyes like the eaves of a white-thatched roof, and, paralleled by deeply jutting cheekbones created dark caverns from which peered large, disdainful eyes. Huge, ochre scimitars rose in long, pale curves from his lower jaw, far outmatching any borne by his minions, and were fronted by two smaller fangs, still the size of modest daggers, growing down from his upper lip. His head was wedged between two boulders of fur-clad muscle which continued as immense bulging arms with biceps bigger than the wizard's head. A cape of fur hung down from his broad forearms as they rested upon the mounds of his knees, the soles of his large dark feet showing through its ragged edge. The monster wore a glistening, silver wristband on one arm that shone with the same enchantment as those of his warriors. The only kingly trapping that the wizard could see on the seated figure was a simple circlet of silver above his heavy brow. At first the wizard could hardly believe that this was an ice demon. Golitha was so much greater in bulk and power than those around him that he seemed to belong to a different breed. He had the long, triangular ears and body fur of an ice demon but his other features bore a closer resemblance to an ice troll or to a ....well, Juvula had never actually seen a gluttung; but the descriptions he had heard of the insatiable ape-trolls of the far north (that reputedly would kill and eat anything and everything that trotted, walked, ran or flew into their path), might well have described the monstrous creature before him.

In truth, Golitha was descended from Golanog the Monstrous, one of the mightiest gluttungs ever to terrorise the frozen wastes of the north. How the blood of this terrible creature found its way into the royal line of the ice demons must, for the present, remain a mystery!

The chamber into which the wizard had been brought was of relatively modest proportions, and was occupied apart from the monarch himself by a seated semi-circle of what the wizard assumed was a council of elder ice demons. It was evidently situated close to the roof of the glacier, as it was illuminated by a flood of daylight, filtered through a vaulted ceiling of interlaced ice spears. The wizard had been subjected to a severe climb up a series of steep passages since leaving his tiny ice cell earlier that day, and therefore had not been surprised to find himself emerging close to the surface of Glanhangel.

The eyes of the great king, not blood red like Graquat's, but a wild, boiling orange, regarded the wizard shrewdly. Then the leader of the hunters dug his claws inside the wizard's collar and yanked the silver talisman out into the light. Golitha's mighty bulk leaned forward and his heavy brow lifted in surprise. A flash of amber fire crossed his cat-striped eyes as he stared incredulously at the glittering symbol. The giant's movement started an object swinging back and forth beneath his own head, and the wizard saw that it too was a pendant, suspended from the King's wide neck by a thick chain of silver. When the pendant's motion slowed, the wizard also saw, to his amazement, that although much larger and more opulent than his, the design was remarkably similar: a wolf's head on a snowflake crystal. For a few moments, the two pendant bearers just stared in silence at each other's talismans, neither of them quite sure what the significance of this unexpected coincidence might be. Then Golitha became suddenly animated and spat a volley of orders at Graquat and the other warriors present. The wizard was allowed to assume a seated position, and the hunters marched purposefully from the chamber.

A hum of discreet mutterings drew the wizard's attention to the crescent of creatures who were seated either side of Golitha's ice throne, their heads inclined to one another as they shared various questions and thoughts. There was no question that these were ice demons of great age. Their faces were deeply lined and sunken, and their fur, where it hadn't grown thin, no longer shone with the gloss of youth. Their once powerful forms were now hunched and shrunken, their limbs no longer swelled with strength; but their eyes, still bright and sharp, were not diminished; and they regarded the wizard with unclouded sagacity.

The noise of a scuffle reached Juvula's ears, and for a moment the eyes of Golitha and all his entourage removed themselves from him to regard the source of the disturbance at his back. The wizard decided not to satisfy his curiosity and turn around. Some instinct warned him that showing one's back to a mighty king was not good policy; especially one that for all the wizard knew had the same ability to summon forth ice javelins as his warriors. As the sounds at his back grew louder, they seemed to suggest that a prisoner was being *helped* into the King's presence by a burly ice demon escort. Golitha was evidently displeased with the conduct of the guards for with a single growl he silenced the struggling. Out of the corner of his eye the wizard saw a dark shape lower itself carefully on to the floor beside him, a gnarled, green-skinned hand emerging from beneath the hem of a black cloak to steady itself. The breath of this newcomer came in short, wheezing puffs, the effort of its labours growing louder in the wizard's ear as it turned to him. Finally, a bass, rasping voice broke the silence.

'My Lord,' it croaked.

The wizard turned at last to look at the figure beside him. Framed by the triangulate profile of a black hood, the withered, green face of an old goblin grinned back at him. Two cat-striped yellow eyes peered out from beneath the shade of a prominent, sagging brow; his nose, hooked like a beak, was scratched and pitted, giving him a bird-like, battle-scarred appearance. The lines in his skin were as numerous as the roots of a tree, mingled and merged into a quilted cross-hatch of antiquity.

'My Lord, Juvula?' The voice spoke again, and this time a fence of brown, splintered stubs that were once proud fangs appeared in a wide, unctuous smile. The wizard smiled nervously back, his greeting tempered by the attention of all in the chamber. He spoke to the old goblin: 'Mummichog.......at last!' he hissed. 'At last you appear!'

The old goblin's obsequiousness faltered only slightly.

'I tried to meet with you at the appointed place,' he told the wizard, 'but I was intercepted by hunters, as were you, I understand.' The goblin gave the slightest flick of his head to indicate the stout warriors standing at their backs. 'Naturally I showed them that I enjoyed the favour of the King.' And with that the goblin drew back the hem of his cloak and bared the underside of his right forearm, to reveal the mark of a wolf's head; an old branding scar stamped deep into the wrinkled flesh. It was pale with age but still grotesquely distinct against the dark tone of his skin. The elder goblin made a show of his arm as he spoke, making sure that all who sat around the fire saw the mark. The wizard detected the faintest trace of gloating in the goblin's earnest expression, as he purposefully caught the eye of every individual seated in the half-ring. The king looked on with an impassive stare but the elder ice demons all nodded appreciatively and indicated similar devices burned into their own forelimbs. The superior glint in Mummichog's eyes faded however, when he saw the talisman lying against the wizard's breast. He looked suddenly crestfallen.

'The pain of receiving this mark,' the goblin continued, in a tone which seemed determined to recover lost ground, 'I gladly endured for the honour of gaining the King's trust!' That said, the goblin covered his arm, and bowed his head respectfully. A murmur of approval broke out amongst the elders, but the expression of the King was unchanged.

The wizard gave the old goblin a wry smile.

'Why do you waste flattery on those who cannot speak our tongue?' he asked him.

The goblin now wore a sly expression.

'My Lord Juvula is mistaken,' he replied. 'My remarks were addressed to him alone.'

'Indeed?' came Juvula's response; and he turned his eyes away from the goblin.

Mummichog placed his wrinkled hand lightly on the wizard's arm, and in the calmest, measured tones said: 'They understand more than you know, my Lord. A man's lies burn brightly in his eyes. And they can tell your motives by the music of your speech, even if they cannot understand your tongue. Beware!'

The wizard stole an awkward glance at the King and his elderly council; a ring of glaring eyes stared back at him.

Golitha's sharp tones stung the air once again; and the goblin obediently turned to listen. The King of the Mountain seemed to be addressing them both, with a long, insistent speech that only Mummichog could understand. His brash, staccato language stabbed at the ears of the wizard in a fractured rhythm. The goblin bowed his head respectfully. Juvula swiftly copied him, his eyes darting constantly between the goblin's face and the floor, fearful in case he should miss some vital act of etiquette performed by Mummichog, and offend his deadly audience.

'What now?' The wizard asked of him after they were upright again.

'What now?' the goblin repeated with sickening calmness. 'Why now is the time, my Lord. This is the moment you have been waiting for. This trinket about your neck has gained you the ear of the great Golitha. Now you must tell him how you come to wear this sacred symbol. To tell him of your dreams.'

Juvula swallowed hard and tried to take a deep breath. Mummichog continued to speak to him.

'Think of me only as a chink in the wall that stands between you,' said the old goblin. 'I am your mouthpiece. I will translate your words to the King precisely as you speak them, and likewise his words to you. I will offer no thoughts of my own either way; I dare not. Both our lives depend on it. Are you ready, my Lord?'

Juvula's throat felt as dry as a desert but something made him nod his head. The old goblin spoke forth to the chamber in a rash of guttural croaks and snarls, and when his introduction was concluded, gave a nod of encouragement to the wizard.

Juvula took a few moments to collect his thoughts, and then, through Mummichog's growling tones, began to recount in brief the tale of his long journey from Anconeus to the Ice Mountain, as a sober preface to the more fantastic accounts of his dreams. The confidence with which Mummichog translated his words and the small number of interruptions he had to endure from Golitha, convinced the wizard that this was a good ploy. After a time, he got to the part where he should have rendezvoused with Mummichog at the gates of the Mountain, and the great dilemma in which he found himself.

'The King says that he was impressed by your bravery,' Mummichog told him, after Golitha's jagged speech reverberating about the walls of the cavern had interrupted him.

'My bravery!' the wizard laughed. 'I was terrified!'

'Yes, but you kept going!' interrupted the goblin. 'You knew the danger but still you came on. You could have turned back a hundred times before it was too late...'

'I had to go on,' the wizard said dreamily. 'I couldn't turn back. I knew that if I did...'

'Warriors have to respect such courage,' the goblin continued. 'even in a sworn enemy. Here bravery is venerated.'

Juvula took a moment to peruse the line of elderly faces listening intently to his story. They all seemed rapt with interest. Even Golitha's fierce features seemed to betray an eagerness to hear more of the wizard's adventures; but then life in the high valleys of Unskara, Juvula supposed, must have been a pretty isolated, insular existence. Since Vrorst's demise, the ice demons would not have dared to venture beyond the gates of their realm, and indeed, had little reason to do so. Therefore, what he was doing with his tale was providing news of the outside world. News that only the likes of Mummichog, and other rare wanderers would bring to the dangerous mountain in the days following the rise of the new power in the South. The wizard knew that the reason for their close attendance to him could not be the result of his word-weaving powers, as it was impossible to work this enchantment through the medium of an interpreter; and perhaps, as Mummichog had intimated, attempting a deception would not have been worth the risk with such a perceptive audience.

Juvula decided it was time to broach the subject of his dreams. His very purpose in coming to the Ice Mountain. He told Golitha and the council of elders, through Mummichog's impassive voice, of the time when Vrorst's Orb was brought to King Hadros' palace at Anconeus by Mezereon and Hexerne. The mention of the Dark Sorcerer's name caused a wave of curses to rise from the ice demons; and Juvula was pleased to see that Mezereon's reputation as a coward and a traitor had spread far and wide amongst the former friends of his master. He told them that although no-one, not even the king from whom the fugitives demanded aid, was allowed to lay eyes upon the precious crystal, he, Juvula, the court magus, a minor sorcerer, had been singled out by the voice of the Orb.

'It spoke to me!' the wizard cried. 'In a voice of such authority that it could only have been His! It told me to leave my worthless place at Hadros' side and look to a greater destiny. Then I saw Unskara, rising like a beacon against a blood red sky. The voice told me to seek out the King of the Mountain: Great Golitha, and showed me the secret symbol that would aid me in my quest. I had the palace silversmiths craft the image which I had drawn for them into this pendant. But why a pendant, I wonder? What power urged me away from asking for a brooch, or a badge, or a shield? And why in solid silver? Why not in gold? Or embroidered in simple thread on a tunic or pennant? It was because the power that sent these dreams to me knew that the King of the Mountain wore this symbol in such a fashion; and that to copy this sacred talisman would buy me favour amongst his people. What other power could invade the sleep of a sorcerer and know of this secret? Only the power of Vrorst himself!'

A hiss of urgent whispers erupted from the seated ice demons and the King as the wizard paused, Golitha leaning right out from his prickly dais to confer with his diminutive advisors.

Juvula silenced them by continuing his speech.

'I was desperate to see the Orb. To lay my hands upon its cool, polished skin and feel its potency. At night, alone in my dark chamber, I could feel it pumping its essence through the empty halls of stone like a beating heart. Long icy fingers, feeling, sensing, probing the darkness, searching for me. And I was not afraid, for I knew I had been chosen.......... then came another dream.'

Juvula paused for his memories to sharpen, his eyes glazing over a little, as if he was trying to recall a scene from the depths of his mind. Mummichog and the ice demons sensed the slightest shadow of apprehension creep across the wizard's expression, as his almost trance-like voice began to describe his vision.

'Vivid pictures that outlived sleep to haunt my every waking hour,' he said at last. 'There was a great cathedral of ice. A vast, vaulted space filled with light. At its heart there rose a high platform, a long flight of steps leading up to it. A throne stood at its summit, and seated upon the throne........ the Lord Vrorst himself.'

The whole chamber gasped in awe.

'I climbed the steps and kneeled before him. He looked down upon me and his eyes were dark and terrible. He placed a hand upon my brow and I was suddenly filled with a pain and energy that burned in every atom of my being. Then he began to draw upon my soul, consuming it like blood. I could feel myself shrinking, fading, and then rising as light as dust into the chill air. And then it was I who was seated upon the throne. His robes about me. His crown upon my head. And I saw the world, the whole world laid before me; and I knew that I saw it through His eyes. We had become one!'

'You were consumed?' breathed Mummichog, for once conveying the emotion along with Golitha's words. The King's eyes burned with wonder.

'But not devoured!' the wizard replied with a faint smile. 'That was what Mezereon, in all his fear and arrogance, failed to see: one sacrifices oneself to rise again in another form. He feared to relinquish his soul and subjugate himself to the will of the power that dwells in the Orb. But I do not fear. I long to exchange this weak, inconsequential body for a new stature. One that can draw upon a well of irresistible power, wreak its vengeance upon the world and reclaim its former majesty. I shall lay bare my soul for such a prize and offer it to the Freezing Fire. A willing slave to His will. The clay from which He shall be reformed.'

Golitha leaned back in his throne, and played with his wristband thoughtfully, a cloud of tiny sparks responding to his touch. His large eyes bored into the wizard in intense appraisal. Eventually his gravely uttering burst forth once more. Juvula turned to the old goblin to hear his words.

'A grand plan,' he said, 'but why did the sacred crystal choose you? As you have said, you are not a High Sorcerer.'

'No, I am not,' answered Juvula. 'But then, was not the Ice Lord's first choice a high sorcerer: Mezereon, the Traitor? And how was that trust repaid? Mezereon refused to obey his master's last command because he feared the Fire! Now it is too late for him, his chance has passed. Vrorst chose Mezereon with his last breath. If he had been given longer to choose perhaps he would have thought differently. I believe it is better that I am a lowly wizard, the son of a half-sorcerer. For if I had any measure of magic, Old or Dark, I would try to subdue the Orb, bend its power to my will. I would want to become its master not its servant; and I would utterly destroy myself in the attempt. Only Vrorst had the strength to rule the Orb, and he is dead. His successor must be willing to become its slave.'

'And you are *willing* to sacrifice yourself? I do not doubt your courage for the task.' Golitha asked.

' I am not a High Sorcerer. I have little power to lose. I am nothing; an unwritten page, an empty vessel just waiting to be filled. I wish only to be a conduit for His power.'

The ears of the King were assailed by no dissenting voices from the council seated at his feet. The crescent of elderly ice demons could detect no deception in the wizard's eyes; he was believed. There was however, one part of the mystery still to be explained. Golitha voiced the question, even though he and his advisors had already guessed at the answer.

'Why did the voice of the Orb send you here?' he said.

The wizard hesitated for just a moment. They were about to discuss the very crux of this meeting. The whole point of his perilous sojourn on the forbidden heights of Unskara. Juvula wanted to be sure to pick his words with care.

'I believe that success on the Ice Mountain is the first link in a long chain that connects me with my great destiny.'

'Define success,' Golitha asked.

'Convincing the great King of the Mountain to lend me his aid,' said Juvula. 'Without the aid of the Ice Warriors I cannot hope to subdue those that stand in my way and find the secret paths to the far north. For I know that your people have a knowledge of the Ice Lord's realm that is unsurpassed.'

'And what prize is there in the far north that requires such favours?' demanded Golitha.

'The haven where my transformation is to take place,' Juvula told him. 'The final destination of the Orb. The secret place that the fugitives are making for. I believe it is called The Spire of the North'

Golitha gave the wizard a scornful look.

'You risk your life to come here on the strength of an old legend,' he barked.

'Mezereon and the girl believed in it,' Juvula responded. 'They spoke about it openly before their servant, thinking she was held in a control spell. Hexerne's sorcery is weak. I was able to break the spell and loosen the elf creature's tongue with little difficulty. And why would the Orb show me images of this place if it did not exist?'

'A pity the Orb didn't show you the way!' said the King, prompting a collective hiss of approbation from the elders. 'Where is this place?'

'I think,' the wizard began, 'the King of the Mountain knows that better than I.'

Golitha glared at Juvula and shifted his bulk on the throne dais, almost as if he was going to rise; but then his eyes narrowed somewhat and he said: ' You mean you *hope* the King of the Mountain knows better than you!'

Golitha punctuated the goblin's translation with a strangled gurgle that might have been a laugh. Whether or not the monster's face was smiling the wizard would not have liked to guess. Ice demons and smiles seemed two of nature's natural strangers.

'Apart from my best guides, you'll want an army I suppose?' Golitha continued.

'I believe it will be essential if I am to overcome my enemies,' admitted the wizard. 'There may still be those willing to offer aid to the traitor and the girl.'

The ice demon king settled himself in his royal seat for his final question, the greatest of them all.

'If I was to give you an army, I risk bringing the wrath of the Golden Alliance to this mountain,' he said, 'What can you offer me in compensation, human, sworn enemy of my people? Why should I help you?'

Juvula held the violent stare of the King, and did not falter in his reply.

'Great Golitha,' began the wizard, 'you were always the greatest ally of Vrorst. Higher placed than any of his loyal friends. Your people the most feared of his warriors. If you aid me in my quest, and see me safely enshrined in His secret sanctuary. As the new Lord of Ice I shall see to it that your favours to me are returned a hundred fold. A kingdom as large as your heart's desire shall be yours within my new world. Any prize that you wish, you have but to name and it will be yours. And your warriors will be the first choice for my armies. My strength will be theirs to captain.'

'This was not always so with the Lord Vrorst himself!' Golitha interrupted.

'But let us not forget,' Juvula told him, 'the Orb chose us both for its deliverance. That proves that of all the kingdoms of the North who once swore fealty to Him, it is the realm of Great Golitha in which He now places the highest faith. Vrorst was ever a generous lord to those that aided him. He will not forget your loyalty when he is restored.'

Golitha pondered at length the wizard's words, and prompted by one of his council, asked a further question.

'What happens if you fail?' he snapped. 'What will my loyalty to Vrorst earn me from his enemies?'

'I will not fail, my King,' said Juvula. 'I have seen my destiny - my doom! It will come to pass, there can be no other outcome! I shall be the next Lord of Ice.'

Mummichog was locked in council with the King and the elders for the next two days, and Juvula had to spend a miserable time confined to his tiny chamber. The occasional visit from the old goblin his only relief from the austerity of his grim cell.

One piece of news that cheered the wizard was that his faithful uskyat had been found alive and well. The terrified beast had been captured and brought within the safety of the city, to save it from attack by the wild wolvines that roamed the Ice Mountain. Mummichog also brought Juvula news of his 'boys': four small dragon creatures that the wizard had nurtured from infants, and looked upon almost as his children. Zemorga, Dragora, Grizzagrim and Zaugros were now in the safe keeping of Mummichog's confederates who were secreted in a hide-out close to Eddilee: The Vale of the Wizards, in the west. The four ugly creatures were to be employed as spies, to help 'The Pretender' as Juvula was shortly to be known, gather the vital information that would help him steal a lead on his enemies.

At last, the old goblin, accompanied by an ice demon guard, released the wizard from his cramped cell and took him to the surface of the glacier. Juvula had not been surprised that Mummichog's counsel had been sought by the ice demons. In his days as ambassador for the Mountains of Menace, during the reign of Hellbender's forebear, Jemlin, he had often been sent to Unskara to cement the sometimes frail alliance that had traditionally existed between the demons and the goblins. Golitha, who had reigned over the Ice Mountain throughout Mummichog's career, had grown to trust the old goblin, who possessed courage and shrewdness in equal measure.

Mummichog's long association with the shadowy sect known as the 'invisibles', a secret brotherhood supposed to be dedicated to self effacement and devout meditations, did much to enhance his image of quiet nobility in the eyes of the ice demons.

In truth the 'invisibles' were a covert force that had infiltrated every part of goblin society. Their membership ranged from the influential to inconsequential. No goblin willing to take the vows and practice the bizarre rituals was refused. Hellbender had always tolerated the sect, and by his preferment of Mummichog had allowed it to enjoy great power. The elder statesgoblin found cause to be grateful for that influence, when Hellbender was murdered, and an unforeseen conspiracy worthy of his own machinations had suddenly threatened his life. He had been ordered by Okra to organise his own execution, and this he had dutifully done. He had only neglected to be present at the time arranged. The 'invisible' network had allowed him to disappear into oblivion; and he had spent the time from then on plotting his revenge.

The old goblin led the wizard along a pathway that wound its way through the forest of spikes and columns that were thrown up from the roof of the glacier. The path afforded stunning views of the summit and surrounding peaks, and was made impervious to airborne attack by the bristling array of ice spears that criss-crossed above it. As they walked together, Mummichog told Juvula of what had transpired in the two days since his momentous audience with Golitha. The wizard listened intently, eager to know if the first link in the chain of his destiny had been forged.

'They are very afraid,' Mummichog told the wizard. 'I have never known such fear on this mountain.'

'I thought they placed great store in courage,' Juvula countered.

'And so they do,' said the goblin. 'They prize it higher than all other qualities.'

'But then........,' the wizard began.

'Imagine your whole existence dependent on ice,' Mummichog cut him off, 'and a new sun rises in the East. A brighter sun. A stronger sun. A sun whose power seems to grow with every passing day.

'The Golden Alliance!' the wizard sneered.

'What if the ice should start to melt in the face of this new power?' the goblin continued. 'Your whole world would be threatened! They fear the Great Thaw!'

'But surely Unskara would be safe from that?' the wizard gasped. 'The snows have never receded this far north, or to this altitude.'

'Never whilst there was an Ice Lord alive in the world to protect them,' the goblin replied. 'But He is dead. Unless one should emerge to rekindle His power and claim His throne, Golitha and his people look to the future with dread.'

Juvula seized the old goblin's arm.

'They do not accept then that I am the chosen one?' he demanded.

Mummichog bared his broken teeth in a wide grin. The wizard grabbed his other arm in frustration.

'Will they help me or not?' he cried.

The old goblin wriggled free of Juvula's grasp and fixed the wizard with an impish eye.

'Let me show you something,' he said at last.

With that Mummichog turned and walked away down the path. Juvula followed in his footsteps, snapping at his heels like an impatient puppy. However, the goblin would say no more until he had brought the wizard to the edge of a deep crater that suddenly interrupted Glanhangel's thorny roof. They looked down on to a wide, circular basin with a flat, open floor. The sheer enormity of the space took Juvula's breath away; and although it must have been a natural feature, the activity taking place on the ground gave it the feel of a vast arena.

The floor of the crater was filled with ice demons. The warriors were engaged in various training activities: hand to hand combat, spear throwing practise on flocks of unfortunate birds released from cages; and other orchestrated war games designed to hone their fighting skills.

Mummichog placed a gnarled hand on Juvula's shoulder and pointed the other at the frenetic occupants of the crater.

'Behold!' he cried. 'The army of Juvula!'

The New Vrorst?

Mezereon and Hexerne rode at the head of a long train of warriors, beasts and wagons. The barbarian army snaked its way through the low hills leading to the deep shadow of the Northern Forest, its weaving body bristling with spears, halberds and standard-bearing pikes. Monstrous ice gracklins strode alongside the fighting ranks, giant wingless lizards as pale as the snow, gnashing their powerful rows of teeth in anticipation of bloodshed. Mezereon had originally developed this murderous reptile in a white form and given them to the Zrobokites to suit their snowbound environment; and over the years the barbarians had put the voracious creatures to devastating use against their enemies. The dragon lizards' bloodthirsty natures being equally matched by that of their masters. The gracklin was now an intrinsic part of the barbarian war machine.

The Zrobok warriors themselves were strong fighters; lithe and agile, and skilled in a fearsome array of weaponry. Heavy scimitars hung from their belts, as well as axes, clubs, bolas and throwing blades. Almost all carried a bow and quiver also, for the archers of the barbarian hordes were famous. The Zroboks were highly skilled at the forge, and had developed a variety of malicious arrowheads: there were those shaped like a sharpened bolt that could pierce heavy armour and shields; barbed points that inflicted terrible mutilation if an attempt was made to pull them out; and arrows with tiny tubular attachments that caused them to shriek like a banshee as they flew through the air - the sound of such a flight falling from the sky in the thick of battle could put a dread fear upon their enemy, and make them believe that the barbarians were in league with demons.

BRIAN BILL

The Dark Wizard and the girl who led this formidable army were mounted on ulrax; tall, shaggy, camel-like creatures superbly adapted for the snowy wastes with their broad, flat feet, and their thick, woolly coats. The deliberate, even flow of their long gait made for an exceptionally smooth and comfortable ride, and the height of their backs elevated the rider from the sweat and drudge of the ranks, affording them clean, unsullied air and excellent views. Little wonder then that these superior steeds were normally the preserve of the King and his generals. Ozzak and Zekkel, the two warlords given to the two fugitives by Kazzak to captain the army if and when the need should arise, also rode on ulrax a little way behind, but they trotted to the front, ordering runners on ahead as the weaving column approached the eaves of the great forest.

When the dark wall of trees was declared safe, the army advanced, Mezereon and Hexerne being guided by Ozzak into the shadow of the forest. The head of the column had to cover quite a distance before the last of the warriors had passed beneath the deep canopy. Once they were all under cover the order was given to halt, and the barbarian horde prepared to make camp.

The ulrax delicately lowered to their knees and then crouched down on to the soft ground to allow the sorcerer and the girl to dismount. The floor of the forest was laid with a springy carpet of dry pine needles, the dense roof of the evergreens permitted little snow to reach the ground, a few isolated patches were its only presence.

Mezereon and Hexerne strolled away from their beasts, leaving them to be attended by others, turning their backs on a growing scene of activity as the gathering barbarians set up their bivouac. The two fugitives wandered a sufficient distance away from the horde to prevent their private dialogue being overheard. They had both been amazed and delighted by the success of their ruse. The barbarians treated them like royalty, especially Mezereon to whom the fierce warriors showed great deference. They truly believed him to be Vrorst, their high overlord, on whose command they would unquestioningly lay down their lives. Such fervent obeisance was a rare treat for the fugitives, who had known nothing but long years of hardship and deprivation since the downfall of the real Ice Lord. They had been furnished with new robes better suited to the extreme cold; fur-lined garments that kept them warm and dry in even the fiercest snowstorms. Hexerne's clothes were made from the creamy pelt of a small ice dwelling rodent, prized for its insulating properties and lightness. Mezereon had been offered a kingly ensemble of ermine, and although tempted (as he always was by the trappings of monarchy), in the end he opted for a more discreet dark fur that would better aid concealment in the deep shadows of the forest. The two of them knew that it would be hard to leave behind the privileges provided by the barbarians when the time came. After all, before their defeat, it was the only life they had been used to; but leave them they must when they reached the last stage of their quest: finding the secret path that would lead them to the Spire.

Hexerne regarded the infinity of trees before them, her eyes wary and watchful. Mezereon withdrew a long pipe, a personal gift from the barbarian king, and with a brief command ignited the weed inside its slender bowl and puffed curling tendrils of blue smoke into the still forest air. He noticed the girl's unease as he sat down on a protruding elbow of root and leaned back against a wrinkled trunk.

'What ails you, Hexerne?' he asked with a plume of smoke.

The girl drew her arms across her chest and shivered a little, her eyes remaining fixed on the forest. Eventually she answered him.

'The trees have eyes,' she said. 'Can't you feel their stare?'

Mezereon threw an untroubled glance at their surroundings, blowing a smug smoke ring through rounded lips.

'Of course I do,' he said at last. 'We are in the land of the Gentlil. They are bound to be watching us.'

The sorcerer continued to breathe shapes into the hushed air beneath the trees, where not even the slightest breeze stirred the branches. Not content with rings, Mezereon began to manipulate his emerging stream of breath into a variety of diaphanous forms: serpents, birds, ghostly figures and as a finale a rising dragon, whose smoky wings seemed to flutter with a shimmering spectrum of iridescent colours. The look of patient contempt on the girl's face suggested that Hexerne was not impressed. Indeed she wore an expression of resolved forbearance that a jaded mother might wear with an irritating child.

Mezereon closed his eyes and let his head fall back against the scored texture of the bark, his pipe hand resting idly on his knee.

'Did you think the elves were simply going to sit back and let us stroll through their realm unmolested?' the sorcerer said with an almost bored tone. 'They are sworn to destroy me. Of course they are out there.'

With that, the sorcerer placed the thin shaft of the pipe to his lips once more and resumed his relaxed attitude.

'I learned a lot about the Northern Elves from the time I spent with Silfaladil,' Hexerne told him, Mezereon's persistent calmness only fuelling her irritation.

'You do surprise me,' came the languid reply.

'Yes, and if you'd had more to do with him, you might have learned something too.'

Mezereon fixed the girl with a cold stare.

'I know all I need to know about the Gentlil: they want me dead!' he told her.

'But they have enchantment, Mezereon!' the girl whined. 'Have you forgotten how Silfaladil got us out of Anconeus? He made us invisible, Mezereon! Don't you remember?' Hexerne threw a sweeping gesture towards the busy encampment beside them. 'The barbarians do not have magical powers. If it comes to that neither do we! The only enchantment either of us seems capable of is the tiny amount required to light your pipe and make your pretty smoke pictures! Do you really believe this horde of thugs is any match for an enemy that can make itself invisible?'

'Yes,' Mezereon answered her, rising to his feet. 'As a matter of fact I do. The truth of it is, my dear Hexerne, the barbarians and the elves have crossed swords before. When Vrorst held court in the Old Frozen Palace, the

31

Zroboks used to make frequent sorties into the forest under Rhazgor's supervision. How else do you think I got my elf prisoners for my experiments?'

Hexerne could not help a shiver slithering down her spine at the thought of Mezereon's old profession, even though at one time she had been his apprentice.

'Over the years,' the sorcerer continued, 'I developed ways of countering the Gentlil trickery. I sent the barbarians ointments to rub on their skin and armour to protect them against the spell webs. They took antidotes to ward off the effects of the poisonous mists. I created enchanted mirrors with which to see an invisible enemy. All of these gifts the Zrobokites still possess. There isn't one elf trick that these warriors have not seen and overcome.'

Hexerne was dumbfounded, this was not the answer she had been expecting. She suddenly began to think better of the vicious horde that was slowly spreading its encampment beneath the trees.

'But Silfaladil must have known this?' she asked at last.

'Of course.'

'Then why did he agree to guide us to Zrobok?'

'He had no choice,' the sorcerer told her. 'How could he refuse and still keep up the pretence that he was trying to help us?'

Hexerne's eyes lowered to the ground and there was an air of sadness about her that angered Mezereon. He had always suspected that the girl's relationship with the elf prince had grown deeper than he would have liked. Mezereon never doubted for a second that the handsome young elf would have betrayed him to the murderous justice of his people at the first opportunity; but whether Silfaladil would have surrendered Hexerne to the same fate Mezereon seriously doubted. The affection the boy had showed in his eyes for the girl had not been feigned. There had been real feelings there, Mezereon was certain of it. Their friendship had been helped by the young prince's firm belief that Hexerne had elfish blood in her. Which indeed by her physical appearance she might well have done. She shared many of the northern elves' characteristics; she had the tall, slender figure, the pale delicate features, almond eyes, and of course the straight black hair that fell as a thick, glossy mane to her waist. Hexerne, of course, was unable to confirm or deny Silfaladil's assertion, being entirely ignorant of her parentage. Only Mezereon could do that, and on that subject he remained resolutely silent.

So, this possibility had added a note of mystery to Hexerne and Silfaladil's relationship that had fast proved irresistible. As far as Mezereon had been concerned Zrobok could not come too soon.

Hexerne had managed her parting from the young prince surprisingly well when the time came for them to descend from their mountain hide-out and approach the barbarian city. Mezereon could only guess that the bonds tying Hexerne to the Orb were stronger than those newly forged with Silfaladil. Nevertheless to the sorcerer's chagrin, the girl clearly remembered the elf prince with fondness.

'You can be sure that no sooner had we left the barbarian settlement with our army,' Mezereon told her, 'than Silfaladil would have raced to the palace of his father at Ckristinial to warn them of our coming.'

'Then they must be well prepared,' Hexerne replied shortly.

The sorcerer shrugged. 'Perhaps,' he said. 'But they will not attack us yet. We are too close to the outside. They will wait until we have reached the deepest parts of the forest where their enchantment is strongest - then they will strike!'

Zekkel approached Mezereon, his eyes deferentially cast down, and the latter visibly grew in stature as he assumed his given role. The barbarian lord informed the sorcerer that the encampment was in place, and his faithful servants awaited further orders. Mezereon congratulated Zekkel on the speediness of the operation and that he would come directly. He was about to follow after the barbarian when he heard Hexerne's sneering laugh.

'It's ironic isn't it,' she said with a bitter smile. 'You were the one chosen to be the new Vrorst, and you refused the honour. Yet, to these pitiful ruffians you are Him! If only they knew that you are too much of a coward to embrace his power!' The girl moved nearer to the sorcerer until their faces were close together; her steely eyes boring into his. 'Enjoy it while it lasts, Mezereon,' she hissed. 'For soon your reign will be over; and you will have to go back to being nothing!'

The girl stepped quickly past the sorcerer and made for the two ulrax which were now surrounded by a deep encampment of hastily erected shelters. Hexerne was going back for the Orb; lately she began to fret if she was parted from it for too long a time. Since leaving Zrobok, the girl had assumed the role of Orb-bearer. The barbarians had provided a strong knapsack for its transportation, and all along their journey the precious crystal had hung from the girl's saddle.

For Mezereon the change was symbolic. It was as if the Orb was using Hexerne as a way of telling him that his chance had passed, the Orb had now moved beyond his reach and was meant for another. Not Hexerne, of course. The sorcerer knew that the girl was not capable of wielding the power of Vrorst's Fire Orb. So this meant there was someone else. A rival, then? Mezereon had consistently refused to accept Vrorst's legacy; but he knew in his heart that he could never suffer anyone else to possess it in his stead. If there was to be a new Lord of Ice, a new Vrorst, then Mezereon was determined that it was going to be him; but not in the way that the Orb demanded. Mezereon would triumph in another way, in a manner of his own choosing. Despite what the likes of Hexerne might think, he, Mezereon, would wear Vrorst's crown; but in his own time and on his own terms. Not as the slave of the Freezing Fire.

The Enchanted Vale

Jonquil's eyes shone with excitement. He had never lost the thrill of dragonflight in all of his adventures. It still filled him with the same gut-churning joy that he had felt on his very first aerial jaunt with the mighty Arangast above the great spread of the Green Sky Forest, when he and Rattajack had helped the three Guardians recover their Sacred Vessels. His present mount might not have been as impressive as the Guardian of Summer but the experience was just as exhilarating. Jonquil was seated behind Tuatara's lieutenant, Hawkhood, on the swift snowcharger known as Silverstreak. Thrace, who was also accompanying them on this flight flew Cloudweaver. Moonrider, Storm-arrow and Snowspear were the other dragons in their small formation, which boasted the magnificent Starblade, flown by Tuatara, at its head.

The banf's lightness of heart was due not only to his present activity but also to the two happy reunions he had recently enjoyed. First with Rattajack at Jacquarondi, after the soaring beam of golden light, projected from the tip of the white tower, had guided Tuatara's dragonflight down through the dense layers of mist to find him, and secondly with Meadolarne at Anconeus.

His joy at seeing the terragon again had been overwhelming, and he had held Rattajack to him with tear-filled eyes. He had been sad to leave Gembranosus and Sheylag after so short an acquaintance, but Tuatara's business was urgent and they could afford no delay. So they left the mist shrouded tower of Jacquarondi and flew on to the majestic fortress of Anconeus, where Gembranosus' seeing-orb had shown Meadolarne to be. King Hadros had taken great pains to protect the young banfina, after she had been left in his possession by Mezereon and Hexerne, not wanting to incur the wrath of Jonquil's powerful friends. The king had been tempted to aid the two fugitives after listening at length to their persuasive demands. It had been Juvula, his chief advisor, who had urged him not to do so. The minor sorcerer persuaded the impressionable king to imprison them instead, and then sent one of his own spies to the castle at Glostomorg to inform the Alliance of their catch. The mystery of how the prisoners escaped was made even more puzzling by Juvula's subsequent disappearance. The hapless Hadros was left with only a young banf female, albeit one of major importance, to show for his involvement in such high matters. Jonquil and Rattajack had run across the floor of the bedchamber in which Meadolarne was being cared for, and all three cried with relief and joy at their happy meeting. The kind attendants who had nursed Meadolarne back to health

after her ordeal at the hands of Hexerne, declared her fit to travel and so Tuatara's flight spread its wings once again, to commence upon the next stage of their journey. Meadolarne had been placed in a position of great honour behind the Ice Witch, and a quaking Rattajack shared Moonrider with Brabast; the terragon had never acquired a love for dragonflight; every journey was an ordeal which he endured with clenched fingers and closed eyes.

The great sweep of land beneath them rose and fell, and tilted this way and that as the dragons soared and planed across the rolling scene of mountains and valleys, seeking the fastest wind currents to carry them along. They were travelling in a northeasterly direction, and Jonquil noticed that the terrain below was beginning to soften a little. The harsh, rugged heights of the mountains that marched eastwards from the wall of Vrorst's kingdom grew further apart; and the valleys that were scooped out between them ever wider and shallower.

Ahead of the dragonflight, a broad furrow of land slung between two craggy ridges came into view. The belly of the smooth trench was covered with a dark growth of evergreen trees, which rose to a stark line against the snow-clad shoulders of the rocky walls. Starblade angled her great wingspan and slipped gracefully into a diagonal descent, the other snowdragons gently tilted their own wings to follow in a lazy, twisting line. Hawkhood reined Silverstreak to do likewise, and Jonquil could not help a grin of delight as the land tipped and turned slowly before them, a great wave of slopes and ridges rising to fill their sight. The line of snowdragons which gradually receded before Silverstreak to a tiny dash of white that was Starblade, slowly wove its way downwards towards the valley until their gliding forms shone boldly against the growing dark stain of the valley forest. Soon they were skimming over the points of the evergreens that filled the gentle curve of the ground like a giant green carpet, the dragons instinctively closing to a 'V' formation beating their wings to a shared rhythm. Suddenly the covering of trees surrendered to a glistening sheet of water that swept away the trees on either side and opened out into a wide, silver lake. The winking surface was lifted into tightly chiselled peaks by the light wind, and at its heart it dipped and rolled with the heavy swell of deep water. As Hawkhood urged Silverstreak forward to take his turn at the head of the formation, the trees marched back in, narrowing the lake to a bending swathe and finally a wriggling forest stream. As Jonquil's mount eased passed the others, the banf waved to a terrified Rattajack and an ecstatic Meadolarne, whose long hair flew out behind her in golden ripples. The banfina gave Jonquil a broad smile, her eyes sparkling with excitement, as she crouched behind the elegant form of Tuatara.

The valley began to turn eastwards, the thick lining of trees that had flowed unbroken beneath them for so long, bending away out of sight in the distance. Silverstreak was replaced at the head of the flight by Cloudweaver, and as the new snowdragon led them through the sweeping curve of the valley, Jonquil noticed that the air was beginning to feel warmer. In fact, when he thought about it he hadn't felt the air's icy bite for quite some time, and the lake they had crossed.....shouldn't it have been frozen? The sea of evergreens, ubiquitous denizens of the colder climes, began to falter, giving way here and there to colonies of broader trees that seemed less jealous of the ground and allowed patches of turf to show beneath the emerald roof of the forest. The snow on the higher ground, thinner and less confident than before, drew itself up on to the loftier levels shunning the lusher scene below. The landscape began to lose its wildness and take on the character of manipulated nature. The trees grew in managed groves, interspersed with flower speckled meadows and crystal pools. The familiar patchwork of agriculture spread across the lowlands, framed with snaking hedges, whilst closely cropped blankets of pasture rose against the shallow slopes. The curved walls of the valley finally opened out to form a broad basin, dammed at its far end by a steep face of pale rock. Cradled in this mountainous embrace was Eddilee; a city of halls and houses, bejewelled with orchards and avenues and all manner of living blooms. The dragonflight rose sharply at Starblade's lead and circled high above the spectacle, an unadulterated shaft of sunlight bathing the sheltered plateau in golden warmth. Jonquil noticed with wonder that the lands beyond the rim of the closed valley were still firmly in the possession of Winter; dull and lifeless, a monochrome of snow and ice. The valley over which they now wheeled in slow, lazy turns seemed to defy the dominant season and shine forth with a blazing spectrum of colour. An old memory suddenly jumped into the banf's mind, and for an instant he was back at the enchanted pool in the Green Sky Forest; an oasis of life and colour that had been transformed by the magical presence of the Summer Vessel. The sight below Jonquil gave him the same feeling of unnatural splendour, of a landscape created by forces working against the continuing legacy of Vrorst's power.

Tuatara took the flight down to a circle of grass dotted with sheep. The oblivious flock scattered bleating in terror as the roar of swooping wings heralded the descending spiral of dragons. By the time they had dismounted and rubbed the stiffness from their limbs, the dragonriders were surrounded by a modest gathering of onlookers. Jonquil and his two companions inspected the ring of faces that surrounded their group. They seemed quite unremarkable. Neither the banf or the banfina could see any clue to the mystery of the extraordinary city in the crowd of people who had collected to greet them. Rattajack, however, could perceive a quality in the gathering; an energy which radiated from each individual in different measure. The terragon had sensed this energy before in some of the characters that he and the banf had encountered during their adventures. To the banfs, these people looked like ordinary men and women, but the terragon knew that they were not.

A tall, slender female approached Tuatara from the circle of inhabitants. To Jonquil's eyes she was young in years, little more than a girl, but her bearing was straight and proud. She wore a simple, full length robe with a neat turban made from a brightly coloured scarf wrapped about her head. She and the Ice Witch exchanged formalities, the girl's expression was stiff and formal, her eyes far from friendly. Indeed, Jonquil noticed a number of scowling glances directed at the graceful form of Tuatara as she followed the girl through the parting crowd. The people muttered and tutted audibly as the Ice Witch passed by them; but no open words of disdain were spoken aloud.

Thrace and Hawkhood followed closely after Tuatara, sensing the coolness of their welcome, the latter beckoning to the banfs and the terragon to accompany them. The remaining three dragonriders stayed to attend to the six chargers, as the beasts would suffer no stranger to lead them to the place of food and rest which awaited them.

The girl, who had introduced herself to the Ice Witch as Ethva, had been sent to bring them to a grand hall which stood in the centre of a large open square. Jonquil marvelled at the surrounding architecture as they walked through the pleasant, tree-lined streets leading to the square. The roofs of the timber-framed houses were tall and steep, and sloped almost to the ground. From the apex of their gable ends extravagant wings of ironwork scrolled forth; great combs of intricate spirals and waves curling into the air, and continuing along the spine of the roof as a rising decorative crest. The great hall which they now approached had been embellished with a wealth of ornament befitting its rank. The majestic fronds which swirled about its long shape had been coated with gold and adorned with crystal, so the fabulous building captured the radiance of the unbridled sun and sparkled with the opulence of a treasure casket.

Ethva was about to lead them inside when she noticed Tuatara staring at the dazzling ostentation. The girl gave a snort of disgust.

'Ridiculous, isn't it?' she snapped. 'You'd think the King of the World lived here!' With that, Ethva turned and entered beneath a glittering arch of golden fretwork, her slender form swallowed by the darkness of the interior.

At the end of a long chamber, illuminated by two rows of tall windows, a figure sat on a golden throne. He had the long, greying hair and beard of a wizard, and a not unkind but not wholly beneficent face from which peered two sharp, amber eyes, warily appraising the approaching group. He was dressed in a richly embroidered robe of scarlet velvet, which fell in luxuriant folds to his jewelled slippers. His tanned, wrinkled hands shone with gold; the huge stone on one of his rings shining from his laced fingers like a star. As Ethva neared him with the small dragon party in tow, he reached across to a velvet hat resting upon a cushioned pedestal and lifted it to his head. The scarlet peak glittered with the precious decoration that had been lavished upon it. Jonquil and the others couldn't help but think that here was the king of the city, such was his apparent wealth and status. Tuatara, however, did not seem overly impressed, and the girl positively disdainful. Ethva turned to address the Ice Witch and her party. 'Behold,

Heskel the Flamboyant!' she proclaimed with a sneering tone.

The seated figure admonished her with a stern bark.

'Ethva!' He then continued in more measured tones. 'Please give me my proper title.'

The girl raised and dropped her shoulders with an angry sigh, raised her eyes to the ceiling and said: 'Behold, Heskel...' she began.

Heskel interrupted her.

'Lord Heskel!' he chimed.

'Lord, *so he insists*, Heskel, *self-proclaimed*, Head of the, *non-existant*, Council!' Ethva bellowed.

Heskel rose to his feet raising his palm to the girl. 'Thank you, Ethva!' he said, before addressing Tuatara directly. 'You must excuse my servant.....'

'Servant!' Ethva wailed.

The regal character continued. 'You must excuse, Ethva. She is an unfortunate victim of the bitterness of youth. We can only hope that experience will sweeten her.'

Another violent gasp burst from the girl's throat and she turned, with a face almost as red as Heskel's robe, and stormed from the chamber.

The robed figure bathed the remaining assembly with his warmest smile.

'Please allow me to introduce myself properly,' he said with a soon-to-be-irritating, patronising tone. 'I am Lord Heskel, Grand Wizard of Eddilee, Head of the Council of Sorcerers. I place myself at your service, Lady Tuatara, and that of your confederates.' The wizard ended his short speech with the merest nod of his head, and then seated himself once more.

Tuatara introduced each member of her party in a brief, perfunctory manner, clearly not deeming the overdressed character sitting before her worthy of any greater effort. Finally she said to him, not unpolitely: 'This vale still falls within the realm of Horcust Rothgilian, High Wizard of Eyesand?'

Heskel looked stung.

'Yes,' he said at last, 'the Dragonmaster is still our High Lord.' Then he followed quickly with: 'But I am the power here! In the city! The people look to me for leadership. Horcust is hardly ever here. He seems to have little appetite for association with his own kind. I think he prefers the company of dragons.'

'When will he come again?' asked Tuatara.

'It is impossible to say,' Heskel replied. 'He comes and goes without word. It is most unsettling. However, he is sure to know of your coming. The dragons keep him very well informed. I have no doubt that he will be here very soon.'

'Let us pray,' said Tuatara, 'that he comes soon enough. Do you have any other news that I should hear, Lord Heskel?' The Ice Witch tried valiantly to keep the tone of mockery from her voice.

'Indeed, I do!' cried the wizard, clearly overjoyed at Tuatara's use of the title. 'I received word only this morning from the South. By advance messenger from the Silk Palace! The Lord Yelver is coming.'

'When?' demanded Tuatara.

'The Spring herald said he had only about a day's lead on his master. So perhaps tomorrow or the day after!' Heskel was evidently quite thrilled at the prospect of holding council with a High Wizard of Spring, he was almost trembling with excitement. 'And,' he continued, 'there is a possibility that the Lord Roshir might also journey here from Dragonskeep. To confer with his brother High Wizard.' Heskel's hands clasped together with joy. 'Oh, imagine it!' he cried. 'Two High Wizards of Light here in Eddilee! What an auspicious gathering we shall make!'

Tuatara fought to restrain a wry smile at Heskel unhesitatingly including himself in the company of the great and the good. A mischevious question formed in her mind. 'Erm.. I wonder, Heskel,' she began, 'this title of Grand Wizard? Where does it come from? I am not familiar with it.'

The smirks of the two dragonriders standing behind the Ice Witch were covered by a sudden feigned attack of coughing. Heskel visibly coloured before Tuatara's inquiring stare; and for a moment his words refused to form on his lips.

'It.. it... is a title given to me by the denizens of this city.. er.. in gratitude for my services.. er.. to them,' he stammered. Then with a huge shrug of false humility, and in quite musical tones he added, 'I am quite unworthy of it, really, but they insist I use it.'

Tuatara's eyes quickly scanned over the richness of the wizard's attire and the decoration of the chamber which he inhabited, and was not fooled for one moment that Heskel believed himself to be unworthy of any honours or gifts, however great. Her gaze returned to the wizard.

'If there is someone who could direct us to our quarters, we have had a long journey and would like to rest,' she told him.

'Of course, my Lady, of course,' Heskel said rising swiftly to his feet. The Ice Witch turned and began to stride towards the entrance, the companions and the dragonriders following in her wake.

'There is one other thing,' the wizard continued, 'I feel I ought to mention.'

Tuatara stopped but did not turn around, her shoulders tightening with a sharp intake of breath. 'Yes, my Lord,' she managed politely.

Heskel stepped down from the small platform supporting his throne and shuffled over to the Ice Witch. He leaned forward to speak conspiratorially over her shoulder. 'Your Ladyship may encounter a little hostility from a few of our inhabitants here in Eddilee. You must understand until recently you were considered a great enemy.'

Tuatara turned to face the wizard, and Heskel took a sudden involuntary step backwards; but the witch's face was not angry, it was sad, her naturally pale cheeks now drained of all colour. She looked visibly wounded. Heskel seemed to sense her distress and tried to mitigate his statement.

'I of course am acquainted with the facts of your great service to the cause of the Three Wizards, so naturally I do not count myself amongst those that...that....' Heskel's voice trailed away, and Tuatara's soft voice, almost a whisper, saved him from the silence.

'There is no need to explain,' she said. 'I understand.'

'Some of them find it hard to forget...... the old days,' the wizard added apologetically.

Tuatara cast down her eyes. 'I understand,' she breathed, almost inaudibly.

The wizard suddenly found himself bereft of words, and could find little sympathy in the eyes of the witch's companions, which now glared at him angrily. Heskel turned and called into one of the dark corners of the chamber. 'Sunjack!' he cried.

A small figure, no taller than Jonquil, stepped into the light. He had clearly been there all the time, standing in the deep shadow, watching and listening. His inconspicuousness had been aided by a full length cloak and cowl of black cloth. The stocky figure had a slightly crouched demeanour, and it wasn't until he stood at his master's side that the group saw his face. Jonquil felt a rash of cold creep across his skin, this creature oozed deceit and mischief like a bad odour; the reaction seemed to be shared by all in the long chamber with the exception of Heskel. The servant had a pallid, slightly green complexion, and the contours of his face bore a trace of the squashed and heavily browed features that betrayed his parentage. His pupils were not cat-like but almost round, and his obsequious smile contained only relatively ordinary teeth, stained and broken as they were. Sunjack was obviously not a full-blooded goblin, but could undoubtedly trace some thread of his lineage back to the Mountains of Menace. However, it was not his mixed blood that made the black robed servant so repulsive to the dragon party, for they were all experienced enough to know that not all goblins of the world were innately evil. There was something deeper with Sunjack. One only had to look into those devilish eyes, shining with a pernicious guile that never slept. It was incredible that Heskel chose to place any trust in this individual.

'Sunjack will show you to your rooms,' Heskel announced with a smile, quite oblivious to the consternation of his guests. 'They are all prepared.'

The servant bowed respectfully to the dragon party, and walked purposefully towards the entrance. 'Follow me, honoured guests,' he said with an encompassing gesture, his oily voice dripping into their ears. Tuatara threw Heskel a questioning glance. It was not common practice for noble wizards to employ goblins or even half goblins as their servants; although it was not unheard of. What made this relationship so surprising was that this unsavoury creature had a devious, repugnancy about him that was apparent at almost the first moment of meeting; and everyone seemed quite aware of it except Heskel. Tuatara addressed the servant directly.

'You! Sunjack. You wear the garb of an 'invisible'. Do you belong to that sect?'

Sunjack was momentarily unnerved by the bluntness of the question; but he gathered his wits and with a well-worn smile delivered his guarded reply.

'It is my humble privilege so to do,' he said.

'Don't try and hoodwink me with your feigned piousness,' snapped Tuatara. 'I know your brotherhood for what it is.' The halfgoblin's serene expression strained a little at the witch's attack; but he resisted the urge to counter. A nagging memory lurked at the back of Jonquil's mind at the mention of the word 'invisible', coupled with the simple black garb the servant wore; but it was too faint and distant to grasp. Tuatara directed a comment to the wizard.

'A strange choice for a servant, Heskel.'

The wizard, finally sensing the unease that had been caused by the discovery of his servant, leapt energetically to his defence.

'Sunjack is an absolute fountain of information!' he proclaimed. 'He has contacts with many races beyond the valley. He soaks up news like a sponge.'

Tuatara was sneering, 'Aye! And just who does he give this news to?'

'Why, to me,' replied the wizard hastily. 'Only to me. The loyalty of my servant is beyond question. He fulfils a very valuable service to our community.'

'Gathering information,' Sunjack interjected in his best silky voice, 'can often be a messy business. Some of the best secrets are to be found in the gutter; but that place is too lowly for such illustrious beings as yourselves. It is better that such work is left for me.'

The witch was about to pursue this matter with Heskel, but then the weariness of the long journey from Anconeus overwhelmed her like a heavy wave dragging at her limbs. Tuatara decided to leave the subject of Sunjack for another time. Then the weaselly voice of the halfgoblin whined in her ear once more.

'Please follow me.'

The dragon party allowed Sunjack to guide them to their quarters and then gladly surrendered to their fatigue.

Jonquil and Rattajack rose with the sun the next morning. They decided to leave Meadolarne asleep, as she was still officially in a state of convalescence after her ordeal with the fugitives; and the banfina's nurses in Hadros's palace had released her only on the understanding that she would continue to receive her much needed rest. The banf and the terragon looked in on Meadolarne in her adjoining chamber, and then emerged into the crisp morning air. Their lodgings were in a large house that easily accommodated all of the dragon party in various chambers. Despite Heskel's protestations Tuatara had insisted on remaining with the group. The wizard had offered her a superior residence that he considered more suitable to her rank, but the Ice Witch politely and firmly refused, not wishing to incur more ill feeling from the citizens of Eddilee by appearing to want to elevate herself above them.

The sun was yet to climb above the eastern wall of the valley, so the quiet streets of the city were lit by a soft, reflected light. Jonquil and Rattajack stood in the middle of the dirt road and regarded both directions. The way to their left led back to the heart of the city and the great hall, the way to the right to what looked like open pasture and then woodland. They didn't take long to make up their minds and set off with a happy stride along the country road.

There were a few of the inhabitants up and about at that early hour; driving carts, herding animals or simply taking the air like the two companions. They all hailed the banf and the terragon as they met them, and stopped their toil or business to engage them in friendly conversation. Predictably, it was Rattajack who attracted the most interest, unique as he was outside the Banf Kingdom, and Jonquil was impressed by how knowledgeable some of the people were on matters that he had come to think of as strictly wizards' business. Why simple farmers and herdsmen should be privy to the ancient articles concerning the arven and the Wells of Hope, he couldn't imagine. There was something else curious about the people of the enchanted vale, for the banf was convinced that the city and the surrounding lands were protected by sorcery, but he couldn't quite put his finger on what it was. Somehow they didn't seem to belong to the tasks they performed, each of them possessing an intellect or capacity far exceeding that required for their function. With these thoughts to mull over, the two companions passed through the outskirts of the city and left the houses and their intriguing occupants behind.

Jonquil and Rattajack were soon striding beside open meadows; rolling slopes of grassland studded with the nodding heads of wild flowers. The sun had cleared the mountains and was pouring its brilliance into the great swathes of vibrant colour. It felt good to feel the warmth of Summer on their backs once again, and to listen to the pleasant hum of busy insects attending the myriad blooms. The bright hues of gorgeous butterflies flickered about the banks and hedges, some of them settling upon long spikes of purple or pink that leaned out over the lane, and flourishing their exquisite cloaks before the eyes of the two companions. Larks lifted from the swaying grass pouring full-throated carols upon the mellow breeze. Their warbling melody, interrupted by scarcely a breath, continued long after their blur of wings had carried them far beyond sight into the cloudless sky. The rasping song of grasshoppers set the whole sensual chorus of sound and colour to a lazy, intoxicating rhythm; and, conspiring with the warmth of the sweet air, slowed the enthusiastic gait of the two companions to a meandering stroll.

Eventually the road faded away until it was merely a grassy path wandering aimlessly through a thick grove of fruit trees. Somehow Jonquil and Rattajack were not surprised to see the branches above them heavy with fruit, even though by rights the trees should not have produced such bounty until the approach of Autumn. To contradict further the conventions of nature, the verdant floor of the grove was inhabited with a full compliment of Spring bulbs: bluecaps and snowbells, and proud regiments of golden trumpets. The two companions had to smile at this bizarre phenomenon. It seemed that whatever power it was that had created this enchanted valley, rather than promote the passing of the Seasons of Light in turn, had decided to enjoy all three at once.

The sun-dappled carpet of thick, emerald grass was soft to the tread, and after picking a small selection of ripe fruit from the hanging larder about them, Jonquil and Rattajack settled down at the base of an old rose apple tree to enjoy a sumptuous breakfast.

'No mushrooms here, Ratters,' the banf said to his friend. The terragon shook his head in agreement. 'At least not in these parts,' the banf added. 'That means that this is not a Well of Hope, doesn't it? Because if it was, the enchantment would come from the ground. And if there was Old Magic here, there would be mushrooms here too, wouldn't there?'

Rattajack piped in affirmation.

'So where does the enchantment come from to sustain this place? From Heskel, do you think?'

The terragon gave Jonquil a look that suggested he did not.

'H'm, I don't either,' the banf agreed. 'Perhaps it comes from this Horcust Rothgilian. The High Wizard who prefers the company of dragons! I like the sound of him, don't you?'

Rattajack nodded enthusiastically.

'He must be a pretty important fellow if this valley is only a part of his domain,' Jonquil said through a mouthful of apple.

Suddenly Rattajack sprang to his feet, ears forward and eyes flashing. Jonquil stopped munching apple and followed the direction of the terragon's stare. The banf's sensitive ears also picked up the soft swishing sound of a movement in the grass. Jonquil had no reason to suspect that there was anything sinister about the noise they had heard, other than the intense reaction of his companion. The fire that blazed in Rattajack's amber orbs gave warning that his special senses had detected something dark.

In the near distance a low shape could be seen, creeping slowly behind the taller growth beneath the trees. It had a dark, stooped appearance, and Jonquil's first thought was that it was Sunjack spying on them. Then two pointed canopies of skin opened out above the undergrowth, and lifted the skulking figure into the low branch of a silver pear tree. The limb sagged beneath the weight of the cumbersome creature, which bobbed and lurched precariously whilst it tried to balance its weight. A small shower of silver sparks flashed against the shaded backdrop of the fruit grove, as a cluster of the tiny pears were shaken from their stems, and fell through a shaft of sunlight on their way to the grass. The creature finally steadied itself and folded its wide wings. It tucked its ugly reptilian head between its shoulders, and sat there motionless, slouched on the gently wagging limb, watching them. It was a most incongruous sight; a creature of such repulsive appearance at rest in a place of such sublime, natural beauty. The banf would have described the beast as a dragon had it not been for its small size: it was no greater in stature than Rattajack. It had the features of a biped dragon (albeit drastically reduced): two taloned feet, a horned head with powerful jaws, a long balancing tail, and broad, clawed wings. It was too large for a widger, and far too small for a carrier. There weren't many dragons of Jonquil and Rattajack's acquaintance that could safely perch in a fruit tree! The banf was intrigued, and started towards the perched gargoyle to take a closer look. A firm grasp on his arm arrested his progress. Rattajack was afraid of the dark creature and wanted to go no nearer. The winged reptile continued to stare impassively at the two companions, betraying no motive for its presence.

'Do you think it's spying on us?' Jonquil asked of his companion who was already backing away nervously. 'If this was the Banf Kingdom we would know that it was friendly,' he continued. Rattajack's fearful expression communicated only too clearly to his friend that he strongly believed otherwise. Jonquil had always trusted in the terragon's instincts in the past, he could see no reason not to do so now. So, the two companions retreated from the creature in the fruit tree, and wended their way through the grove.

They wandered beneath the sun-glittered bower of trees for some time, sampling a variety of delicious fruits, and marvelling at the way nature had been so manipulated in that place as to allow budding leaves, clouds of blossom and mature fruit all on the same tree. Jonquil held a ruby plum up to a beam of golden sun, and the scarlet globe filled with light, just like a jewel. When he bit into its succulent flesh, the sweet juice spilled from his mouth in sparkling rivulets. By the time they reached the border of the luscious grove, the banf and terragon had thoroughly slaked both thirst and hunger in one, Jonquil's pockets and pouches bulging with more plunder for future meals. They emerged from the eaves of the fruit wood on to a sweeping slope of pastureland, an occasional cluster of tall, broad-canopied trees, giants compared to the diminutive denizens of the grove, rising from its smooth rolling contours. The two companions decided to climb to the top of the slope, to see what view it might afford over the lower lying areas of the valley. They were barely half way up the slope when a large shadow swept over them. Rattajack instinctively flattened himself against the short grass with a note of alarm. The banf dropped to one knee and shielded his eyes against the glare of the sky with cupped hands to try and see what manner of beast it was. Eventually the banf focused on the winged shape of the same small dragon that had intruded upon them in the fruit grove. It flapped ahead of them towards the brow of the hill and casually alighted on the very spot that they had been making for. Just as before, the languorous creature folded itself into a torpid slump and just stared down at them. Jonquil clenched his fists.

'Come on, Ratters,' he cried. 'That ugly lizard isn't going to scare us off this time!'

And before Rattajack could stop his friend, the banf was ascending the upper half of the sloping greensward with purposeful strides. The creature moved not a single muscle as the banf approached, but its eyes fixed Jonquil with an evil glare. Undaunted, the banf pushed on until he was within ten strides of the hunched beast. Then the creature visibly tensed, its limp form rising to attention. It hesitated for a moment as if it thought the banf might think better of his bold advance, but when Jonquil didn't falter, it let forth a complaining croak, threw open its long wings and trotted into the air. Its wide span carried it away from the banf in a low skimming flight that followed the gentle undulations of the grassland leading towards the rim of the basin. When it had covered sufficient distance to deter pursuit, Jonquil saw wings like dark banners push against the air and its body drop to the ground. As Rattajack scrambled up the slope beside the banf, the distant creature resumed its characteristic, slumped attitude and stared back at them.

'It must be love!' Jonquil sighed ironically.

Meadolarne awoke from a blissful sleep, feeling fresh and calm. The terrible dreams that had plagued most of her nights in the palace at Anconeus now visited with less frequency and horror. Her dreams had been partly the reason why her nurses had agreed to her leaving so soon, thinking that the forbidding castle itself might have been responsible for some of the banfina's nocturnal demons. In truth, as Tuatara had suspected, Meadolarne's nightmares had been mostly the work of the Orb, using its subtle powers of suggestion and thought-control to torment her sleeping hours. The mighty globe had no other purpose for inflicting such misery upon the unfortunate female than the sheer devilment of doing so; and also, perhaps, in some way, the torture of Meadolarne was a form of revenge against Jonquil, whom the Orb had marked as its greatest enemy. Now she had left the deep shadows of Hadros' palace, and the Orb was far away, Meadolarne felt a lightness in her heart that she had almost forgotten how to feel. Her memory of the dark days she had spent with Hexerne, and later Mezereon, were still mostly a blur. The girl's holding spell had taken control of her conscious mind and forbidden remembrance. Meadolarne was glad of this, for she did not wish to remember; and she hoped the recollections of her time as Stobe, Hexerne's handmaid, stayed locked in the depths of her subconscious mind forever.

The banfina slowly opened her eyes and gazed about the room. Slivers of sunlight poured through the slats of the wooden shutters, painting bright bands upon the facing wall of her chamber; each one a pale, distorted impression in light of the scene beyond her window. She turned over on to her stomach and lay rapt with fascination, as tiny blurred figures made up of hazy patches of colour that were cloaks, robes, shirts, topped with blobs of pink that were faces, moved back and forth along the narrow pictures. With childlike wonder Meadolarne realised that she was watching the bright images of people moving about in the street outside. She could see them talking to one another. Pulling carts or pushing barrows. Bright white shapes, that her ears told her were horses, entered and departed from the living pictures, crossing the wall in blurry, liquid movements. The banfina wasn't sure whether this wonderful phenomenon was the work of enchantment or not, but it was certainly magical in her eyes; and she would make sure that she showed the delightful spectacle to Jonquil and Rattajack, if it was still there when they returned. For without even climbing from her cot, and going into the next chamber, she knew that the two friends were not there. They would have woken early and left with the dawn to go exploring. As much as she adored adventuring with her loved ones, that morning Meadolarne was grateful they had left her to her bed. Her long, dreamless sleep had left her feeling strong and refreshed.

Meadolarne wondered if Tuatara had a similar light show taking place across her bedchamber walls, and decided to go and see. She knocked lightly at the witch's door, and hearing no answer tentatively pushed the door open. Just as the banfina's had been, Tuatara's chamber was still shuttered against the morning. There was a strange, reflected glow flickering on the walls as if a fire made of blue flame was burning in the grate. Meadolarne searched the gloom of the interior and saw the Ice Witch. She was sitting erect and motionless at a small table, her eyes pressed shut, as if it took great effort to keep them so, her palms held against the round form of a crystal globe. Flashes of ice-blue lightning flickered inside the orb, splinters of its profound brightness leaking through the witch's fingers to dance on the darkened walls. Without willing it, the banfina found herself calling out the Ice Witch's name. The fine, aristocratic head that was being held so stiffly the tendons of her neck stood out like wire, slowly turned as if to look at the banfina. Meadolarne stared at Tuatara's closed eyes, and she thought she could see pale lights playing behind her taut eyelids. Then the eyes flew open, and to the banfina's horror, the whole of the witch's eyes were blazing with blue fire. Meadolarne screamed in terror and backed against the wall. In an instant Tuatara peeled her palms from the skin of the crystal and was herself again. She rose swiftly from her chair and lightly grasped the banfina's arms. Meadolarne flinched at her touch but the Ice Witch soothed her with gentle tones.

'It's all right, Meadolarne,' she said quietly.'There is no need to fear.'

The banfina's eyes were wide with apprehension as they stared into the face of the statuesque figure that towered over her.

'I am not one of your demons,' added Tuatara.

The Ice Witch lowered herself to her knees and took Meadolarne's hands in hers. She smiled warmly at the banfina, and waited until she felt some of the tenseness ease between them.

'Are you still afraid of me?' she said at last.

'Y-your eyes,' Meadolarne stammered.

'I know,' said Tuatara, the same eyes now full of sympathy. 'It was the blue fire from the crystal. We ice enchanters need to call upon it at times. It is a powerful, sometimes dangerous force that can be harnessed to cleanse and change. But I fear there is a poison deep within me that even its great potency cannot reach. A poison that threatens to overwhelm me.'

'Did you draw upon it because of what that Heskel said to you,' asked a somewhat recovered Meadolarne. A shadow fell across Tuatara's face and her eyes lowered in shame.

'Perhaps,' she said softly, 'It is true that I will never be able to undo the great wrongs of the past. I can only try to be worthy of the trust that the Three Lords have placed in me.'

The witch rose and walked to the window, a flood of sunshine burst into the room as the shutter was pulled back. Tuatara smiled. 'These things should never be discussed in the dark,' she said.

Meadolarne moved closer to her.

'What is this poison that you speak of?' she asked the sorceress

'The same stuff that your dreams are made of, I think.'

'But my dreams have got better,' Meadolarne told her. 'In time they will fade altogether.'

Tuatara's troubled gaze returned. 'Perhaps,' she said.

'What do you mean?' the banfina insisted.

The Ice Witch ushered Meadolarne to the chair by the small table, the banfina keeping a wary eye on the now dormant power globe. Then Tuatara knelt down beside her and once more took her hand.

'You and I both have secrets locked within us,' the sorceress began. 'Yours of the time when you were under Hexerne's controlling spell. Mine of the life I knew before Vrorst turned me into Tuatara, the Ice Witch; and banished all former memories to the furthest reaches of my mind. I don't even know who I am. Where I belong. All this he stole from me.'

'But it is different for me,' Meadolarne replied. 'I know who I am; and I do not wish to know whom it was Hexerne turned me into.'

Tuatara spoke again. 'But don't you see, Meadolarne,' she began, 'it is not wise to leave these things buried. For they cannot lie quietly. They fester and grow black, and work evil within us. We will never find peace until they are confronted and laid bare.'

The banfina's eyes were heavy with concern, and they were slowly drawn to the crystal Orb.

'Is that what you were doing with the blue fire?' she asked Tuatara.

49

The witch's face brightened into a weary smile.

'Partly,' she said. 'And as I told you in that respect I failed. But I was also searching the labyrinth of my mind for another buried memory. One that it is possible Vrorst placed there intentionally; in case he should ever have need to call on me to use it. I am afraid in this task I also failed. But Meadolarne, forgive me. I have filled your heart with woe. Be of good cheer. The harm in you is small, and can soon be mended. And then the dreams that come to you in sleep will be light and joyful.'

Meadolarne seemed to take comfort from these words, and her smile returned. The shadows lifted from her green eyes once more. She stayed and shared breakfast with Tuatara, and then the two of them stepped out into the bright morning; the road beside their lodgings already bustling with industry.

The two companions rested on the brow of the hill for a while, enjoying the view across the roof of the fruit grove to the hazy rise of the far mountains. Every now and then, Jonquil fancied that the breeze brought him faint snatches of music. Soft, enticing ripples of whistling notes that tantalised the senses. Rattajack also stirred when the distant tune came, his ears swivelling to try and catch the tiny string of sounds; but as soon as he and the banf began to focus upon it, it was gone. With a few backward glances at their distant watcher they set off again; this time to descend on the other side of the hill, which sloped down to a smooth grass-lined trench. Once the two companions were out of sight of the dragonwatcher, they ran as fast as they could along this meandering trail, until once again they found themselves beneath the shade of trees. They peered out cautiously from behind the stout trunk of an iron beech, whilst they caught their breath, half expecting to see the winged silhouette of their reptilian pursuer swoop into view. To their delight, the only beings they saw fly across the sky was a small flock of white doves. The banf and the terragon exchanged a smile of relief, and began to wend their way through the trees.

It was a modest wood, tall and airy, with broad stripes of sunlight slanting through the high canopy. A girl's voice was calling softly in the stillness of the trees, and as they drew nearer to the tuneful sounds they saw a figure, tall and straight, bathed in a bright pool of light, her arms uplifted to the sky. She continued to call, oblivious to her audience, and as the two companions watched, a string of white doves fluttered down to her from above, their pristine plumage making them shine like stars in the wide, golden beam. The delicate birds hovered about her, some of them alighting on her fingertips and then lifting away again. Jonquil hailed the girl, and Ethva smiled when her eyes readjusted to the shade and she recognised the two companions.

'I wondered who they belonged to,' the banf said as two of the white birds fluttered down to investigate him. 'We saw them flying about up there.' He strolled up to the girl with a dove perched contentedly on each index finger. Rattajack had acquired a third, which peered at him curiously from the top of his head.

'They follow me everywhere,' Ethva told them. 'I hatched them from eggs.'

Suddenly a shadow crossed the sun, and the six birds leapt into a twisting cloud of wings and sped through the hole in the canopy. The girl and the two companions peered at the patches of sky through the ceiling of leaves to try and catch sight of what it was that had just swept over the trees. Jonquil and Rattajack could guess only too well.

'Something scared them,' Ethva said, shading her eyes with her hand. 'I hope there isn't a hawk flying today. Some of the wizards keep them.'

'The wizards?' Jonquil asked.

'Yes, the likes of Culzean and Nedwen,' the girl replied. 'Glazzabal keeps eagles in his treehouse; great, monstrous birds that could carry off someone of your size.' Ethva absently measured Jonquil's height with a flat hand, and then compared it against her own body. 'But they are very well trained,' she continued, seeing the look of alarm in the banf's eyes, 'and he never lets them fly free without a controlling spell.'

'How many wizards are there here?' asked the banf.

'How many!' Ethva cried, raising a hand to her cheek as if this was an almost impossible question. 'Why, hundreds! Several hundreds perhaps! Students and masters. Not counting an equal number of enchantresses of course.'

Jonquil and Rattajack stared at the girl with utter astonishment. She laughed at their dropped jaws and wide eyes.

'But surely you knew?' she giggled. 'This is Eddilee, the Vale of the Wizards. Everyone here is an enchanter of some sort.'

Jonquil assured Ethva that they had not known of this amazing fact. There had been no time for Tuatara to explain the details of her important journey to the three companions. She had simply whisked them away from Anconeus on the pretext of urgent business, and the next thing they knew they had landed in an obviously enchanted valley, and were being introduced to some richly dressed stranger who described himself as the Grand Wizard of Eddilee.

'Heskel!' the girl hissed. 'That pompous buffoon!'

'Who exactly is he?' asked Jonquil.

'Nobody!' she snapped. 'He's just a sad old fraud who invents ridiculous titles for himself to make up for his lack of craft.'

Ethva's countenance grew dark with anger, and as she gave out about Heskel, her particular bugbear, she gestured to the two companions to follow her. She eventually brought them to what she described as one of her favourite places in the valley. A pretty spot where the trees of the wood parted to permit a chuckling brook to weave between their feet. In an open patch of sunlight, the sparkling thread of water ducked beneath a low slab of rock supported by two boulders to make a primitive bridge. Ethva sat down upon the warm slab which was just wide enough to accommodate the two companions either side of her, and all three dipped their feet into the cold, bubbling water.

'This is one of my thinking places,' the girl told her two new friends. 'It's so restful here.'

Ethva leaned back, closing her eyes until her face was fully tilted into the sun, and then with one flourishing movement, pulled the wrapped scarf from her head and shook free a shiny cascade of silky, brown curls. Jonquil then realised that the tall young woman seated beside him had the same elegant, refined features as all the other sorceresses that he had come to know during his long adventures; and perhaps, he thought, that was what had been niggling him about the other inhabitants they had encountered in the valley. They all comported themselves with a genteel aplomb that seemed somehow at odds with their apparent occupations. Like a population of gentlefolk who, for reasons best known to themselves, were simply playing at being farmers, fruit-pickers, blacksmiths, stockmen, handmaidens, washerwomen, etc. In short, they all felt like impostors, which in a sense they were. That wasn't to say that the individual wizards and witches were not any good at their uncharacteristic roles. For when Jonquil put these points to the girl, she assured him that they were all encouraged to develop a level of skill at least equal to, if not superior, to that normally required for the job. Indeed, according to Ethva, many of the valley's inhabitants had become master craftsmen in skills not usually associated with their calling. Jonquil was quite intrigued by this enchanted valley, and was eager to hear more. Rattajack seemed more interested in the five doves that had followed them to the brook, settling a short distance from the bridge, and were now sipping their fill along its glistening edge. After all, the terragon had sensed a difference in the people of the vale, at their very first meeting. Therefore this was not really news to him, even if it came as a great revelation to his beloved companion.

'It is a place of great learning,' Ethva told the banf. 'Our kind come here from the length and breadth of Enchantica to study with the great masters.'

'Your kind?' inquired Jonquil.

'Someone who shows signs of the gift. It can happen at any age. And when it does one is sent here to the valley as a postulant - to learn and develop in the craft. Of course, not all of us are destined for greatness. Some will leave here as only simple conjurors, astrologers, herbalists and the like. But a select few, those with the greatest skill and aptitude will rise to become the High Servants of the mighty.'

'And where does the power come from,' Jonquil asked, 'to sustain this wonderful place?'

'From those that dwell here, of course,' replied Ethva. 'We aren't here because the valley is enchanted,' she told the banf. 'The valley is enchanted because we are here. The magic comes from us, its inhabitants. We sustain this undying blend of the seasons with our own will. It is one of the first things we learn how to do. Whether by growing and harvesting crops, making tools, rearing livestock, befriending wild animals or cloud-herding. Each of us must work our own tiny miracles, that by themselves are nothing, but combined with our brothers and sisters build into a mighty, irresistible force.

'And what tasks do you perform?' asked the banf.

'I have an empathy with birds and animals; and so I watch over the small beasts of the woods and forests, and the delicate souls of the skies.'

Jonquil smiled as five of the delicate souls jostled with each other for prime position on Rattajack's head and snout, the terragon playfully twitching his ears or flicking his nose, causing the pearl-white doves to flutter like large, hovering butterflies before his amber eyes.

'But I have ambition,' Ethva continued. 'One day, in many years time I too hope to enter the Pit of Enlightenment, and set my wits and craft against a mighty dragon like Aznargen.'

Jonquil felt he ought to know what the Pit of Enlightenment was, but decided to hide his ignorance and let the girl go on.

'Verne, my - er - friend, has just completed all his training, and has been chosen to leave for the Storm Mountains with a batch of other lucky hopefuls. He's very highly thought of by his masters. When I see him again he will be a High Wizard. That's if he graduates of course. If he manages to subdue the mighty dragon of the Pit with the power of his sorcery alone.'

'What if he doesn't?'

The girl gave Jonquil a grimace, her eyes fearful.

'Well, there have been some terrible rumours about the Pit,' she said. 'And it's true that those who fail never again return to the valley; but I don't *think* the dragonmasters allow Aznargen to eat the candidates if they don't manage to bring him under their control. Throstle will never give a straight answer on the subject. He says if I have ambitions in that quarter then the least I know about it all the better. Of course, Throstle has faced the great dragon Aznargen himself, and come through it successfully, so he knows all there is to know. He's always telling me things for my own good. Or not telling me.'

Ethva's mock frown was then replaced by a dreamy smile.

'I hope to be like him at the end of my training: at one with the dragons. Throstle says I'm making good progress with the birds and the small beasts, and that's how he started. Also,' the girl added with a tone of doom, 'as penance for my short temper, and a valuable study in humility, Throstle suggested that I spend part of my day in attendance to Heskel.'

As the despised name passed her lips, the girl petulantly flicked up one of her legs. A fan of water droplets was flung into the air which spattered on to the trembling surface of the brook in a long chain of rings.

'That's why it was I who met you at the landing meadow, and had the *honour* of bringing you to his Lordship. But I am not his servant!' she cried. 'The trussed up old charlatan! Even though he likes to treat me as one.'

'I thought Sunjack was his servant,' Jonquil said.

'He is, the grovelling little toad!' came the reply. 'I stay as far away from that mealy-mouthed mongrel as I can; and I counsel you to do the same. He is not to be trusted! Heskel likes him because he flatters the old fool. He's the only one who does. Everyone else laughs at his pathetic pretensions. He is not the power in the city, except in his own mind. He is not a Grand Wizard, except in his own imaginings. Throstle is the power in the city, as he is in the rest of the valley and beyond. All that gold and glitter! Camping it up like a king! He's an embarrassment! Grand Wizard? Grand Jester more like. I shudder to think what wicked little plots he and his halfgoblin brew up together behind closed doors. I shouldn't really say this, Jonquil; but I think Throstle tolerates Heskel's outrageous coxcombry in order to distract the rest of us from the fact that he spends so little time with us. I suppose a pretend leader is better than no leader at all. Or at least it would be if it was anybody other than Heskel!'

'What about this Dragonmaster the Grand Wiz... er ....Heskel spoke of?' asked Jonquil. Rattajack suddenly became interested in the conversation at the mention of this intriguing character, and much to the annoyance of the doves, who were suddenly left without a perch, the terragon rejoined the other two on the bridge.

'Oh, he is wonderful!' Ethva crooned rapturously, lifting her eyes to the sky, her face lit by a beaming smile. 'Throstle is everything that Heskel is not!'

'Throstle?' the banf asked a trifle confused. 'Who is this Throstle?'

'The High Wizard of Eddilee.'

'But I thought that was someone called Horcust,' Jonquil said.

'It is!' Ethva laughed. 'Horcust Rothgilian, Dragonmaster of Eyesand, Lord of Eddilee; but known to his intimate friends, of whom I include myself, as Throstle! He much prefers it to all his other names. Unlike Heskel, Throstle has earned more titles and accolades than you can shake a stick at, but he hates using them. He doesn't need to invent authority for himself. Oh, just wait till you meet him, you'll love him. He's so ordinary and modest, and yet so wise and powerful. And just wait till he meets you, Rattajack. I bet he's never seen such a handsome creature like you before.'

Rattajack piped forth with excitement. The more he heard about this Throstle fellow, the more he liked him.

'And then there's little Addax, his dragonet,' she added. 'His constant companion and most trusted friend.'

An image of the ugly gargoyle that had haunted the two companions' wanderings through the valley came into Jonquil's mind. He wondered if the spying gargoyle and 'little Addax' were the same creature.

'Is he about Rattajack's size?' he asked the girl. 'Quite dark in colouring.....'

'Who, Addax?' she giggled. 'Why bless you, no! He's only a dragonet. He's tiny. Throstle carries him about on his shoulder! He's so sweet.'

Jonquil then told Ethva about the small dragon that he and Rattajack had seen in the fruit grove, and how it had followed them like a shadow ever since. The girl's eyes narrowed in thought as Jonquil described the reptilian's habit of just sitting and watching, but there was no light of recognition in her face. He then told her that the winged shadow that had frightened the doves had most probably been the same creature.

'Do you think it might belong to the Dragonmaster?' the banf asked.

The girl considered for a moment.

'I shouldn't think so,' she said at last. 'I can't imagine Throstle having anything to do with such an ugly beast.'

'Perhaps it was one of his spies,' said Jonquil.

'Oh, no!' replied the girl. 'Throstle's dragons fly so high in the sky that you can't see them; but they can see you!'

'He never uses spies on the ground?'

'Well, if he did, you'd never know!' the girl told him with a mischievous smile. 'His dragons will have seen Tuatara's arrival. He is sure to come and meet with her. The Queen of Witches! There's another pretentious title for you.'

Jonquil smarted a little at this brusque reference to Tuatara. Someone for whom he had slowly nurtured a great respect. Despite her status as a former arch enemy.

'And see how she just strolls into our valley,' Ethva continued. 'As free as you please. As if she was our greatest friend - instead of our deadliest enemy!

'Ethva....' Jonquil tried to interrupt.

'I tell you, Jonquil,' she continued, 'there are some here in the vale that would rather see her cast under a hold spell and tried for her crimes, than sit with her at a council.'

'But Ethva....' the banf tried again.

'I don't know why the Three Wizards have decided to trust her, and far be it for me to question their great judgement; but there are people here who lost loved ones, some their entire families to the armies of Vrorst, whom she served so effectively. Are we expected just to accept this incredible change of loyalty? Forget her former deeds? Welcome her into our hearts as a new found friend and ally? Well, I'm sorry but I for one won't do it!'

'Ethva,' Jonquil said again, with a calm, quiet voice. 'If your Throstle is as wise as you say, then I think he would ask you not to be so hasty in your judgement of these matters.'

The girl opened her mouth as if to make some reply, but the commanding tones of a third voice booming from the shadows behind interrupted her.

'He would indeed, my friend!' it said.

All three figures seated on the stone slab bridge turned as one to face the newcomer. Suddenly the girl erupted into a howl of delight.

'Throstle!' she squealed.

Ethva scrambled to her feet and ran to greet the tall figure emerging from the generous shade of a large iron beech. If Jonquil and Rattajack had been anticipating a personage with an appearance similar to the richly-adorned Heskel, they could not have been more mistaken. The wizard that stepped into the sunlight was clothed in a simple, dowdy robe made from plain, earthy coloured cloth woven for strength rather than show. The first thing to notice was the well-worn wide brimmed hat, its long thin point bent in half and weighed down with dangling beads and charms. The broad band above the brim was stuffed with a variety of herbs, feathers, grasses, sticks, and protruding into the air most notably a long, beautifully carved flute. The wizard (who like most of the wizards Jonquil had encountered seemed to fall into an indeterminable middle-age) was clearly a traveller, judging by his sturdy boots, sensible dress and abundant baggage. A springy step suggested a hardy athleticism borne of a life of walking.

He was laden with bed roll, assorted bags, pouches, and flasks of all descriptions. All of them hanging on straps from his shoulders, or tethered to a thick leather belt. He carried a stout staff made from a twisted, wind-blown branch, bands of runes and other mysterious symbols carved at intervals along its length. Shards of sunlight glanced off the facets of a power crystal held perpendicular to the staff by the jaws of a carved dragon head rising from the top.

The face of the wizard had the same strong commanding features that Jonquil had come to expect from the high sorcerers. His long, almost white hair was tied back into a bushy tail. His beard, streaked with pearly grey, had also been tied at intervals along its length, and threaded into the criss-cross of straps at his chest to keep it out of the way. His keen, hazel eyes were warm and befriending, and like the rest of his face prone at any moment to light up in joyous laughter.

Almost indistinguishable from the other shapes and bundles that were attached in some manner to the wizard, was a diminutive figure perched on his shoulder. Sheltering beneath the shade of the large brim, the small creature was only visible as the wizard drew nearer. As Ethva charged towards the traveller, her arms outstretched to wind themselves about his neck, the figure fled from its resting place with an annoyed squawk, and swept into the sunshine on a blur of flashing wings. The miniature dragon made a beeline for Rattajack, and surrounded the astonished face of the terragon with a swirling, balletic flight. Addax finally came to rest again on the very tip of Rattajack's nose, and peered into his large eyes with intense fascination, the dragonet's tiny head alternating from one amber globe to the other with sudden, bobbing movements. When the terragon's eyes finally managed to focus on the swift creature, he let out a flurry of piping calls in greeting to his little visitor. The dragonet leapt into the air with a brief trill of response; and then spiralled over to Jonquil, circling madly around his head and perching quite boldly upon his shoulder. Addax fixed the banf with a bright steely eye.

The wizard gave the girl an affectionate hug, and then brought her back to the bridge, his arm about her shoulders. Ethva was bombarding the newcomer with so many questions about where he had been, what he'd been doing, why he had stayed away for so long, that all the wizard could do was laugh in response. Finally he gripped her shoulders and pushed her to arms' length, staring deeply into her eyes.

'Never mind all that,' he chuckled. 'I can see that your impetuous nature has improved not a jot since I was last here. And what's happened to your manners, in my absence? Aren't you going to introduce me?'

A spark of mischief glittered in the girl's eyes as she uttered a brief apology, and then stepped forward to present the wizard.

'Jonquil the banf and Rattajack the terragon, allow me to present the Lord Horcust Rothgilian, High Wizard of Eddilee, Dragonmaster of Eyesand, Pergoral of Kaerlaverog......,'

'Thank you, Ethva!' the wizard groaned, silencing the girl with a hand over her mouth. 'Merely my name would have sufficed!'

A muffled giggle began behind his hand. She playfully broke free and ran over to the two companions, who were standing rather awe-struck by this being whose radiant character shone more brightly than all of Heskel's gold and jewels.

'See,' she said to them, 'I told you he hates his titles.'

The wizard bowed courteously to each of them, thrilling them even more.

'I insist that my friends call me either plain Horcust or Throstle. Call me whichever you please.'

The banf politely introduced himself and the terragon, and thanked the wizard for his courtesy. Of course Horcust was well aware of their identities and their fame, and lost no time in quizzing the pair on their adventures. Jonquil was pleased that the wizard paid special attention to Rattajack. His bright, hazel eyes gorged themselves on the terragon's rare form, and the curious patches of silence that interrupted the wizard's speech made the banf wonder if Horcust was communicating with Rattajack in that secret, silent language that only other dragons could hear. After all if the wizard truly did use dragons as his news-gatherers then he must have mastered the silent tongue. He turned again to Jonquil, with Addax still perched on the banf's shoulder.

'Well,' he said. 'My little friend here seems to have given you his seal of approval.' Horcust offered a finger to the dragonet who snapped at it playfully. 'You are honoured, Jonquil. There aren't many shoulders that he will abide.'

The wizard turned to the girl.

'I heard what you were saying about the Lady Tuatara, Ethva,' he said with a more serious tone. 'And Jonquil is right. You are too hasty with your judgement. And your knowledge of the great matters of the world is small.'

The young sorceress's smile began to fade as she recognised the approach of an admonishment.

'But Throstle....' she moaned, attempting to forestall him.

'I too have looked upon Vrorst's awesome majesty,' Horcust began, denying her protesting looks. 'I have felt the lightest touch of the smallest claw of his mighty hand, and I was as helpless as a child before it. When the Lady Tuatara finally found the courage to defy him, even if it was only inspired by revenge, she knew that she would face the full wrath of his will; and still she chose to resist him. He could have crushed her like an eggshell, but still she stood against him. Alone. Without a single ally to aid her. Could you have shown such courage, Ethva? With the Lord of Ice and the great Orb of Winter as your foes?'

The girl's eyes dropped to the bubbling water about her feet. Her brow knitted into a frown of uncertainty.

'She didn't have to raise her hand against the Ice Sorcerer,' the wizard went on. 'She could have just remained as she was; his mighty slave; tolerating his scorn and contempt to continue his deadly work. If she had, my dear Ethva, Vrorst would still be King of the World; and you and I would not be standing here in this pleasant spot talking as we are. This exquisite valley, for all its strong enchantment, would have been swept away as if it were nothing, by an unstoppable storm of snow and ice. Our wonderful city crushed like a house of straw. I think, Ethva, if the Lady Tuatara found the strength and heart to stand alone against the most powerful, evil being Enchantica has ever seen, then we who have known suffering at the hands of Winter can surely find the will to offer her our forgiveness and understanding. She committed her former crimes in another life; a life created and manipulated by Vrorst. She is no longer the same person. She has turned her back on the ways of the Ice Sorcerer. She is changed; and by the time the tale of the Orb has reached its last chapter, I suspect that she will have done more than enough to earn the respect of all of us.'

Whilst Horcust talked to Ethva, Jonquil's thoughts travelled back to his own previous encounters with Tuatara. His capture over the snowfields of South Enchantica, where now the great verdant plain containing the Canvas City lay. His long journeys to the Mountains of Menace and later to the Throne Citadel; and the three occasions the Ice Witch had saved his life. First when he and Charlock had been about to be slain by Hawkhood and his fellow dragonriders following their capture. Then, deliverance from the hungry jaws of Hellbender in the goblin city. Finally, the incredible scene he had witnessed alongside a sleeping Thrace in the high dungeon of the Throne Citadel, when a lizard had entered the dark cell and in a pool of bar-striped moonlight 'grown' into the person of Tuatara. She had set him free from the dungeon, saving him from a slow, terrible death at the hands of the young Hexerne. Jonquil had never really understood why the Ice Witch had helped him on those occasions. Perhaps she did not even know herself; but as a consequence the banf found it hard not to hold Tuatara in some degree of respect and affection.

Horcust lifted the girl's chin with his cupped hand. He smiled warmly. The girl's countenance began to lighten in response.

'So quick,' he said to her. 'So fiery! For the life of me I can't imagine why I am so fond of you!'

Ethva's face beamed with pleasure at the wizard's words.

'I'm sorry, Throstle,' she said earnestly. 'I'll try to think more carefully before I bluster in future.'

'It might be better,' the wizard answered, 'if you thought better of blustering altogether!'

Ethva burst into laughter.

'I know. I know,' she cried. 'My temper is too short and too hot! But I can't help it.'

'You can at least try and help it!' Horcust told her with a smile. 'And will you also try and spread a little of your new found wisdom amongst the others in our city who harbour enmity against the Lady? I know they listen to you, Ethva.'

The girl sighed heavily.

'It won't be easy to persuade someone who lost their family in the war to forgive one of its grand architects.' she said. 'But I'll try!'

Horcust fixed her with a steely, knowing stare.

'I can ask no more,' he said with a grin and a small deferential nod. 'Now come, my friends,' the wizard added. 'We are awaited by the great and the good! We must return to the city.'

Horcust made as if to stride forth, and immediately he did so, Addax lifted on to his shoulder vacating that of Jonquil. The wizard moved swiftly off into the trees, Ethva hot on his heels extracting firm promises from him that he would stay long enough this time to give her all the news of his travels in the long interval since his last return to the valley. As he walked the wizard plucked the long flute from his hat band, and began to play a stirring reel to set the pace for the long hike back to the city. The flurry of lively notes lifted into the air in a seamless scroll of sound, almost begging the feet of the listeners to move to its charming rhythm. The spiralling tune was all pervasive beneath the mottled shade of the beeches, and at the same time as natural as birdsong. Ethva turned back to the two companions.

'Now you know why he is called *Throstle*!' she cried.

And indeed there was a quality in the delightful noise the wizard made that resembled much the endless, hypnotic cadences of the thrushes or the larks. Jonquil and Rattajack looked at each other, and the mystery of the far away music on the hill was solved.

Suddenly the girl remembered her pearly white charges still bathing and drinking at the brook. She ran back to the bridge and called them up, counting them by name on to her arms.

'Strange,' she said to herself, 'there's only five here. Where's Serenity?'

There was no sign of the sixth dove. Eventually Ethva forced herself to turn away from the water and catch up with the fading flutesong. She scurried after the others with many backward glances, fearful in case her sixth charge should be looking for her. At last, the girl resolved to go back to the city with her friends, and await there the return of the absent member of her flock. Such was her concern that Ethva would stop Throstle's playing every now and then during their long walk back to the wizards' settlement, and call out her plaintive carolling to the open sky. The others tried their best to allay the girl's fears and by the time they had reached the open sunshine and the start of the rolling flower meadows, Ethva had been persuaded to sing a joyous song of Summer, accompanied by a lilting melody from the flute of her illustrious friend.

High up in the thickest part of the proud iron beech canopy, its ugly, dark features well camouflaged by the dense foliage, a terragon sized dragon creature peered down through the leafy layers to watch the departure of the wizard, the girl and the two companions from the small bridge. Its acute hearing had strained to catch as much of the distant conversations below at the brook as it could. All of these it would report back to its master, as was its instruction. The reptile yawned a glistening barricade of sharp pegs, its active tongue snaking around the rim of its scaly jaws to claim any snagged morsels of its last meal. With a loud snap, the long jaws closed, and a single pearl-white feather attached by a spot of blood to the corner of its wide grin, was loosened by the sudden draught to begin its long floating spiral down to the brook, to join a number of similar downy plumes that had been left by the waterside.

To Seek a Way North

The High Council was to take place in the splendid round chamber in the Great Hall, and many weighty matters were to be aired and discussed. None heavier, of course, than the fate of the mighty Orb of Winter, and the two fugitives who bore it.

An elite assembly had gathered in Eddilee for this urgent conference. Yelver and Roshir, High Wizards of Spring and Summer respectively, had arrived to join Horcust and Tuatara at the council table. Jonquil, Rattajack and Meadolarne, had been included amongst the honoured guests, as was Heskel, who despite his comparatively lowly status had insisted on attending the meeting. Not wanting to be distracted from their important business by a petty wrangle over protocol, the high enchanters had agreed.

The prestigious company sat down to begin their congress on the third morning following the two companions' first meeting with Horcust, and the celebrations that had broken out on his return.

The two newly arrived High Wizards seemed quite youthful for such important sorcerers. Roshir had a pleasant, darkly skinned face with keen deep brown eyes. His light beard and hair were black, the latter tumbling from his head in a wild cascade of beaded braids. Yelver, who like his Summer brother was garbed in the colours of his respective season, had pale, angular features with sleek black hair drawn back into a thick tail. His chin was completely bare, indeed his ivory skin looked too smooth to have ever sprouted hair. His eyes were a sharp blue - cool and insistent. The Spring wizard was said to have a good deal of elf blood in him, and he did share many physical characteristics with the enchanted folk of the far north. As Jonquil looked from Yelver to Tuatara, he was struck by the similarities between the two of them: did this mean that the Ice Witch was of elvish descent also?

It was Roshir who began on the subject of the Orb, and he shared with the assembly the news that he brought from Halmarand at Dragonskeep. The High Wizard, who was acting as deputy to Carobus, told the council that Mezereon and Hexerne had been traced to the isolated barbarian kingdom of Zrobok, high in the rim of snowbound peaks that bordered the eaves of the great northern forest. Desperate for aid, they had decided to approach the king of that wild, almost inaccessible land, and see what support he would lend them. The Zrobokites had always been amongst the staunchest allies of Vrorst. Never failing his call to arms when he had need for their ruthless, bloodthirsty style of warfare. Even a few of the goblin tribes balked at some of the Zrobokites' excesses when the smell of blood sent them into one of their infamous killing frenzies. Vrorst, of course, only encouraged these atrocities. He liked his servants to be feared; feared to such a degree that merely the threat of deploying them was enough to gain victory.

The barbarian homeland was so detached from the rest of the world (virtually the last proper settlement before the great North Forest), that its fierce people knew little of what transpired beyond their borders. The two fugitives, with the aid of Silfaladil, Prince of the Northern Elves, who they seemed to have adopted as their guide since his hand in their escape from Anconeus, had found their way there along the perilous mountain trails; and, sensible of the insularity of the Zrobokites and their zealous loyalty to Vrorst, decided to attempt a most audacious deception.

As most of those around the table knew, Mezereon had always borne a slight resemblance to his dark master. Indeed, in later years he even modelled his appearance after Vrorst. To anyone who saw them both together, the two could never have been mistaken for the same person; but as far as the Zrobokites were concerned, of whom it was almost certain none had ever laid eyes on the Ice Sorcerer or Mezereon at close quarters, the Dark Sorcerer possessed enough similarities to pass himself off as Vrorst. He was gambling that such was the isolation of the barbarian settlement, that although they might have guessed at Vrorst's defeat, their information would be based on vague speculation and rumour. Whispers that might have circulated about their camps concerning the Ice Lord's death would be swiftly laid to rest by the appearance of the great sorcerer himself; if such a surprise visitation could be believed. It was a bold ploy, and one that could easily fail and lead to horrible reprisals if even one of King Kazzak's court had firm knowledge to the contrary.

Mezereon and the girl had been determined not to make the same mistakes as they had with Hadros; requesting aid, in the name of old loyalties. They had decided it was time to be bold, and so Mezereon had come before Kazzak and his court, in the persona of the Ice Lord, and demanded they help him escape to his sanctuary in the Far North. It had been a daring scheme, Roshir told the company, considering that Mezereon's robes must have been badly travel-worn by that time, and that his character simply did not carry the authority, no matter how good the disguise, of his former master.

'Personally, I find it hard to believe that such a deception could have been possible considering the fugitives' desperate circumstances,' Yelver interrupted. 'Mezereon trying to pass himself off as the former King of the World? After seven hard years in hiding? He must have looked more like a beggar seeking alms.'

'Ah yes,' countered Throstle, 'but you are forgetting the one factor which would have overruled at a stroke the two fugitives every disadvantage.'

'Yes,' concurred Tuatara. 'The Orb!'

Roshir nodded. Mezereon had shown the Zroboks Vrorst's Orb of

Power. Without knowing of Vrorst's death and the intimate history of the crystal globe following that event, the sight of a sorcerer standing before them holding the great Orb of Winter, would have convinced the barbarians without doubt that they were in the presence of the Ice Lord himself.

The gloved hands with which the Dark Sorcerer would have undoubtedly handled the great crystal, so as not to risk touching its dangerous surface with his bare skin, would have detracted little from the potency of the image; and Kazzak and his people could not have failed to have been impressed by the sight of it.

'No doubt the Orb itself contributed to the ruse by the creation of a little visual splendour of its own,' Roshir told the council. 'A few strategically thrown bolts of blue lightning about the courtroom, the odd demonic apparition let loose amongst the gathering of warriors; effects guaranteed to convince even the most sceptical of Zrobokites that it at least was the genuine article. After all, the Orb also had an interest in the success of Mezereon's performance: the fulfilment of its own destiny depended upon it.'

Roshir also said that he believed the presence of Hexerne helped in Mezereon's deception. Kazzak and his people would have taken her to be a disguised Tuatara, faithfully following her lord to his final refuge. After all the resemblance of the girl to the Ice Witch was far greater than that of Mezereon to Vrorst. That imposture would have succeeded with little effort.

Tuatara shifted uncomfortably at the Summer wizard's words. She was only too well aware of the rumours that had abounded in the Winter camp concerning herself and Hexerne; but as the Ice Witch had no knowledge of the time before she became the Lady Tuatara, she had been unable to deny the insinuations with any confidence; she only prayed that it was not so.

The Summer High Wizard told the assembly of how the awe-struck barbarians had cowered before the figure of whom they believed to be their overlord, and offered him all that they might need for the long journey ahead: guides, beasts of burden, and an army to see them safely through the darkness of the great northern forest, and beyond.

'So this was how Mezereon, Hexerne and the Orb left Zrobok,' Roshir told them. 'At the head of a fearsome column of bloodthirsty warriors. Thoroughly rested and refreshed, riding instead of walking, and probably feeling more confident in the prospect of their success than they had done since the day they threw in together.'

'And what of Silfaladil?' asked Throstle.

Roshir blew air threw his lips in a vague manner, and showed his palms as if this question was still to be answered.

'As for the Prince of the Elves,' the Summer wizard replied, 'we can only rely on inspired speculation as to his movements following the two fugitives entry into Zrobok. We are all familiar with elven secrecy.

'As you may be aware, the Zrobokites and the Northern Elves are sworn enemies, so Silfaladil's accompanying Mezereon and the girl to the barbarian settlement would have been out of the question. They must have left him in a hide-out somewhere in the hills. Elves can move far swifter than mortals if they have a mind, and we assume that after being abandoned by his charges, the prince hurried into the forest ahead of the barbarian army and sought out the sentinels of his people keeping constant watch over the borders of their kingdom; and through them sent word to his father the King.

'The Lord Carobus returned the dragonflight to Halmarand by which he had travelled to Ckristinial. With it he sent a report of all he had been able to learn from the elvish king and his people. Unfortunately, the contents of Silfaladil's message to his father were withheld, and could not be ascertained by other means as the Kingdom of the Elves is protected from the prying eyes of sorcerers' power globes (even those of the greatest) by strong enchantment.

'As for Silfaladil's motive for lending his aid to the two fugitives; for we now know that even if he was not directly involved in freeing them from the castle at Anconeus (there is good reason to suspect Juvula of that particular crime), Silfaladil almost certainly aided them in escaping the fortified city itself. He undoubtedly did not do this through love of Mezereon, whom the northern elves hate above all other enemies; but it is possible, as the Lord Carobus and the good general suspect, that Silfaladil's offer to guide them to the far north was all part of an elaborate trap to capture the Dark Sorcerer on elvish ground and bring him to elvish justice.'

The assembled high enchanters agreed that although the two fugitives had accepted the elf prince's aid (and when faced with the choice of freedom or recapture by Hadros' guards, who would not?), Mezereon clearly had trusted Silfaladil to guide them no further than Zrobok. He certainly would not have tolerated Silfaladil as a guide through the elf prince's own kingdom; the homeland of Mezereon's sworn enemies. Now Silfaladil's plans had been temporarily thwarted, it was assumed he had returned to his own domain to devise another scheme for the capture of the Dark Sorcerer. Only time would tell what form this new plan would take.

Roshir told the council that Carobus was bringing the full weight of his authority to bear upon Rilfinnian, the elf king; and trying to dissuade him from any action that might endanger the Wizards' own efforts to recover the Orb.

Halmarand was already hot on the fugitives' trail having descended on Zrobok only days after they had left with Kazzak's army. The greatly reduced strength of warriors in the settlement had put up little resistance against the superior force of lion dragons, and despite Kazzak's initial obstinacy, the general was eventually able to learn from him the details of the two fugitives' sojourn at the barbarian kingdom.

Next to speak at the council was Yelver, the Spring High Wizard. Having only recently left the great community of the Canvas City, he was full of news from all parts of Enchantica on a wide variety of subjects. Eventually, however, he also turned his attention to the subject of the Orb; this time from the viewpoint of the Three Wizards, in whose august presence it had long been his privilege to serve.

The far sight of the Lords Fantazar, Orolan and Waxifrade had long been hampered by the Orb of Winter; which had shrouded itself in an impenetrable shadow of enchantment, concealing its whereabouts from the Three Wizards' Fire Orbs. This was only possible because all four Fire Orbs, Spring, Summer, Autumn and Winter, had originally been cut from the same block of crystal, and so had a unique dependency upon each other - a shared circle of power which bonded them together. The Three Wizards had reiterated their warning that the Winter Orb must not be destroyed; but delivered safely into their hands.

Yelver, on behalf of his great masters, could not impress upon the council strongly enough the importance of discovering the location of the place known as the Spire of the North, and their reaching it before those bearing the Orb. The Three Wizards greatly feared Vrorst's powerful tool of sorcery entering the portal of his secret refuge. A haven which was sure to have been constructed atop a mighty well of Dark Magic, and therefore protected by the strongest, blackest enchantment imaginable.

The Spring wizard then introduced a note of warning concerning the fate of the Orb of Winter and the previously little known Mage of Anconeus: a minor sorcerer with the name of Juvula.

Just as Gembranosus' seeing globe had shown the face of Juvula to Jonquil following his vision of Meadolarne, the Three Fire Orbs had repeatedly thrown up the same image to the Great Lords. For some reason the minor mage from the court of Anconeus was causing a significant disturbance in the interwoven threads of Old Magic that lay across the face of Enchantica like an intricate web; and to which most crystals (to a greater or lesser extent) were sensitive. Such activity was invariably the portent of approaching danger. The Three Wizards could not yet be sure what manner of threat Juvula posed, as previously his ambitions had always exceeded his powers as a wizard; but they knew better than to ignore the warnings of their magic globes.

Heskel, who for much of the council had been quite vociferous, making frequent contributions of varying quality to the different discussions (clearly trying to impress the illustrious company with his interest and knowledge), became curiously quiet and withdrawn on the subject of Juvula; even when pressed by Throstle to make some comment on the achievements or otherwise of the aforementioned character during his time as a student in the Enchanted Vale. Heskel was brisk and evasive in his reply. He mumbled something about Juvula not being particularly memorable in any of his studies. An average student who failed to distinguish himself. Throstle threw a significant glance at Tuatara, and then proceeded to shed a little more light on the former inhabitant of Eddilee.

'Juvula was a troublemaker,' the Dragonmaster began. 'A schemer and a deceiver, who was constantly coaxing others into mischief and then skilfully side-stepping the blame. At the time of his leaving, when his masters had decided that there was nothing more that they could teach him, Juvula had acquired only one skill - his voice. He had mastered the art of word-weaving.'

A wave of puzzlement swept over the lesser beings present at the table, and even some of the wise seemed to know less than they ought. The only one of them to show no outwards signs of either surprise or interest was Heskel. Throstle tried to explain:

'Word-weaving is a way of twisting and manipulating words to gain mastery over the will of others,' he said. 'It is an invidious and unworthy gift. Or in the words of one of my own wise old teachers: *The skill of coating poisoned words with the glaze of diamonds.*

'It seemed inevitable that he would eventually find service in the treacherous world of court politics, and is believed to have been responsible for persuading Hadros to ally himself with Vrorst rather than the Wizards of Light. Juvula no doubt did this believing that his own chances of advancement were much better on the side of Winter than amongst the ranks of those who knew him. However, to his eternal chagrin, and despite constant efforts to impress, Vrorst failed to honour him with high office amongst his own servants. Consequently the Mage of Anconeus grew into an increasingly bitter and jealous character, ever mindful of his shortcomings as a wizard.'

Before the proceedings of the council went any further, Throstle made a mental note of Heskel's behaviour; his unwillingness to speak on the subject of Juvula. He had never known the pompous fool to be so reticent to talk about anything before.

'One thing that does baffle me though,' Throstle continued, 'is Juvula's suspected involvement in the freeing of Mezereon and Hexerne from the dungeons of Anconeus.'

This statement was greeted by a general murmur of agreement. The behaviour of the minor sorcerer towards the two fugitives had perplexed both the powerful and the wise.

Juvula had commenced his part in the action by persuading King Hadros, his liege-lord, to deny Mezereon and the girl aid and imprison them in the dungeons; sending one of his own servants to the Alliance garrison at Glostomorg to inform them of the capture. This could be interpreted as the act of a character eager to ingratiate himself with the new power in the world. Juvula then, inexplicably, released them from the dungeons and set them free into the city, or so it was strongly suspected. This bizarre deed closely followed by his own disappearance from Anconeus.

The reason for this extraordinary duplicity was still unknown. Yelver told the council that the only explanation which carried any weight with the Three Wizards was one which suggested the involvement of the Orb. Could it be that following the two fugitives incarceration, Vrorst's power crystal had begun to work its influence on Juvula?

'It is not inconceivable,' Tuatara declared. 'The further north the Orb travels the greater its power will grow; and the more the Forces of Light make plans for its seizure, the more the Orb will hatch counter schemes of its own to thwart its enemies. It will spread its dark influence far and wide to recruit those that might in any way aid its journey northwards. There is an intelligence and brooding purpose inside that crystal globe that feels very familiar.'

For a moment the eyes of the whole council stared at the tense countenance of the Ice Witch, her haunting tones almost transfixing them.

'And do you believe that this Juvula has been recruited, Lady Tuatara?' Roshir asked at last.

The memory of the Winter Orb's cruel power was still too clear for Tuatara, and if the Mage of Anconeus truly had been claimed by the Freezing Fire then she could not help feeling a stab of sympathy for him.

'It is not inconceivable, my Lord,' was her answer to the Summer wizard.

'If it is true,' Throstle added, 'then he will need the aid and support of some powerful allies to become a contender.'

'A contender for what?' asked Roshir.

'Mastery of the Orb,' the Dragonmaster replied.

There was a collective gasp of amazement from the two High Wizards of the Seasons, and they exchanged looks of incredulity with each other.

'A minor sorcerer gain mastery over the Orb of Winter, Horcust?' Yelver exclaimed. 'How is this possible?'

The elfin wizard's eyes were large and questioning. They searched Throstle's face for a clue to the truth of his extraordinary statement.

'Have you news concerning Juvula that you are yet to share with us?' Yelver asked further.

Throstle lowered his eyes to the polished face of the table, and did not speak for a few moments. Eventually, with a brief glance at Heskel, the Dragonmaster turned again to Yelver.

'Nothing substantial,' he said. 'But there are whispers...'

'Relating to what?' Roshir interrupted.

Throstle paused for a moment as if to gather his thoughts, and then leaned in towards the table, resting his weight upon his forearms.

'There are rumours concerning Rhazgor,' he said at last.

A ring of furrowed brows greeted this statement. Heskel's eyes dropped smartly into his lap when Throstle threw a glance at him. In the end it was Roshir who broke the silence.

'What rumours, Horcust?' he asked. 'The last we heard he was still holed up in his ice fortress with the indomitable Corracrist standing guard outside.'

Rhazgor, the one time deputy of Mezereon, and the sorcerer who had personally overseen the capturing of prisoners for his dark master's

experiments, had fled to his remote fortress after the demise of the Lord of
Ice. Corracrist, a huge dragon given to Rhazgor by Vrorst as a reward for
some service, was set to guard the entrance to the frozen refuge against all
attackers; and this he did with unfailing success. Consequently Rhazgor had
become one of the few sorcerers from the upper echelons of Vrorst's regime
to remain 'at liberty' after his death. Rhazgor had been amongst the many
high captains of Winter who had made their mass escape from the high
tower of Dragonskeep after the fortress had fallen to the might of
Halmarand and his lion flight. Most of his confederates had since been
taken but every effort to prise Rhazgor from his icy sanctuary had failed, and
he had remained safely incarcerated in his self-imposed confinement during
the several long years since Dragonskeep had fallen. Or at least that had
been the situation until Throstle's dragon spies had brought him news of a
change. Corracrist, the mighty dragon had disappeared. He was no longer
guarding the frozen fortress from attack. In Throstle's mind this could mean
only one thing: Rhazgor had emerged. As to the motive for this bold move,
the Dragonmaster could not be certain; but he knew that the Winter
sorcerer would not have abandoned his impregnable haven on a mere whim.
Rhazgor had evidently stridden forth from his hiding hole with a grave
purpose.

'This is indeed astounding news, Horcust!' exclaimed Yelver. 'Will you
not tell us more?'

Throstle leaned back into his chair and clasped his hands beneath his
chin, his two raised index fingers beating softly against his lips.

'It is only a whisper at present,' he told them. 'And I believe that less
harm will be caused by keeping secret a thing which is only thin rumour,
than speaking of it openly. I anticipate knowing more of this matter in due
course; and I crave your indulgence in respecting my silence for now.'

Roshir and Yelver shared a thoughtful moment, clearly somewhat
disturbed by Throstle's news and mysterious conclusion, and then agreed
that they would do as Throstle asked; adding a request that as soon as the
Dragonmaster had any firm tidings he was to acquaint them with it forthwith.
Throstle said that he would.

Heskel had looked decidedly uncomfortable during the
Dragonmaster's brief account, and had flashed what he thought were
surreptitious glances at Throstle as the Dragonmaster had spoken. Almost as
if he had some secrets of his own that were beginning to trouble his
conscience, or at least make him fearful. His wayward eyes had been
observed, however, by the keen gaze of Tuatara.

The council eventually concluded that the subject of Juvula would
have to be continued at another time. For only time could tell what part the
Mage of Anconeus would yet play in the fate of the Orb.

The two banfs and the terragon had sat in silence for most of the
council, unless questions had been addressed to them directly or they felt

they had some relevant point to contribute to the topic under discussion. They were quite happy just to listen - it was enough for them simply to be present at such an august gathering, privy to the great works of the world.

Meadolarne had perhaps spoken the most out of the three. The gathered enchanters had wanted to know about Juvula's behaviour at Anconeus whilst the Orb had been present in the great palace; and although her memory of that time was vague, the council seemed to glean more information from her fractured reminiscences than the banfina thought they contained. Meadolarne had clearly answered one question that had been troubling one or two members of the group: why after the two fugitives' imprisonment, Juvula or anyone else, had not taken the Orb from Mezereon? The banfina had described in her answers how fearful everyone in the palace had been of Vrorst's great instrument of sorcery; from the King to the lowliest servant. No-one had wanted to even go near it let alone handle the crystal globe; so when the Dark Sorcerer and the girl had been made captive, the Orb had been imprisoned along with them. Its terrifying presence removed to the deepest regions of the old fortress.

Jonquil, Meadolarne and Rattajack appreciated that the fate of the world was wrapped up in the fate of the Orb. Even though they did not fully understand what the terrible consequences would be should the Orb be lost or broken. For his part, Jonquil had no reason to suspect that he and the others had any further role to play in the matter, despite a niggling desire to be there at the grand conclusion; when the whole business was laid to rest once and for all. Indeed, the banf had no reason not to believe that in a short time he, Meadolarne and Rattajack would return to their homeland; reunited and safe once more.

The council was nearing its conclusion. Roshir announced his intention to return to Dragonskeep and assume the governorship of the great fortress whilst Halmarand was engaged in the pursuit of the fugitives and the Orb. There he was to rendezvous with his Autumn counterpart Hergest, before his brother High Wizard flew on to aid Halmarand with his quest in Northern Forest. Yelver announced his intention to stay on in Eddilee for a short while, and then to make the long journey to Ckristinial, the royal city of the Northern Elves. There to aid Carobus in his delicate negotiations with Rilfinnian.

Tuatara announced that she too had a desire to go to the elf kingdom, for she had heard of one known as Arubal. An ancient mortal female of the race of the Lake People, who lived in the enchanted realm, and was said to have a skill with crystals unsurpassed by even the mighty. The Ice Witch needed to try and exorcise the last residue of Vrorst's power that still dwelled within her. She also felt an inexplicable power drawing her to the kingdom of the elves; as if a voice from deep in her past was calling her there.

The feelings of joy and release that had swept over Tuatara at Vrorst's death had soon been overshadowed by an inescapable sense of dread slowly creeping over her soul. As if there was a splinter of the Ice Lord's power left within her, a dark malignancy that could once again rise up to consume her and cast her back into slavery, if the Lord of Ice should ever return to the world. If it was possible to break through the wall of darkness that sealed in the black poison, and release it into the light, there was a chance she might find true freedom - true peace!

Tuatara clung to the hope that if Old Arubal could reach, and purge from her, the venomous pool that lay at the roots of her soul, she might also reveal long buried treasure. Memories of the life she knew before Vrorst; of the person before Tuatara. If the dam which held back all these secrets could be breached, then along with the flood of corruption, out would flow the last trace of Vrorst's influence over her; and Tuatara, or whoever she then discovered herself to be, would finally be free.

After a brief private conference with the two seasonal High Wizards, Horcust accompanied Tuatara and the three friends as they walked out into the noon-tide sun. He led them towards the shade of a fat drum pear tree; Addax who had been stationed on top of the ornate roof for the duration of the conference swept down on to the Dragonmaster's shoulder.

Jonquil noticed something sparkling in the strong sunshine on Throstle's breast. On closer examination he saw it to be a pendant made from a cluster of crystal shards.

'Throstle!' the banf cried. 'Where did you get that?'

The wizard laughed and raised the glittering object up for all to see.

'A present from the Three Wizards,' Throstle told them. 'Carried all the way from the Silk Palace by the Lord Yelver.'

'What does it do?' Jonquil asked.

Throstle laughed again, his eyes beaming fondly at the banf.

'You have been in the company of wizards too long, my friend,' he said, patting the banf's shoulder affectionately. 'Who says it has to do anything? Let's just hope it brings us luck, eh?'

Whilst the three friends entertained themselves with a game of goblin-in-the-middle with a large drum pear, the wizard drew Tuatara away to take a short walk with him in the bold sunlight.

'This Arubal,' he said to her when they were alone, 'she is from the lake dwellers of Manaslangua, is she not?'

'That is what I have heard,' the witch replied.

'They say that all those who dwell on the lakes have skill with crystal.'

Tuatara nodded.

'They are but infants compared with the arts of Arubal,' she told him.

'Then she is skilled indeed!' the wizard gasped. 'It is said that the lake people believe crystals to be tears from the stars.'

Tuatara smiled, and then her face darkened a little as a troubling thought occurred to her.

'You were not pleased with Heskel at the council?' she said.

Throstle expelled a sharp puff of air and shook his head.

'He told the assembly less than he knew concerning Juvula, of that I am certain!' the wizard declared.

'You don't think there might be some ......connection between them?' Tuatara asked.

'Well, if there is,' Throstle replied, 'we both know by what means, don't we?'

'Sunjack!' the witch hissed.

The wizard raised his eyebrows in concurrence. The witch fixed him with a cool stare.

'What do your spies tell you, Horcust?'

Throstle sighed, and his hazel eyes took a wide sweep of the surrounding square before he answered.

'That at best he is involved in serious mischief that threatens the peace of this valley,' the wizard began. 'At worst - that he is the ringleader of a conspiracy!'

The Ice Witch's eyes widened in surprise.

'A conspiracy?' Tuatara breathed. 'In favour of Juvula?'

The wizard nodded.

'Do you know who they are?' the witch asked further.

Throstle's face darkened with anger and his brows knitted into a scowl. He snorted with distaste as he reeled off the names of those he suspected.

'Gristmire, Shirene, Mequinda, Harlas! All of them respected members of our illustrious community. Small in number but great in power! I shudder when I think of the harm they could generate between them!'

Tuatara laid a hand upon his sleeve.

'Do you really believe that Juvula will try for the Orb, as you hinted at the council?' she asked.

Throstle did not answer immediately. He held the witch's stare for a short while, letting his gaze sink deeply into the two sapphire pools that were her eyes.

'My instincts tell me that he has been touched by its influence,' he said at last. 'For what purpose I can only guess. All I can do for the moment is watch Heskel closely, and hope that before too long he leads me to the truth.'

'So that is why you let him attend the High Council,' the witch smiled. 'To force his hand.'

Throstle nodded and stroked his beard thoughtfully.

'I was careful to see that no secrets of grave importance were discussed before him; but enough juicy snippets to raise his hackles and make him afraid. Of course for the immediate future he will be guarded and careful; but eventually he will want to communicate with his friends, and ultimately with The Pretender himself!'

'And Rhazgor?' Tuatara asked with a worried tone.

'It may only be a coincidence,' Throstle answered. 'But something has persuaded him to leave the sanctuary of his ice fortress; and I do not believe that it is a desire to try for the Orb himself!'

Tuatara breathed deeply and placed a tender hand on the wizard's shoulder.

'It seems there is a storm cloud threatening this sunny haven,' she said. I only wish I could stay and help you ride it out; but I am afraid I have my own battle to fight. A battle against an enemy I thought long dead.'

The wizard squeezed the witch's hand.

'You will be victorious, my friend,' he told her. 'I have no doubt. And have no fears for me. For the High Wizard of Eddilee has returned, and his eyes are upon this valley once more. Let his enemies beware!'

Tuatara smiled encouragingly at Throstle and then took her leave of him. The wizard watched her tall, statuesque form stride gracefully over the cobbled ground towards two tall figures who were waiting to escort the Ice Witch back to her dwelling place. Thrace and Hawkhood bowed respectfully as Tuatara approached them, and they all turned together to depart from the square.

Throstle turned his attention back to the small group still tossing the large round fruit to one another beneath the shade of the drum pear tree; a leaping Rattajack playing the goblin between the two laughing banfs. With a glad smile, he snatched his long whistle from its home in his hat band, and placed it to his lips. As a delightful cascade of the sweetest notes tumbled from his fingers, the wizard lifted his feet into a merry little jig and skipped his way back to the three friends.

A Silver Surprise

Jonquil and Rattajack stayed in the centre of the landing meadow until Starblade was a tiny speck in the eastern sky. Tuatara had directed the snowdragon carrying herself and Meadolarne to circle the open field of pasture three times before the white beast had finally begun the task of spiralling upwards to harness the power of the high winds, essential for long distance flight. Starblade's bold shadow had raced across the emerald turf drawing a wide ring about the two standing friends; her dark profile growing larger and fainter on the grass as she steadily pulled out of her low glide.

They had waved eagerly to the banfina as she had swept past repeatedly, and continued to do so long after Meadolarne would have been able to see them. Then the banf and the terragon started back towards the city with heavy hearts. Jonquil understood why the banfina had wanted to accompany the Ice Witch to the land of the elves, he just hadn't anticipated being parted from her again so soon. For the first time in his adventurous life, he was the one having to stay behind and worry.

Meadolarne's dark dreams had begun again shortly after her attending the High Council. Perhaps it had been all the talk of Juvula at the conference table that had rekindled her nocturnal demons. Whatever the cause, she had decided to accept Tuatara's offer of accompanying her to Ckristinial to seek the aid of the one known as Old Arubal: Mother of all Crystalcraft. The Ice Witch was confident that the ancient one would be able to cure the banfina's cursed sleep, and exorcise all of her demons once and for all.

Jonquil could still hear Tuatara's words to him before his farewell greeting to Meadolarne.

'Have no fear, Jonquil,' she had said in a reassuring tone. 'Meadolarne will come to no harm whilst she is under my protection. Moreover it is to save her from the harm of her nightmares that I take her away from you - if only for a little while.'

Meadolarne had squeezed Jonquil tightly in her arms, and pressed her cheek close to his. She told him not to worry and that they would soon be together again. Jonquil had smiled at his banfina as strongly as his heavy heart would allow, and before she left him to climb into Starblade's saddle beside the Ice Witch, he handed her the slipper nut, which he had originally made for her, and also the precious acorn lamp containing the rare blue fire lantern mushroom.

'Well,' he started to say, shrugging his shoulders, 'it might be quite dark in the Northern Forest. You might be glad of something to light your way!'

With a final kiss, the banfina had run to the waiting snowdragon and clasped Tuatara's proffered hand which helped her up on to the dragon's back.

'Take care!' Jonquil had shouted after them, as Starblade had began her long charge to take-off speed; and then the banf had pulled Rattajack to him as they stood together to watch Meadolarne's departure.

No sooner had the two companions left the green meadow than a familiar voice hailed them from further along the road. It was Ethva. She quickened her pace when she saw that they had heard her and ran to greet them.

'Good morrow to you both,' she said heartily. 'Throstle sent me to find you. We are to meet him at the house of Indlewick.'

'Who's Indlewick?' inquired the banf.

'A healer,' the girl said simply, skipping on ahead with childlike abandon. 'Throstle thinks it's time something was done about your wings!'

Ethva suddenly stopped, clapped her hand to her mouth and turned quickly back to the banf. Her eyes stared at Jonquil with a wide, apologetic expression; her hand eventually slipping down to her chin.

'Oops!' she exclaimed. 'I wasn't supposed to tell you that. It was meant to be a surprise!'

Jonquil laughed and patted the young sorceress's arm.

'Don't worry, Ethva,' he said reassuringly. 'I'll act surprised!'

The girl smiled weakly.

'I am sorry, Jonquil,' she sighed, as they continued on their way. 'Throstle's always saying my big mouth will get me into serious trouble one of these days. I think he's probably right.'

Jonquil and Rattajack did their best to convince Ethva that spoiling the surprise was not that grave a crime, and after a short while the girl's spirits returned to normal. Unfortunately, so did her sense of discretion.

'Well, at least I didn't tell you that Indlewick has got a terragon,' she blurted.

This time it was Jonquil and Rattajack's turn to stop dead in their tracks; it took the girl a little longer to realise her slip. When she did, both hands flew to her face and a long, pitiful wail emerged from her horror-struck countenance.

'Oh, no! I've done it again!'

The two companions bounded up to the young sorceress, who this time was beside herself with remorse and foreboding.

'There's another terragon here?' Jonquil asked excitedly, Rattajack piping with eager anticipation at his shoulder.

'Oh, Throstle's going to kill me!' Ethva whined. 'What have I done? I'm not usually this stupid! I don't know what's wrong with me!'

Jonquil and Rattajack persisted with their inquiry, 'Is there really another terragon here?' the banf asked again.

Ethva evidently decided that although closing the dovecote doors after the birds had flown was a little pointless, she was determined not to let any more secrets out of the bag, and so finished the remainder of the journey to the house of the healer in closely guarded small talk; much to the frustration of the two companions who plagued her every step of the way to expand upon her last accidental revelation. As if to demonstrate that the young sorceress could conduct herself with discretion, if a little late, Ethva's mouth was as tight as a clam on any subject other than the weather and each other's health.

When they reached the house of Indlewick, the two companions saw that it was set aloft a low mound, built within the embrace of a ring of squat trees, whose stouter boughs formed part of the dwelling's structure. The large house was round in shape and built entirely of wood with a central stone chimney. A deep balcony ran around the second storey supported from below by thick wooden poles that were carved and ornamented in the most exquisite detail. The high conical roof of Indlewick's house was thatched with iron beech leaves, a traditional roofing material in all corners of the Commonlands. The effect was to have a lid on your home which shone with a metallic brilliance, the colour of dried blood.

The gentle slopes of the mound surrounding the house were covered in a vivid mosaic of colours. Various herbs and other medicinal plants and shrubs grew in kaleidoscopic profusion, broken only by a network of snaking stone paths. Plants and flowers also grew in window boxes and hanging baskets, or climbed ornate trellises, so that the whole building was edged and draped in living colour. A ragged curtain of faded stems hung in bunches or garlands from the eaves and beneath the balcony: a varied crop of valuable flora harvested from the magnificent garden, and tied up in the warm air to dry. Indeed, there was so much plantlife on or about the house that from a distance little of its true structure could be seen; it might almost have been constructed from leaves and flowers. The ring of old trees, which looked as though they might have gathered to hold up the place with their wide, outstretched limbs, cast a softly dappled shade over the dwelling and nearby edge of garden, their twisted branches vibrant with green leaf and heavy with long, pendulous fruit, as purple as a bruise.

At work amongst this fragrant jungle were a small number of attendants, whose heads bobbed up and down amongst the stems and branches as they stooped to pull out unwanted weeds, take cuttings or generally tend to the plants' needs. One young woman spotted Ethva and called out to her, then the rest of the bent figures straightened up and hailed a hearty, 'Good morrow' to the three visitors. Each of the workers, male and female, wore a simple, habit-like robe in green and brown that was the uniform of those who served at the house of the healers. After passing a few pleasantries with the newcomers, the mainly youthful gardeners returned to their labours.

Ethva and the two companions approached the main entrance along one of the thin winding paths. As one might expect, the thick beds of luxuriant blooms that raised their gaudy heads to the sun were crowded with insects, their generic hum setting the exquisite scene to music. Clouds of tiny flying bodies rose and fell on to the colourful faces of the flowers, their crystal wings glinting like diamonds as they rummaged between the brilliant petals for nectar.

Sitting at his ease in the shade beneath the balcony, alternately sipping a most delicious looking cordial from a glass bowl, garnished with fresh herbs, and sucking on a long, delicate clay pipe, was Throstle. The High Wizard was a picture of relaxation; slumped in a comfy chair with his feet propped up on a stool, a thin haze of smoke hovering in the air above him. He let out a contented sigh as Ethva led the banf and the terragon on to the deck.

'You know, sometimes I forget just how wonderful home comforts can be,' he said to them. 'Greetings, my friends, and welcome to the house of Indlewick. Some cordial?'

Throstle gestured towards a small table beside his chair containing a glass pitcher two thirds full and three bowls. They all readily accepted. The wizard filled the bowls, rose from his chair and offered them to his three friends.

'Come,' he said, after draining his own bowl, 'let me take you to the master of the house.'

Jonquil was dying to ask Throstle about the terragon the girl had spoken of, prompted by equally impatient looks from Rattajack, but to save Ethva from the inevitable embarrassment that would cause, he resolved to be patient.

The interior of the house seemed to contain almost as many plants as the outside. Clay pots of all shapes and sizes were crowded on to shelves, tables, chairs, cupboard tops, in fact, almost any flat surface that was able to share in the available light; all of them bursting with some manner of greenery. Every last patch of wall space was lined with shelves and cabinets packed with a breathtaking array of bottles, flasks, jars and phials, each filled with a rainbow of colourful liquids and powders. There were rows upon rows of canisters, urns, boxes and bags, stacked against tall wooden chests with a myriad tiny drawers. Every vessel and container had been labelled with its precious contents, the writing small and spidery. Jonquil had never seen such a collection of potions and powders, it made the healing grotto of Queen Abalarne in the Banf Kingdom look positively measly.

The whole of the downstairs was one enormous, circular room, made light and airy by many tall windows. The fully stocked walls and counters were attended by a few industrious figures, who turned politely to greet the visitors before carrying on with their various tasks. Like those who tended the plants in the garden, these conscientious characters also wore the distinctive costume of the healers.

Rising from the centre of the spacious chamber was a spiral staircase leading to the upper floor. They climbed the stairs and found themselves on a circular landing with a ring of archways leading off it into separate rooms. Throstle guided them towards one of these openings and ushered his three companions inside. The chamber was like a condensed version of the great room down below; floor to ceiling shelves crammed with vessels and containers, a window crowded with plants, large areas of work surface strewn with books and papers. In addition to this already familiar paraphernalia, there were tables piled high with interconnected tubes and flasks, mysterious liquids contained within bubbling away over naked flames. Bending over before one such precarious construction with his back to the entrance was a large figure, broad in the beam, and when he straightened up taller even than Throstle.

Indlewick was a jolly character, his full round face seemed to wear a permanent smile, and was frequently prone to bellowing laughter. He was as big as a bear and as gentle as a butterfly. He covered his bald crown with a pudding shaped cap, short cropped wisps of greying hair poking out beneath. His brown eyes were kind and reassuring but as sharp as a blade. A thick hedge of ginger-white hair sprouted from his brow, matching a similar goatee tuft on his chin. He was dressed in a modest style, if a little grander than his workers to denote his rank, but still in the same drab shades of green and brown.

Rattajack saw that a far corner of the room was screened off from the main part by a decorative curtain. He seemed to be the only one of the four visitors who had noticed it, and this was because he felt himself strangely drawn to whatever it was that lay behind that curtain. Rattajack's attention was so distracted by this sensation that he only half heard Jonquil being introduced to Indlewick and then himself. A large, warm hand gently squeezed one of his ears, and then the big frame of the healing wizard squatted down beside him. The terragon gazed into the wide, beaming face, and at once decided that he liked this friendly character. Indlewick spoke softly into his ear.

'Why don't you go and see,' he said with a chuckle.

This statement may have seemed somewhat cryptic to the others in the room, but the terragon and the large wizard understood it perfectly. With a quick look at Jonquil who was pleasantly intrigued, Rattajack cautiously approached the curtain. A sense of excitement began to flutter in his stomach that he could not quite explain. There was a presence behind the veil of cloth, a being who was radiating feelings of quiet contentment that only he could sense. Rattajack slowly drew back the curtain with his hand and peered within.

Curled up in a nest of sheep's wool, eyes tightly closed was an exquisite creature, who drew a gasp of admiration from Rattajack. Jonquil came up beside him and shared in his companion's delight. The sleeping form had all the shape and bearing of a beautiful she-terragon, but instead of the usual forest green colour, Trea, for that was her name, had scales of silvery-pearl, and crest and wings of the softest shade of blue. Both Rattajack and Jonquil were entranced, and as they gazed down at this remarkable vision, Rattajack began to call to her in his silent language. At first there was no response. The silver terragon remained deep in slumber; but then, the closed eyelids twitched a little and then slowly blinked open. Two pale, amethyst orbs stared up at the two companions. Rattajack gave her a soft trill of greeting, and Trea rose from her nest and nudged his snout with hers. Indlewick squealed with delight at this touching scene, and clapped his hands with joy. It was quite an incongruous sight to see such childlike enthusiasm in such a large person. This was clearly the reaction he had been hoping for. With a soft, enticing voice he called the she-terragon to him. She hesitated for a second, a little unnerved by his excited behaviour; and it was evident to the banf that Trea and the wizard had not enjoyed a long acquaintance. She was strangely unsure. Eventually the silver terragon conquered her fear and trotted into the fat healer's arms, who had dropped to a crouch so as not to appear too large and forbidding. Trea could not help looking back at Rattajack whilst she was being fussed, her eyes incredibly large and doleful. The male terragon just stood transfixed, and Jonquil noted with a smile that his companion's mouth had remained open since he had first laid eyes on the beautiful female; and when the banf placed his hand on the terragon's shoulder, he could feel that Rattajack was trembling.

Indlewick suddenly announced that all this excitement had made him hungry, and that he was sure it must be time for breakfast. With that he led his group of visitors into a large room on the opposite side of the building, that seemed to serve as some manner of refectory for the household, and sat them all down to a delicious meal. Much to the two companions' frustration, the healer wizard kept the conversation at the table on the subject of herb lore. He questioned Jonquil relentlessly on what medicinal plants or substances were to be found within the confines of the Banf Kingdom; and having quickly exhausted the banf's knowledge of such matters, he then addressed his insatiable curiosity to Throstle, demanding to know what new plants the High Wizard had discovered for him on his long sojourn in the wilderness of Dragongorge. Jonquil spent the whole duration of the meal waiting for an opportunity to ask some questions of his own: chiefly about the silver terragon and where she came from.

Some time later when Indlewick finally got around to attending to Jonquil's wings, the story of Trea came to be told, and what an enlightening tale for the banf and his terragon companion it turned out to be. Stranger yet, it was Throstle, not the healer, who was to tell it. The High Wizard talked whilst Indlewick set to work on Jonquil's long neglected wounds, throwing in occasional comments and interruptions of his own whenever he saw fit; and receiving a sharp, 'Who's telling this story?' admonishment from Throstle when he did.

One of Throstle's apprentices, Karreg, an adventurous soul who like his intrepid master liked to wander far abroad, had one day found himself in a remote, snowy chasm at the northernmost tip of the range of tall, white mountains known as the Marble Fortress. His feet having a habit of moving faster than his brain, as Throstle put it, the foolish young wizard soon got lost. Despite long consultations with his charts, copies of those drawn up by Throstle with the accumulated knowledge of years of exploration, Karreg was still no nearer to working out just where he was. One further worry for the young wizard was that he thought he must be relatively close to the area containing the high fissure ruled by the great dragon Vladdigor. Stumbling accidentally into the jealously guarded territory of that vicious legend was something he wished to avoid at all costs; but was he north of the dragon or south of him? To the east or west? In the end he chose his path with a flip of a wishbone, and set off Northwest.

Eventually, the young explorer entered a valley of towering cliffs; perfect dragon country, though not much like the descriptions he had read of Vladdigor's domain. That did not mean that he should not be on his guard however, there were other dangerous dragons besides the infamous blue tyrant inhabiting the mountains and valleys. Karreg guessed that he must have wandered into the tail end of one of the main tributaries of Dragongorge, that eventually wound its way through the mountains, growing deeper and wider, until it joined with the great canyon itself. Such secluded ravines were often chosen by the more secretive dragon races, who preferred an environment far removed from the sometimes intense competition of the larger chasms. The paladris or paradise dragons were a good example of such species; and Karreg saw with a quickening heart that he had entered a valley which was home to a colony of these rare and beautiful creatures.

Belonging to the family of skydancers, the paladris needed clear, open spaces to perform their stunning courtship displays, and so sought out lonely, unpopulated areas that they could claim as their own. It was considered to be one of the greatest privileges to catch a secret glimpse of the brilliant males as they soared and dived before an audience of females, displaying their rainbow majesty and aerial prowess. Like giant, fabulous kites they would twist and spiral on the surging draughts, flourishing harlequin spans of wing, fin and tail. Their aim was to entice the females from their cliff-ledge perches, to join with the males on the boisterous breezes and dance the hypnotic, synchronised nuptial flight.

'Imagine a flock of these handsome dragons,' Throstle said dreamily. 'A mesmeric sky dance, a bright, airborne kaleidoscope, whirling against a backdrop of dark, frowning cliffs, caught in the last searching beams of the evening sun. Karreg was blessed with good fortune indeed to witness one of the rarest sights in the dragon kingdom. I myself have only seen it a handful of times.'

Throstle eventually moved his apprentice on from this point in the tale, reluctant as he was to leave the cliffs of the paladris. Karreg had wished he could record the location of this thrilling scene on his charts for future reference, but as he was ignorant of his own precise location, at that moment, this was sadly impossible. Beyond the valley of the paradise dragons, the young wizard entered a wide basin containing a large frozen lake. The surrounding walls were formed from gently sloping ridges, honeycombed with a broad swathe of caves and holes about half way up. It was then that the young wizard committed his most foolish act so far. As is so often the case with those of tender years, he allowed the child within him to outrank his common sense, and instead of keeping to the anonymity of the rocks, he could not resist venturing out to leave his mark on the pristine, white crust covering the water. The lid of the ice was at least a man's height thick at the lake's centre, and therefore strong enough to support a whole army let alone one, solitary lost youth. The ice was not his danger. His danger was in removing himself from the relatively safe background of the frost-mottled rocks and shale, and setting his dark form against a glaring white canvas of pure snow. Karreg could not have made himself more obvious to the hungry eyes of a predatory dragon, if he had built a huge smoking fire and blasted a long fanfare on a giant bugle. Therefore it was only a matter of time before his foolishness brought its inevitable reward.

About the same time as the young wizard reached the heart of the frozen lake, he thought he spied an unusual shape lying at the edge of the shore furthest from him. The light seemed to catch on this mysterious form in a shimmering, silvery hue. Being a wizard, and therefore insatiably curious, he set off to find out what it was. Unfortunately, Karreg did not see the silhouette of a large dragon alight on the top of the high ridge behind him.

The dragon, known as Grymwarg, was the scourge of the lake basin and surrounding valleys. He had been idly planing above his territory, casting a watchful eye over the sprawling, barren landscape below, when his keen sight had spotted the tiny black speck moving across the white disc of the lake from high up in the sky. Being a dragon, and insatiably curious (and hungry), he had decided to investigate. Grymwarg was a terrifying specimen of a dragon. He was mainly steely-grey like a falcon, with mottled flanks and black detail about his face. A long, sleek crest rose at the back of a savage head, which flared like a flag when the beast was enraged. Like most dragons, he never rushed into an attack, but watched with cool interest until the situation had been fully appraised. He was especially wary with Karreg, for his special dragon senses warned him that this was no ordinary trespasser, but one who carried the protection of enchantment. A wizard. To make such an obvious target of himself, the enchanter was either very confident in his powers or lacking in wit. Which was it? Grymwarg could tell by the distant figure's ease of movement that he was relatively youthful. That might tip the scales in favour of naivety over wisdom. It was intriguing; and the dragon decided that the prospect of sweet, young flesh made it worth testing the wizard's mettle. Grymwarg raised his great wings and sprang into the updraught.

At first he thought it was dead, but when he bent down and laid a gentle hand upon its flank, the limp form gave a weak whimper. Karreg had never seen or even heard of a terragon, so to his inexperienced eyes this poor creature was just an infant dragon. A baby, lost just like him, far from its nest and parents. There were no visible injuries on its shiny body, apart from the leg on its underside which seemed to be bent at rather an unnatural angle; but there were deep scratches on the wing limbs, and a few tears in the bluish flight membranes. What this rather pretty little creature was doing down by the frozen water, Karreg could only guess. The marks at her back suggested that she had been seized by sharp talons, and the youth wondered if she had been stolen from her eyrie by marauding hunters, as was the practice of snowhawks, and dropped by mistake as her abductor flew over the lonely crater. Karreg gently stroked the delicate head, and to his delight the terragon's eyelids parted a little to reveal sparkling slithers of amethyst. The young wizard tried to reassure the pitiful creature with soft words, and as he did so, slid a hand underneath the silvery body and carefully raised the terragon to her feet. Her whimpers became louder, and it was evident that the twisted leg was broken. However when Karreg finally got her to remain upright, the moaning she had done over her pain was nothing to the piercing cry that erupted from within her as her drowsy eyes fixed on something fast approaching at the wizard's back. Karreg spun around and bawled in horror at the sight of Grymwarg gliding low over the frozen lake towards them, a storm of white snowpowder curling about his wings. For a terrible moment the young wizard froze with fear, and then, like a miracle, the words of his master came flooding back into his frantic mind. Karreg lunged for his staff that he had laid down beside the terragon's body. Uttered the secret word which awoke the sleeping power in the crystal housed at its tip, and then readied himself for the approach of the monster.

Remembering his lessons, Karreg noted that Grymwarg's rear talons remained tucked back against the base of his tail, which meant that this was to be a reconnoitring pass rather than an attack. Most fighting dragons sized up their opponents before committing themselves to battle. Karreg held his nerve as the winged terror grew vast before him, suppressing the urge to engage the dragon too soon.

'Warring with dragons,' Throstle had once told him and his fellow apprentices, 'is as much a contest of nerve and wits, as brute strength; and if you're lucky, you'll face one who is more interested in the fight than the kill!'

Karreg made a silent wish that this dragon foe shared his master's philosophy.

The slipstream from the dragon's pass nearly knocked the wizard from his feet, and the blizzard of snowpowder that tore along with it stung like grit on his cheeks. He quickly turned to watch the speeding form of the grey dragon bank across the grim face of the rock ridge and rise once again on the mighty draughts.

What now? Had the dragon seen enough or would he make a second pass? Karreg's limited experience of the wild warriors of Dragongorge was little help to him, and as he did not know what species he was being assailed by. The lists of predictable behaviour for certain dragon types, that he had learned by rote in the classroom were of no use to him either. All the young wizard could be sure of was that the dragon was very large and very close.

He tightened his grip on his staff as the distant winged shape turned back towards the lake and dropped swiftly below the skyline. Grymwarg's grey body against the slate-grey background made his manner of approach difficult to see. Unlike his first pass, the dragon was deliberately flying within the strip of rock between snow and sky to mask his intentions. Karreg realised that this wily old fighter was so intimate with the lie of his domain, that he could use his knowledge to utterly confound the wizard's learned etiquette of engagement; if the youth could not see Grymwarg's rear claws, how could he know if they were up or down? It was at this highly inappropriate point that Karreg chose to admonish himself for his present peril; if only he had not been in such a hurry to explore the mountains; if only he had listened to the wisdom of his master and learned to walk before he tried to run.

The roar of the wind beneath the outstretched wings of the dragon grew louder in the youth's ears. Almost without intending it, the charging word slipped from his lips, and his staff crystal sparkled with power. Whether as a consequence of the sudden light from his staff, or simply the following through of his original intention, the dragon thrust his bared talons at the wizard. Had Karreg not been prepared for an attack, he would have seen the claws drop from the dragon's rear too late, and been unable to shoot a shrieking, golden bolt at the hurtling bulk. The fiery streak of power smote the dragon hard in the underbelly, causing his lowered feet to spring back up in reflex. Grymwarg roared as his huge form swept unfulfilled over Karreg's head, the dragon sounding his thunderous voice more from surprise and rage than a feeling of pain. The young wizard's assault could have felt little worse than a pin prick against a hide as ancient and thick as that of Grymwarg's; but it had been a long time since the old monster had crossed swords with an enchanter, and the sting of Old Magic came as something of a shock after the feeble weapons of his normal prey. The dragon screamed up into the sky once again, casting angry glances beneath him at the smouldering wound that still trailed a smudge of smoke as he flew.

Karreg looked about him for anything that might offer him and the terragon shelter; for he knew that if the dragon came again this time it would be to the death. Apart from the belt of caves high up on the slope of the ridge there was nothing, not even so much as a large rock or boulder. The caves would have been ideal, but as Karreg was only too well aware, the dragon would reach him and his little friend before they reached the caves. The terragon may have been just able to hobble along, but she was in no condition to make a mad dash for anywhere; and now that the youth had made the acquaintance of the enchanting creature he was not about to save himself and leave her to the dragon's mercy. He was confident that with his unconditional love for all dragonkind that was something that Throstle, his master, would never do, no matter how dire the consequences.

There was nothing else for it then. He would have to make his stand where he was, on the edge of the frozen lake, and, as his friend Yandreas would have said: either die or earn the next notch on his staff!

Grymwarg slowly traced the perimeter of the basin, planing just above the ragged line of the ridge. He had no need to hurry to begin his next attack; the young wizard was trapped in the open, and they both knew it. The dragon was far too fast for his foe to make it to the caves, so the youth had nothing to do but wait for the inevitable; and Grymwarg intended to make him wait. The dragon had suffered the indignity of a wound at the hands of an audacious novice, and for that he was going to suffer. Unfortunately for the wizard, Grymwarg was not a firebreather, so death from him was seldom swift. The dragon put down on a raised pinnacle of rock to take his ease, and give an occasional soothing lick to his smarting injury.

Karreg sighed as he watched the dragon's distant silhouette alight atop the dark band of rock. He was not sure whether he wanted it all over with or not, but the waiting was awful. He glanced once again at the far off caves, and then down to his injured companion. The silver terragon had fallen asleep again despite her fear, a sure sign of her weakened state. Perhaps it was for the best, the young wizard thought gloomily. Let death come swift and unseen to the poor creature, for in all probability it would not be so for him. The power in his staff was not enough to slay the dragon, only anger him further; and as Throstle had often warned them, 'A vengeful dragon can be a slow executioner!'

A high pitched shriek from high in the air behind him wrenched Karreg away from his maudlin thoughts. The young wizard's heart raced as the hovering form of another dragon hung menacingly above them. The beast resembled the family of fleet creatures known as swifts. A rapid search through his memorised lists reminded Karreg that this fast flier shared many characteristics with the snowhawks, of whom they were part ancestor. The hovering dragon was barely two thirds the bulk of Grymwarg; its body much sleeker and streamlined, its wings long and pointed like blades. Sandarach was a known marauder of the isolated vales, and had clearly returned to the great basin for its lost meal. Karreg could not quite decide if the murderous beast was dismayed or delighted to find its tender morsel in the company of another potential prey.

A deep roar carried on the breeze to the young wizard from across the wide floor of the basin; and Karreg turned to see Grymwarg's broad wings embrace the air. A ray of hope brightened the youth's gloom. The great grey dragon was now faced with a dilemma; should he continue with his attack on the young wizard, or should he turn his fury against Sandarach, the interloper? Karreg decided to gamble that the large dragon would choose the swift as his first target, and firing a warning bolt at the smaller dragon still hovering menacingly above, he scooped up the dozing body of the terragon and struck out for the distant caves.

Grymwarg surged across the expanse of the lake like a tornado, his cry of outrage shaking the air. This was to be no reconnoitre, the dragon was charging straight for the kill. Sandarach, peeved at being denied his catch, delayed his inevitable exit from the crater, by attempting an impudent strike at the hurrying wizard. Despite his burden, Karreg was still able to manoeuvre his staff, and the swooping swift earned itself a burning hole in its wing for its impudent aggression. Sandarach screeched in agony and then, foregoing its prize, bent all its determination on gaining height for a fast escape. For all its speed and agility, the swift could not make up for its foolish delay, and Grymwarg cannoned into its lithe form like a flying battering ram. The smaller dragon was punched into a violent spin which eventually brought it crashing down on to the shale beach. The large dragon's velocity necessitated a wide sweep to bring him back round again to the lake, and by that time the young wizard was half way to the caves and safety. With a growl of disappointment Grymwarg banked into the surging updraughts and leisurely spiralled down to the twitching mass of wing and limb that was Sandarach. Grymwarg was not in the habit of eating dragonflesh; so, rather than drop like a vulture on to the marauder's body and consume it, he seized the smaller dragon by the wing and carried it bodily from his domain.

'I found the crippled form of Sandarach some days later,' Throstle told his audience, 'and with skills I learned from the master here, healed his wounds. Despite old Grymwarg's might, the injuries were not that great; dragons are made tough in Dragongorge. I'm glad to tell you that wicked Sandarach changed his opinion of wizards following his recovery, and is now one of my most reliable scouts. Still a little too fond of nest robbing for my liking, but I'm working on him!'

'What about Karreg and the terragon?' asked Jonquil

'Oh, well, they made it to the caves of course; and Grymwarg isn't a vindictive dragon, he gave young Karreg the battle. With the help of our little friend here, whom Karreg called Trea (which in his native tongue means 'precious'), they wound their way through the network of tunnels and emerged on the outside of the basin's rim. They were then discovered by friendly dragons, and word was brought to me of my long lost apprentice's whereabouts and adventure.'

'Trea, of course, was then brought to me,' Indlewick chipped in. 'For her wounds needed urgent tending; but as you can see her broken leg is as good as new.'

Jonquil extended a friendly hand to the silver terragon, to stroke her forehead. Trea seemed to be soothed by the banf's attention.

'Ah, I can see that you have the touch, Jonquil,' said Indlewick.

to reveal a thin, dark red kernel and a thick cladding of the yellow wool; which pulled out of its leathery shell in soft, stringy tufts.

'One of the commonest trees in Eddilee,' Indlewick continued, 'eight of which are currently helping to hold up this house!'

'Orchin's healing powers are legendary,' Throstle said to the banf. 'Almost as legendary as Indlewick's here!'

The healer gave a burst of dismissive laughter, and then began to apply a thick layer of the yellow wool to Jonquil's wings.

'I am confident,' the fat wizard told the banf, 'that when this poultice has done its work, your wings will be as good as new!'

'They feel better already,' Jonquil admitted.

'I am afraid the dressings will have to remain in place for some time for the orchin to do its work properly. I shall have special covers made for you, to keep the poultice clean and safe.'

Indlewick continued with his laborious task, carefully placing the cool, damp strips on the densely layered feathers. Jonquil could almost feel the stiff, ravaged tendons easing beneath the healer's gentle hands.

'Why don't you tell us some more dragon stories, Throstle?' Ethva urged. 'Whilst Indlewick applies the orchin. I'm sure Jonquil would like to hear more.'

'Oh, indeed I would,' the banf agreed.

'Tell us about Eyesand,' the healer piped up from behind a broad, outstretched span of Jonquil's primary feathers.

'Oh, yes!' the banf cried. 'I would dearly love to hear about the dragons of Eyesand!'

Throstle assumed an expression of mock astonishment, and glowered at each of them in turn.

'Pah!' he exclaimed. 'Here we all are on the brink of disaster, and you want to hear dragon stories!'

'Of course!' Ethva replied cheekily, making them all laugh.

Throstle flicked his eyebrows, gave a quick shrug and said, 'All right then.' He refilled his pipe, strode out on to the balcony, settled himself into a large, comfortable chair set against the wall, and added, 'We'll just have to save the world tomorrow!'

Honour Among Thieves

'Eyesand!' said a dark voice. 'The Dragonmaster of Eyesand!'

'Horcust Rothgilian?' said another. 'What of him?'

'I hear he is sheltering a rich prize, my Lord. One that will be of great interest to you.'

'I should hope so, Mummichog,' snapped Juvula. 'I have had to leave my army and fly halfway across Enchantica to be here. It had better be worth my trouble!'

The old goblin grinned and drew his master further into the cave, as if there was a need to keep secrets even from their own servants loitering outside on the valley side. The depths of Mummichog's suspicions sometimes outweighed reason, and Juvula wondered if the old goblin trusted his own shadow.

'Sunjack has sent word to me that Jonquil the Hero is at Eddilee,' Mummichog hissed in a conspiratorial whisper.

The wizard's eyes ignited with interest. 'And his little dragon friend?'

'Terragon,' Mummichog corrected him. 'Rattajack, the terragon.'

Juvula paced through the gloom of the cave, his head bowed in deep consideration.

'Was I right to send for you, my Lord?' the old goblin asked with a smug glint in his yellow eyes.

The wizard turned and gave Mummichog a severe stare that slowly dissolved into an evil smile. 'Yes,' he said eventually. 'You were right.'

Juvula strolled past Mummichog's hunched form and back out into the daylight. The sweeping view of the snow-kissed valley unrolled before him; and on the horizon the high rim of the golden basin of Eddilee. Mummichog joined him at the bright vista.

'I never thought I would ever return to this place,' the wizard murmured dreamily, almost to himself. 'My experience here was not exactly profound!'

The old goblin cleared his throat sensible that he was intruding upon private reminiscences.

'Er ...... what would you like us to do, my Lord?' he inquired.

Juvula looked around at the two groups of attendants that stood idly about awaiting instruction. One made up of 'invisibles' - goblins in black cloaks - the other his own men; neither group eager to mingle with the other. Juvula's eyes returned to the distant Vale of the Wizards.

'I want them!' he hissed. 'I want both of them! Especially the one known as Jonquil; the elf creature. The Orb spoke of him!'

'Er... banf, I believe, my Lord,' Mummichog interrupted.

'Whatever!' the wizard snapped.

The old goblin gave Juvula a broad, servile smile - as he always did when someone had just given him offence, and he was silently fantasising on ways he would like to repay that insult. So he was a pedant! He remembered his preciosity used to infuriate Hellbender also; but if correctness was a crime, Mummichog was glad to be guilty.

'Do you want them taken - alive?' the old goblin asked, knowing full well the answer.

'Of course! They are the sworn enemies of He-that-is-to-be-reborn-in-me! Therefore it is only fitting that I should be the one to slay them.'

'They hardly ever venture out alone, according to Sunjack,' Mummichog told him. 'Although your four dragon spies take it in turns to keep a close eye on their activities.'

The wizard gave the goblin a sly, insistent look. 'I am sure the artful Sunjack can devise some means of distracting them,' he said.

Mummichog nodded in compliance. 'I will despatch Zemorga at once with a message for our brother,' he said solemnly.

Juvula smiled, 'The old devil beast is here? I should like to see him before he leaves again.'

'At the rear of the cave, my Lord,' Mummichog replied, gesturing inside. 'He's eating ... er ... something... at the moment.'

The two of them walked back into the shadow of the cave, and eventually the wizard could hear the noisy sounds of something being devoured: juices slavered and bones cracked. Juvula greeted the ugly dragon creature with terms of affection usually reserved for something pink and fluffy. Zemorga, for his part, gave a gurgling croak in response, a long, thin portion of his meal dropping from his jaws as he did so. The wizard stooped to pick it up, and as his eyes slowly grew accustomed to the gloom, he saw that it was an arm.

'What is this?'

'Horolog,' said the old goblin.

'What's a horolog?' the wizard asked in disgust.

'It was not a what - it was a whom,' Mummichog replied with a casual air. 'He failed to live up to expectations.'

Juvula stared into the shadowy face of the old goblin, unable to conceal the shock from his face.

'All the brothers know the price of disappointment!' Mummichog added.

The wizard emitted a long gasp of disbelief, the old goblin wrongly interpreting the wizard's reaction as faint-heartedness.

'You are feeding *your* people to *my* dragons? Juvula asked with an indignant air that caught Mummichog unawares. 'Well?' the wizard demanded.

'Only the ones who displease!' Mummichog finally managed to say.

'But these beasts are used to good meat!' Juvula exclaimed, 'I hope you wash them properly first!'

'Who, my Lord?' asked the goblin, a little confused. 'The dragons?'

'No!' the wizard roared. 'The victims! Who can say what effect unwashed goblin meat might have on my special boys!'

The old goblin looked at the hunched form of Zemorga and tried to see what was so special about the living gargoyle that chomped merrily down upon the mortal remains of his former postulant.

'They look pretty well on it to me, my Lord,' he said quickly.

Juvula offered the cold damp limb to the monstrous reptile who snatched it from his hand with eager jaws, crunching it greedily between his racks of sharp teeth.

'Yes, well, just you see that you look after them. They are all very precious to me!'

The wizard left the darkness of the cave and returned to the barren landscape, the rugged contours of the anonymous valley glazed with a grey dullness. Only the distant slither of green, brief snatches of a deep trough of fertile land, broke the dismal patchwork of sombre tones. The Vale of the Wizards was showered with a radiant torrent of golden beams; the choking cloud cover of the Winter world held back by invisible hands.

'Has his eminence the Grand Wizard thrown any tasty morsels of news in our direction lately?' Juvula asked with a tone of mockery.

'I fear that spring of information has become somewhat stifled of late,' Mummichog replied. 'The Lord Horcust returning has something to do with that, no doubt. Also two high emissaries from the Three Wizards arrived from the South a short while ago. There was a High Council.'

'What was discussed?' the wizard demanded.

The old goblin shrugged his shoulders.

'What's the matter, shiny baubles not enough for Heskel any more? Did he not like the ring I sent for him? That came from Hadros' personal treasure box!' Juvula sneered.

'He has to be careful,' Mummichog explained. 'In such illustrious company.'

'Then what of Sunjack? Has he suddenly lost his eavesdropping skills?'

'Sunjack was ordered to stay away from the Great Hall by Horcust Rothgilian,' the goblin answered. 'He even had him watched by the girl, Ethva. She followed him like a shadow. He could not get near to the place.'

'Then what of the others?' Juvula demanded. 'Is there any news of my power crystal? The final endorsement of the valley's elite!'

The old goblin shook his head. 'Not as yet, my Lord.'

The wizard scowled and angrily hurled a fragment of rock that he had been toying with into the great void before him. Then he sighed reflectively, turning to stare at the eastern horizon.

'I must return to my army soon; and prepare a welcome for our new found friend,' he said. 'If they do not send the crystal in the next few days, it will be too late.'

'Where is the army, my Lord?' Mummichog inquired.

'Camped just outside the eastern wall of the forest.'

'And the Orb?'

'The Dark Sorcerer and the girl are bivouacked just inside the western border in the company of a Zrobokite horde,' the wizard told him.

'Zroboks!' the old goblin gasped, his face creased with trepidation. 'Fearsome fighters!'

'Indeed!'

'My lord Juvula is very well informed,' Mummichog said with an uneasy smile.

'I make it my business to be,' Juvula replied slyly.

'Dragon spies?' the goblin fished.

'Amongst other things,' the wizard said in a tone which effectively closed the subject.

Mummichog grinned and cast his eyes deferentially to the ground. The wizard suddenly remembered something he had meant to ask the goblin. He coughed awkwardly.

'Mummichog,' he said.

The old goblin slowly raised his eyes to the wizard's face.

'My Lord?'

Juvula took a few steps away from the listening group of goblins and gestured Mummichog to follow, the old goblin dutifully complied.

'Graquat said something to me before I left, which he would not translate,' the wizard said in lowered tones. 'I need you to tell me what it means.'

'Certainly, my Lord,' answered Mummichog. 'Can you remember it?'

The wizard gave another embarrassed cough, and then with as much dignity as he could muster, proceeded to give as accurate a rendition of the ice demon's grating speech as he could manage. To his great annoyance the old goblin's face began to twitch with suppressed mirth.

'What's so amusing?' Juvula demanded testily.

'Nothing, my Lord.' replied Mummichog, his face suddenly becoming serious.

'That is pretty much how it sounded to me!' the wizard insisted, his eyes glaring defensively. 'Now, as you know my grasp of Unskaran is basic to say the least, and I only recognised one word: eat. What was the rest of it?'

The old goblin sighed deeply, his breath rippled with swallowed laughter. When he spoke he had to keep clearing his throat to conceal any errant chuckles.

'Are you sure that is what he said?' Mummichog asked with a tremulous voice.

The wizard snorted angrily, his normally short temper strained to its limits and replied through gritted teeth, 'As best as I can remember, yes! What does it mean?'

'Well,' Mummichog began expansively, 'it is a very old ice demon proverb. A gift of invaluable advice passed down from father to son......'

The wizard's mood seemed to improve a little at the goblin's words. It pleased him to think that the general of his ice demon army held him in such regard that he would recite an ancient saying at their parting.

'....which loosely translated means,' Mummichog continued. 'don't eat yellow snowhoppers!'

It took a moment before the wizard's face came to terms with what the goblin had said. Mummichog clamped his lips together and defied them to grin.

'What?' Juvula roared.

The old goblin could do no more than nod his head and shrug.

'That's all I need!' the wizard raged. 'An ice demon general with a sense of humour!'

With that he turned and stormed back into the cave. His thunderous voice could be heard a little while later when he evidently surprised his men somewhere inside taking their ease, and vented his fury upon them without mercy.

Mummichog stopped grinning; his face quickly darkening to a troubled scowl as he watched Juvula disappear into the black yawning gape of the cave.

In reality, the old goblin had not been amused at all. His suppressed convulsions of mirth had all been an act. He was in fact very angry.

Graquat was getting bold. Too bold. And the old goblin had suddenly found himself having to give the wizard a false translation of the ice demon's parting quip. After all, Mummichog had not survived the reigns of four goblin monarchs without having the ability to think on his feet. However, he resented being forced to do so by another's folly. There would be time enough for himself and Graquat to vent their bile against Juvula when the Orb was theirs; but they did not have it yet! If Graquat did not learn patience and restraint, then their arch scheme would surely fail.

The plot was simple enough: wait until Juvula won the Orb from the fugitives and then relieve him of it. Not to use it themselves of course. Mummichog would never presume to such status; after all he was an 'invisible' - modesty personified! However, the old goblin knew that he who possessed the great crystal could command a high price for its safe delivery to whichever side desired it the most. All of his ambitions would be realised from the proceeds of such a bargaining; and the old goblin's ambitions were high indeed. Not for himself, but for his son. After news had reached the Dark Mountains of the death of Bledderag, the last of the king's sons, Mummichog had secured a secret agreement with Hellbender that Gamling, the old goblin's own son, would inherit the throne on the great king's demise. When Okra had surprised them all and murdered her father, seizing his throne, Mummichog's great hopes had been dashed. However, with the Orb as a bargaining tool, the old goblin would be able buy all the power he needed to reinstate the rightful king of the Dark Mountains: his son. Gamling was safe in a secret location only waiting for the day when his father would call upon him to reunite the great tribes of the goblins once again. Okra and Gremba had lost everything that Hellbender, aided by Mummichog, had achieved following their disastrous involvement in the Battle of Dragonskeep. The tribes were now dissipated and disordered; warring against each other as was their old, old habit. Mummichog had a dream that his son, Gamling, would be the one to lead the goblin nation to new glories, greater than before.

For the time being, however, both he and Graquat would have to be patient and careful. They were still a long way from their goal, and they still had need of the wizard. Juvula was no fool, and they could not afford to give him any cause for suspicion. He was already picking up a few ice demon words and phrases, and it was only a matter of time before the contents of Mummichog and Graquat's casual dialogue, which they exchanged quite openly before the wizard, was no longer secret. The old goblin ground his teeth at the thought of Graquat's reckless arrogance and loose tongue. The true translation of the ice demon's words was, 'When this is over, human, I eat your heart!' Mummichog had dredged up the old joke on the spur of the moment; and if Juvula had been just a little further on with his understanding of the language, then all of their grand schemes would have crumbled into dust. Juvula may not have been a great, all powerful wizard, but Mummichog had seen enough over the many years he had schemed with him to know better than to idly incur his enmity.

Stories and Adventure

Throstle continued to enthral his small audience with his tales of the dragons of Eyesand. So much so that Jonquil and Indlewick moved all of the healing paraphernalia - stool, orchin basket, table, implements, etc. - on to the balcony to better enjoy the High Wizard's colourful renditions of his favourite legends. Ethva was already installed in a voluminous hammock, often used by the fat wizard on warm afternoons, and was lazily taking her ease, swinging gently back and forth and sipping from a bowl of the delicious herb cordial. Throstle himself had resumed the attitude in which they had first seen him that day, and was speaking in a lilting, rhythmic voice, his eyes staring into the sun-dappled weave of grizzang branches.

He was now speaking of Eyesand itself; a city, once mighty and prosperous, that was built by men on the floor of the great canyon known as Dragongorge. The city sprawled over the dry bed of the chasm like a small mountain range; its valleys: labyrinthine streets, and its peaks: great soaring towers of stone.

The people of Eyesand had lived in harmony with the dragons of the gorge, by whose consent they dwelled there, for many generations. Sharing the bounties of their trading with the peoples of the upper world with their dragon neighbours. Inevitably, however, there has to come a day when evil nature - a characteristic unique to neither man nor dragon - sets its hands to work against the noble peace. Greed and envy came to live amongst the denizens of the city and the cliffs. An attitude of resentment was born and swiftly spread throughout both populations. Some of the city dwellers began to begrudge the portion of their wealth and good fortune which they felt obliged to share with the dragons. A few of the dragons began to despise the presence of men in their ancient homeland - ever expanding their city, plundering the precious natural resources of the great gorge, and seeming to grow endlessly both in numbers and arrogance. In the end the dam of high emotions burst and war erupted between man and dragon; but it was an uneven fight and was brought to a tumultuous climax when a vast army of dragons descended on the beleaguered city and tore it down, blackening the sky in a great avenging cloud.

Those who did not flee were either crushed beneath the crumbling masonry or despatched by the enraged dragons. Never again would the race of man attempt such a venture in the homeland of the dragons. Smaller, more discreet settlements have existed on the fringes of the gorge and in its distant tributaries, and nomads have occasionally wandered through its empty chasms, pitching their encampments and taking water from the falling streams. Yet no more great cities have risen from the dusty floor of Dragongorge itself. Over the centuries, the dragons of the great canyon learned tolerance towards the other races of the Commonlands; that is as long as the outsiders remembered that Dragongorge is for the dragons alone.

So what of Eyesand during the time of Horcust Rothgilian, so called Dragonmaster of Eyesand? After the sacking of the great city, the dragon host dispersed and returned to their caves and cliff ledges to continue the timeless ritual of their long lives. They soon forgot about the smouldering ruin and the war with the people who once lived there. That is until a few dragon species decided that broken walls and blackened windows were not that dissimilar to their own cliffs and caves, and began to inhabit the old ruin. Over the years more and more dragons were attracted by the growing community until Eyesand once again became a thriving city of life: dragon life. Being intensely curious the dragons explored what was left of the ancient corridors and deep chambers and came across great stores of grain and wine, abandoned by their fleeing owners; but most exciting of all - secret hoards of gold and treasure were uncovered, amassed by rich merchants who had been forced to leave them behind.

If there is one thing that is guaranteed to cause normally peaceable dragons to quarrel like avaricious children, it is gold and jewels. As soon as the treasure was discovered the strongest and most powerful beasts waded in and claimed as much of the sparkling wealth for themselves as they could feasibly defend. One such dragon was Urlfang, later to be called Glimmerscale by the nomads and the cliff top settlers, and the steady stream of adventurers who came to the ruined city to try for a share of the dragon's hoard.

Glimmerscale had removed a sizeable portion of wealth to an old guard tower. A large, cylindrical building half of whose height had been ripped off during the city's destruction, and was laid bare to the stars as a wide circle of ragged stone wall. Beneath it there was a capacious chamber that was formerly sleeping quarters for a whole battalion of guards. Laid on the floor of this large subterranean space was a huge pile of gold, silver and gems. Laid on top of the dazzling hoard, when not feeding himself or driving off would-be thieves, was Glimmerscale.

So large and heavy was the dragon and so long did he remain on guard in the bowels of the ruined tower, that a second skin of princely treasure became permanently attached to his underside. This meant that when he rose out of the dishevelled turret and reared his formidable shape before the trembling figures that had dared his wrath, his whole trunk sparkled and shone with a priceless coat. The effect by torch light in the dead of night was spectacular; the soaring torso of treasure glittering before their naked flames like the evening sun on a breeze-kissed river. Before very long the reputation of the dragon they learned to call Glimmerscale began to spread far and wide.

Urlfang known as Glimmerscale was not the only dragon to win fame for himself. For the ruins of Eyesand seemed to attract a host of inhabitants of an unusual or remarkable nature. Whilst Glimmerscale sat upon his pile of wealth, Magmaroth 'Bloodhorn', a fearsome firedrake, occupied another buried chamber elsewhere in the city. As Throstle explained to his avid listeners, most male dragons were highly territorial and had an innate disposition to protect. This quality made them ideal guardians; whether for a prize belonging to another, such as a wizard or a king; or some possession of value that they had discovered for themselves. The firedrake 'Bloodhorn' was no exception. Like Glimmerscale, he too had found a precious thing to guard. It was not treasure, although throughout the long years it remained in the city, it attracted almost as many thieves.

Magmaroth was a huge dragon whose thick scaly hide was as red as blood and had long, scarlet horns rising from his head, hence his familiar name. His fire was as hot and bright as any breathed in Enchantica save the four Guardians of the Seasons, and he used it to full effect on the succession of knights and other challengers that came to lay hands upon his precious charge. The object of the red dragon's guardianship was in actual fact prized higher than mere jewels and gold; it was a symbol of great power; and lured those who hungered to possess the gifts they believed it might bestow. It was the tomb of Shadragora: the first Dragonmaster of Eyesand, and the very individual who had negotiated consent from the dragons of the gorge for the building of the great city. The wizard had never lost the affection of the dragons with whom he could converse in their silent tongue, and also managed to retain the veneration of his people. Therefore during the conflict that eventually followed, Shadragora became a unique figure: an individual respected by both sides. The young

Horcust Rothgilian, a native of the city, had been a student of the great wizard for many years, and owed much of his skills with dragons to the teaching of his beloved master. Horcust had been a postulant in Eddilee during the time of the war, and did not learn of his city's demise until it was too late. When the young wizard returned to Eyesand, which was now a desolate scene of destruction and ruin, he also learned of the death of the old wizard.

Shadragora had been lifted from the sea of rubble in which he had perished and reverently carried to a high place of mourning by the dragons. Recognising Horcust as the old wizard's student, the citizens of the cliffs allowed him to view his dead master's body, and eventually remove it to lay it in a tomb within the ruins of Shadragora's beloved city.

Eyesand had been the old wizard's dream; a great city of stone where men and dragons could live in harmony for all time. He had worked tirelessly to ease the tensions that steadily grew between his two constituencies; but in the end was unable to contain the evil powers that sought to destroy that which he had striven so hard to create. Too late the warriors realised the consequences of their bloodlust, and the evil insanity which had driven them to war, and when the hostilities had ceased discovered that the wizard had been killed in the fighting. As the last survivors of the city's army limped away from the burning ruin that had been their home, their sombre victors bore away the wizard's body.

Horcust dressed his old master in his finest wizard robes and laid beside him in the tomb the many artefacts that had been his tools of sorcery; but such was the intensity of his grief that the young wizard could find no tears to weep for his dear departed teacher.

After a while the tomb of Shadragora became a thing of great myth and legend. Tales were told of how the secret of mastery over dragons was contained within his stone resting place. The worth of such a legendary power was deemed immeasurable; for it was believed that such a gift could not only provide its possessor with an invincible army, but also, as dragons were reputed to be the hoarders and keepers of untold treasure, a fortune beyond compare!

With such a fascination growing around Shadragora's tomb it became necessary to ensure that the stone coffin could never be defiled or robbed. For not only were the old wizard's robes and artefacts perceived as talismans of great power, but even his bones. Hence the arrival of Magmaroth 'Bloodhorn', the red firedrake, whose hot breath provided the warmest of receptions for any would-be grave robbers. The red dragon it was who kept the old wizard safe in his eternal rest, rising from the hidden chamber in a furious cloud of smoke and flame, an avenging demon ready to reward those who would dare to desecrate the remains of Eyesand's most favoured soul.

One artefact that had not been placed in the tomb, and of all the old wizard's relics was the one that could truthfully be said to possess real power, was his staff. An ancient length of yox or 'wizard's oak' carved with runes and enchanted symbols, rising to a carved horizontal dragon's head in whose wooden jaws a beautiful power crystal was held. This potent rod was kept by Craagnagar 'Old as Mountains', an ancient and wise dragon revered by all who dwelt in the great gorge, and a former friend and confidant of Shadragora. The elder dragon had never fully shared the old wizard's dream for the city that was to become Eyesand, but nevertheless had played his part in convincing the denizens of Dragongorge to give their consent to its construction. Craagnagar told the grieving Horcust of his own sorrow at Shadragora's death, and that he believed the old wizard would eventually have named the young apprentice as his heir. The ancient dragon promised the youthful Horcust that if he proved himself worthy, then the staff and all the respect and title that had formerly been his master's would one day be his. In the meantime the young wizard was named Dragonfriend and given leave to move freely within the dragon homeland. Many years passed before Horcust Rothgilian earned the right to hold the staff of Shadragora and call it his own. He had more than doubled his years since the building of the old wizard's tomb, traversed most of Enchantica in all directions on all manner of perilous quests, survived the ultimate ordeal of the Pit of Enlightenment and the terrible Aznargen, consequently became a High Wizard, and was named Lord of Eddilee by the Three Wizards. On his eventual return to the ruins of Eyesand and the cliffs of Dragongorge, Craagnagar finally bestowed the title of Dragonmaster upon him, and when he visited the tomb of he that had first borne that noble title, Throstle fell to his knees before the stone bier and was finally able to weep for his beloved master.

All three listeners were visibly moved by Throstle's telling of this very personal chapter of his extraordinary life. Even the High Wizard himself had tears in his eyes as he spoke of those far off days and the characters he had known and loved.

Jonquil said how he would dearly love to visit the ruin of Eyesand and the high cliffs of the gorge and meet the famous dragons that dwelled there, especially the old monarch Craagnagar. What stories must that ancient dragon be able to tell of the history of Dragongorge? The banf wagered that if any creature in Enchantica would know for certain the whereabouts of Trea's family group, then it must surely be Craagnagar. The ancient monarch of the gorge received dragon messengers from far and wide, therefore the silver terragons must have been known to him; all dragon life was known to him. Throstle considered that a visit to Craagnagar might turn out to be a profitable enterprise for them all, and announced that before long he would arrange such a venture for the banf and the two terragons. Jonquil's eyes gleamed with pleasure at hearing this, the banf well aware that Rattajack would be equally thrilled at the prospect of such a trip.

To round off his bout of storytelling Ethva urged Throstle to tell them a tale from the early days of Eyesand, when men and dragons had lived in harmony and peace with one another - happy to share in the splendour of what must have been a wondrous city at that time.

So, Throstle recalled the story of King Khastamir, and his three daughters: Sekala, Miliska and Azura. The dragon princesses of Eyesand.

In those days the dragons were an integral part of the fabric of Dragongorge's first and only great city of men. A visitor to Eyesand - of which there were many, for at that time the city was deemed to be one of the great wonders of the world - would watch spellbound the comings and goings of the dragons and the easy way they mingled with the city people. Most outsiders travelled from places where dragons were rare; and those that they had seen would have been the sole preserve of their king and his generals, kept well apart from everyday life. To see the skies full of leathern wings and proud beasts striding majestically through the streets amongst the crowds of citizens would have been most extraordinary to their eyes. The new arrival would see dragons flying into open buildings with large hooded roofs and gaping, arched mouths, where the heavy burdens slung beneath their chests were unloaded. Other dragons would be having their carrier sacks filled; the variety of goods dependent upon the size and strength of the beast concerned. The larger specimens flew out of the dragonports with loads of weighty mineral ore hanging from their powerful shoulders, the smaller ones with only a few barrels of wine or fruit. The visitor might be amazed that none of these dragons had riders to direct them. Their attendants just spoke a few words into the ears of the patient beasts and then away they flew, rising above the towers of the city to destinations near and far.

The dragons of the gorge not only aided the citizens by fetching and carrying the produce of trade; they also participated in the hunting and gathering of food; the unearthing of gems and precious metals, and of course the protection of that wealth. The unparalleled synergy of dragons and humans bestowed an advantage upon the city that elevated its wealth and prominence to legendary status.

Khastamir was a wise and benevolent king, who held the dragons of the gorge in the highest regard. In recognition for his respect and favour towards the inhabitants of the cliffs, Craagnagar gave the king three orphaned dragon infants as gifts for each of his daughters. As they grew up, the young women became so close to their dragon companions that before long they were known as the dragon princesses.

Sekala, Miliska and Azura, grew into fearless dragonriders. Valiant and reckless, they conducted themselves more like warriors than princesses. Much to the concern of their father, they would take to spending long periods away from the city, exploring the more remote regions of the smaller chasms that branched off from the main body of the gorge. Shadragora, who alone of the royal household appreciated the exceptional skills of the young women as dragonriders, often used the brave princesses as emissaries to far off lands, where they helped forge new friendships and trade alliances with foreign powers.

To the frustration of their father, it soon became clear that the three princesses preferred the company of their dragons to that of any man, and showed little interest in taking husbands. They had no patience for idle courtship, preferring to fly off to new horizons on the backs of their faithful beasts, as wild as the storms that carried them. They seemed addicted to adventure, and were forever seeking foreign wars to fight in or dangerous quests to embark upon. Such as the time the three sisters sought for the legendary dragon, Karaxus.

This beast of myth and rumour was the rarest of creatures: a dragon with powers of enchantment. Its skin was reputed to shine in the sun like precious argent, and at certain times to shed scales of real silver. The scales of Karaxus were said to possess remarkable powers. If one was used to make a vessel in which a medicine was prepared then that remedial draught became an enchanted panacea to cure all ills. A beauty cream applied as a mask with a scale spatula transformed the face of the subject into one of great loveliness. A mail shirt of layered silver scales rendered the wearer impregnable to injury, be they set upon by sword, lance, arrow or even dragon fire. Little wonder then that the scales of Karaxus were valued highly. The silver dragon was said to be the slave of an evil old sorceress called Melidan, who kept the noble creature prisoner in a high tower in a far off lonely valley. Melidan kept the dragon hostage so that she alone could have possession of its precious gifts; and charge a high price to those who had need or were desirous of the silver scales' unique powers.

Melidan's castle clung precariously to the sheer, craggy face of a high cliff. It was a small cluster of crumbling towers the largest of which had at its base a great arch sealed with a strong web of iron bars. Imprisoned in the chamber within was the silver dragon.

The sorceress had a special chariot in which she transported herself to and from her lofty refuge. It was suspended by chains from two mighty bat-like dragons who carried her for many leagues over the barren landscape of her mountain home. It was whilst abroad in this bizarre vehicle that the three princesses came upon her. They forced Melidan to turn back to her castle, and finally brought her to bay on the edge of the cliff. Using counter-spells given to them by Shadragora to protect them from the sorceress's venomous magic, Sekala, Miliska and Azura eventually overpowered and subdued the evil Melidan and took from her the keys to the great dungeon.

Karaxus was released from his confinement and soared joyously into the open air like a great silver dove finally released from its cage. The three dragon princesses forced the old sorceress into the dark prison and locked her inside; leaving her to free herself if she could. Then the silver dragon indicated a smaller dungeon in another part of the grim castle, and there the princesses found a young man. He was a warrior from the distant kingdom of Gyre in the east, and had been following the dragon - intending it no harm - but hoping to pick up some of its discarded scales along the way. When Karaxus stumbled into the sorceress's trap the valiant young fighter rushed to his aid but not having the protection of a wizard's enchantment he was struck down by Melidan's poisonous powers, which acted upon his body like the bite of a venomous snake. Caring little if he should live or die, the old witch threw him into a cold dark cell and left him to his fate. Eventually the sorceress remembered the young warrior, who was called Sarnau, and ever with a mind to profit, wondered if he might be worth a ransom. She decided to keep him alive, and grudgingly did so by feeding him with food laced with just enough antidote to keep her spreading poison at bay, but not sufficient to cure him. She would only deign to do that if she was paid a good price for his life.

Sarnau was tall and dark with eyes of deepest brown. His walnut skin was smoothly sculpted by a taut, statuesque figure. Despite the shadow of pain cast over him by Melidan's sorcery the three sisters were each immediately enamoured of his handsome bearing.

In gratitude for his freedom, Karaxus gave each of the princesses one of his enchanted scales, and then flew away into the empty wilderness to seek a refuge where he might be safe from the greedy desires of those who hunted him.

The three sisters returned to Eyesand with the young warrior who without the witch's antidote began to slide into a permanent veil of sleep. The princesses took Sarnau to Shadragora to see if the old wizard's skills could save him. Despite the apparent devotion of the three sisters, Shadragora suspected that only one of them was truly in love with the young warrior. For many days the great sorcerer battled with the venomous power that gripped the young life, but eventually the sorcerer had to admit defeat and declare the young warrior beyond his aid. According to Shadragora there was only one thing that could bring the young Sarnau back to life: one of the silver scales of Karaxus.

First he asked Sekala, the eldest, if she would give up her scale for the life of the young man she claimed to love; but Sekala answered that she had already had the silver scale melted down and crafted into a new hilt for her sword. She now had a blade that could cleave any armour and would never fail her in battle.

Miliska, the wizard asked next as she too had declared her love for the ailing Sarnau. The middle daughter could only shrug her shoulders and show six new gleaming arrow heads in her quiver. With these enchanted arrows Miliska's aim was ever straight and true, and the silver points deadly to her foes.

Shadragora turned at last to Azura, the youngest of the king's three daughters, and the only one of the three to remain at the young man's bedside since his arrival at the wizard's chambers. Without hesitation the dragon princess lifted a chain from around her neck and hanging from it by a jewelled clasp was the third of Karaxus' silver scales. The precious disc was still warm from the girl's breast when the wizard placed the chain around the neck of the youth, laying the enchanted scale against his heart. Shadragora and the princess then left Sarnau alone for the power of the dragon's scale to do its work.

It took two days for the young man's eyes to open, and when they did they first focused upon a tall elderly looking figure with a long white beard, dressed in flowing robes decorated with mystical signs and runes: every inch a wizard. Another figure followed the wizard into the chamber, a young woman with olive skin and dark brown almond eyes that almost stifled the young man's tender breath. Her robe was a simple shift of shimmering blue cloth, her long serpentine hair falling upon it like black silk. She smiled warmly into the deep brown eyes of the youth and Sarnau had not looked upon the girl for more than a few moments before his heart was captured.

To the joy and relief of King Khastamir, one of his three rebellious daughters had finally expressed a desire to take a husband. Azura and Sarnau were married with all due pomp and ceremony. Azura's sisters found themselves quite relieved that they had not been truly in love with Sarnau, and celebrated their sister's nuptials, and their narrow escape, by challenging all comers at the banquet to a drinking and wrestling contest.

Sarnau was named Khastamir's heir in due course, and together with Azura founded a new dynasty of Kings of Eyesand.

Sekala and Miliska, now relieved of all royal duties, devoted themselves entirely to the pursuit of adventure, and screamed into the pages of history and legend by overthrowing tyrants, rescuing pretty dragons from evil princesses, seducing handsome young virgins, and generally bringing murder and mayhem to the enemies of their people.

A collective sigh of satisfaction rose from the small audience as Throstle concluded his tale. Ethva had to be the one to ask if the tale was really true, and, with a teasing smile, the High Wizard said nothing but reached inside the neck of his robe. His hand emerged grasping a silver chain which he slowly pulled out in a deliberate, dramatic fashion. Eventually a flat glittering object swung into the light beneath Throstle's upheld hand, its brilliant metallic surface flashing with bright stars of sunlight. When the object finally came to rest, they all saw that it was a roughly disc shaped plate of silver, its shiny skin ringed like the bole of a tree. Ethva squealed with delight when she saw it, and gingerly extended a finger to touch its precious form. Throstle told them that the object was indeed the third scale of Karaxus which Azura, its rightful owner, had left in the keeping of the wizard Shadragora. On her death, the scale was bequeathed to the old sorcerer, and on his death it passed to Throstle. It was one of his most prized possessions, not solely because of its enchantment which was still as potent as the day the silver dragon plucked it from his body, but because of its long and eventful history and the good deeds it had performed in the hands of its keepers.

Indlewick concluded his treatment on Jonquil's wings and the banf and Ethva went out into the sunshine to watch the two terragons at their play in the lily pond. The two wizards remained behind in the cool shade of the balcony to exchange a few private words on a matter that was of great concern to them both.

Throstle had always had a keen ability to acquire information in a subtle, unobtrusive manner. He had spies in more places than the sky; and all of them invisible to his enemies. Indlewick himself was no slouch when it came to gathering news and harvesting gossip. Being a healer, the large wizard had access to a wide circle of Eddilean society, and was often taken into the confidence of his patients who wished to share with him more than just a description of their ailments.

Both wizards, therefore, by their own methods, had come to hear worrying rumours of a conspiracy nestling within the upper ranks of the valley's enchanters. Threads of deceit and treachery linking powerful names in the city with that of Juvula. Heskel's infidelity in that quarter had long been suspected, but now there were sinister whispers concerning a few other wizards and witches of note. The discovery that a circle of betrayal had grown from the scheming of the Grand Wizard had both surprised and dismayed the two wizard friends.

Indlewick was bemused by this strange association, and failed to comprehend why illustrious beings such as Gristmire, Shirene and Mequinda would throw in their lot with an insignificant wizard like Juvula, whom they far outranked in power. Throstle sucked on his pipe and nodded slowly as if he agreed they did make unlikely confederates.

'Perhaps because like him they believe he has been chosen,' he eventually offered as an explanation.

The healer wizard considered this for a moment and then shook his head confidently.

'Shirene? Gristmire? Mequinda?' Indlewick said with an air of incredulity. 'The likes of those would not join with Juvula on the strength of some dreamed up destiny. They must believe they have something to gain by aiding him. But what?'

Throstle did not answer straight away but leaned back in his chair and exhaled a long chain of colourful smoke rings, each one interlinked with the next. The spectral chain undulated slightly in the soft breeze and then slowly dispersed.

'Where one leads many may follow,' Throstle sighed almost to himself.

'If the one is strong enough!' Indlewick interposed.

The Dragonmaster expelled one large ring that seemed almost to glow in the shade like silvery moonlight. He then cast a lazy glance at his friend.

'Or perceived to have the strength,' he said raising his eyebrows.

Indlewick's eyes were drawn from Throstle to follow the sedate journey of the great circle of smoke, as it steadily grew in size and diminished in vigour until it reached its zenith and faded from sight.

'Perhaps Juvula will similarly outgrow his abilities,' the healer said to the patch of space where the smoke ring had been.

'But tell me, Throstle,' Indlewick spoke again, 'do they honestly believe that if Juvula is successful in this mad quest he will look favourably upon a valley that practically kicked him out as a failure?'

Throstle plucked the pipe from his lips and shook his head.

'Not upon the valley,' he answered, 'but, as you said yourself, Gristmire and the others must have been offered some personal reward for their loyalty.'

The Dragonmaster paused for a moment to consider a further point, his eyes narrowing in thought. 'And no doubt some tasty morsel of news that gives them confidence in Juvula's prospects.' he added. 'For they are not likely to commit themselves to supporting the son of a half sorcerer without some expectation of his success!'

Indlewick tugged irritably at his tuft of beard.

'Such as?' he asked the High Wizard.

Throstle pondered for a little while.

'Some ally perhaps,' he said at last. 'That we are yet to learn of.'

Indlewick's face was a picture of puzzlement.

'A new adversary?' the healer asked.

'Or an old one,' Throstle answered in his usual cryptic manner.

The healer wizard smiled wryly, gave a deep sigh, and reached for his own pipe, which was primed and ready nearby. Throstle clearly knew more about this subject than he was prepared to reveal at once. Indlewick suspected that it was going to take time and patience to prise this new information out of his friend. So, he propped his feet up on a stool, filled his throat with the sweet smoke of the burning herb and settled himself in his chair for a long session.

'Now, Throstle,' he said when he was comfortable, 'suppose you tell me just exactly what it is you're thinking.'

For the next few days Jonquil and Rattajack further acquainted themselves with the wonderful valley that was Eddilee. They made frequent return visits to Indlewick's house to visit the healer and his special lodger, Trea. Rattajack and the silver terragon had struck up a firm friendship, and the banf could not help wondering if when all their adventures were finally done Trea might be persuaded to return with himself, Meadolarne and Rattajack to the Banf Kingdom; For Jonquil would have had to have been a blind fool not to have seen the bond that had grown between the two terragons. There was always the possibility that the silver terragon would want to try and find her family group in the frozen wastes of the north. A venture which might also include Jonquil and Rattajack, if the she-terragon wished it. Whatever the outcome should be, of one thing the banf was sure:

Rattajack was going to find it hard to say farewell to his new friend, and would go to the greatest lengths to ensure that he need not do so. For his part, Jonquil was delighted that his beloved companion had found Trea; she was a delightful creature, and it was high time that the terragon enjoyed some female company of his own kind. The banf had an image in his mind of the two banfs and the two terragons eventually going home together. Somehow it just felt right.

When the two companions were not frolicking in Indlewick's pool or taking the silver terragon for long walks into the meadows with Ethva as their guide, they accompanied Throstle on his many visits to the houses of mighty enchanters.

They called upon Glazzabal, a relatively youthful wizard, with a thick powerful frame and a mild nature; and saw his stunning collection of hawks and eagles. As Jonquil gazed upon the awesome birds at rest on their various perches in the wizard's treehouse, he realised that Ethva had not been exaggerating; the largest of them probably could have carried him off in their talons.

Jonquil and Rattajack also met the other hawk fanciers Ethva had mentioned: Culzean and Nedwen. Two manic artistic wizards who lived in a small rickety house perched on a steep grassy slope some distance from the city. Culzean told them that the valley was in for some rain before very long, and as a special treat for the population, he had been commissioned by Heskel to design a rainbow to rise at the conclusion of the downpour. Throstle explained to the two companions that Eddilee's rainbows were legendary, and were always used to sweeten the visitation of rain, which of course was a necessity for the maintenance of their rich pastureland.

A long succession of wizards and witches were

introduced to Jonquil and Rattajack as Throstle continued to renew his acquaintance with the city's noted. These included Tudwile, Pulverbatch, Rishangles, Mayslin, Rhosgoch, Nanpantan, Skerrie, to name but a few. Most of these powerful enchanters Throstle counted amongst his friends and loyal confederates; but there were a few to whom he seemed to feel little regard and even less affection. One of these was the aforementioned Gristmire, and the banf and the terragon found themselves taking an instant dislike to this sinister character. Gristmire kept close company with a young enchantress of startling appearance called Shirene, and an older witch with a permanent supercilious scowl and the longest fingernails Jonquil had ever seen known as Mequinda. The banf and the terragon could tell that there was little love lost between Throstle and these three arrogant characters; and as soon as it was polite for them to take their leave of Gristmire and his friends, they did so and gratefully.

One afternoon when the normally clear Eddilee sky was marred by a thickening bank of heavy cloud - the first signs of the oncoming rain - Throstle was walking the two companions back to their lodgings along the avenue which entered the wide square in which stood the gaudy spectacle of the Great Hall. Jonquil had made a treevine ball during one of their woodland treks with Ethva, and he and Rattajack had been delighting the High Wizard and Addax with the many games they had invented to play with it. As they neared one of the smaller side entrances of the large building, the door opened and the lavishly costumed person of Heskel stepped out, glancing cautiously up and down the avenue as he emerged. He carried a small casket in his hands which, as he caught sight of the High Wizard and the others, he hastily thrust behind his back. They fancied they saw another smaller figure following behind him, but the Grand Wizard's sudden halt and frantic efforts to conceal what was in his hand must have sent him scuttling back indoors. The mystery character must have quickly relieved Heskel of the casket for when Throstle and the two companions approached the Grand Wizard, his hands returned empty to clasp against his chest.

The smile which exploded across Heskel's face was most exuberant, and he was suddenly very glad to see them all. He greeted them warmly as he stepped forward to meet them, clearly quite keen that they should not get too close to the open doorway behind him. If Throstle was intrigued by the other wizard's furtive behaviour, which he undoubtedly was, he showed not a sign of it as he engaged Heskel in some cheery small talk.

'Rain clouds!' Throstle exclaimed with forced joviality. 'By my stars! That's not a common sight in Eddilee. Are the cloudherders on strike, Heskel?'

Heskel flicked his eyes skywards and then after a slight pause answered the High Wizard in an enthusiastic and somewhat relieved manner; as if he had been anticipating a more difficult question.

'Erm...the..er.. farmers on the northern slopes have been

complaining about the lack of rain,' Heskel gushed. 'The pasture for the livestock, you know.'

He waved his hand dismissively as if such matters were beneath his concern.

'I usually arrange for the rain to fall at night, of course,' he continued. 'Only this time for a change I thought.....well...you know...a rainbow might be quite inspiring, especially for the younger ones.'

'Oh, yes!' Throstle said encouragingly. 'One of the legendary Eddilee rainbows!'

'Well...yes...' Heskel concurred, his speech a little strained. 'Culzean is supposed to be designing one for us. That's if he can tear himself away from his precious birds.'

The conversation continued in the same vein for some time until Throstle decided they should take their leave of the Grand Wizard, and no sooner had they started along their way than Heskel turned to go back into the hall. He hesitated for just a moment before entering, as if it dawned on him how suspicious it looked him going back inside without having been anywhere; but after a half-glance behind him he went in anyway and closed the door.

Throstle gave a deep sigh as he stared back at the glittering pile that was the Great Hall.

'It seems to me,' he mused, 'that in my absence a web of intrigue has been spun across this valley; and now it is my task to try and distinguish the flies from the spiders!'

Jonquil remembered the clumsily concealed casket and the fleeting glimpse of the other figure.

'Heskel doesn't seem much like a fly to me,' he said to the wizard.

Throstle smiled down at the banf and raised his eyebrows.

'He doesn't seem clever enough for a spider either!' he replied.

The High Wizard and the two companions said their farewells to each other as their paths now lay in opposite directions. It was only a short stroll for the banf and the terragon to reach their dwelling house. Throstle strode out purposefully towards his own home and as soon as he had moved out of sight, stopped and set the dragonet to watch the Great Hall.

As the wizard continued on his way Addax rose on to the nearest roof and surreptitiously fluttered his way to a good vantage point, where he could see all the comings and goings of the extravagant building without being seen himself.

Throstle proceeded briskly along the flower bordered avenue that led to his dwelling, and was just about to pass by a side street which led back to the main square, when two malignant characters stepped out into his path. He immediately bristled, tightening his grip on his staff when he recognised them, and met them both with a hard stare.

One of them was a witch of striking appearance. Tall and graceful with a long, thick mane of bright auburn hair that flowed from her head like a bronze waterfall; two broad bands of golden hair rising from her temples to join with the luscious cascade. Her eyes and lips were heavily painted in bold, dark shades which gave her an intense, almost alarming expression. Her dress was tight fitting and opulent, with wings of layered cobweb lifting from her sleeves and bodice in the light breeze. The spider motif was clearly favoured by the lady for she wore it as jewellery and embroidered decoration. She even bore a spider tattoo in violet dye upon one of her exposed shoulders. The colour of her robe was tantalising to the eyes for it had the same protean quality as the iridescent hues found on the carapace of some exotic beetles. As she moved through the splintered sunlight a dozen shades of violet fought with each other across the witch's curves each one striving for dominance over the cloth. Throstle found himself almost mesmerised by the pulsating colours of the witch's robe; and then his attention was drawn to the other figure. A tall wizard, made even broader in the shoulder by a heavy cape of dark fur atop a flowing gabardine of rich jade velvet. His stern features were framed by a dense mop of black hair and a neatly tailored beard. Two piercing blue eyes glared from beneath a thick hedge-like brow, and despite the wizard's smile they remained cold and calculating.

They both offered a warm greeting to the Dragonmaster, but the coldness of their eyes made it a lie. Throstle returned their courtesy.

'Shirene, Gristmire,' he said. 'What an unexpected pleasure. Are you on your way to see Heskel at the Hall?'

The witch chuckled and strolled around Throstle with slow, liquid movements. She even cheekily stroked the carved dragon at the head of his staff as she passed.

'Actually no, Throstle,' she said, blatantly using his pet-name in a slow sensual voice. 'We have just come from there.'

'Important business?' the Dragonmaster inquired, choosing to ignore this breach of decorum.

'Nothing that need concern you, Horcust,' the other wizard spoke. 'At least not yet!'

Shirene giggled and completed her circle of Throstle by leaning languidly against the broad figure of Gristmire. She gazed licentiously into the eyes of the tall wizard whilst her fingers drew lazy circles in the dark fur of his collar. She turned again to Throstle.

'I suppose you have heard the news about Rhazgor?' she asked him. 'But then of course you have. You know everything, Throstle.'

The second usage of the name that the Dragonmaster reserved for his friends brought a mocking grin to the lips of Gristmire, but Throstle kept his composure and continued to smile courteously.

'But did you know that he has joined with Juvula?' the witch added with a note of feigned concern.

The Dragonmaster's smile faltered slightly at this revelation, and his two enemies seized upon it as their victory. Their eyes were as bright as vultures witnessing the death throes of their next meal. The witch was in no mood to stop now.

'He has offered himself in service to the Chosen One,' she said excitedly, stepping closer to Throstle. 'His staff is Juvula's to command!'

Gristmire moved up behind the witch and wrapped his large arms about her shoulders, pressing his cheek next to hers; his chilling stare fixed on the Dragonmaster.

'The Mage of Anconeus will be a worthy adversary for you now, Horcust,' the tall wizard sneered. 'With Rhazgor at his side!'

Throstle stared at the two gloating faces pressed one against the other, and then smiled to himself. He tugged at the wide brim of his hat in salute and said in a bright voice: 'Thank you!'

The faces of the witch and the wizard darkened a little.

'I knew your confidence in Juvula was not fuelled by mere bravado; or that old destiny thing,' the High Wizard continued cheerfully. 'And I suspected Rhazgor's involvement, but I could not be certain. That is, until now! Thank you again for your candour. It is always best to know these things. After all, forewarned is forearmed! Good day!'

With a second respectful tug at his hat brim Throstle quickly removed himself from the company of Gristmire and Shirene (always a pleasurable thing to do); and left the two enchanters looking after the High Wizard with expressions somewhat less smug than they had been when they had first met.

Jonquil and Rattajack resumed their antics with the vine ball, intending to play their way back to their lodgings. Their game involved keeping the ball in the air as long as possible; whether by kicking, punching, heading or any other method; the only rule was that the ball must not hit the ground. As it was difficult to steer the game in any one direction, the two companions found themselves moving back towards the Great Hall. Jonquil hit the ball high into the air with a two-handed punch. Rattajack tried to get underneath it but his feet slipped on the dusty road so that instead of a clean header back to the banf, the ball deflected off the terragon's head sending it flying into the branches of one of the long row of trees lining the avenue next to the hall. Jonquil and Rattajack waited for the ball to drop through the leafy boughs, so that they could catch it before it landed and carry on with the game. However, the ball did not come, and the noise of its descent suddenly ceased. The banf and the terragon looked at each other mournfully, and then stared up into the thick layers of foliage. There was only one thing for it; Jonquil had sat for too long making the ball just to leave it stuck in a tree, it had to be rescued. So, without another thought, they both grabbed hold of the lowest branches and climbed up into the tree.

A few moments later the side door of the hall slowly opened once again. Heskel's anxious face peered around it, trying to see as much of the avenue as he could without revealing himself. Eventually satisfied that the coast was clear he crept out on to the pavement and signalled to one inside that it was safe to follow. A short shadowy shape stepped out beside the wizard, his yellow eyes darting quickly this way and that scanning their surroundings to see if they were observed. Jonquil and Rattajack froze as soon as they heard the low voices below them; hardly daring to breathe when they realised who it was, and the nature of their conversation. Heskel had the small casket once more, and before he would entrust it to the keeping of his servant he made him listen to a list of instructions. The half-goblin's impatient attitude suggested that this was not the first time he had heard this speech, but he nodded dutifully in the right places and gave the Grand Wizard the assurances that he wanted to hear.

'Remember the false bottom of this casket conceals a sheet with the names of all those who I believe may be sympathetic to our cause,' Heskel said to Sunjack. 'It also contains a crystal wrapped in silk; but not an ordinary jewel, oh no! A power crystal! A gift from all of his friends here in the valley. A crystal for his staff! And don't forget, if you are stopped, you are simply delivering last minute instructions to Culzean about the rainbow; that's near enough the direction you will be taking. I've put a few relevant papers inside the box to verify your story.'

The half-goblin nodded disinterestedly, this level of espionage was clearly far below his abilities, he was capable of much greater feats of scheming than just the delivery of a box. However, he smiled reassuringly as he humoured the wizard, and promised him that he was in full possession of all the necessary information.

'Off you go then,' Heskel urged, pushing the casket into Sunjack's hands. 'And offer my salutations to the next Lord of Eddilee!'

The black draped servant pulled the flaps of his

BRIAN BILL

114

cloak about himself and stole swiftly along the line of trees, keeping to the pools of shadow they cast upon the road. Heskel threw a few cautionary glances here and there across the square, and then swept back into the building. Barely a moment after the two companions heard Heskel close the door, their vine ball dropped from its cradle of branches and hit the ground, only a few paces from where the wizard and the half-goblin had been standing. Jonquil looked fearfully at the departing form of Sunjack to see if he might have heard the noise, but the dark shape continued its rapid progress along the avenue undeterred.

Jonquil and Rattajack descended from the tree and retrieved the ball. Their first instinct was to go for Throstle and acquaint him with the skulduggery they had just witnessed; but when they looked after the dark form of Sunjack stealing speedily into the distance, they realised that by the time they roused the wizard, the half-goblin would be gone without trace. So instead they decided to follow the cloaked figure on their own and discover his destination. They suspected that he was on his way to Juvula, or his agents; and the two companions knew that they would be doing a great service to the valley if they were able to bring back to Throstle the location of the enemy's hide-out.

Addax watched the banf and the terragon set off in the direction that Sunjack had taken. Not having been close enough to hear the clandestine conversation between Heskel and his servant, the dragonet was not aware of Sunjack's errand. He did know, however, that the two companions were not heading for their lodgings as they were supposed to do; and so he waited for them to gain some distance before he lifted into the air and skimmed the treetops in invisible pursuit.

The late afternoon sun streamed through the rolling bank of grey clouds like golden sand filtering through a giant fist. The broad beams cut through the gloomy sky to paint bright swathes of colour upon the subdued landscape. The banf and the terragon had followed Sunjack's shadowy figure through a maze of streets and lanes, across meadows and along winding forest tracks until he brought them to the edge of the trees, at the foot of a shallow incline which was the start of the long verdant climb up to the rocky rim of the valley wall.

The way ahead lay across a landscape that was open and smooth, and there were few opportunities for shelter upon the wide grassy slope. Pursuing Sunjack through such bare terrain presented many difficulties; the greatest of which was how to keep themselves hidden from his sight as they followed him. As they rested beneath the cover of the forest eaves, watching the distant cloaked shape tirelessly ascend the turf before them, the banf and the terragon resolved to let the half-goblin build up quite a lead before daring to resume the chase.

Sunjack had almost disappeared from sight before Jonquil and Rattajack emerged from the shadow of the forest and stole up the slope after him. The rain which had been so long threatened had mostly fallen whilst they had been under the cover of the trees, and so had been hardly noticed. They could now feel the last few drops of the vast grey curtain as it swept through the valley, and as they crouched beside a lone outcrop of boulders nestled against the sloping turf, they looked back along the vast expanse of Eddilee to see a most fantastic spectacle.

Painted upon the departing backcloth of weeping cloud, the shimmering form of an immense eagle spread its great wings across the valley in a multicoloured embrace. The varied hues of its feathers shone brightly with the last strength of the waning sun which beamed its golden glory through the thinning remnants of cloud. The tips of the eagle's mighty span fell across the rolling flanks of high pastureland as long spears of transparent colour, gently staining the dull turf with limpid shades. Culzean would have been rightly proud of his rainbow, and Jonquil and Rattajack fancied that some distance along the valley side before them, they could just see the ramshackle house that was his and Nedwen's; the two wizards would have enjoyed an enviable view of their marvellous creation.

When they peeped over the top of the boulders the two companions found that Sunjack had disappeared. They searched the broad face of the emerald slope as it swept up before them, but could see no sign of their quarry. The half goblin had clearly not been moved by the splendour of Culzean's eagle, and had continued his relentless ascent unhindered by distraction. There was always the chance that Sunjack was hidden in some unseen dip up ahead and would eventually reappear. If he did not, the two companions would have to face the fact that they had lost him, and return to the city with their task unfulfilled. The banf and the terragon crept cautiously around the rocks, mindful of the cover they afforded them, and began their long scramble up the next bank of lush turf, made slippery by the sharp downpour.

Sunjack, at this point in time, had no idea that he was being followed. He was not usually this careless; it was simply that his mind was occupied with other considerations, and he was impatient to reach his destination. He was excited at the prospect of meeting Juvula, whom he had heard so much about from Heskel and Mummichog. Although the leader of his goblin sect had never made any overtly negative remarks concerning the Mage of Anconeus, Sunjack suspected that Mummichog's respect and loyalty for the wizard were not as deep as he professed. Heskel on the other hand was quite besotted with Juvula, and talked of him in the most affectionate and reverent terms. Sunjack decided that he would make up his own mind about The Pretender as he had heard the wizard called, when he had the opportunity to meet him face to face.

The half goblin had almost climbed out of the depression that preceded the final push for the Giant's Cleft, the high gate in the jagged ridge which led to the sombre world beyond the enchanted vale. Sunjack threw a glance over his shoulder at the fading colours of the great ethereal eagle, its magnificence now somewhat diminished.

'Pathetic!' he cursed to himself.

Sunjack had never had much time for wizards' fancies. He respected the rock shattering might of a power bolt - that was a talent worth having; but he could never understand the fascination with frivolous endeavours like customised rainbows, fountain carving, funny smoke rings or any other way of wasting good power. These wizards should be wreaking havoc amongst the weaker races; shrivelling their bodies with their infernal fire: that is what Sunjack would do if he was a wizard. If the half goblin suddenly acquired the enchantment of someone like Gristmire or Maldreth, or even the great Horcust himself, he would not squander it making pretty pictures or useless ornament; he would use it to blast a few holes in his enemies - explode a few heads! There were quite a few scores Sunjack would love to settle in Eddilee by such means; and beyond. Thoughts similar to these kept the half goblin company as he began the final leg of his long climb.

The orange ball of the sun slipped into a pale envelope of cloud; its last rays fanned across the burnished sky in broad swathes of golden chiffon. The menacing cloaks of grey were now tamed and dispersed, and in their place only drifting tufts of gilt edged ochre. The first lamps of Eddilee glowed against the growing pall of gloom slowly creeping over the valley floor.

Sunjack clambered into the tall gap in the rock wall, trying hard not to think of the legend which told of a mighty giant striking the hard rim of the valley with his axe for no apparent reason: the half goblin had no time for silly legends either. He was about to hurry through, sensible of his profile being visible against the sky to any watchful wizard in the city with a telescope, when a sudden rugged bark drew his attention to one of the pinnacles of rock above his head. Staring down at him from its lofty perch was one of Juvula's ugly dragons, its silvery eyes glowing red with the reflected light of the sunset. Eventually Sunjack recognised it as Zemorga, and signalled for the creature to come down to him. Instead, the dragon motioned with its head at something back down the slope. Sunjack suddenly broke into a cold sweat and a terrible fear gripped him. The dragon's warning could only mean one thing: he was being pursued. The memory of his imprudent journey from the city rushed back to chide him, and he was horrified to realise that he had reached the Giant's Cleft with scarcely a look over his shoulder to see if anyone might be following. The half goblin's imagination began to run wild, conjuring images of some powerful avenging wizard, like Horcust, striding after him, waiting for him to reveal the whereabouts of Mummichog's lair.

The half goblin could stand the suspense no longer. He threw himself down on to the ground and wormed his way back towards the brink of the slope. Hardly daring to push his head over the edge, he peered fearfully down to see what Zemorga had spotted from his high vantage point.

At first Sunjack could see nothing; the vast, majestic slope of undulating grassland yielding not a single figure; but then he realised he was expecting to see the tall frame of a wizard standing out from the slanting turf. As he began to scrutinise the descending vista in greater detail, his eyes finally locked on two low shapes crawling over the lip of the shallow depression just below him, hardly discernible from the patchy greensward in the half light of early evening. The two figures were probably no greater in size than himself. They were moving as close to the thick grass as they could manage, and kept throwing cautionary glances up at the gap. Sunjack studied them for some time before he recognised them, but as soon as he did he scrambled to his feet and gave a predetermined sign to the watching dragon. Zemorga gave a short bark of comprehension and then watched the cloaked figure beneath him scuttle out of the valley and along the narrow cliff path which eventually led to the evergreen slopes.

A Brave Sacrifice

The two companions tentatively crept up to the great cleft. They breathed a sigh of relief when they discovered that Sunjack had already moved on. They had been afraid of breasting the ridge and stumbling into the half goblin still at rest. Before moving on, they turned to gaze upon the valley below them, which even in semi darkness was a stunning spectacle. The dark rash of trees and houses at the centre of the great trough was studded with a subdued constellation of lighted lamps. The jagged edge of the opposing valley wall was now masked in deep shadow, soaring like the broken ramparts of a giant's fortress against a blood red sky; and at their backs, shining over the world of Winter, a scattering of stars was already lighting the way for the oncoming night.

It was only now that the banf and the terragon realised the folly of their impromptu pursuit. They had no food, no lantern, and no idea what they were going to do when they had followed the half goblin to his final destination. Neither of them had imagined that Sunjack would lead them right out of the valley. He had carried no provisions himself, so they had assumed that his journey would be relatively short. As it turned out they had travelled half the width of the Vale, and taken only water from the streams and fruit from the trees to sustain them. Of course the aptitude of goblins for marching was legendary, they measured distance by the mountain - not leagues or days; and Sunjack needed no lantern to find his way for his feet clearly knew this path well.

Jonquil and Rattajack stood on the crest of the ridge trying to decide whether to go on into the danger of the unknown or turn back to the safety of the city. They looked at the deep sprawl of the enchanted vale, and then the grim spectacle of the world beyond; a world of snowy peaks and valleys that glowed in the pale starlight like bleached bones. They knew in their hearts that they should turn back, that bravado should not be allowed to eclipse good sense. However, having come so far it seemed silly not to venture a little further. After all, Sunjack's secret destination might only be a short distance down the trail. Jonquil and Rattajack stared into each other's eyes, neither of them wanting to be the one to make the decision.

Suddenly, their road was decided for them by the screeching fall of a winged demon. The dark shape dropped to the ground blocking their way back into the wizards' valley with a malevolent snarl and a quivering span of leathery wings. Jonquil recognised the creature as the same ugly beast that had shadowed them so closely during their first exploration of Eddilee's forests. Only now it was far more animated, very different from the sluggish, lethargic gargoyle that had slumped about the place, barely sufficiently awake to keep itself upright. Nevertheless, the banf had scared it away once so there was no reason to suppose that he could not do so again. Baring his fists as before Jonquil advanced upon the growling creature roaring his challenge. Zemorga's growls elevated to a piercing defiant screech, and it soon became obvious that he was not going to yield. In fact, instead of flying away as Jonquil hoped, the beast lunged forward snapping its steel trap jaws only inches from the banf's face. Rattajack, sensing the grim determination of their foe, sprang forward and pulled Jonquil away from the killing jaws. Zemorga, enraged by the banf's attack, dropped its head and arched its back, assuming its threat pose and prepared to charge. The awful din of its battle cry chilled the blood of the two companions as they stood helplessly waiting for the monster's assault. Then an even shriller cry pierced the turbulent air and a flash of pale wings swept past the eyes of the two fearful friends. It was Addax.

The faithful dragonet had secretly shadowed them all the way from the Great Hall, and of course, had spotted Zemorga long before the banf and the terragon had been made aware of his presence.

The tiny dragon flew at the dark monster, his shrieking battle cry striking a sour harmony with the dreadful voice of his opponent. Zemorga was easily three times as large as the diminutive dragon, but Addax did not falter; he swooped boldly into the fray, thrusting his needle sharp talons to the fore. The dark dragon retreated from this furious advance, wrapping his wings about him to fend off the scratching claws and stinging bites of the other; but this was no surrender. After a few moments the evil beast recovered from the surprise of Addax's attack, and readied himself to strike. Zemorga's lethal jaws burst through his shield of wings and smote the air only a hair's breadth from the dragonet's throat. Addax threw himself backwards as the monster tensed for a second lunge, and using the hard ground almost as a trampoline the dragonet launched himself into a different direction.

The battle progressed with the tiny dragon buzzing the dark beast like an angry hornet. Spinning him this way and that with mesmeric spirals that turned his pale form into a milky blur. Zemorga snapped vainly at the air now and then as the dragonet circled him but failed to find the swift creature. Addax's wings beat so fast they made a loud thrumming noise which only added to the impression of a giant revenging insect; and he could sting too. In the course of the battle Zemorga sustained deep scratches on his head and chest; the dragonet also accounted for some painful tears in the gargoyle's flailing wings.

Suddenly a third dragon voice assaulted the air, and Jonquil and Rattajack turned to see another terragon sized monster, like Zemorga, sweeping down at them out of the ruby sky. Addax disengaged from his ugly foe just as the other gargoyle joined in the battle. The dragonet sped between the two companions as if urging them to follow him down the cliff trail. Dragora, the new protagonist wailed his outrage as the banf and the terragon sprinted off along the path to chase the fluttering shape of Addax.

The two monsters skipped along after their prey, with a hideous vulture-like step, their broad wings fully outstretched to give them size and balance. The dragonet had not led his two friends far along the trail before he abruptly drew himself up into a defensive hover. A piercing curse hissed through his bared teeth as two more hideous beasts appeared on the path before them; wings wide and heads low mimicking the threat pose of their two brothers. Grizzagrim and Zaugros sang a terrible duet with their croaking growls as together with Zemorga and Dragora they trapped the dragonet and the two companions. Addax squealed his defiance at the four gargoyles and flew a furious circle about the banf and the terragon to keep their attackers at bay. The dragonet would willingly have done battle with all four adversaries had Jonquil not urged him to depart from that lonely place and fly back to the city for help. Addax was clearly reluctant to leave the two companions to the mercies of the monsters that had them surrounded, but after stooping at each of the ugly beasts in turn making them duck or flinch to avoid his raking claws, he lifted up into the darkening sky, hovering for just a moment as if considering a change of heart, and then swept over the dark wall of the ridge and was gone from sight.

Jonquil and Rattajack moved closer together as the four dark dragons began to circle. Their cruel, unblinking eyes fixed the banf and the terragon with a ravenous stare, and the two friends were alarmed to see swaying tendrils of drool oozing from the creatures' powerful jaws.

Then a sharp cry, unintelligible to the companions but effective on the monsters, caused their attackers to cease their malevolent stalking and

hearken to the mystery voice. Another command was barked into the air and the two monsters who now barred the way, hopped aside to allow Jonquil and Rattajack to move forward. A chorus of angry growls from the two ugly beasts at their rear ensured that they took this opportunity, and began to walk cautiously along the trail.

The four gargoyles nipping at their heels kept the two companions at an acceptable pace, and before long standing just ahead of them on the path, barely distinguishable from the growing gloom, was a hooded figure cloaked in black. Despite the dim light they recognised him as Sunjack. The shadow from his hood effectively extinguished his features, but even so when he spoke they could tell that he was wearing his usual slippery smile.

'A little out of your way, are you not, my friends?' he sneered.

Jonquil did not answer, but stared defiantly into the hole of darkness that was the half goblin's face.

'You will both pay a dear price for your curiosity!' Sunjack continued. 'And just in case you might be considering the merits of an escape attempt, allow me to tell you that on this side of the path we have a continuous high wall of rock, and on this side a sheer drop to certain death.' The goblin turned his head as if casting his eyes over the rising arches of Jonquil's wings, which had been freshly wrapped in Indlewick's special covers only that morning. 'Unless, of course,' he said, 'you can fly!'

The banf thought he could hear traces of derisive laughter gurgling under the half goblin's breath.

'But then I see that you at least cannot,' Sunjack added pointing a finger at Jonquil. 'If your dragon friend should decide to use his wings to escape, then my four companions here will simply fly after him and tear him to pieces!'

Zemorga and his brothers all growled encouragingly at this statement, and shook their wings as if to show their eagerness for such a chase. Jonquil had no doubt that Sunjack was telling the truth; and although Rattajack's wings may have saved them both from a few sticky situations over the years, he was no flier, not in the dragon sense of the word. The four gargoyles would have been able to catch him with barely a flap of their strong wings.

'What a pleasant surprise the two of you will make for Juvula,' the half goblin said with obvious glee.

Sunjack then turned to Zemorga, and ordered him to go on ahead and warn the hide-out of their coming. The dragon creature gave a short bark in response and trotted across the path to fall headlong into the great void of the frozen valley beyond the cliff. They watched the ugly beast rise from the dark depths and plane out across the snowy backdrop of the distant landscape on its wide, voluminous wings; slow, lazy beats carrying it along a path that mirrored their own.

'Shall we continue on our way?' Sunjack said in his mocking tones of respect. 'We shall have to keep to a brisk pace, as it is quite a step to our destination. Come along!'

With that the half goblin swept about face and strolled down the cliff trail affecting a jaunty, carefree style. A sharp growl from the beasts behind the banf and the terragon encouraged them to follow. Whilst they were marched along the steadily descending pathway, Jonquil's thoughts centred around two things: getting his hands on the casket Heskel had given to the half goblin, and which was still tucked under his arm; and secondly devising a plan to escape. The banf decided that it was not inconceivable that the two things might be connected.

Just as Sunjack had said the cliff path offered no escape routes on either side for many a mile; but after some time the thin ledge abruptly disappeared into a tumbling black mass that turned out to be an evergreen wood; an overspill from the lush vegetation of Eddilee that had evidently taken a liking to the austere chill of the dark side of the valley wall.

Under the trees it was as black as night, and it was some time before the hunched profile of Sunjack, striding purposefully ahead of them, was visible in the darkness. The lack of light was clearly no handicap to the half goblin. He trod the path through the tall conifers with the confidence of long familiarity. In the deep shadow, sound took precedence over sight. The progress of their assorted feet crackled over the light carpet of pine needles, from the hard crunch of the half goblin's boots at the front, to the soft plodding tread of the taloned feet at the rear. The sounds told Jonquil, who, as a creature of dark forests, was evolved for listening, that the small dragons behind them were moving in single file, even though the path had now grown wide enough to accommodate himself and Rattajack two abreast. The three gargoyles had obviously struck up a steady rhythm, one behind the other, and were reluctant to break their stride.

Despite their dingy surroundings Jonquil could see that the high wall which had bordered the trail for so long had finally given way to a steep slope, to which the plucky fir trees clung with all their might. Jonquil noticed that his companion trotting by his side was more animated now that they were once again under the shelter of a canopy of branches. This of course was because the forest was their natural habitat, and they always took strength from a close community of trees. Jonquil knew that he and Rattajack would stand a better chance than most at liberty in such a place, even in the pitch dark. They were forest born and bred; and if they were to effect an escape from their captors before the endless cliff path brought them to Juvula, the evergreen wood was the best place to do it.

Jonquil let his hand nearest to his friend brush against the terragon's flank, and once he sensed he had Rattajack's attention, he pressed a series of signs against his scales with his fingers. Signs that they had originally devised for use when baiting trolls in the Green Sky Forest. Forest trolls may have been as stupid as any other, but they had one advantage: the gift of excellent hearing. Even a whisper was not safe from the keen ears of the monsters. So the banf and the terragon had invented a basic language of hand signals relating to a small number of manoeuvres. Jonquil pressed the sign for 'honey pot' against the terragon's side, and Rattajack gripped the banf's hand to show that he understood. It was a bold plan, and one that might well result in serious injury or worse for the both of them; but then the prospects of them surviving long after their introduction to the evil Juvula seemed small. The banf decided that it was worth the risk.

Jonquil feigned a trip, and Sunjack, who had been pressing on with gusto, suddenly sensible of the opportunity the forest might present to his prisoners, spun around on hearing the banf's cries and hastened back to him.

'Get up!' he hissed. 'This is easy walking here, there's no reason to fall!'

Jonquil slowly rose to his feet, and judged as best he could where in the formless black shape that was the half goblin the casket would be found.

'My ankle,' Jonquil gasped; and as if to prove his infirmity he tried to walk and stumbled awkwardly against the body of Sunjack; his groping hands eventually touching the cold metal ornament of the wooden casket.

'What the...!' Sunjack exclaimed.

A cry of 'now!' rang out from the banf, and Rattajack who had been crouched down in readiness suddenly sprang up with a loud trill and launched himself up into the air. His small wings beat valiantly and just gave him the lift he needed to start him up the steep slope rising away from the path. A general shriek of alarm erupted from the three following dragons, and for a moment they were torn between giving chase to the terragon or responding to the cries of the half goblin as Jonquil tried to wrestle the small box from his grasp. This slight hesitation gave Rattajack enough lead to at least make something of the chase, and he scrambled as fast as his legs could carry him higher into the ranks of trees. Eventually the gargoyles sorted themselves out and two of them flapped up the slope after Rattajack, whilst the third, Dragora, charged at the writhing mass that was Jonquil and Sunjack. Using the keenness of his ears, the banf tracked the advance of the snarling monster, and at just the right moment swung Sunjack around so that Dragora's lunging bite closed on the goblin's arm. The cloaked figure screamed in agony, and at once the casket came free in the banf's hands. Without a moment's delay, Jonquil leapt from the path and fell into the plunging slope of undergrowth that swept down towards the wide floor of the frozen valley. As soon as his feet met with the slanting ground, the banf instinctively tucked himself into a ball, enclosing the casket with his body, and allowed himself to be rolled and buffeted down the valley side. A greater scream burst from Sunjack as he realised his loss, and following the noise of Jonquil's tumbling descent, he beat the dragon's jaws from his arm and jumped down from the path, the mortified Dragora swooping after him.

Jonquil eventually came to a jarring halt at the base of a stout pine. It took a few moments for the world to stop spinning before his eyes, and then he crawled away over the ground, searching for deep shadows to hide in. The banf found that his eyes had grown accustomed to the gloom beneath the trees quite quickly, and he was able to negotiate a safe path around fallen trunks and noisy dry thickets without too much difficulty or mishap. His greatest concern now was for Rattajack; but he comforted himself with the thought that the terragon had always had a great aptitude for troll-dodging; and as gargoyle-dodging could not be that different there was every chance that his friend would successfully evade his pursuers for some time. In clinging to that hope, however, Jonquil secretly knew that he was ignoring two important differences: the fact that the terragon was trying to manoeuvre himself across a terrain pitched at an impossible gradient, and that like Rattajack, his opponents could fly.

The banf eventually discovered the massive rootcage of a fallen giant; its unending bole reaching away down the slope towards the floor of the valley. It was ingenious work climbing almost blind into the tower of tangled roots, requiring slow and supple movements. The task was not helped by only having one hand free with which to climb, but finally he made it to a safe crevice, and clutching the casket to him, tucked himself inside.

Sunjack, closely followed by Dragora, wandered franticly through the thick soup of darkness searching for Jonquil. He could not believe that in such a short space of time he had lost everything that he had been bringing to the hide-out: his captives and the casket with its priceless contents. His head had been so occupied with thoughts of the reward and praise that he would receive from Juvula and Mummichog for his good work, that he had become neglectful. He told himself that he should have bound the two prisoners before they entered the accursed evergreen wood. Better yet, he should have slit both their throats at the start and had done with it. One thing was for certain: Juvula was expecting that box. There was no way that Sunjack could go on to Mummichog's lair without it. The half goblin had been present when Horolog's misdemeanour had been punished; and that poor wretch had only fallen asleep whilst on watch. Sunjack dared not imagine what delights Mummichog would dream up for a fiasco such as this. The half goblin was guilty of arrogance, carelessness, not to mention gross stupidity; if he did not recover the casket, he might just as well slit his own throat.

Sunjack lowered himself down on to the prostrate bough of a huge fallen tree. He felt sick with fear, and just at that moment could think of nothing to do but weep. It was too dark to look for tracks, and Dragora seemed more interested in snapping at passing bats than sniffing out the banf's trail. He would have to wait until first light, and pray that Mummichog did not send a search party out for them. Zemorga was bound to have reached the hide-out by now, and their arrival would be awaited.

A triumphant chorus broke the silence of the slanting forest wrenching the half goblin back to his senses. A flurry of mad thoughts blew into his mind: could they have found the casket? The banf? Had someone arrived from the hide-out already? Juvula, impatient for his power crystal! Sunjack leapt to his feet, his heart racing. Should he run towards the sound or away from it? Was it success or disaster? In the end his curiosity overpowered his fear, and calling Dragora to heel, the half goblin began to clamber hastily back up the slope towards the thin path now high above them.

Jonquil had heard the cries of the dragon creatures also, and in his heart of hearts knew what it must mean. The urge to rush to his friend's rescue was almost overwhelming, but to do so would be to wreck their plan. He had to sit tight and let the events unfold, otherwise he would ruin everything and endanger both their lives.

The half goblin eventually staggered back to the path and was met with the sight of an exhausted Rattajack slumped on the ground with the two victorious gargoyles stooping over him with murderous intent. He shrieked at them to withdraw and then pulled the terragon roughly to his feet.

'Can you find him?' he screamed into Rattajack's ear. 'In the dark?'

The terragon made no answer but just looked vacantly at the half goblin as if he could not comprehend Sunjack's meaning. Sunjack gripped Rattajack's snout and pressed his face very close.

'I know you can understand me,' he hissed. 'And I'm in no mood for games! If you don't lead me to him I swear I will feed you to these three - limb by limb!'

A collective slaver from the surrounding monsters greeted this last statement, and with a worried glance at the drooling jaws and bared teeth of his proposed executioners, Rattajack turned back to Sunjack and with a look of abject shame slowly nodded.

They all returned to the part of the forest where Sunjack had given up the chase for Jonquil, and Rattajack reluctantly assumed the role of bloodhound. He sniffed the ground here and there until he picked up his beloved friend's scent. Then he moved off, the half goblin letting out a whoop of joy as he followed on. Dragora, Zaugros and Grizzagrim all barked in unison after Sunjack's cry and stalked after the terragon. Rattajack took them on quite a tour of the forest. So much so that at one point the half goblin yanked the terragon upright by his collar, and assuming his former threatening tone, warned Rattajack not to trifle with his patience. It was then that the terragon casually pointed to the base of a prickly bush with his snout. The half goblin looked at the spot, and his voice suddenly burned with joy. He reached down and plucked the casket from the thorny stems, hardly feeling the scratches that he sustained in doing so, and held the precious article aloft like a great trophy. When he lowered it again, he planted an affectionate kiss on its wooden skin and cuddled it like a puppy. Although it was dark Rattajack could tell that Sunjack's face was glowing with relief and ecstasy, and when he next spoke to the terragon it was almost with a note of kindness.

'You are a clever boy, aren't you?' he crooned.

Then a dark thought must have crossed his mind, for he started to fidget franticly with the body of the box. There was the sharp squeak of wood drawn across wood, and then a hollow fumble, a rustle, and a deep sigh of relief. Whatever it was the half goblin had suspected might be missing was evidently still there.

Suddenly Sunjack seemed to recover his former authority, and began to bark orders at the three attendant gargoyles. Rattajack was to be taken on ahead to the hide-out by Zaugros and Grizzagrim. The half goblin and Dragora would remain behind a while with the casket to see if they could find the banf's body. Sunjack clearly believed that Jonquil had lost his grip on the precious box as he tumbled uncontrollably down the slope.

'He probably broke his neck!' he cackled. 'There's some big rocks at the bottom of the drop!'

Rattajack with his special senses knew differently. He could feel that the banf was very close by. He only prayed that his friend would stay hidden and not attempt to rescue him. The terragon did not have the power to tell the future, but he did not feel as if he was in any imminent danger. After all, if Sunjack's orders had been to kill the two companions if he ever got the opportunity, he would have done so before now and saved himself a lot of bother.

For Jonquil's part, he had never deserted his terragon companion in times of peril, and it was all he could do to stop himself from rushing to his aid at that moment; but the banf knew that if he was to attempt a rescue against such odds, the best he could achieve was his own capture. Moreover, the banf reasoned that Juvula and his cronies were almost certain to keep Rattajack alive and unharmed, especially as they would know him by now to be a friend of Throstle's; that association would make the terragon a valuable hostage. Even so, the logic of this argument did little to dispel the feelings of guilt and betrayal that began to claw at Jonquil's heart, at letting his beloved friend be led away as a captive.

As if to allay Jonquil's fears, Rattajack let forth a sombre call which seemed to carry through the stillness of the forest far into the distance. Sunjack was somewhat surprised at this uncharacteristic outburst, but interpreted it as a cry of mourning for the banf.

'Aah!' the half goblin offered a mocking tone of sympathy. 'He's crying for his friend! Ain't it sad, boys?'

If terragon sized dragon creatures with the ugliest steel trap faces imaginable could execute a collective snigger, then that is what they did in response to Sunjack's jeering. The terragon hung his head low and allowed himself to be led away by his two dragon guards.

Jonquil let his head fall on to his knees as if not wanting to see his friend's removal; but his ears still recorded Rattajack's weary footfalls passing by the giant rootcage. The banf had finally been persuaded not to intervene on his friend's behalf by the special call which Rattajack had made. The call was another of their old signals: it meant 'all is well'. The terragon had told his friend in the clearest way he knew not to reveal himself. Their plan had worked like a dream so far, and now they must let it continue unhindered.

Sunjack and Dragora carefully wove their way down the slope hoping to find some sign of the banf's demise, but the half goblin eventually conceded to the darkness and settled down to wait for morning; holding the casket tightly to him as if even the air itself might try to steal it away from him. Jonquil wriggled about in his crevice until he found a comfortable position and then finally closed his eyes on the dark night.

Dawn slowly crept its way beneath the deep canopy of the evergreen wood, where the darkest shadows of the night seemed to have taken refuge. Sunjack's eyes suddenly snapped open, and in the split second of time it took for him to realise that the casket was still held in his arms, he panicked.

Dragora was standing nearby chomping on the remains of some woodland mammal that had come a cropper inside the monster's killer jaws. The gargoyle croaked a greeting to the half goblin, and in doing so dropped half of its breakfast on to the needle strewn floor. Sunjack climbed to his feet and retrieved the limp morsel from beneath the ugly creature's mournful expression. He picked the hard spines from the wet meat, and then, remembering his own hunger tore off a small portion and tossed the rest upwards. The pick-axe jaws of the dragon snatched the body from the air with a lightning strike, its bite echoing through the empty wood like the fast closing of a large leather-bound book. As Sunjack started for the bottom of the slope he stuffed the handful of bloody flesh he had stolen into his mouth, and mumbled as best he could for the dragon to follow.

The two of them scoured the pile of large boulders at the foot of the valley wall until the sun itself began to peep over the ragged horizon of distant mountains. They then moved off along the bottom of the slope, abandoning their search and gradually making their way up through the trees to rise once more on to the narrow path and finally leave the forest behind them. The open side of the trail became a sheer drop once again as the cliff path began a wide sweep around a great bay of open space.

Sunjack had decided to be philosophical about the exercise. He did not have the body of the banf, or rather some recognisable portion of it that he could show to his masters; but he did have the casket, and one valuable prisoner as well. After he had given his hastily devised explanation to Mummichog for his tardiness, he felt sure that he would escape without any major reprisals. If he managed to make his explanation especially convincing, Sunjack fancied that the delivery of a significant captive like Rattajack might still earn him a reward of some kind. It was whilst enjoying thoughts such as these that Sunjack led Dragora along the ever descending cliff path.

The half goblin and the dragon had not proceeded far along the trail when a rumble groaned through the heavens above them. Sunjack stopped to look at the sky, and where a little while ago there had been a perfectly clear expanse of blue, there now hovered a dark cluster of angry grey clouds, moving swiftly over the high ridge of the valley. At first, the half goblin dismissed this sudden gathering as merely a continuation of the rain contrivance for the Enchanted Vale; but then the thunder drummed again, louder than before, and Sunjack began to get an uneasy feeling in the pit of his stomach. The wizards never used thunder during their rainmaking. It was always reserved for spectacular displays on special days (when the lightning was forged into the images of fiery dragons and other infernal creatures) and only ever practised by the most powerful. A sharp wind suddenly blew down the trail, scooping up great waves of pine needles and hurling them against the two figures, forcing them to shield their eyes and faces from a veritable hail of stinging darts. The glare of lightning momentarily brightened the rocks about them, and the accompanying report tore through the ether like the stampede of a thousand gracklins.

Sunjack started to run; natural storms did not brew up in a matter of moments, there was clearly some enchanted hand at work with this one. Lightning reached for the cliff in a brilliant branch, striking a lone fir tree struggling up from the rock wall a little way ahead. The tree exploded into a great plume of fire and crashed on to the path in a sweeping arc of flame.

The half goblin skidded to a halt before the burning tree, Dragora almost ploughing into the back of him and pushing him into the wall of fire. They were trapped. They could go no further forward. The only road open to them was the one that led back into the eye of the oncoming storm. The wind began to roar with a supernatural fury, rifling through the canopy of the evergreen wood behind them, transforming it into a slanting swathe of storm-lashed waves. Sunjack thought he could hear another sound mingled with the hoarse wail of the wind; a sound reminiscent of wind-chimes, only stronger, coarser, blown with aggression. Then it came to him. It was the voice of a flute; only a flute amplified almost beyond recognition and played by a demon.

Sunjack held the casket to him as if yet again he feared its loss. He cast a glance at Dragora who stared back at him intently, waiting to take his lead from the half goblin. As loathed as he was to part from his prize, he knew the choice he had to make. Sunjack pushed the casket into the dragon's wing claws and was about to instruct him to fly ahead with it to the hide-out, when he heard his own name bellowed by a voice more terrible than the storm.

The half goblin and the dragon turned as one towards the crest of the ridge, and standing high above them against the blackened sky, his hair and robe billowing in the driving gale was a wizard. Held firmly in his hand was an ancient staff whose crystal sparkled with the potency of Old Magic.

Sunjack let out a scream of horror and virtually pushed Dragora off the narrow ledge into the air. The gargoyle very nearly lost his grip on the casket as he tumbled from the path, and only just managed to juggle it into his talons before thrusting wide his wings to save himself from the fall. As the dragon creature rode out from the cliff on the violent draught, Sunjack cried after him to go on to the lair and get help. The half goblin threw a quick glance at Throstle, another at the burning tree which still effectively barred his progress, and then fled back up the narrow path towards the dark wall of the evergreen wood.

Throstle followed the small dragon with his eyes and summoned a lightning bolt from the bruised clouds overhead. The gleaming thread of light wriggled through the air and smote Dragora's right wing, throwing him into a wild, swerving flight. He tipped and reeled in the teeth of the storm but held on to the casket with grim determination. His injury was to prove insufficient to disable him, for after dropping briefly from sight he rose once more on the buffeting wind and beat a hasty rhythm for home. Throstle watched the dragon until he disappeared around the far headland of the great bay. He could have sent another lightning bolt against Dragora, one that could have killed him outright; but the wizard's love of dragons stayed his hand, and allowed the casket-bearer to escape.

The Dragonmaster of Eyesand bore no such love for goblins, however, and he now turned his wrath on the fleeing figure below whose black cape sailed out behind him in the face of the howling gale. Assuming that Sunjack had witnessed the wizard's assault on the dragon, Throstle aimed a streak of white fire a few paces ahead of the half goblin. Sunjack suddenly froze in his tracks, staring transfixed at the smoking hole in the path. He had seen the attack on Dragora; and had no intention of showing disrespect to such power by trying to outrun it. At the sound of Throstle descending the slope, Sunjack's hand almost imperceptibly drifted towards the hilt of his dagger.

When Throstle reached the path the storm abruptly ceased. Sunjack did not turn around to face him. He continued to stare at the blackened hole before him as though he could not tear his eyes from it. The wizard approached the half goblin from behind and placed a firm hand on his shoulder. Suddenly Sunjack spun around and thrust his dark blade towards Throstle's stomach; but the dagger met an invisible wall of resistance that would not yield to the goblin's efforts. The wizard laughed.

'For shame, Sunjack!' he said. 'Do you not know that a mortal cannot strike a wizard and survive the stroke. I should have thought you had sneaked around wizards long enough to have learned that much. My enchanted armour is more than a match for your puny blade, and it has saved you from causing your own disaster!'

Sunjack's fearful yellow eyes peered up sheepishly at Throstle, and then dropping the dagger, the half goblin sank wailing to his knees, grabbing fistfuls of the wizard's robe and begging to be spared. Throstle reached down and pulled the half goblin to his feet by his hood.

'Where are my friends?' he roared at Sunjack.

The half goblin wrung his hands and moaned pitifully.

'Good Horcust, kind Horcust,' he snivelled, 'great Lord of Eddilee...'

Throstle pulled him on to tip-toe by a fistful of collar.

'I'm sorry, Sunjack, but your flattery will not work on me!' he growled.

The half goblin tried to loosen the wizard's grip at his throat but as he did so Throstle's fingers tightened. Sunjack desisted and commenced to croak his reply. He spun the wizard a tale of how he quite innocently came across the two companions on the cliff path set upon by four hideous gargoyles who were after their blood. Naturally he had tried to intervene on the victims' behalf and fight off the bloodthirsty creatures; but alas to no avail: the banf had been hurled from the path by one of the monsters, and the terragon had been carried off by another two. The fourth one was the creature that Throstle had assailed with his lightning. Sunjack had been trying to catch this creature to avenge the deaths of the two brave travellers when the wizard had arrived on the scene and allowed him to escape.

Throstle listened impassively to this fantastic tale, and at the end of it breathed a weary sigh and then abruptly lifted Sunjack off the ground, took two steps towards the edge of the path, and thrust him out over the void. The goblin gurgled in terror, his eyes ready to burst from their sockets. His legs kicked madly in the air as if searching for the ground that was not there. Throstle's intense hazel eyes bore into the turgid yellow orbs that were Sunjack's, and his voice had an edge of steel.

'Now listen to me, you snivelling lickspittle!' he snarled. 'I want the truth, and I want it now!'

The half goblin made no reply but just stared horror-struck at the wizard.

'I recommend you start talking before my arm gets tired,' Throstle added with a menacing glint in his eye.

This seemed to galvanise the half goblin's senses, and he began a mumbled confession concerning the fate of the two companions.

'And what of Heskel's casket?' the wizard demanded.

At first, a shocked whimper was Sunjack's only response; but when Throstle feigned losing his grip, the whole sorry story was hastily blurted out.

The wizard stared long and hard at Heskel's servant dangling like a terrified rat from his fist. He knew Sunjack to be the thread that bound all the treachery in Eddilee together. An evil courier connecting the valley's highly placed traitors with the servants of Juvula. A wave of anger rose within the wizard at the thought of such malefactors inhabiting his city; but with it came a twinge of guilt. For had it not been his long neglect of Eddilee that had allowed such disaffection to flourish? Heskel was always accusing him of preferring the race of dragons to that of wizards. Perhaps in his heart of hearts Throstle had to admit that it was true. He was in love with Eyesand and the dragons that lived there. The inhabitants of Eddilee had never been able to compete with that affection. A flush of shame at what his selfishness had allowed to happen amongst the people who looked to him as leader washed over him, and he brought his arm back and placed Sunjack safely on the path. In all fairness, Throstle decided, the half goblin was no more entitled to blame than himself.

The wizard made Sunjack lead him to the place in the evergreen wood where Jonquil had jumped from the path. The two of them then descended the slope to roughly the place where the half goblin, with Rattajack's help, had recovered the casket.

Sunjack slumped down on to the exact same limb that he had sat upon the previous night, when his own search for the banf had been equally fruitless. Throstle stared thoughtfully at the ground and allowed his eyes to wander freely over the confusion of tracks that scarred the thin loam. For some reason the wizard found himself being repeatedly drawn to the great rootcage that rose from the sparse scrub like a monstrous, ancient flower. The tangled roots were as bleached and bare as old bones, and as Throstle looked deeper into them he suddenly became aware of two bright green eyes staring back at him. A familiar voice lifted into the air from within the massive ball of roots.

'Throstle!'

The banf's head suddenly popped out into the light.

'Jonquil!' Throstle exclaimed.

A cursed profanity dropped from Sunjack's lips before he remembered himself and quickly followed it with praising the gods out loud for the banf's deliverance. Privately he could not believe that he had been so close to Jonquil's hiding place and not known it. He then realised how clever the terragon had been in leading him to the casket and in so doing distracting him from searching properly for his friend. Sunjack may have been duped by this tricky pair, but at least he had the comfort of knowing that the precious box was out of Throstle's reach and safely on its way to his masters; and in all likelihood a team of rescuers, sent by Mummichog, would be along at any moment to liberate him from his captors.

The wizard and the banf could not have been more delighted to see one another. The former because he feared Jonquil to be dead, and the latter because now they could get on with the matter of rescuing Rattajack. Throstle wanted to hear the whole story from the banf just to see if it varied in any significant way from Sunjack's; and it transpired that it did. Not because the half goblin had lied - he had been too genuinely terrified to do that - but because he had not known about the two companions' little ruse; which had all centred around the casket.

'Sunjack has already told me what was hidden inside it,' Throstle told the banf. 'Although I had guessed as much. I ran into Gristmire and Shirene shortly after they had visited with Heskel, and they as much as admitted they had been engaged in some mischief with the old reprobate.'

Throstle removed his hat and sat himself down upon the horizontal bough next to the half goblin; and for the first time Jonquil thought he saw the shadows of real foreboding darken the wizard's countenance.

'And now he has a power crystal to add to his ever growing list of prizes!' the wizard sighed. 'And a master sorcerer in Rhazgor to teach him how to use it.'

'No he doesn't,' said Jonquil sitting down on the thick branch beside Throstle.

The wizard did not appear to have heard the banf, so lost was he in his dark mood. He gazed dolefully into the distance and continued to voice his gloomy thoughts.

'If only I was not so soft hearted when it comes to dragons,' he said. 'I should have dropped that dark creature carrying the casket, and saved us all a good deal of trouble! If only we could have prevented Juvula from getting his hands on that stone!'

Jonquil casually tossed something sparkling into the wizard's lap.

'We did!' the banf exclaimed.

Sunjack gave a gasp of horror and started from his seat as if a live scorpion had been thrown at him. The wizard gazed down in wonder at the fabulous object which now lay in his lap. It was the colour of amethyst, the size of a widger's egg, and it shone with the vitality of a star. Throstle gave a sigh of amazement, and turned a face bathed in a soft purplish light towards the banf.

'But Sunjack said when he recovered the casket the stone was there!' the wizard said in astonishment.

'It was! It was!' the half goblin cried, jumping excitedly, hardly able to believe his eyes. 'I felt it with my own hands, Horcust. Still wrapped in its silk pouch!'

The wizard and the half goblin both looked expectantly at the banf. Jonquil gave them a cunning smile.

'You felt a stone all right, Sunjack,' he explained. 'One like this!'

Jonquil stooped to pick up a common pebble from the ground. He held it up for the half goblin to see, and then tossed it to him. Sunjack caught the stone, examined it in his palm, and then turned deathly white.

'I swapped it for the power crystal whilst I was hiding in the root cage,' Jonquil continued. 'And then when you returned to the path to investigate that awful cry, I crept out from my hiding place and stashed the casket in the thorn bush.'

'And Rattajack knew of this deception?' asked Throstle.

'Oh yes!' replied Jonquil. 'It was the old honey pot trick that we used to play on the forest trolls back home. We used to creep up on them, steal their honey pots and get them to chase us. Then Rattajack would let himself be caught whilst I found a place to hide. I would tip all the honey out into our own container and then stash the empty pot somewhere. Rattajack would then lead the troll to the abandoned pot. The monster would be so overjoyed at recovering his prize that he would allow Rattajack to escape. Then he would discover his loss.'

'A little hard on the trolls,' Throstle said with a wry smile.

'Honey used to make them drunk,' Jonquil told him. 'And that's the only time when they were really dangerous!'

Throstle gently picked up the glinting crystal and held it before his eyes.

'Honey, eh?' he chuckled.

Jonquil nodded.

'Our trolls would do anything for honey!' he said, and then added with a sombre tone: 'Only this time, of course, Rattajack did not escape.'

Sunjack gave a sour grunt as if the terragon's capture was poor compensation for the ruination the two companions had brought on him. When Dragora arrived at the cave with the casket, and it was discovered to contain nothing more than a worthless pebble, his masters were bound to think the worst of their suspiciously absent servant. Accuse him of sabotage, duplicity; and the most skilful word-weaving in the world on his part would not convince them otherwise.

Throstle found a small velvet bag for the power crystal, rose to his feet and buckled it safely inside one of his leather pouches. He then grasped his staff purposefully, noted the position of the sun through the roof of the wood, and told the banf that Addax would be looking for them before long, and they should move on. He turned at last to Sunjack, who was a perfect portrait of wretched misery.

'By now your part in this mischief will be known or guessed in both the city and the hide-out,' the wizard told him, 'and you know well enough that death awaits you in either camp!'

The half goblin nodded slowly and sank to his knees with a pitiful whimper.

'I will not ask you to make yourself known to your masters' lair, but I will not set you free until you have revealed it to us. Do you understand?'

Sunjack lifted his miserable face to the wizard and in a voice cracked with fear and grief said he did. Throstle then turned and commenced the hard climb to the path with renewed vigour, his long legs making short work of the steep woodland slope.

They struck out along the cliff path, passing the place where Sunjack had been dangled over the edge and the burning fir tree had blocked the way. The half goblin's dagger was still lying where he had dropped it. Jonquil picked it up and pushed it into his belt. He could not imagine himself ever using it in anger; but if he and Throstle were about to embark upon a rescue errand, then a sharp blade might prove to be a useful thing.

The fir tree was little more than a smouldering stick now and presented no obstacle to proceeding down the trail. The wizard flicked it into the void with the end of his staff, and marched forward.

After skirting the far headland of the great bay of rock, the path began to weave its way purposefully towards the wide valley floor. They crossed over to the foot of the opposing ridge, and Sunjack told them that the hide-out was situated at the rear of a deep shoulder of rock near to the summit; but he knew the way to a vantage point where they could observe

Mummichog's cave in secrecy. As this had been Throstle's intention he commanded the half goblin to lead the way. Sunjack took them along an old wild goat trail that snaked up the snow-dusted slope to a grand buttress of rock standing proud of the smooth wall of the valley with a broken crown of ruined pinnacles.

If they kept themselves low, this high bastion afforded a safe and excellent view over the broad shelf of rock before the cave. Three large dragons were at rest there; a swarm of busy attendants scurrying to and fro with baggage and provisions, clearly preparing the recumbent beasts for an imminent journey. There were few figures present who did not run about or carry things. Figures who moved with an air of authority, overseeing this feverish industry. Sunjack's vantage point was too far from the hide-out for them to be able to recognise any of the individuals, but by the marked contrast in height of those gathered around the dragons, it was obvious that the hide-out was populated by goblins and men.

Suddenly the purr of small wings sounded close behind the three watchers, and before they had time to twist around, Addax had trotted up to Throstle's prostrate form. The wizard praised his loyal dragonet for finding them, and then the pale creature informed his master that he had found Gracewing as Throstle had requested and that the faithful steed was secreted, in readiness, nearby. The wizard told Addax that this was well done, and that he had another little task for his dragonet to perform.

'I want you to get as close to yonder cave as you can without being seen,' he said. 'Try and discover where they are holding Rattajack, and bring back the names of all those you recognise.'

Addax's head bobbed twice in a rapid acknowledgement of his task, and without hesitation charged into the air and banked swiftly towards the white face of the slope, using the snowy wall to disguise his approach. Like a small pale bird he raced towards the distant shelf and was soon lost to the eyes of those who watched him.

Throstle drew back from the edge of the rock, and signalled for the other two to follow him. He clambered back down to the head of the goat trail and before long brought them to a space beneath a deep overhang of rock. A great cushion of snow had been blown into this large cavity, and to the astonishment of the banf and the half goblin, the wizard suddenly began to speak words at it. Jonquil stared at the sculpted mound of white not knowing what to expect. He saw a movement, and then the whole surface of the snow seemed to shift and rise up. As they watched, the majestic person of a white dragon took shape from the snow; a creature of supreme elegance and beauty lifting himself out from his frozen bed, and shaking his crumpled wings free of the clinging powder. A fine, aristocratic head, which reminded Jonquil a little of the noble Charlock, trumpeted softly to the wizard in greeting. Throstle approached the exquisite being with extended arms and embraced the handsome neck of his old friend; Gracewing reached down and nuzzled the wizard's back in return.

Throstle introduced Jonquil to the white dragon in the warmest possible terms, and in his usual polite fashion, the banf bowed deeply. Sunjack refused to go anywhere near the dragon, even though the wizard assured him that there was no danger.

The banf saw that Gracewing's body was laden with a long saddle and assorted baggage, all of it made from materials as white as his scales. It was no wonder therefore that he had been able to lie down upon the snow mound and practically disappear. There was never any chance of an enemy spying Gracewing as long as there was snow on the ground for him to stand against.

Throstle told the statuesque dragon the story of the casket and as he did so he inspected the array of bags and satchels, which had been specially made and packed by Indlewick. There was a plentiful amount of food and water, blankets, a small tent, and of course a fully stocked medicine roll containing every herb and tincture for the healing of injuries. There was also a change of clothes for Jonquil - some better suited to the Winter climate; and Throstle even found a spare pipe and a pouch of smoking herb tucked away. Gracewing was carrying sufficient provisions for a long flight, just as Throstle had requested, for that was what he believed awaited them.

With a shrill salute to Gracewing, Addax swooped beneath the overhang and fluttered on to Throstle's proffered fist. The dragonet stared avidly into the wizard's hazel eyes, and in his silent tongue reported what he had seen. When the small creature had given his last nod and twitch to emphasise his unheard speech, and fluttered on to his perch at the head of Gracewing's saddle, the wizard called Jonquil to him and gave voice to Addax's message.

'Both Juvula and Mummichog are present at the hide-out, but as we suspected they are preparing to leave,' Throstle began. 'Addax tells me that there was great consternation at the discovery of the empty casket and Sunjack's name was held up for blame.'

The half goblin groaned aloud at this news and wrung his hands in despair.

'What about Rattajack?' Jonquil asked anxiously. 'Is he all right?'

'He has been bound to the flank of Skuldrax, Juvula's own dragonsteed; and that is how he is to travel to the great northern forest,' Throstle replied, laying his hands compassionately upon the banf's shoulders. 'Addax was able to communicate with Rattajack, and though he says that he is not looking forward to the journey, he is well! He sent a message for you - now is not the time for rescue!

'Juvula is flying to rejoin his army camped just beyond the great forest's eastern wall. He is expecting to meet with someone of importance there. Rhazgor, no doubt! They have already waited overlong for Sunjack's arrival, and have assumed that either he has taken the power crystal for himself or it is in the hands of the enemy - us! They will depart as soon as they are ready, and according to Addax that will not be long.'

The wizard threw a brief glance at the dragonet and the pale creature squawked in response and lifted from his perch to fly up on to the rock and stand watch over the activities at the hide-out.

'Do not fear, Jonquil,' the wizard continued. 'Gracewing will follow them to the ends of the world if necessary. They will be expecting us to follow them of course, and that is exactly what we shall do. We will let no harm come to Rattajack. And when the time is right we will claim him back from his captors!'

A short while later Addax called Throstle and the others back up to the vantage point. Juvula had emerged from the hide-out and was holding last minute consultations with his captains. One of whom was barely half his height: Mummichog. Jonquil had only the barest recollections of Hellbender's chief advisor, from the brief time he spent in the Mountains of Menace as Tuatara's prisoner. For some reason he seemed to remember the old 'invisible' as having being executed by the new regime: Okra and Gremba.

'They're slippery characters these 'invisibles',' Throstle told him, throwing a cautionary glance back at the skulking Sunjack. 'Very difficult to keep hold of!'

More dragons fully laden for the journey were led from the wide mouth of the cave into the bright light of midday. Juvula's eagerness to make amends for their delay and return to his army was illustrated by his risking the journey in the full light of day, rather than under the cover of darkness as was more customary. This ill-advised bravado was an indication of the importance Juvula had placed in the power crystal sent for him by Heskel and his fellow conspirators, and subsequently lost by Sunjack. Juvula had waited past the time when it was considered safest for his dragonflight to travel across the skies, and clearly had no intention of wasting yet another day waiting for the night to come again.

The first outriders urged their beasts to the lip of the shelf and took to the air. Throstle clasped Jonquil by the shoulder and indicated that it was time for them to make ready to fly. Sunjack watched them climb aboard the beautiful white dragon, and make their preparations with the various harnesses and buckles, his expression that of a lost child. He seemed completely bereft and bewildered, as if he needed to be told what he should do next. Gracewing strode elegantly towards the edge of the slope; Addax perched on the horn of his great saddle, Jonquil sat behind the dragonet, and the wizard behind the banf. Before the white dragon unfurled his long blades of skin, Throstle turned back to address the half goblin who was still following them like a pathetic dog.

'You must serve yourself now, master spy!' he called back to two of the most forlorn yellow eyes any of them had ever seen. 'Become your own master! And may fate deal more kindly with you than you deserve!'

Throstle was just about to give Gracewing leave to fly when another thought occurred to him. He lifted the pendant of crystal shards brought for him by Yelver from the Three Wizards from around his neck, and placed it over the banf's head. When Jonquil felt the weight of the crystal cluster on his chest he turned around to Throstle with an inquiring expression. The wizard smiled and shrugged his shoulders.

'For luck!' he said.

Skuldrax shifted irritably against the restraints of his harnesses. He resented having to carry a prisoner, as he considered himself to be first amongst the dragons of Juvula's flight; and therefore above such menial tasks. He cursed Rattajack for his presence, and threatened to bite him if he so much as twitched a muscle during the forthcoming journey.

He was a mean tempered dragon at the best of times. A bully, who felt a constant need to assert his superiority over the other dragons. He had an ugly, bony face with thick set jaws and cruel teeth which he kept needle sharp by chewing on granite rocks. His eyes were pale, small and cruel, and set into dark channels beneath his horny brows. He was a powerfully built quadruped, with a long low-slung body and short muscular limbs. Skuldrax's thickly textured hide showed a bold pattern of marks that were a testament to the dragon's aggressive nature: deep scars earned from his frequent skirmishes with the other beasts of Juvula's flight who were unfortunate enough to attract his wrath.

The terragon was bound in a close fitting sack, drawn tight around his neck, and strapped to the monstrous dragon's flank directly underneath his wing alongside all the other baggage. Even discounting Rattajack's intense dislike of flying it was going to be a very uncomfortable passage for him. He almost wished they had not left his head protruding from the sack, so he did not have to witness the visual glory of his long ordeal.

Juvula approached his dragon mount in the company of Mummichog. They were finishing a conversation regarding the manning of the hide-out after the great departure. Juvula could see no point in leaving anyone to guard the cave beyond that day as they were unlikely to have any further use for it. The old goblin, however, had decided to leave a small number of his 'brothers' behind to try and find out what happened to Sunjack and the power crystal. Mummichog did not tell the wizard but he had given his servants orders to kill the half goblin whatever the truth turned out to be. As for Juvula's four 'boys' they would fly alongside the main contingent; the wizard had decided that he had been parted from them for long enough; and he wanted them all with him at his moment of glory.

'Let us hope,' Mummichog said in a faintly critical tone, 'that we are not intercepted by an Alliance flight before we reach our army!'

'I have already explained to you why I am taking this risk,' Juvula responded with an impatient sigh, as he pulled on thick gauntlets. 'I dare not delay any longer. I have an important rendezvous to keep, and I cannot allow Mezereon to steal too great a march on us into the forest.'

The old goblin considered for a moment pursuing this already contested argument, but then thought better of it. The wizard stooped to peer beneath the great ruffle of skin that was Skuldrax's folded wing. He tested the bonds which held the dragon's living cargo in place. Rattajack stared back at him with accusing eyes.

'And as for you, my little beauty,' the wizard crooned to the terragon, stroking one of his long ears, 'you will net me a fine fish before this business is over, if I'm not very much mistaken. Perhaps more than one!'

With that the wizard hauled himself into the saddle and urged Skuldrax towards the edge of the flat shoulder of rock. He turned back to Mummichog before allowing the dragon to leap into the void.

'You will follow on in the rear?' he shouted back.

Mummichog smiled and gave his reply.

'My only aspiration is to follow, my Lord,' and then added under his breath. 'Until the moment I have you at my mercy, Mage of Anconeus!'

Juvula gave him a half smile and then raised his hand to those who were to leave with him in the second wave. The four gargoyles, led by Zemorga, trotted out from the cave to take up their positions around Skuldrax. They would fly near to their lord, but not too near lest they should be in range of his dragonsteed's jealous bite.

The old goblin watched the second flight drop from the ledge and then rise again some distance away, the broad spans of the dragons' wings lifting them up from the snowy sweep of the wide valley.

When the last group were ready to depart, Mummichog summoned forth his own means of transport. Dragon flying was not something that came naturally to goblins. They usually preferred to keep their feet firmly on the ground. Mummichog, however, had come to appreciate the freedom and opportunity that a dragonsteed could bestow on a traveller; and so had suffered himself to learn the necessary skills and acquire a suitable beast. The beast was Mothmog, and bore more resemblance to a huge, naked carrion bird than a dragon; and yet with its ungainly appearance and voluminous black wings that covered most of its body like a vast, wrinkled cloak it seemed as if it had been spawned to bear no other creature but a hunched old goblin garbed in a black sheet.

The other fliers may have sniggered at the sight of Mothmog as the awkward creature was led out into the daylight for the old goblin; but Mummichog knew his dragonsteed to be a resolute and faithful beast that was slow to tire, and would go on beating her wings in the service of her master long after the more attractive creatures had been dropped by fatigue.

Mothmog spread her deep cape of skin as she dived from the ledge and swept up on a rolling bank of wind that cruised the valley. With the remainder of Juvula's flight following in her wake, Mummichog's dragon led the way into the north eastern sky.

The Battle for the Orb

The thickening weave of contorted, lichen-draped branches made it difficult for the barbarian army to negotiate its way through the intrusive reach of the trees. The marching warriors found themselves having to duck or fend off voluminous curtains of damp growth as they made their way beneath the lower limbs of the evergreens. The straight, regimental conifers had now been replaced by gnarled, unruly moss pines, a sure sign that they were entering damper climes.

Mezereon had decided before they entered the forest that the journey through the trees would be too difficult for the tall ulrax, and too uncomfortable for their passengers. Consequently they had not journeyed far into the forest before the army had been halted to enable the two fugitives to dismount. A wall of warriors had formed around Mezereon and the girl, each one bearing a tall shield to fend off any chance arrows from the nearby undergrowth as they walked to two armoured litters specially provided for them.

For three days the Zrobokite horde wound its way through the major part of the great forest with little interference. There were the inevitable minor ambushes, when small numbers of unseen bow-wielding elf snipers fired short volleys of their enchanted arrows from deep cover at the snaking column. These half hearted assaults were little more than tail tweaking exercises on the part of the enchanted folk. Little stabs at the barbarian army to test the discipline, the strength and above all the precautions that the elves knew their sworn enemies would have taken to protect themselves from their elven magic. The barbarian commanders knew that the main attack would come as they approached the upper reaches of the vast forest, where the elves brewed their strongest enchantment. Ozzak and Zekkel also suspected that the elves would try to entice large numbers of the Zrobok warriors to split away from the main body of the army and charge into the depths of the forest in pursuit of their unseen attackers, thus allowing the elves to divide their force. With this old tactic in mind the barbarian warlords had commanded their troops to remain in formation no matter how great the provocation, until the proper time came to retaliate.

A few flights of lethal arrows were exchanged between the dense banks of undergrowth and the marching wall of ferocious figures, but still the Zrobok horde remained as one.

Strange palls of luminous mist drifted through the twisted ranks of trees surrounding the army. Hexerne watched them nervously as the barbarian column moved ever deeper into the enchanted region of the forest. A few elven shots had already fizzed past close to the litters during the long march, the sleek darts leaving a trail of enchanted luminescence in their wake.

The head of the column abruptly halted, and Ozzak called Mezereon and Hexerne forward to look at something that the Zrobok commanders had found. When the two of them reached the front line, and the warriors parted to admit them to the warlords, the sight which greeted them drew an involuntary gasp of horror from Hexerne.

Stretched across the gap between two ancient, gnarled trunks was a huge shimmering web. The delicate strands gleamed with the strange light of enchantment, and tiny stars sparkled into the air sporadically as if the power within the web was impatient for a victim. Drawing his long scimitar which had been smeared with one of Mezereon's special tinctures, Zekkel hacked through the enchanted trap, and the great web shrank back into the trees its malevolent potential foiled.

The army encountered many more elven traps artfully woven along their path as they continued their advance, some of them only single strands strung at calf level to evade the sharp eyes of the lookouts; but as Mezereon had predicted, the Zroboks were alert to the tricks of their enemy, and scrutinised their path through the forest with the greatest care.

Hexerne started as the two warlords called another halt. Mezereon once again joined them at the head of the column and the three of them looked out at their dingy surroundings. They had reached a place where the trees had begun to thin a little to allow patches of open ground. Shrouds of mist hovered over dark rashes of bog, and strange calls occasionally rang out in the distance, echoing through the confined space beneath the dark canopy. They all agreed that the terrain was growing ever more suitable for warfare, and therefore the inevitable clash with the elf army could not be far away.

Mezereon peered up through the layers of branches to try and catch a glimpse of the sky. The morning was now well advanced above the roof of the forest - although it made little difference to the world beneath the trees where it was forever twilight.

The Dark Sorcerer returned to Hexerne, whose face was taut with fear.

'What is it?' she demanded.

The sorcerer ignored her and told her to rest while she had the chance, for soon they would be moving again. Hexerne eased the knapsack containing the Orb from her shoulders and sunk down onto a soft sack hastily placed there for her by an attendant warrior. Before they took their leave of the sorcerer and the girl, the team of bodyguards thrust their shields into the soft ground to form a ring of protection and privacy around the two fugitives. Hexerne pulled the knapsack between her feet and then stared gloomily at Mezereon, who was similarly seated and just about to light his pipe.

'They're near, aren't they?' she asked tremulously.

Mezereon exhaled a long plume of blue smoke.

'They've always been near,' he replied.

The girl scanned the makeshift wall of shields about them as if the elves might suddenly rise over the top at any moment. She could not remember a time when she had felt more frightened. The air reeked with the smell of looming death, and her fear gave her the courage to ask the one question that had never been allowed an answer.

'Mezereon?' she asked in the tone which had always made the sorcerer visibly wince. 'Can I ask you something?'

For a while he did not answer, but continued to suck gently on his pipe, his eyes lazily regarding the patch of the shield ring which happened to fall under their gaze. Eventually he turned to her with accusing eyes.

'What?' he said darkly.

Hexerne buried her hands between her knees just as she would do as a child when she knew she was about to try the patience of someone important.

'Won't you tell me about my parents?' she finally asked in the most innocuous tones she could muster.

The Dark Sorcerer gasped in astonishment, his eyes wide with disbelief.

'You want to talk about that at a time like this?' he sneered.

'I can't think of a better time,' the girl quickly replied. 'I am afraid, Mezereon. Afraid that one of us, both of us, might be killed in this battle. And I don't even know who I am!'

Mezereon let out a deep sigh, half closing his eyes to show his weariness with this interminable subject.

'Look, Hexerne, I have told you....'

'I know what you have told me and I don't believe it!' the girl interrupted leaping to her feet. 'You know who my parents were. You have to!'

The girl suddenly flung herself down on to her knees, her hands clasped to her chest like a supplicant.

'Tell me, Mezereon, I beg of you!' she moaned. 'I don't want to die not knowing who I am!'

The sorcerer stared down at her slightly unnerved by this sudden passion.

'You are Hexerne, the little sorceress,' he said through gritted teeth.

'No!' the girl cried. 'That is what Vrorst made me! Who was I before?'

Mezereon turned his head away and gazed stonily at the ground. The muscles in his cheeks rippled the neatly trimmed pelt of his beard as Hexerne's insistence started to disturb his controlled demeanour.

'Will you just tell me this, Mezereon,' the girl breathed. 'Are the rumours true about Tuatara?'

The sorcerer tensed at the sound of the Ice Witch's name, his brow wrinkling slightly as if in pain.

'Is she my mother?' came Hexerne's strained voice again.

The silence succeeding this question was almost violent in its intensity. Mezereon bowed his head and slowly turned back to the girl, but he could not meet Hexerne's eyes. In a voice barely audible he gave her his answer.

'Yes.'

Hexerne's hands flew to her face and she crumpled to the ground, a desperate wail rising from her shaking form.

'I prayed that it was not true!' she cried. 'I would rather it was anyone but her!'

Mezereon rose swiftly and hauled the girl to her feet. The face that she lifted up to him in surprise was wet with tears.

'You have the blood of the most powerful sorceress in the world flowing in your veins. You should be glad!' he snarled at her.

'Glad!' she cried. 'She killed my Lord! She betrayed us all! Is it not because of her that Vrorst is dead?'

'No!' Mezereon roared, shaking the girl in a sudden rage. 'Vrorst was killed by arrogance! Ambition! He was so blinded by his own magnificence that he allowed pride to mar his judgement!'

The sorcerer's eyes glared with anger, Hexerne fancying she could see tiny sparks of blue fire glinting deep within them. It had been a long time since she had seen her companion so impassioned, and she began to grow a little afraid.

'If you must have someone to blame for His death,' Mezereon continued, 'then blame the banf, Jonquil! For he it was who first infected Tuatara with the contagion of Old Magic! Those wretched mushroom eaters carry it like a plague! They wreak of it. They sweat it through their pores! Tuatara only started to change after she had come in contact with the pestilent vermin! She is as much a victim of their vile enchantment as Vrorst, or us!'

Hexerne's fearful stare slowly softened into a half smile. The sorcerer frowned at her.

'Why are you looking at me like that?' he demanded.

The girl took a step backwards from the sorcerer, a look of mild amazement haunting her features.

'If I didn't know you any better,' she said. 'I would think that you were defending my ...mother!'

Mezereon was visibly stung by this remark.

'I might almost believe that you admired her!' the girl sneered.

There was a noise at the shield wall which caused a shriek of alarm from Hexerne. One of the tall components was pulled aside and Ozzak pushed through. He bowed respectfully to Mezereon murmuring something in his abrupt, whining tongue. The Dark Sorcerer gave him a stiff reply and then made to follow the barbarian warlord out of the shield ring. Hexerne was suddenly galvanised into action, calling after the disappearing figure.

'No, wait!' she cried out. 'Mezereon! My father! Who was my father?'

In another part of the forest, far removed from the barbarian horde, beneath the lofty canopy of the mightiest pine trees ever to take root in Enchantica, a great host of armed elves were gathered together in a clearing; males and females both bearing bows, javelins and swords. The wide space opened out before a great embankment of grass covered earth that was but a small glimpse of an immense ring encompassing the secret elven city of Ckristinial. A single gate of modest proportions served this part of the fortification, and through it poured yet more tall, sinewy figures to join the mass gathering.

Great sheets of glistening web were drawn between the mountainous trunks of the trees surrounding the high wall to create an encircling labyrinth of special pathways known only to the elves and those they trusted. Thick, clinging mists also haunted this mighty ring of enchantment, designed to bemuse and deceive, and led the uninvited visitor into the enchanted embrace of one of the delicate traps which hung in the still forest air like glistening filigree.

The elven crowd continued to be swelled by the endless outpouring of armed bodies, whilst at its centre a joyful ceremony was taking place. A raised dais had been placed at the heart of the gathering, and standing upon this was a small number of auspicious figures. One of them was a female dressed in long flowing robes, her black hair which fell freely to her waist shone like moon-kissed water, and was threaded with silver bells and precious stones. A wreath of star orchids she wore upon her brow, and before her stood the King and Queen of the Northern Elves and their son Silfaladil.

A princess of the elves, long thought lost, had finally returned to her people, and rediscovered her true identity. Daughter of Rilfinnian's murdered brother she was, and her name had at long last been returned to her: she was the Princess Shoshonia.

At the age of only eight years she had been stolen from her people, her parents both slaughtered by a Zrobok raiding party. The barbarians had been in the service of Mezereon and the girl was eventually presented to him by Rhazgor as yet more fodder for his unnatural experimentation. However, some rare quality in the child caught his eye, and rather than subject her to the terrors of his potions and corruption, he kept her as a special prize for his master.

Vrorst was delighted with his gift and took charge of the girl, personally tutoring her in the ways of witchcraft and great sorcery; and as his influence over her grew, so her memories diminished until by the time she reached adulthood she could remember only the Ice Lord: his kindness, his generosity, his love - and nothing of the grief that had brought her to that fate. The Lord of Ice used his dread power to build walls of darkness in the mind of his protégé, behind which he would harbour valuable secrets, the nature of which only he could perceive; the elf girl's past not least of all.

The first great feat of sorcery that she had mastered under his tutelage had been to transform herself from a young elf woman into a small lizard. This powerful performance so impressed Vrorst that he decided to give her a name that would forever remind him of her first great triumph. He used the word for 'lizard' in the old tongue; and so the Princess Shoshonia became the feared sorceress Tuatara.

All this the former Queen of Witches learned from an ancient old woman crouched over a table strewn with crystals, who with her inimitable skill had managed to forge a key to unlock the many doors of Tuatara's mind.

And then she had remembered everything; and just as Old Arubal had warned her, it was not a joyful thing. The grief which brought the end to her innocent years blended with the dark guilt of a long life in Vrorst's evil service overwhelmed her with an avenging storm of pain and regret. An endless catalogue of malevolent deeds was revealed to her, all of which the Ice Lord had commanded her to forget. A great cache of long hidden secrets the old mystic drew forth, whilst they sat facing each other across a small table in a dimly lit hovel, formed by the squirming roots of one of the giant trees. The rain shower of crystals that hung each from its own thread from the ceiling had shaken with the force of two embattled energies. An evil shadow had been purged from Tuatara's soul, and it had taken every ounce of the ancient one's strength to drive it out. The effort of the long struggle had left them both exhausted, and it was well that Arubal had first seen to Meadolarne's malady, which had been a small task for the mother of crystalcraft, for the old one was left weak and helpless as an infant for many days after her curing of the Ice Witch.

Tuatara now remembered her former name, and her long lost family and people. She remembered her dead parents and her enslaving by Mezereon's agents. She remembered everything that Vrorst had concealed. All the terrible actions and episodes that he had forced her to commit, the memories of which he evidently feared might threaten her loyalty to him if he allowed them to remain in her waking mind.

Such as giving birth to a daughter! The creation and existence of whom had been denied from Tuatara's consciousness for all eighteen years of the girl's life. The pain of this revelation had been the worst to bear. It had skewered her heart like a searing pike. The feelings of loss and violation warring with each other for command of her spirit.

Vrorst had used the Ice Witch as a means to create a new protégé. A child who would inherit the acquired powers of both her mother and father; an embryonic queen the Ice Sorcerer could mould from birth to his own design. And he had called her 'little sorceress' or in the old tongue: Hexerne. Rumours had surrounded the Ice Witch and the girl when they had both dwelled at the Throne Citadel; but Vrorst had created a false history for Hexerne, claiming her to be an orphan. Tuatara had found no reason to suspect this story. Although she had not laid eyes on Hexerne for several years, the rumours of their relationship had not died, and the reports of their remarkable likeness had no doubt continued to haunt them both.

Eventually Tuatara emerged from the great ordeal of her freed secrets, her spirit healed and at peace; and she now felt she had the strength and confidence to face the last chapter of the war against Vrorst without fear of her soul. She also had a new purpose to drive her onward: the saving of her new found daughter.

As the great celebrations drew to a close, a sizeable party of elves withdrew from the main host and wound their way through the misty labyrinth to do battle with the enemy army that had condemned itself by entering the forbidden realm of the enchanted forest. The remainder of the elven force witnessed the final formalities of the ceremony to welcome Shoshonia back to the kingdom of her people.

A string of elf maidens ascended the dais and surrounded the elf princess with a sheet of silk. Behind this screen her long robes were removed and she was clad anew with the garb of an elf warrior. The multitude raised a mighty cheer when she was revealed to them in her new attire; and she opened her arms wide to them as if to embrace the love they offered her.

Then the great elf host began to lead off into the labyrinth, to make its way to a part of the forest pre-ordained as the spot where the two armies were to meet for the final reckoning. The battleground, as Mezereon suspected, was to be the place where a great well of enchantment rose to the surface, offering the optimum chance of victory to the elves. Silfaladil and his father Rilfinnian had given the strictest orders to their fighters that the Dark Sorcerer was to be taken alive, and had equipped their warriors with special webs impregnated with the strongest magic for the purpose.

The elf prince was himself preparing to leave for the great battle. He was to lead a hundred elf horsemen against the barbarians, all of them mounted upon strong resilient ponies that blanched at nothing. As Tuatara made her way to Starblade, upon whom Meadolarne was already secured, Silfaladil approached her astride his beautiful white steed, Elseshelle. The elf pony was adorned with a fabulous battle harness of ornate straps of green hide chased with silver. Strings of bells looped across his sleek snowy form from an exquisite saddle studded with polished gems. His royal master wore a breastplate bearing the insignia of the elven kings: a circle of star orchids enclosed in a wreath of pine needles. The emblem was repeated on his round shield which rested on the pony's flank, and the silver armour which the beast wore upon his noble face.

Tuatara bowed respectfully to the prince and he saluted her with her old name of Shoshonia. He was a handsome youth with bright, commanding eyes, his wild black mane restrained by a thin circlet of engraved silver. An oval occold, the royal jewel, had been set into the front of the engraved band, and as Silfaladil countered Elseshelle's impatience to join his fellows, the stone at his brow sparkled with purple fire.

'Whither are you headed?' the prince asked of the witch.

Tuatara did not answer him until she had risen into the snowdragon's saddle.

'North,' she told him.

'On what errand?' asked Silfaladil.

'To see if I can find the place which draws the Orb bearers like a great beacon. For someone should be there ahead of them to block their path.'

The elf prince laughed confidently, his hand coming to rest on the hilt of his sword.

'You are mistaken, princess,' he said. 'They shall not leave this forest. The Orb and its followers will be taken or slain.'

'I pray you are right, noble prince,' the witch replied. 'But I fear that the Orb will do all in its power to evade capture.'

The prince drew himself up in the saddle until he was straight and proud.

148

'It will not succeed!' he declared.

A slight grin played across Tuatara's mouth, although her eyes carried a glint of foreboding.

'We shall see,' she said simply, and then urged Starblade to proceed with their long walk to the small secret clearing where they would take to the air.

Silfaladil watched them depart and then turned his white pony and galloped to the head of the horse column, the tiny bells on Elseshelle's harness sounding his progress with a musical rhythm as he rode between the great boles of the giant trees.

As Starblade sidled through the forest, Meadolarne turned back to ask a question of Tuatara.

'I imagine the Roof of the World to be a big place!' she began. 'How will we find the place we seek?'

Tuatara smiled and leaned forward to address the banfina.

'Many secrets the Ice Sorcerer buried in the deep corners of my mind; thinking them safe forever,' she said. 'But Vrorst did not reckon on the skill of Arubal. She uncovered them all!'

Meadolarne's eyes suddenly grew bright with excitement.

'And the whereabouts of the North Spire was amongst them?' she asked.

Tuatara gave a half sigh and her eyes seemed less than certain.

'There is a picture in my mind,' she told the banfina, 'of a lone, snow-clad peak rising above an ocean of mist. If we can find that peak, then it may lead us to our goal. Vrorst must have placed the knowledge within me, in case one day, if things went ill, he had need for me to find the hidden sanctuary to fulfil some purpose. You can be sure that the same information was similarly secreted in Mezereon's mind.'

'Then Mezereon will know the way also,' Meadolarne added.

'Undoubtedly,' the witch answered. 'But they will not need his knowledge. The Orb will direct them. The Orb is the only guide my daughter and her .....*companion* will need!'

The snowdragon increased its steady gait to a slow trot and before long the witch and the banfina could see up ahead of them the place where the trees had been cleared by the elves to permit a modest visitation of dragon borne visitors to their forest.

The eastern wall of the forest towered over the modest encampment of tents and resting dragons that nestled against the feet of the great trees. An angry snowstorm raked across the circle of bowed shelters as Juvula's dragon flight tilted towards them out of the raging sky. The meagre settlement was almost completely veiled by a slanting curtain of hurtling snow, the furious blizzard lashing against the rippling fabric of the tents and the stoical figures of the dragons.

Juvula was almost blown down from Skuldrax's saddle with the force of the wind when he unclasped the safety harnesses; and after watching over the untying of the terragon, led his small band of fliers towards the largest of the snow buried mounds at the centre of the group.

Once inside, Rattajack was lashed to a stout pole whilst Juvula and his confederates unwrapped the thick layers of tuthras and fur that had protected them from the icy gales. A generous fire rolled upwards from a large stack of logs and gradually the group of figures gathered around it to warm their chilled bodies. Food and drink had been laid in readiness upon the lid of a large chest, and the tired group made free with it.

More figures entered the domed space of the tent. It was Graquat and two of his lieutenants. Ice demon guards, the only creatures who could bear to stand outside in such conditions, had alerted their chief to the wizard's arrival. Graquat informed Juvula that the main body of their army was now well inside the borders of the forest en route for their planned encounter with the barbarian horde. As soon as the goblin interpreter that Graquat had brought with him had completed his translation of the chief ice demon's words, Juvula let it be known that he was satisfied. His instructions had been complied with and all was well. Graquat then told him that his visitor had arrived, and the light of excitement brightened Juvula's eyes. He urged the ice demon to fetch him to him, and then prepared to meet his new prestigious ally.

Rhazgor entered the fiery glow of the shelter, and the light from the flames was immediately captured by a glistening robe of black dragonscale mail, the fabulous garment reflecting a myriad sparks of golden fire. In his right hand he held an ancient staff capped with a spearhead of blue crystal, which despite the glow from the fire remained filled with a cool, azure light. The aged face of the wizard was framed by a wild shock of white hair streaked with two opposing plumes of black. A sharp dagger of a beard thrust down from his chin starkly white against the colour of his magnificent robe; and as he approached, Juvula saw that his eyes were grim discs of jet set in wide pools of ivory.

A cloak of white fur was removed from the wizard's shoulders by an attendant and after a moment of mutual appraisal the two wizards clasped forearms in a brotherly greeting. A relieved ripple of laughter and appreciation broke out amongst the onlookers, and with a warm smile the former Mage of Anconeus invited Mezereon's former lieutenant to sit with him in council beside the fire.

As Juvula held conference with Rhazgor in the main dome of stretched nalzarg skin, Mummichog led his flight down to the encampment seated between the great black cape of Mothmog's wings.

Graquat was there to meet the old goblin as he staggered into the nearest of the smaller tents to escape the vicious onslaught of wind and snow. Mummichog threw a displeased glance at the chief ice demon as he shook the debris of the weather from his cloak. Graquat dismissed the other occupants from the tent his intuition telling him that the goblin had private words to share with him. As soon as they were alone Mummichog diplomatically admonished the ice demon (as much as he dared) for his brazen affront to Juvula, even though as far as they could tell, owing to the wizard's ignorance of the ice demon tongue, it had fallen upon deaf ears.

'Juvula is no fool!' Mummichog warned. 'And the folly will be ours if we treat him as one.'

Graquat narrowed his blood red eyes and told the old goblin that his lieutenants were primed and ready to act upon his word. They needed only a sign of assent to spring into action. Mummichog raised his hands in a gesture of caution, his yellow eyes darkened by a frown of foreboding.

'We must be especially careful now that Rhazgor has joined our camp,' he told the ice demon. 'We cannot afford a single error in our behaviour, or we will be suspected!'

'We will have to kill him too!' Graquat growled.

The old goblin's eyes widened in alarm at this sudden expansion of their plan; almost as if he had just had a premonition of a forthcoming disaster. For a moment he felt a rush of panic as though control was being slowly twisted from his grasp and events were beginning to gather their own cataclysmic momentum. Then Mummichog calmed himself and gently tried to reassert his steadying influence over the zealous ice demon, and through him his volatile underlings.

'We must be patient, my friend,' he said softly. 'If we act a moment too soon we will fail! We must also be careful not to over reach ourselves. Together Juvula and Rhazgor will make a formidable foe. I would be content with only one death if it wins us the Orb. Let us not lose sight of the fact that that is our main objective!'

Graquat grunted a grudging agreement and settled down with Mummichog to discuss the finer points of their plot. The old goblin making doubly sure that the ice demon was willing to adhere religiously to the crucial timing of their plan. Later, when he had sufficiently recovered from the long gruelling flight he had just endured, Mummichog presented himself to the minor wizard and his powerful new supporter. The look of thinly veiled suspicion in Rhazgor's dark eyes that greeted the goblin as he entered the main dome, filled him with renewed apprehension, and if the old goblin had not had so much invested in the success of his bold scheme with Graquat, he might have turned tail and fled at that very moment.

The distant bank of mist crept its way over the ground towards the barbarians. Like a pale, hazy river, almost luminous against the gloom of the forest, it snaked between the contorted feet of the moss pines. Thin tendrils like long glowing fingers felt their way forward, the tall curling mass following on behind.

Ozzak, Zekkel and Mezereon stood at the head of the halted column regarding the approaching wall of mist. As soon as the large pale cloud had been spotted far off in the distance, the Zrobok army had been called to a state of readiness. Arrows were set to bows. Shield walls were lifted into place. Hundreds of pairs of barbarian eyes stared suspiciously at the floating bank of mist that was moving swiftly to within bowshot.

Hexerne looked out at the glowing cloud also, from behind the raised shields of her bodyguards. It was clear from the tense anticipation of the warriors around her, their eyes to a man fixed rigidly on the shifting wall, that no-one believed the mist to be a natural phenomenon. The Zroboks seemed to be expecting a host of elves to rush forth from its billowing mass at any moment.

Suddenly a cry rang out from the flank of the barbarian column furthest from the creeping cloud, and the eyes of the fighters on that side turned to see a second bank of mist fast approaching from the opposite direction. A fence of shields suddenly clattered into place along the previously only lightly defended flank, and the army leaders decided it was time to act.

The twin patches of mist covered an expanse of ground equivalent to about the first third of the barbarian column, and it seemed to be the head of the army that they were targeting. On the relayed orders of the Zrobok warlords scores of archers ran in an ordered stream towards the front of the column, using the long strip of ground between the two walls of shields like a protected highway. The bowmen massed in thick lines behind each of the defensive walls and on the signal of their leaders let fly two simultaneous clouds of black arrows at the opposing banks of mist.

No sooner had the barbarian arrows left the strings of their bows in screaming shadows of death than an answering wave of lethal darts lifted from each of the glowing banks. A warning cry went up from within the Zrobok lines and those that stood inside the protective walls raised their own shields above their heads in anticipation of the deadly downpour. The arrows of the elves rained down upon the barbarians in converging swarms rattling against the upturned shields or thudding ominously into both the ground and any exposed flesh. Specially chosen Zrobok captains were observing their ranks with close attention, their long curved knives drawn in readiness. For the arrows of the barbarians were tipped with a mortal poison, but those of the elves were charged with enchantment. An enchantment caused any victim not killed outright by the arrow to be thrown into a murderous fury, and run amok amongst his fellows slashing and stabbing in a fit of frenzy. The watchful captains were ready for any such mischief to manifest itself amongst their men, for despite the antidotes that each warrior had taken before entering the forest, there was always the exception, when a quick slit of the throat was the only cure.

The walls of mist continued to roll towards the barbarian column until the upper third was completely engulfed. Rows of vicious pikes were thrust out between the shields like the raised oars of a mighty longship; a thorny reception for the elves' anticipated charge.

For a few tense moments nothing happened. Not a single sound broke the silence of a massed horde holding its breath. The enchanted mist wrapped itself about the frozen figures of the barbarians whose eyes strained to try and pierce the milky fog without.

Suddenly with a noise like a hundred whiplashes, a blizzard of gleaming arrows filled the air, each drawing a line of light across the greyness. The arrows came in a flat horizontal assault fired directly at the walls of shields, now parted slightly by the rows of pikes. The elf archers clearly hoped to breach the protective fence and find unprotected targets within. A few agonising cries went up from those caught by the arrows that found the slim gaps between the shields, and the vigilant captains made short work of any whose antidote had failed. The barbarian archers answered the elf bows with a shrieking volley of their own noisy darts; but not a single cry of pain was heard from the concealed ranks of the enchanted enemy.

Sensible of the temptation the elves were presenting to the warriors, the Zrobok captains ran back and forth along their lines urging their men to restrain their wrath and hold their formation. Meanwhile other figures were sent down through the column to the middle section of the army where the first of the gracklin packs were to be found. Closing ranks after them the shield wall permitted two groups of the terrible dragon-lizards and a small host of accompanying fighters to break from the main body of the column and advance outside its defences towards the cloud of mist obscuring the head of the army. The striding white monsters had been clad with armour for the battle. Spiked face shields gave an added bite to their charge; heavy, layered chest armour protected their hearts from the penetrative points of elven arrows; and long shin plates guarded against the concealed enchanted strands the elves drew between the trees. The beasts' handlers gave their wild cries to charge and the dozen or so gracklins on either side of the army let forth a great bellowing chorus of rage and thundered into the fray. A mighty cheer rose up from the mist-bound warriors who, although able to see nothing of the battle being conducted just beyond the reach of their pikes, could at least satiate a little of their fury by listening to the murderous lizards and their howling brothers engaging with the elves.

Then, as if dispersed by a sudden rush of wind the mists disappeared. The gracklins and their accompanying force were suddenly visible in their blind rampages, and they were alone. There was not a single elf to be seen anywhere in the forest on either side of the column. Mezereon saw with a twinge of disappointment, though not surprise, that the Zrobok archers had not claimed a single victim with their flights of poisoned arrows. Or if they had their bodies had not been left behind by their fellows. The only injuries that the dragon-lizards and the attacking warriors had inflicted had been upon their own number; driven to assaulting any figure that came close in the maddening fog.

This frustrating skirmish was proof, if the two experienced Zrobok warlords needed it, that the enchanted mists were only a handicap to the elves' enemies. The forest folk themselves clearly had eyes that could penetrate the dense clouds they created and perceive all.

Mezereon instructed Ozzak and Zekkel not to dwell in that place but move the army on through the forest. Although he did not say as much to the two warlords, he was mindful that they were getting ever closer to the northern wall of the great forest. The Dark Sorcerer did not want the main battle to take place somewhere that was still a long march from the edge of the elves' kingdom and influence. The further north he could push the army before it was waylaid by open warfare, the greater his and Hexerne's chances of escaping the forest.

The army started off again at double pace, the two fugitives having climbed back into their armoured litters to be jogged along with the rest of the column. A few more sinister mist patches loomed at them out of the forest as they proceeded but these were largely ignored by the barbarians, save for the brief exchanges of a few flights of arrows. The Zrobok warlords had clearly decided to save the ferocity of their fighters for the great conflict that lay ahead.

After being jolted and thrown about for a while the two fugitives came to the conclusion that they would probably be far more comfortable on their feet. The four warriors that carried each litter trotted along before and aft more careful to keep up with the pace than to give their charges an even ride. Hexerne had to hold on to the sides of her cabin to stop herself from being spilled out, and the Orb, lying at her feet in its satchel, alternated between thumping against the wooden floor and the girl's shins. Mezereon was just about to command the litter bearers to halt, when the monstrous blare of a host of war trumpets suddenly rang out. The hellish sound must have originated some distance away for there was no sight of the authors of the noise for some time.

As the barbarian army halted and stared away to their right flank they thought they saw another pale line of mist brightening the darkness of the furthest trees. Was this to be the great battle? Had they finally reached the place of great enchantment where they were to meet the massed host of the elf kingdom? Ozzak and Zekkel had no reason to suppose otherwise and so gave instructions to their army to assume battle formation.

Mezereon stepped away from the litter and the frenzied industry of the warriors, to get a better view of the oncoming foe. Battle horns were not a usual feature of an elf attack. They preferred stealth and surprise even when attacking in massed numbers. Moreover, the pale line spreading across the dark horizon seemed more solid than mist; its movement more like the rapid approach of charging figures than the rolling billow of fog. A sorcerer's keen eyes see further than those of a barbarian, and what Mezereon saw in the oncoming wall of white filled him with dread.

The Zroboks readied themselves for war but a strange sound caught them at their work and forced them to stop and listen. All eyes turned towards the nearing wall of white and a sound like faint thunder began to build in their ears. A dull drumming that seemed to rise up from the ground itself in a pulsating crescendo. As the noise increased it gave rise to other sounds: gnashing, snarling, roaring, screaming. The sound gradually became recognisable as that of a stampede of many large animals, the rasping of their breath keeping time with their furious pace.

The floor of the forest trembled before them. A thousand heavy paws beat an awesome battle rhythm, in concert with the wailing call of the horns to produce the terrible music of war. A vast wave of white figures swept over the ground towards the barbarians: huge wolves in their hundreds thundering between the trees, maniacal white-furred riders urging them on towards their foe. With their great manes thrown up by the wind the wolvines charged onward, a snarling sea of flying fur. The screaming ice demons mounted upon their galloping forms rode them without reins or saddle. A fistful of mane and what fur they could grip with their clawed feet was the only purchase they had upon their ferocious steeds. As the thundering multitude drew nearer to the lines of the Zrobok army, the riders raised their free hands and conjured glistening spears of ice from the air.

The barbarians realised too late the nature of their foe. They had been preparing to meet a hail of arrows not a charge, and as before had erected a strong barrier of shields lined with banks of archers. They frantically tried to reassemble their defensive lines, sending forth teams of pikemen to make a hasty stand against the closing wall of wolves. The slavering jaws of the first gnashing monsters could now be seen, and the clamour of their growling voices chilled the blood of the stoutest warriors. The ill prepared fences of pikes that were desperately thrust into the soft ground and lowered at the surging wave of fur and fangs proved little worth against the first line of wolvines, who smashed through the rows of pikemen wrenching their long spears asunder. A shower of light shards glinted amongst the flights of ice javelins that were hurled from the wolves backs, the shiny projectiles reaching deep into the ordered lines of the main column. A flurry of arrows exploded from the ranks of the barbarian archers but it was too late, the mounted army of bounding white monsters were already upon them. With a great crashing sound that must have carried far into the surrounding depths of the forest, the wolvines ploughed into the Zrobok shield wall; their terrific charge meeting more than three parts of the entire column. The barbarian warriors were instantly released from the shackles of discipline and restraint. Ordered warfare had been thrown to the wind; confusion now reigned and at last the Zrobok fighters were free to do what they did best: fight!

The demolition of the shield wall brought Hexerne to the opening of her litter where she had been cowering ever since the enemy had been sighted. She peered out into the frenzied confusion, only one line of her bodyguards remaining in their protective formation. The previously ordered lines of the column had dissolved into a screaming melee of chaos. Suddenly a familiar voice tore through the din to arrest her attention. She turned to see the tall figure of Mezereon standing a short distance away franticly gesturing at her to go with him.

'Hexerne!' he screamed. 'Come on! We've got to get away from here!'

The girl glanced nervously about her, seemingly fearful to leave the close confinement of the litter, as if she felt it somehow afforded her a measure of protection. Her foot emerged from the opening and trod warily upon the soft ground. Her body slowly followed, her wide sapphire eyes constantly darting this way and that as if she expected to be set upon by the enemy at any moment. Mezereon called to her again, urging her to make haste; and, hitching the knapsack up on to her shoulders, Hexerne steeled herself to make a dash for it. Suddenly a wild cry went up from the line of bodyguards and a mountain of pale fur rose above them, rows of gaping fangs snarling at its centre. The wolvine leapt clean over the shield wall and the warriors who supported it and pounded into the covering of dry debris that lay between the bodyguards and the girl. Hexerne screamed in horror and sank helplessly to her knees, the jaws of the monster snapping only inches from her head as it bounded past. The draught of its passing threw Hexerne on to all fours and she scrambled to her feet and staggered towards the Dark Sorcerer's outstretched hand. Mezereon instantly swept his black cloak about the girl's pale clad form and stole away with her towards the banks of barbarian archers where the two Zrobok warlords were trying to bring some order to their army's defence.

Wave after wave of wolf-mounted ice demons charged into the seething mass of barbarians, who had now abandoned all attempts at a disciplined response and simply thrown themselves into the fight like incensed hornets. Spears of ice flew against swarms of black arrows and lances, filling the air above the combatants like mosquitoes over a pond.

The fierce white attackers produced an endless succession of gleaming javelins in their fists, which they deftly threw one after the other into the ranks of their enemy; the cruel frozen spikes slipping through the air to evade the raised shields of the foot soldiers. Despite the irresistible force of the wolvine charge, the Zrobok fighters were still rushing out to meet them with bared teeth and lowered pikes. With the shafts of their long spears planted in the earth, they raised the riders from their fearsome steeds like maggots wriggling on hooks; until they themselves were trampled underfoot by the furious onslaught.

The gracklin packs that had been driven up from the rear of the column now entered the fray. Unrestrained by their handlers, who simply stood back and let their murderous charges attack at will, the great dragon-lizards thundered towards the action, heads bowed low as they were trained, to demolish and crush all that stood in their path. The powerful reptiles ploughed a wide furrow into the dense rows of wolvines that had built up on the outward fringe of the battle. The agonising yelps of the giant wolves testified to the might of their assailants. As the gracklins lifted their armoured heads from their devastating work, the spikes of their face plates scarlet with blood, they employed their cavernous, dagger-laden jaws to pluck the cowering riders from the backs of their dying steeds and crush them. Long files of fresh warriors so far untouched by the battle followed swiftly in the wake of the rampaging reptiles, to set upon the beleaguered wolvines and ice demons like avenging army ants. Scimitars rang against barbed swords, halberds grappled with silver shields, the Zroboks and the ice demons flew at each other with primal screams, each side driven by an entrenched hatred of the other.

Mezereon and Hexerne had taken shelter between the massed ranks of the barbarian archers, who were all fiercely focused upon the great violent sprawl of the conflict. Ozzak and Zekkel were still attempting to impose a degree of control upon the conduct of their forces, but with limited success.

The gracklin advance had given the two warlords heart, for it was the first substantial blow that the barbarians had struck since the assault began, and they had urged the Zrobok bowmen to send forth their arrows with renewed vigour. The sorcerer and the Zrobok leaders were still reeling from the shock of this unlooked for attack. Their minds had been so tightly focused on meeting the threat of the elves that they had anticipated no other foe. Mezereon and Hexerne were both bewildered by the sudden appearance of Golitha's power, so deep in the forest, but suspected that the motive behind the action was in some way connected to the Orb. Vrorst's great tool of sorcery seemed to be working itself like a beacon, drawing the greedy and ambitious from far and wide. What the ice demons hoped to gain from its capture, apart from the ransom of its great value, the sorcerer and the girl could only guess.

After a while the two sides became too embroiled for a blanket bombardment of arrows, and the archers had to pick their targets carefully lest they should hit their own warriors in the wild confusion of bodies. The host of wolvines that had been driven back from the fray by the gracklin charge now skirted around the edge of the melee seeking another way in to the fighting; the roaring sweep of monstrous cavalry thundering uncomfortably close to the dark pool of massed bowmen.

Mezereon tried to assess how the battle was going, and which side if any was gaining the upper hand. The reinforcements from what had been the rear of the column had boosted the strength of the barbarians, although the giant wolves were exacting a terrible toll on their numbers as they set upon them with fang and claw. Something made the Dark Sorcerer turn away from the battle and regard the quieter stretch of forest to the north. Mezereon's eyes grew wide with alarm as he saw that the vista of endless trees, as should have been, was entirely swallowed up by a thick wall of mist rolling in towards the battle like a vast ghostly tidal wave. His keen sorcerer's sight was able to pierce the milky veil a little, and with a sinking heart he saw the floor of the forest moving with the stealthy approach of a great elf host. Mezereon smiled ironically to himself; so Rilfinnian had sent his army against them at last. Only now each of the three armies had two foes to defeat instead of one. The elves had no doubt waited for the two warring powers to weaken each other before making their own advance, but the enchanted folk still had a mighty task to perform to drive the massed interlopers from their realm. Mezereon decided that his and Hexerne's only chance was to try and make their escape alone during the worst of the confusion.

As if three armies coming together, each one the sworn enemies of the others, was not enough. A fourth force was at that time cautiously

C DAVISON

creeping forward towards the sounds of the great battle. They were an army of dismounted dragonriders, who had been forced to leave their fierce steeds before the eaves of the forest. Their armour clanked noisily about them as they progressed, although the sound was barely a whisper compared with the mighty clamour of the battle ahead of them. The vast chorus of rage and pain reverberated beneath the dark canopy like an imprisoned storm. A bright emblem they bore upon their breastplates: the image of a golden dragon rising against the emergent rays of the rising sun; though there were few amongst the company of three hundred, including their leader, who were confident that the insignia would buy them favour with any of the three warring powers.

A tall figure clad in long robes of Autumnal shades, a slightly incongruous sight in an evergreen forest, strode beside the shorter figure of Halmarand. The crystal housed at the tip of the sorcerer's staff burned with the light of primed potency, and his dark brown eyes searched the twisted trees about them with unblinking watchfulness. Hergest leaned towards the general and spoke softly into his ear, Halmarand raised his hand to halt his force and the trailing line of dragonriders instinctively lowered themselves to the ground in an effort to conceal their bright armour. The long sight of the sorcerer had perceived the battle in the distance and the great blanket of mist that was slowly engulfing it. Halmarand knew that this heralded the entry of the elves into the bloody contest, and that if he was to advance his dragonriders into the great milky shroud, they would simply be added to the list of foes that the enchanted army strove to destroy. Moreover, he had been charged by the Three Wizards to recapture the Orb of Winter and, if possible, the two fugitives who accompanied it. He had not been given leave to enter into a war, unless such action was unavoidable in the recovery of Vrorst's power globe. Halmarand was torn between employing his old tactic of holding back to let the enemy, or enemies, destroy themselves, and pushing on towards the fighting lest their quarry should give them the slip.

After a brief consultation with Hergest, who advised the general that although the Lord Carobus would have worked hard to persuade King Rilfinnian not to interfere with the Alliance's efforts to intercept the Orb, the desire to capture Mezereon and bring him to Ckristinial would take precedence over all other agreements.

'Then we must endeavour to separate Mezereon from the Orb,' Halmarand decided. 'Without getting drawn into the main conflict.'

The general let it be known to his men that he intended to divide his force into two halves, and that each group would circumvent the great turmoil and take up positions on the northern side. They would then lie in wait for the two fugitives, and whatever escort they could muster, when they made their inevitable break for the north wall of the forest. With his orders relayed to the end of the line, the dragonriders split into two companies, their respective commanders leading the way around the furious field of warfare.

Hexerne found herself staring blindly into a thickening wall of white. The battle had gradually faded from her sight as the great fog bank gently drifted over the field of conflict. The noise of the fighting was undiminished but the massed combatants themselves were lost to her eyes. She suddenly felt a strong grip on her arm. She turned to see the stern countenance of Mezereon.

'Come, Hexerne,' the Dark Sorcerer hissed. 'It's time to take our leave.'

The girl's eyes stared at him in horror, and she shrank back from his grip.

'But the elves are out there!' she whined. 'We will be heading straight towards their army!'

Mezereon grasped the girl's chin, pressing his face so close to hers that she could hardly focus upon his glaring eyes.

'Listen to me!' he rasped through gritted teeth. 'The Gentlil are all around us! To escape this forest we will have to cross their lines whichever direction we take. And our path lies yonder! To the north!'

'But...' the girl began to protest.

'If we stay here the elves will take us for certain!'

Hexerne peered around the sorcerer to regard the opaque bank of white that should have been the northerly forest, her wretched expression growing more fearful.

'Can you see through this mist?' she asked of him.

Mezereon glanced in the direction of the battle and then turned towards their intended route.

'Not as well as those that created it,' he said, 'but well enough to choose a path. Come on!'

With that the Dark Sorcerer pulled the girl out into the swirling mist, once more wrapping his black cloak about her body as he led them towards the dim outline of a stout trunk whose roots were smothered by a thorny brake. Before they could reach the cover of the tangled undergrowth, the pounding footfalls of a gracklin thumped into their left ears whilst the baying barks of two wolvines assaulted their right. Mezereon threw himself and the girl to the ground, as the various monsters approaching from opposite directions met before them.

Only one of the wolves bore an ice demon, and the heavy beast leapt and dodged like a nimble cub to save its rider from the lunging jaws of the striding monster. The gracklin also bore a rider: a barbarian perched on a small saddle just above the great lizard's shoulders. A deep quiver of throwing spears positioned beside him, and whilst the gracklin and the wolvines snapped and clawed at each other, the two riders exchanged a volley of javelins and screamed profanities. The fearsome talons of the reptile tore deep gouges into the soft ground as it spun itself in wild circles to reach the fast moving bodies of the wolvines who worked together instinctively to outmanoeuvre the slower giant. Suddenly the spiked head of the gracklin swung out like a mighty mace as the wolves raced past, its deadly thrust connecting with the flank of the riderless creature bowling it across the ground in a hurtling roll that carried it right pass the prone bodies of the sorcerer and the girl. A roar of triumph bellowed from the dragon-lizard and it charged after the injured wolvine, the inside claw of its leading leg trampling the splayed material of Mezereon's cloak into the earth. The monstrous creature's second step landed a short distance beyond their feet, and the draught from its tail snaking above their heads ruffled the fur of the sorcerer's collar. The ice demon urged the second wolvine after the gracklin, and the enraged creature leapt high on to the reptile's back as it lowered to finish off the stricken wolf. The long fangs of the wolvine bit deeply into the exposed spine of the great lizard, causing it to erupt into a terrible scream of pain and surprise. The barbarian turned in his saddle to try and fend off the mighty animal but before his hand could grasp the shaft of his first javelin, the ice demon, still clinging to the bristling fur of his steed, impaled him with a whiplash spearshot.

Mezereon rose quickly to his feet and scooped up the girl from the ground, and before anything else could come along dashed beneath the cover of the thorn bushes. There they took a brief rest and calmed their shattered nerves.

Juvula and Rhazgor stood outside the vast arena of carnage, in the company of the last wave of mounted ice demons. Graquat sat proudly at the head of the pack, his muscular steed clawing at the ground in his impatience to enter the fray. The two sorcerers stood side by side in a magnificent silver chariot drawn by a team of four powerful wolvines. His faithful gargoyles stood huddled together like four old crones by one of the large wheels. Mummichog was mounted on Juvula's uskyat, preferring speed to brawn, in case of the need for a swift withdrawal. The old goblin would have brought Mothmog with him into the forest if such a thing had been possible. As it was, the bat-like dragon had been left in the base camp beneath the eastern eaves, in the company of Skuldrax and the magnificent Zorostra - Rhazgor's steed.

Rattajack had been left under guard in a small clearing not far from the sorcerers and the muster of wolvines.

Juvula was kept informed of his army's fortunes by a constant stream of scouts riding in and out of the thick wall of mist which shrouded the heart of the battle. Inevitably news was sparse and almost certainly inaccurate. The air was now so cloudy in parts of the fighting that the combatants could barely distinguish the nature of the warrior they were standing shoulder to shoulder with. The news that Juvula wanted most of all was that concerning the Orb, and he had sent rider after rider in search of a sighting of the two fugitives and their precious cargo.

Graquat was growing restless. The sounds of the battle before them was stirring his blood and he longed to sheath an ice javelin in the belly of a man: the sworn enemies of his people. The Zrobokite barbarians were men, and the fingers of his spear claw itched with anticipation at the thought of them. The ice demon captain turned to the hunched form of Mummichog perched on his biped steed beside the silver chariot. He barked a request that he be allowed to lead his pack in a charge at the enemy. The old goblin demurely interrupted the plotting of the two wizards and passed on Graquat's words. The request was flatly denied. The pack was to remain with the chariot to guard any tactical retreat. The ice demon captain made a noisy show of spitting when he received the reply and the expressions thrown at him by the two sorcerers would have terrified any lesser spirit. A huge roar of demon voices erupted from the unseen melee, as if their side had inflicted some major triumph over the barbarians. Perhaps the felling of a gracklin or the breaking of some troublesome defensive position. Whatever the cause of the roar, it was to prove too much for the warrior that inhabited Graquat's skin. Without another backward glance, he raised his fist to the milky air and uttered the piercing battlecry of his fearsome clan. The host of creatures - steeds and riders - took up their captain's cry and a forest of arms lifted into the air behind him; each of them tinged with a sparkling plume of blue stars. As Graquat urged his wolvine forward a long spine of ice grew swiftly from his raised fist. The air behind him suddenly glittered with the advent of fifty ice javelins as the screaming pack surged forward in his wake. Juvula and Mummichog's simultaneous cries of protest as their rear guard disappeared into the mist were only heard after the war cry had faded away. The Pretender cursed the name of Graquat aloud as he seized the reins of the silver chariot and drove himself and Rhazgor northwards from the sounds of the battle in search of deeper cover in which to shelter. The four small dragons flapping after them like angry geese. Graquat's charge had left only a handful of ice demons behind to continue with the reconnaissance vital to Juvula's plans.

Graquat's pack bounded towards the cacophony of rage and death, which was their only guide to the whereabouts of the battle. A grin of evil anticipation bared the fangs of every wolf and ice warrior. The rhythmic thumping of the monstrous animals' paws pounded in the ears of their riders, quickening their heartbeats and boiling their blood. They stormed through the fringes of the battle running down any figures in their path that were not obviously ice demon. Graquat renewed his ice spear three times before his wild cavalry reached the concentration of writhing bodies, and then buried his fourth in the flank of a stalking gracklin mauling the limp remains of a dead wolf rider. A barbarian pikeman spotted the ice demon captain through the veil of mist and lowered the head of his long spear to charge. Graquat turned his steed and flew towards the Zrobok warrior, his fifth ice spear filling his grasp. Beyond the advancing barbarian the awesome profile of a gracklin loomed out of the milky void, striding after the running figure as if compelled to follow him. A blast of fury bellowed over the barbarian's head as the great reptile recognised the pale shape of Graquat and his wolvine charging towards him. The wolf steed ducked beneath the barbed blade of the pike and then nudged the shaft upwards with a flick of his huge snout. This slick manoeuvre enabled the ice demon to glance the cruel spearhead aside with his sword and then drag the jagged blade across the throat of his foe as he followed through. The blood stained jaws of the mighty reptile plunged downwards to seize Graquat's head, but the ice demon flattened himself along his charger's back and rode between the gracklin's legs. His fifth ice spear he thrust upwards into the soft flesh of the giant's underbelly as he was carried through. The gracklin's bellow of rage rose to an ear-splitting shriek of torturous agony before his powerful legs buckled beneath him and he crashed headlong into the soft ground; the force of his fall showering the surrounding figures with a hail of leaf litter and soil. A raucous cheer erupted from the ice demons at the death of yet another of the great dragon-lizards; and Graquat conjured forth his sixth ice javelin and searched the mist for his next victim.

Suddenly a new host of riders thundered into the fray, and greeted their fellow combatants with a searing blizzard of sparkling arrows. The brilliant swarm streaked into the mass scrummage and almost before their bowshots found their marks the archers turned and were gone. This new cavalry had been mounted upon sleek, nimble ponies who galloped through the mist negotiating turns and jumping obstacles as if the opaque air was no hindrance to them at all; and the bells which the graceful steeds bore upon their harnesses, rather than giving the ponies away in the fog only added to the confusion. The gentle metallic tones hung in the air long after the elf mounts had passed by, leaving misleading peals to tease the tortured senses of their enemies.

Then another sound erupted from the tight knot of warring figures. It was the chorus of madness. The trumpeting voices of those who had suddenly lost all reason and focus, and had been possessed by the spirit of raving insanity. Graquat looked on in horror and dismay as ice demons he knew began to hack at each other in frenzied convulsions of hate; conjuring forth their lethal ice spears only to bury them in their own kind. Wolvines threw their riders and trampled them into the ground, only pausing to tear out their throats before leaping at some other unsuspecting soul. Some of the barbarians began to laugh at this grisly spectacle, pointing to the still smouldering arrows which had injured the rampaging individuals, until some of their own number began to be affected. The ice demons and the wolvines were not protected by Mezereon's antidotes and the elves cruel enchantment was able to work its full menace upon them. Even those that had not been pierced by the sparkling arrows were not safe, for their deranged brothers set upon them with insatiable fury, rivulets of angry foam pouring from their bloody jaws.

Suddenly Graquat's faithful steed who had carried him through countless battles over the years, reared up beneath him and tossed the ice demon captain over his head; Graquat flying through the air in a high arc before crashing to the soft floor. The ice demon sprang back to his feet and turned to see his beloved steed bearing down upon him, his bared fangs gleaming with white spittle, a sputtering arrow glimmering in his flank. In an instant a new ice spear was in Graquat's fist and with it he felled the magnificent monster as it reached for his throat. The ice demon paused to share a moment of mourning with the twitching wolvine before he stole away from the battle and lay amongst the dead until he was passed over by the advancing elf lines.

Jonquil crept forward as quietly as he could; and as he was a banf and a forest dweller, his skill of the noiseless tread was second to none. The small clearing lay ahead of him, and the handful of ice demons that were guarding Rattajack. His terragon friend had been tied to the jagged remains of a tree stump, and sat with his head slumped as if he might be asleep. As Jonquil neared the opening, however, he fancied he saw the slightest flicker of Rattajack's eye, and knew that his beloved companion had sensed his presence.

The four ice demons were pretty bored with their tedious task. They longed to join their brothers in the fray; the occasional sounds of warfare carrying from the battle only adding to their frustration. They resented their prisoner for his need to be guarded, just as Skuldrax had resented having to carry him on the long journey from the hide-out.

It was only natural then that when the sudden bright light appeared in the distant murk, encapsulated by a glowing sphere of mist, it succeeded in attracting their attention. One reacted to it first and then the others sprang to their feet to peer inquisitively through the trees. The strange light caused a great deal of excitement amongst the ice demons. They debated and gestured to one another in an effort to reach a consensus as to what it might be. Jonquil of course knew that it was the crystal on the top of Throstle's staff, from which the wizard had conjured forth a brilliant incandescence. Eventually, the four guards decided that they should investigate, and three of them stepped cautiously into the trees leaving the fourth to guard the prisoner.

This was pretty much as the banf and the wizard had predicted, and so it was now time for the second diversion that they had devised to come into play to deal with the one remaining ice demon.

Stretching on to tiptoe to watch the progress of his fellows, the fourth guard became aware of a loud rustling in a thick patch of evergreen bushes just inside the clearing at his back. The ice demon slowly turned around to stare at the rash of verdant undergrowth which was visibly shaking as if some

168

small creature was trapped within the cage of rough stems. With a caution borne from a warning to trust nothing and suspect even the smallest things whilst inside the enchanted forest, the fourth guard gingerly approached the trembling bushes. Jonquil gulped when he saw the long ice spear grow from the creature's raised fist, and his body half assume the throwing position. He tentatively approached the feathery foliage of the low plants, his eyes fixed upon the waggling stems, his movements slow and deliberate. Suddenly a blur of white wings erupted into his face from the dense foliage. The ice demon cried out in alarm and staggered backwards trying to beat off his flying assailant. Then Addax dropped to the ground and scurried off into the shadow of the trees, flapping his pale wings as if they were injured. The guard screamed his outrage at the retreating creature and hurled his glassy spear after the dragonet. If Addax had been the tiniest amount less agile he would surely have been skewered by the ice javelin. As it was, the nimble reptile leapt aside in the nick of time and the cruel point thudded safely into the earth. The dragonet fluttered on through the trees in the manner of a frantic, disabled creature, and the incensed ice demon without another thought for his valuable prisoner, conjured forth another spear and charged after the hobbling form of the tiny dragon.

Jonquil sprung into action the moment it was safe to enter the open space. A low pipe of greeting was the only sound that passed between the two companions as the banf went to work on Rattajack's bonds with Sunjack's knife. As soon as the terragon was free, the two friends stole silently into the cover of the trees and made good their escape from the clearing.

After leading their respective pursuers a merry dance through the mist veiled forest, Throstle and Addax finally ended their games: Addax ceased to feign injury to his wings, and Throstle simply extinguished his enchanted lantern.

The wizard and the dragonet eventually rendezvoused with the two companions at a pre-decided location, and the re-united banf and terragon decided that probably the best way to meet up with Meadolarne again was to join with Throstle and Addax in the hunt for the Orb. For as Roshir said during the High Council at Eddilee: 'In these dark days, all paths, good and evil, lead to the far north. And that way lies the destiny of us all!'

Catch-as-Catch-Can

Juvula was growing anxious. His last two messengers had failed to return from their errands and he only had a handful left to send forth into the dense pale shroud, which still lay over the forest, for news of the Orb.

Mummichog was also growing anxious. Graquat had been a long time at the battle, and if he did not return soon, the old goblin feared that he would have to face the prospect of wresting the Orb from his master single-handed; if and when The Pretender managed to acquire the valuable prize!

For his part, Rhazgor was also uneasy. Not for any fears of the Orb: the Winter sorcerer had absolute faith in the destiny of his confederate, even if Juvula was only the son of a half-sorcerer, and therefore in wizardry far beneath him. The dreams that had visited Rhazgor in his frozen sanctuary had told him of Juvula and the great quest he was embarked upon; and the images of The Pretender victorious within the power chamber of the North Spire had convinced him that Vrorst's spirit truly was alive and continuing to work its influence upon the world; and that Juvula not Mezereon was now his chosen heir. Such was Rhazgor's fealty to Vrorst and the Power of Winter, that it never occurred to him to question why a minor enchanter from an inauspicious kingdom like Anconeus should have been chosen to embrace the greatest enchantment the world had ever seen, before a powerful wizard such as himself. The wisdom of the mighty was not always clear to those that followed them; but Rhazgor was and had always been a faithful servant, and that was undoubtedly why the spirit of the Orb had chosen him to serve the one who had been chosen to rule them all. There was obviously some unseen quality in the former Mage of Anconeus that singled him out for greatness: a quality that only Vrorst's Orb could perceive.

Rhazgor's disquiet was caused by more immediate concerns. His heightened sorcerer's senses warned him that there were unfriendly eyes upon them, and that their small group was in imminent danger.

Juvula called another of his ice demon scouts to him and was just about to inform him of his errand when a bright line of light suddenly flashed before the wizard's eyes, and embedded itself in the ice demon's shoulder as a sparkling arrow. Such was the shock of the surprise blow that the creature was knocked off his feet, only to spring back at the chariot a moment later with the fire of madness burning in his eyes. The ice demon raised his fist as if to conjure forth a spear but before the frozen weapon could materialise, Juvula thrust his boot against the creature's chest and heaved his assailant back to the ground. Rhazgor was about to execute the offending ice warrior with a bolt of his blue fire when the milky air about them seemed to fill with a gleaming rain of arrows. The four wolves harnessed to the chariot exploded with rage and violence, and leapt upon each other with unleashed savagery. They then turned their fury to speed and lunged forward through the trees, biting and bellowing at each other as they ran. The sudden lurch of the wolves was too fast for Rhazgor and he toppled off the back of the chariot before he could save himself. Juvula just managed to hang on as the wolvines pulled him in a terrifying charge between the twisted trunks; the low branches of the moss pines thrashing the body of the wizard, flinging him wildly against the sides of the speeding vehicle. The maddened wolves veered this way and that in their frenzied flight, weaving through the trees in a savage, aimless gallop. Eventually one of the wheels struck a low obstacle and tipped over, the wizard jumping clear before the chariot was mangled against a stout trunk. The wolves broke free from their harnesses and chased each other into the mist, their booming roars carrying far into the surrounding forest.

Juvula rolled along the ground and finally came to rest against a fallen log. For a few moments he just lay there dazed. The hazy network of contorted branches above him spinning uncontrollably before his eyes. When his senses returned to him, the wizard slowly rose to his feet and regarded his surroundings. There was no living soul to be seen in any direction, and as far as he could tell he was alone.

Juvula staggered over to the upturned chariot and gazed miserably upon its broken form. Then he saw something moving in the corner of his eye, something paler than the mist. He turned to look at it, and at first his eyes could make no sense of its ethereal shape. It might have been a figure, although one so faint and transparent that it could belong to no living being. The thing began to move or float between the trees, in places passing right through the craggy boles to appear again on the other side. Despite the ghostly nature of this strange apparition, Juvula found that he was not afraid. Indeed, he was possessed by an irresistible fascination for the pale spectre and felt himself compelled to follow it.

Mummichog leaned forward in his saddle to try and keep within sight of the four gargoyles who were trotting before him, snouts held low to the ground pursuing the trail of their master's chariot. The uskyat could probably have followed the trail for itself but the old goblin preferred to have Juvula's 'boys' in front of him where he could see them. As a consequence of Mummichog's ruthless discipline with the 'brothers', the four foul creatures had developed a strong liking for goblin flesh during their time at the hide-out.

They had all left Rhazgor to deal with the elf archers alone; Mummichog secretly hoping that the forest bowmen would emerge victorious. Rhazgor dead or captured was one less obstacle between the old goblin and the Orb.

Hexerne's tired feet stumbled against the hem of Mezereon's cloak and she fell heavily against him. Mezereon tried to haul the girl back to her feet but she begged him to let her rest a little while. A short distance ahead of them a cluster of lichen stained boulders stood in a modest clearing. The wizard agreed to a brief pause at the rocks and dragged the moaning Hexerne towards them.

The girl slumped on to the nearest stone, leaning the weight of the Orb against its taller neighbours, her body racked with exhaustion. Mezereon stood nearby watching the forest warily. They had covered a good deal of ground since leaving the barbarians, and to Hexerne's amazement had managed to pass safely through the elf lines and evade their keen scrutiny. The girl sat watching Mezereon with half-closed eyes. He was agitated and restless. He tried now and then to sit down and take some rest as she had done but his heightened senses were constantly alert to sounds or movement to which she was oblivious, and a moment later he would be back on his feet. He wrapped his long cloak about himself, pulling the hood over his head as if feeling a sudden chill. Hexerne continued to observe him as the sorcerer slowly turned his back to her in his constant vigil of their surroundings; his wizard's eyes seeing much further than hers. Then the girl blinked and looked again. The figure of Mezereon had somehow melted into the trees beyond. He had not become transparent, but Hexerne's eyes simply refused to see him. At first she blamed the fatigue for affecting her vision, but then the sorcerer turned to face her parting the cloak to reveal his robes beneath. His robes and the part of his face not obscured by the hood were perfectly visible, the rest of him was lost in the background. A gasp of wonder escaped from the girl's lips, and the eyes of the wizard caught her stare. A long moment passed between them and with it a jolt of understanding.

'So that's how we passed by the elves unseen!' she breathed. 'A cloak of invisibility!'

Mezereon made no answer but continued to stare with a dispassionate countenance. Hexerne eased the heavy knapsack from her shoulders and rose sluggishly to her feet. She approached the sorcerer and stroked the smooth fur of the cloak, as if it was the first time she had laid eyes upon it.

'The Zrobokites supplied the fur,' she murmured almost to herself, as she followed the sweep of the material around Mezereon's figure. 'But they do not have enchantment.'

The girl stepped around to the front of the cloak and looked up into the sorcerer's eyes.

'You must have imbibed the cloak with your own powers,' she said to him.

Still the sorcerer made no reply. Hexerne returned to her seat on the rocks and leaned back to regard the silent figure before her.

'Only a powerful sorcerer could create such a cloak; and you have always let us believe that your powers had gone. That you left them behind with your sorcery crystal, when you fled from Dragonskeep. But you have been a mighty wizard all along: you have just pretended to be weak!'

Mezereon maintained his silence but stepped closer to the knapsack containing the Orb, which lay beside the girl. Hexerne instinctively laid her hand upon it as if claiming ownership. Then the dawning of another realisation crept across her face.

'Our escape from Anconeus!' she gasped. 'It wasn't Silfaladil who made us invisible. It was you! Wasn't it?'

Hexerne glared at the sorcerer her eyes a mixture of amazement and contempt.

'It was you!' she repeated in a whisper.

Mezereon lifted the cloak from his shoulders and laid it upon the rocks. He then seated himself next to the girl. His expression was almost one of affection, or pity.

Hexerne gave him a wry smile. 'No wonder you weren't afraid of the forest. You knew you had the means to evade the elves all along!'

Mezereon shrugged.

'I could not be sure,' he said at last. 'The Gentlil have strong enchantment. There was no guarantee that I could best it. But I do concede that I had more cause for confidence than yourself.'

'Why the pretence?' Hexerne asked.

'I needed to share the burden for a while,' he replied. The girl's eyes narrowed in confusion. 'The Orb!' Mezereon said in answer to her unspoken question.

'For a while?' Hexerne said warily. 'You intend to take it back then?

Mezereon gave a dark smile as his answer; and the girl slowly rose from the rocks, grasping hold of the knapsack, and backing away into the open space. Her face was white with apprehension and she was shaking her head at the smiling sorcerer.

'Do you know what will happen to you, Hexerne, if you enter the North Spire with the Orb?'

'It is my destiny to do so!' the girl hissed.

'You will be utterly destroyed!' Mezereon told her. 'Consumed by the Freezing Fire before you could even cry out.'

Hexerne began to visibly tremble, and naked fear was now upon her face.

'I was chosen for the task!' came her quaking reply.

'You have the seed of great power within you, Hexerne,' the sorcerer continued. 'Your parentage gives you that; but it is sleeping, unrealised and that makes you vulnerable - and weak!'

Hexerne held the round shape inside the sack to her breast, cradling it in her arms. Tears began to glisten in her large eyes.

'It is enough for me to fulfil the quest,' she said. 'I do not care what comes after.'

Mezereon's smile finally faded, and he looked upon the girl with a stern benevolence.

'I do not wish it!' he said.

Hexerne was bewildered. She suddenly realised that she was in the presence of a complete stranger. Every word that the sorcerer spoke to her sounded as if it belonged on the lips of someone else.

'Why should you care what happens to me?' she breathed. 'I am nothing to you!'

Mezereon rose from his seat and took a step towards the girl. Hexerne responded in kind with a nervous retreat. The Dark Sorcerer seemed to have grown in stature, and seemed taller and more terrible to the girl.

'You must give the Orb to me now,' he said in calm, commanding tones.

'But the Orb was yours for the taking for seven years!' the girl whined. 'And you did nothing.'

'It was not the time,' Mezereon told her. 'I was too afraid. Its threat was too close, too strong. It took every ounce of my strength just to resist it. Then when you came and took the Orb upon your shoulders, for the first time in seven years I felt its grip upon me lessen; its deadly focus shift to another. And I have been free ever since to regain my strength, and discover its faults, its weaknesses. My eyes are open once again and I can see the Orb for what it truly is: an imperfect thing. An instrument of great power that I now have the means to subdue to my will!'

Hexerne stared intently at the face of the sorcerer, hardly able to comprehend the words that she was hearing.

'You see, Hexerne,' Mezereon went on, 'Vrorst did not bequeath his power to me. He bequeathed me to his power! And that was not acceptable to me. I always intended to embrace the power of the Orb. To accept my legacy. But at the time of my choosing; and on my own terms!'

'Terms?' the girl breathed. 'You intend to bargain with the Orb?'

'I intend to become its master not its slave!' the sorcerer replied with a smile.

'You used me!' Hexerne accused him. 'I was your packhorse. A diversion, whilst you prepared yourself!'

'And in so doing I have saved you,' Mezereon replied.

The girl was gripped by a sudden surge of rage, and with a boldness that overruled her fear she took a step towards her protagonist.

'Who asked you to save me?' she growled. 'It is my destiny to carry the Orb to the Spire! I cannot be parted from Him now. Without the Orb I am nothing! I have nothing!'

'You have life, child,' Mezereon countered; his voice strange, almost kind. 'And the chance to take a different path.'

Hexerne drew her mouth into a tight line, and slowly retreated from the sorcerer, her head shaking in time with every step.

'My path was chosen for me before I was born,' she said tremulously. 'And I will follow it to the end!'

Mezereon raised an upturned palm, his cobalt eyes seeming to burn with an inner fire. Instantly, the girl felt pressure build at her back, as if she was retreating against the strands of a giant web whose tolerance was reaching its zenith.

'Give me the Orb, Hexerne,' the sorcerer asked in soft, dream-like tones. 'You are powerless to resist me; but you must give it up willingly. I do not have the strength to fight you both.'

The strings of the web began to draw the girl towards the sorcerer, her heels ploughing two furrows in the soft forest earth as she tried to hold back from him. Mezereon's eyes blazed like sapphire stars, and Hexerne felt icy fingers begin to close around her will. Her eyes were unable to break away from the sorcerer's burning stare, and a dark viscous numbness was slowly engulfing her struggling body. Mezereon continued to call softly to the girl, as he drew her towards him, but his words reached Hexerne's mind as a confused drone of distorted sound.

Suddenly, a glittering net of jewel-like threads fell between them, and with a great roar of vexation Mezereon's hold over Hexerne dissolved. The girl was thrown backwards on to the ground with the force of her counter struggle, and as she lay there she watched, dazed and mesmerised, as web after glistening web folded themselves about the sorcerer's writhing form. The eyes that had formerly shone with such potency at Hexerne now gazed alarmingly at her, pale with pleading. The girl could not be sure whether the fear that haunted Mezereon's eyes was for himself, or for her and the Orb. Like a fierce animal brought to bay, the sorcerer fought against his shimmering bonds; but his struggles were in vain, for the more he resisted, the tighter the enchanted threads drew about him.

Hexerne slowly became aware of a half circle of dark figures standing just inside the clearing. They were as tall as she; with skin as pale, eyes as blue, and hair long, silky and black. They were dressed in close fitting warriors' garb: layered rows of leaves made from a material of an indefinable colour covering their lean, willowy forms. A longbow and quiver was carried by each of them; a haze of enchantment hovering above the collected flights of their arrows. As Hexerne looked on, two of the shadowy figures, whose clothing seemed to share the same camouflaging quality as Mezereon's cloak, stepped towards the sorcerer, and, in a similar manner to a fisherman casting his nets upon the water, added their magic webs to those already drawn about him.

Hexerne scrambled to her feet and turned to flee from the clearing, and as she did so her eyes met those of Silfaladil. The elf prince was standing before the graceful form of Elleseshelle, and his piercing blue eyes stared out from a face whose expression was struggling with conflicting emotions.

The girl clutched the knapsack to her and backed away from the prince. The smile which eventually stayed on his lips was warm but uncertain. Hexerne stared at him impassively, like a cornered animal trying to conceal its thoughts of escape.

'Hexerne,' Silfaladil said breathlessly. 'We meet again.'

The girl did not reply, but tightened her hold on the Orb.

'You are free now, Hexerne,' the elf prince continued. 'Free to give up this insanity. Mezereon is taken. His hold over you is broken.'

Hexerne threw a brief glance at the pathetic face of the sorcerer, peering out from behind a glimmering mesh of elf web. Her eyes then returned to the prince.

'You do not understand, Silfaladil,' she answered him. 'Mezereon is as much a slave of the Orb as I. I must go on.'

Silfaladil's smile faded, and a frown darkened his eyes.

'Give up your burden, Hexerne,' he said, 'and return with me to Ckristinial. I promise you all will be well.'

The girl slowly shook her head, her eyes never straying from his.

'I cannot,' she replied. 'I implore you to let me pass!'

A look of entreaty suddenly spread across Silfaladil's face, and his arms swept open to embrace her.

'Hexerne.....'

The girl retreated from him, her eyes burning with hostility and alarm.

'I cannot go with you, Silfaladil!' she cried. 'Let me pass! I have not wronged you. You have Mezereon. That's what you came for!'

The elf prince stopped, surprised and hurt at the ferocity of her rejection. He could see that the girl was still deeply under the influence of some jealous power, and that it would take more than his gentle persuasion to release her from its grasp.

'The Orb will not suffer you to stand in my way,' Hexerne warned him. 'If you do not let me pass it will destroy you!'

Silfaladil looked upon the girl with an expression of affectionate pity, and drew from his jewelled belt what looked like a small ball of shiny thread. With a deft movement of his fingers, the prince transformed the ball into a wafting sheet of sparkling gossamer, which hung from his hand by a single metallic thread. Hexerne stared at the floating web with horror, only too sensible of its menacing purpose.

'Even if my heart would allow such a thing,' Silfaladil said, 'my loyalty to my people would not. Your burden is a powerful force for evil. A great weapon used against us by our former enemy, and one that may be used again by any that come after him. For the sake of our future, I cannot let you pass.'

The elf prince caught the net in his fingers and held it up for Hexerne to see, its glimmering threads forming a curtain of bright lines between them.

'Once inside the web,' Silfaladil continued, 'you will be freed from your suffering, and relieved of the torment of your burden forever.'

Hexerne backed suddenly away from the figure of the prince. A scream of 'No!' burst from her throat as she retreated towards the middle of the clearing, and Silfaladil spun the enchanted web above his head in readiness to cast it over her. A moan of despair or rage burst from the strangulated body of the sorcerer at the elf prince's advance; and unseen by anyone a thin tendril of pale blue light snaked out of the dull wrappings of the Orb and along the ground towards Mezereon's boot.

Before Silfaladil could let fly his magic web, a brilliant starburst of fiery blue light erupted from the figure of the sorcerer. The brilliant fronds of power streaked outwards towards the surrounding figures of the elves knocking them off their feet and filling their bodies with a cold clinging lethargy that bewildered their senses. Hexerne remained in the clearing long enough to see the Orb's power set to work upon melting Mezereon's enchanted bonds, and then with a quick sorrowful glance at the stricken figure of the elf prince, she grabbed the magic cloak from the rocks and ran into the trees.

By the time the sorcerer was able to break free from the last of the elf webs, Hexerne had made good her escape. With his cloak upon her she would be impossible to follow by sight, and Mezereon knew that he would have to rely on his special sorcerer's wits to find her. It would also take every ounce of his powers to conceal himself from the many elf patrols that still roamed the forest; but not for an instant did he consider not pursuing the girl and the Orb. For as he stood there staring into the mist shrouded trees, trying to feel the direction Hexerne had taken from the clearing, the words she had spoken to him in the goatherd's shack all that time ago drifted back into his mind: 'Abandon the Orb! I could no more leave the Orb behind as tear out my own heart! We are both bound to it ...... to the bitter end!'

Hexerne ran blindly on through the trees, taking any path that presented itself to her. At first she was more concerned with putting as much ground between herself and Mezereon as she could than making sure she was heading in the right direction. She was careful to keep the sorcerer's cloak wrapped well about her as she made her way in case she should fall under the gaze of unfriendly eyes. However, after she had fled without rest for a good while Hexerne decided it was time to seek a more sensible route. Mezereon had taught her how to tell directions from the sky and the stars, and even from the forest itself. As the mist was too thick to use the sky as her compass, the girl was forced to resort to the latter method.

She looked about her and soon found the thing she needed: a ruby spruce. The tall slender tree had just come into fruit, and as she had been shown, Hexerne looked to see on which side the deep scarlet berries grew thickest. The greatest showing of fruit always faced south, to save the precious berries from the worst of the cruel gales which frequently blew out of the north to assail the uppermost lip of the forest. To double-check, Hexerne looked to see in which direction the needles of the moss pines were lying: for they always grew pointing into the teeth of the wind. Satisfied that she had found north, the girl moved quickly on, fearful to remain in one spot for too long a time.

Juvula's feet began to drag as though his boots were filled with lead, but the urge to follow the pale spectre floating through the mist ahead of him kept him staggering forward. Despite the blurred outlines of the apparition, he had decided that it was a figure draped in long flowing robes of white. There might have been some manner of crown or headdress above what he assumed to be a face, but the fabric of the vision was so delicate and shifting, like a wisp of smoke carried gently on a breeze, that it was impossible to be sure of its form.

The shimmering plume of light led the wizard to a place where the mist began to lessen and the trees to thin. Although Juvula could not be certain of his whereabouts, he had an idea that he was now in the furthest reaches of the forest, not far from the north wall.

Juvula watched the spectre pass through the wide bole of an ancient moss pine and then disappear from sight. The heavy feet of the wizard stepped into the nest of writhing roots that sprang from the base of the crooked tree, and promptly snagged in a proud loop, bringing him crashing down on to all fours. Juvula rolled into the cradle of twisted limbs and immediately surrendered to the weight of the fatigue which lay upon him. The effort to rise again was too great, and even the fear of losing sight of the pale apparition could not stop his eyes from closing. In an instant he had slipped into a deep sleep.

When the wizard awoke it was as if a veil had been drawn from his eyes. The mist had gone. Once more he could see the trees about him marching away in their endless ranks into the distance. A flash of bright light caught his eye, and Juvula turned his head to see the ghostly spectre once again, closer now than it had ever been, and somehow more intense, more substantial. During his time of slumber, it seemed to have acquired shape and detail. The blurred strokes of its robes now showed distinct folds and decorations. There were the features of a face inside its hazy coccoon of glow, and what appeared to be a crown of ice rising from its regal brow. Juvula lay in the embrace of the tree roots, bathed in the light of the splendid vision; but just as a soap bubble shows its finest colours before bursting, the spectre similarly abruptly disappeared, leaving the wizard once more in the gloom of the forest. In its place however, another strange vision appeared: a shifting smudge of confused outlines with the watchful face of a young elf woman peering out from within. If Juvula had been any distance from the bizarre figure, it would have eluded his eyes completely, but the girl was drawing ever nearer to the old moss pine and as she did so slithers of her under robes showed through the enchanted shroud. The wizard recognised the face, and cried forth her name as he rose before her. Such was Hexerne's surprise at this sudden meeting that she dropped the knapsack, the shiny globe bursting from its dull wrappings to roll a short way across the forest carpet of pine needles.

A gasp of awe escaped the body of the wizard, and then Juvula suddenly became aware of movement about him and the hoarse rasp of panting creatures. The four gargoyles nudged against him in greeting, and then split off to encircle the frozen figure of the girl. Mummichog trotted into view astride the uskyat, the eyes of the old goblin fixed like wide yellow saucers upon the Orb as he slid from the beast's saddle.

For a few tense moments, all eyes regarded the shiny skin of the crystal globe, and then Juvula took a step towards it. Hexerne was too shocked by this unexpected encounter to move, and all she could do was watch the Mage of Anconeus as he approached the great sphere. Juvula's eyes lifted from the Orb to Hexerne, and a smile of absolute triumph illuminated his face. The girl felt her heart pounding in her chest as the wizard stooped to lay hands upon the globe, a terrible cry of anguish slowly building within her. Mummichog also felt the pain of longing burning through his veins, and as Juvula's fingers spread to encompass the crystal, his own hand flew to the hilt of his dagger. A roar of victory slowly rose from the wizard, his triumphant voice lifting into the still air of the forest. The sound tore through Hexerne's charged senses setting every nerve on edge. Tears of frustration and sorrow welled up in the girl's eyes, as she saw her dreams crumble into dust. Then Juvula's voice changed from a cry of exultation to a scream of agony, and when he straightened up again it was not the Orb of Winter that he clasped in his hands but the shaft of an ice javelin which protruded from his shoulder. The Wizard staggered backwards from the Orb crumpling against the craggy trunk of the old moss pine. Mummichog stared at him in wonder, and the four gargoyles hissed and growled as they flapped over to their beloved master, outraged at this unseen attack upon him.

Then another figure stepped out of the gloom. His pale fur catching the eyes of those mesmerised by the wounded image of Juvula.

'Graquat!' Mummichog cried, the old goblin's face suddenly beaming with joy. 'I thought you were dead!'

'Not so,' the ice demon snarled, his eyes burning with bloodlust.

'Your timing is impeccable,' the old goblin continued. 'I thought I would have to kill him by myself. Quickly, help me gather up the Orb. We must be away!'

The ice demon ignored Mummichog walking past him with barely a glance. He had eyes only for Juvula; and as he approached the fallen wizard a second ice spear was summoned from the air. For the moment the Orb of Winter held no fascination for Graquat. His only interest was the death of Juvula.

The four reptiles crowded around the body of their master, wings spread protectively, as if to shield him from further attack. Graquat stood before them, coolly calculating how many of the ugly beasts he would have to despatch before the air was clear between himself and his prey.

Mummichog, irritated at the ice demon's indifference to him, turned his attention back to the shiny object lying naked on the ground. He

179

cautiously crept towards the Orb, his dagger drawn so that he might be prepared against another unseen attack. The old goblin's eyes burned with awe and craving as the reflection of his own cloaked figure fell across the polished face of the globe. Then his gaze shifted to the empty knapsack still lying at Hexerne's feet, and then up to the wild eyes of the girl herself. Mummichog held the knife before him and advanced upon the girl, expecting her to retreat and give him the sack. She did not. The old goblin hesitated not anticipating heroics; but it was not bravado that kept her still. Hexerne was simply transfixed with fear and an insurmountable loathing to place any distance between herself and the Orb. Mummichog was a little unnerved by the dissembling quality of the enchanted cloak, and decided against attempting a struggle with a body half of which his eyes refused to see. He tossed the knife in his hand catching its blade in his fingertips, and slowly raised his hand to throw.

A roar of defiance went up from the four gargoyles as Graquat also raised his arm to strike. The four creatures swayed and snapped before the body of their master like a furious nest of vipers. The noise distracted Mummichog and he turned to see the long splinter of ice glinting menacingly in his confederate's grasp. A smile crept across the goblin's face and he anticipated with relish the sound of the javelin thudding into Juvula's breast, and the agonising strangled scream that would follow. Mummichog's yellow eyes gleamed with pleasure as he waited for Graquat's arm to drop. Then a dark movement from behind the stout tree drew the goblin's attention, and a flicker of fear crossed his face. Suddenly the glassy spear held aloft in the ice demon's fist lit up with an intense glow, and the body of Graquat shuddered and convulsed as if struck by a powerful force. As Mummichog looked on, a brilliant tongue of blue flame burst through the thick fur of the ice demon's back, and he was launched backwards on to the soft ground, a grimace of pain frozen on to his rigid countenance. The dagger fell from Mummichog's fingers as his eyes beheld the majestic figure of Rhazgor standing beside the twisted trunk of the great moss pine, his finger still pointed at the place where Graquat had stood; the sapphire stone atop his staff incandescent with livid power.

Mummichog fell to his knees in abject supplication. The Winter wizard ignored the old goblin and crouched down to examine the stricken form of the minor sorcerer. The four reptiles backed away to give Rhazgor access to their master, but stayed nearby like worried children to watch the sorcerer's administrations. Rhazgor applied the fingers of his free hand to the bloody flesh surrounding the body of the spear, and with the power of his staff froze Juvula's shoulder. The ice javelin was then wrenched out, and the resulting hole sealed with a new skin of ice.

Juvula was helped to his feet, and brought carefully away from the tree. His eyes fell upon the wretched form of Mummichog and then frantically searched the ground about him, a look of desperation haunting his white face. The cry of loss that burst from his lips alerted the others to the

disappearance of the girl. Mummichog turned to look behind him and where the precious Orb had lain only moments before there was now only a shallow depression in the soft bed of pine needles.

Juvula staggered forward screaming in disbelief, throwing wild, forlorn glances into the trees. Rhazgor took the wizard's arm and steadied him, and with his sorcerer's eyes calmly pierced the gloom of the surrounding forest for signs of the girl.

Eventually they both turned their attention to the cowering form of Mummichog. Juvula lunged at the old goblin seizing him by the throat, and demanding to know what he had seen.

'I saw nothing, my Lord!' Mummichog wailed. 'I was too busy trying to stop Graquat from carrying out his terrible scheme!'

Juvula slowly raised himself and looked down upon the old goblin with a cold smile.

'Is that so?' he breathed. 'You know the price of disappointment don't you, Mummichog?'

The old goblin nodded quickly, snuffling and pouting his lower lip in as great a performance of pathetic contrition as he could manage. He wrung his hands before him, assuming his best attitude of servile humility; but it was all to no avail. He had been discovered, and his former friend was clearly in no mood for forgiveness. Rhazgor raised his hand to point at the goblin, the head of his staff blazing with light; but Juvula caught him by the wrist, crying: 'No!'

A spark of hope fluttered in Mummichog's heart, perhaps the Mage of Anconeus had no appetite to kill him after all. Perhaps he would be satisfied with simply sending him forth into the forest to take his chances with the elves? Mummichog's heart raced as he waited for the minor sorcerer to speak. When at last Juvula did speak, it was to Rhazgor not to the old goblin.

'No, my friend,' he said. 'That is not the way. Mummichog always took such great care of my 'boys' for me. I think it is only fitting that now my 'boys' should take care of him!'

Juvula then caught the eye of each of his four faithful dragon creatures. The gargoyles responding with an eager hiss. Mummichog glanced at the four monsters who had now turned their malevolent eyes upon him and screamed at Juvula to show mercy. The minor wizard just gave him a hollow smile and said to his 'boys': 'Kill him!'

Mummichog sprang to his feet and darted through the trees, the snarling jaws of the four gargoyles lunging after him. The old goblin did not get far before the growling monsters brought him down and unfolded their leathery wings about his squirming form. First they tore his clothes from him and then his flesh; the four monsters had waited a long time to satisfy their lust for goblin meat, and they fed with frenzy; the screams of the old goblin carrying a long way through the empty vault of the forest canopy.

As soon as the creatures were satiated, Juvula sent them into the forest to hunt down Hexerne and the Orb; the minor sorcerer promising them elf flesh as a second course! The four gargoyles filed into the trees, Zemorga at their head, their ugly faces held low to the ground to sniff out the girl's trail. Rhazgor helped Juvula on to the uskyat and the two wizards followed swiftly in their wake.

A wizard with a tiny dragon perched on his shoulder and two smaller figures arrived at the ancient moss pine a short while after the two sorcerers had left the scene of death. They regarded at a tasteful distance the remains of first Graquat and then Mummichog.

'To think that Rattajack and I were at the mercy of such killers ourselves not long ago,' Jonquil mused.

'Indeed,' Throstle added with a sigh, 'and now they are on the trail of the Orb, no doubt.'

'That means we must be also!' the banf exclaimed cheerily.

'I suppose it does,' the wizard responded with a smile.

Throstle then turned to the tiny figure on his shoulder.

'Addax, my friend,' he said, 'do you think you could fly on ahead and see if there is a way we can steal a lead on our quarry? The Orb will probably set them a winding trail to follow. A nice short cut is what we need!'

The dragonet trilled his assent, and after a brief circle above their heads darted through the upper branches and disappeared into the darkness of the thick canopy. With Rattajack's special senses to guide them the three remaining figures started off from the great tree, following in the footsteps of those that pursued the girl.

Mummichog's scream had been heard by Hexerne as she fled through the trees. The bloodcurdling cry had caused her to stumble such was the fear it inspired, but after the silence had returned her legs had moved with renewed vigour and urgency. Although she followed no visible trail, it was almost as if thoughts were being placed in her mind as to the best route to take. She hoped the directions came from the power that dwelt in the Orb for the protection it afforded her was now her only hope.

At last she fell against a scabby trunk and took a few precious moments of rest. The trees were plainly growing thinner, the daylight stronger, although she knew that there could be little of the day left. Mezereon had told her that they had been less than half a day's march from the north wall when the battle came. The girl prayed that before long she would see the light of day reflected from the snowy mountains through the trees ahead, and she would be finally free of the accursed forest.

Hexerne took a deep breath, hitched the knapsack a little higher on to her shoulders, gripped the edges of her enchanted cloak, and resumed her long northwards run. As she set off, however, she fancied she heard other footfalls trampling through the pine litter a short way down the trail. A rash of icy fear swept over her skin, and when she halted to peer anxiously behind her, she met with the sight of Grizzagrim and Zaugros leading the team of gargoyles after her. A cry of alarm escaped her and Hexerne dashed forward to try and out sprint the monsters, who half ran, half fluttered over the roots and fallen boughs that lay in their path. The sound of their snarls rang in the girl's ears, the steady drumming of their talons growing louder and faster. Hexerne raced on through the trees, her feet driven by the power of blind panic, the occasional desperate glance that she threw behind her only confirming her worst fears: her pursuers were gaining on her.

Grizzagrim stooped low as he ran, his flapping wings giving him extra propulsion over the ground. He was moving at just below take-off speed which made it easy to give that little added spurt when he and his brothers needed to rise over the occasional obstacles which presented themselves along the chase. All the dragon creature could see of the girl was her legs, exposed by the breeze-lifted hem of her magic cloak, as they pounded along the soft ground between the trees; the cloak itself was a confused blur of shifting shades.

The leading gargoyle was closing on Hexerne, its glistening fangs only a few paces behind the trailing edge of the enchanted cape. Suddenly the girl felt a tug at her throat, as if something had snagged the hem of the cloak. With a terrified squeal she pulled herself free and with a last surge of strength increased her speed. The next tug came shortly after and was much stronger; disrupting her stride and threatening to drag her down. This time she could feel more than one force pulling on the cloak, and knew that fighting for it was futile. Hexerne grasped the clasp at her throat and forced it over her head. The cloak flapped into the air to land upon the two figures of the leading gargoyles, bringing them to a sudden stop. The two trailing creatures flew over the tangled bodies of their brothers and sped after the now fully visible figure of the girl.

Dragora and Zemorga would have known nothing of the concealed swords as they swept down from the screen of dark foliage and cleaved their necks. Their headless bodies continued to run blindly on through the trees for some time before yielding to the impossibility of their existence and crashing down amongst the undergrowth. Their two disembodied heads rolled along the ground after the fleeing girl, jaws still snapping wildly as if death was no obstacle to their purpose.

A fence of crossed swords halted Hexerne's flight, and the two gargoyles that had finally freed themselves from beneath the enchanted cloak took to their heels in squawking retreat when they laid eyes on the armoured figures emerging from the forest about them.

Hexerne glanced about her like a trapped rabbit as a circle of helmed soldiers formed around her. A stab of despair pierced her stomach when she recognised the symbol the armed figures wore upon their breasts: the rising of the golden dragon. Their captain stepped forward to address her, his eyes looking with unrestrained pleasure at the knapsack the girl now cradled in her arms. He gave her a small bow before he spoke.

'I am Saxel,' he began, 'and I believe that is the prize we all seek!'

Hexerne made no reply, her glaring eyes straying from the face of the captain to the figure of one of his men who was approaching with Mezereon's cloak folded casually over his arm; the dragonriders seemed not to notice anything extraordinary about it.

'You will now surrender it to us,' the officer said, unable to conceal a note of glee in his voice. The young man could not wait to see the general's face when he presented the great Orb of Winter to him. He would probably be made a general himself for having achieved such a task; promotion for all of his men a certainty. An unsettling smile formed on the girl's lips as she once again met his eyes.

'Do you dare to take it from me?' Hexerne said in a low breathless voice, that hardly seemed as if it could belong to a young woman.

The young officer suddenly blushed as he realised the eyes of his whole company were upon him. He took a bold step forward and made to reach for the bundle in the girl's arms, but at the last he could not make his hands touch the round shape inside the sack. He gave an awkward cough and then stepped away from Hexerne.

'The Orb is too dangerous to be handled by a mortal,' he announced more confidently than he felt. 'We will hold the girl here until one of the sorcerers arrives. Both General Halmarand and the elves have wizards amongst their companies.'

With that the young captain strode away and the circle of dragonriders slowly dispersed. None of them keen to stand too close to the girl and the knapsack. A guard of four was placed around Hexerne and she was made to sit on a nearby fallen bough and await the coming of one who could take her burden from her. The magic cloak was hung over a low branch a short distance from the girl, and she eyed it longingly. One of her guards saw her mournful expression, and took pity on her.

'Are you cold?' he asked Hexerne.

The girl was a little startled at first, and did not quite take the guard's meaning. Then she understood the reason for his question and nodded with a sweet smile.

'My cloak,' she said softly to him. 'The air is so damp and chill. Might I not have my cloak?'

The guard hesitated for a moment as if considering whether this request merited troubling his superiors for permission. In the end he decided that the prisoner had the right to expect the granting of so small a kindness, and retrieved the cloak from the branch. Hexerne rose quietly from her seat as the guard approached her. She smiled her gratitude at him and he nodded in acknowledgement, courteously opening out the folded material to wrap around her shoulders. Hexerne allowed him to drape the cloak about her and then whilst the guard looked on, fastened the clasp about her throat, pulled the hood down over her face and walked slowly away into the trees. For a few astounded moments the guard just stood there watching the girl stroll away from him. Then it struck him that he should do something, and with a cry of alarm he alerted the company to Hexerne's escape. Swords were drawn and heavily shod feet crashed into the undergrowth. Bushes and low foliage were slashed and prodded in an effort to find the girl's hiding place; for no-one seemed ready to believe the unfortunate guard who claimed that his prisoner had simply disappeared into thin air!

Addax found Throstle, Jonquil and Rattajack beside the bank of a small forest stream. The wizard and the two companions were discussing the tracks pressed into the damp earth beside the chuckling water when the pale dragonet swooped on to a nearby branch, announcing his presence with a bright trill. The tiny dragon then proceeded to recount to the wizard all that he had seen concerning the two sorcerers, the four gargoyles and their quarry. A look of relief swept over the wizard's face when he heard of the ambush involving some of Halmarand's men; for that meant that Juvula was most likely cut off from Hexerne and the Orb. A look of dismay then furrowed Throstle's brow when Addax described the enchanted cloak which the girl had employed to make her escape.

'Such deviousness and deception!' the wizard exclaimed. 'How are we to counter such tricks?'

The dragonet then informed the wizard that despite the enchantment of the cloak, he was still able to track the girl, and could, if Throstle wished it, lead them to her along a swift path that would outrun Juvula and Rhazgor. The wizard considered this for a moment and then shook his head.

'I cannot simply pass them by,' he said. 'Juvula poses no immediate threat but Rhazgor is yet capable of great harm.'

'But if we do not go after Hexerne now,' Jonquil countered, 'she may get too far ahead for us to catch her! One of us at least should go with Addax.'

Throstle looked horrified at this suggestion.

'Are you proposing dividing our company, Jonquil?' he gasped. 'I cannot countenance such a thing! How can I protect you if you go off alone into the forest?'

Jonquil placed a reassuring hand on the wizard's arm.

'Throstle,' he said, 'Rattajack and I are forest folk. We have survived many great dangers in the Green Sky Forest without a wizard's protection. Have no fear for me!'

The wizard's troubled expression did not lighten at Jonquil's words, but he seemed to have resigned himself to a decision.

'I am uneasy at this parting, Jonquil,' he began. 'But I see that we must take different paths. The girl must be pursued, and I must find Rhazgor, to draw the sting from his tail.'

Throstle placed his hand on the banf's shoulder and turned to the dragonet perched on the branch.

'Addax, take good care of this brave soul. And Jonquil, I will do likewise for Rattajack. If by some chance your chase should lead you out beyond the north wall of the forest, send Addax back to me, and we will come for you on Gracewing! Find yourself a good hiding place until we arrive. And by the means of Rattajack's special senses we will soon be reunited again.

'Beware the Orb, Jonquil! Do not be tempted to take it upon your own shoulders. It is possessed by an evil, treacherous power, and will lead you to disaster if you allow it to tempt you.' The wizard gave the banf a grave but admiring smile. 'Good fortune go with the both of you, my friends!'

The two companions embraced and said their farewells, and then Jonquil and Addax and Throstle and Rattajack, took their leave of each other and went their separate ways into the forest.

The ghostly spectre shimmered and swayed in the fading light of late afternoon. Its ethereal form floated through the semi-gloom of the forest unhindered by branch or bole. It had first appeared to the girl shortly after her escape from the dragonriders, when a safe and speedy path was required to move her swiftly on towards her goal. The apparition was simply the final proof for Hexerne, if such a thing was needed, that she truly was the one chosen to carry the Orb to its place of triumph. It had now led her to the very edge of the great forest and the white slopes of the far north glinted tantalisingly through the thinning wall of trees.

Hexerne came upon a circle of open ground with a large flat rock at its centre. At the far side of this small clearing began a long slope down into a tree-lined valley, after which rose the barren, snowbound ridges and peaks of the land beyond the forest. The girl slumped down on to the low slab of rock, and gazed in awe at the snatches of brilliant landscape that peeped through the screen of dark foliage that rippled in the gentle breeze before her. Despite the daunting journey still ahead, there was a strange comfort in those distant mountains. For the first time in seven years, Hexerne felt close to home.

The girl had no notion of how long she sat on the flat rock staring into the haze of the distant land. It might have been hours or merely moments, but a sharp noise quickly sharpened her senses when it invaded her coccoon of silence. A twig snapped close behind her, and the girl instinctively grasped the straps of the knapsack, preparing to flee. Then a familiar voice broke the tense silence.

'Hexerne.'

The girl spun around to see the bedraggled figure of Mezereon standing just inside the circle of open ground. Exhaustion weighed heavily upon him, and his former haughty countenance was now bowed and weary. The girl stared at him in incredulity, as if the figure before her could not be real; another visiting spectre, only this time to haunt and torment her instead of deliver her from her enemies. The dark figure staggered forward and propped himself against the rock, his eyes seeming to share in some of her disbelief.

'It really is you,' he gasped. 'Beyond belief!'

The girl moved away from him her eyes filling with desperate tears.

'It cannot be!' she cried. 'How is it possible that you found me?'

'The vision,' Mezereon answered breathlessly. 'The pale vision. It led me to you.'

'The vision?' Hexerne repeated incredulously.

The Dark Sorcerer nodded and sat himself down upon the rock.

'It led me to you,' he said again.

Hexerne remembered the ghostly figure that had guided her to the edge of the forest. She then looked down at the bundle in her arms, and wondered if the power of the crystal within had not just been working for her benefit alone. Hexerne realised that Juvula must also have received the attention of some guiding hand. How else could he have been lying in wait in the precise place where she was destined to pass by? And now Mezereon had been lured after her. No doubt to try and take again what he considered to be his property! Hexerne fought back the tears as she tried not to believe that she had been allowed to carry the great globe all this way only to lose it at the last.

'So you've come for the Orb!' she hissed at the sorcerer.

Mezereon lifted his head to look upon her.

'Does not the fact that I am here prove that I am chosen?' he asked her wearily.

Hexerne threw him a bitter smile.

'That is what I was thinking before you arrived.'

The sorcerer looked quizzically at her.

'I too have seen the vision,' she told him. 'And I too thought it appeared to me alone!'

The girl held up the knapsack as if offering it to the sorcerer.

'Here is your prize, Mezereon,' the girl continued. 'Here is your destiny!'

The sorcerer hesitated for a moment, the wild gleam in the girl's eyes making him unsure. Then he slowly began to reach for the proffered bundle. Suddenly, the girl twisted her body and heaved the knapsack into the air as hard as she could. A cry of horror burst from his lips as Mezereon watched the bundle fly through the air and land at the foot of a dense thicket of undergrowth; a nest of feather-like fronds saving the precious cargo from disaster. The sorcerer leapt to his feet and rushed over to the bundle, his face flushed with fear and rage.

'You little fool!' he roared. 'You might have broken it!'

'I wish I had!' the girl screamed back at him, the sobs of despair she had resisted for so long finally taking hold of her. 'Then none of you would have had it! For none of you are worthy!'

The girl dragged herself back to the flat rock and fell upon it, her body heaving with grief. Mezereon regarded her pitifully, the heat of shame replacing that of anger.

'This forest is full of thieves, deceivers!' she said through her tears. 'You are all like magpies chasing a glittering bauble. You see only the sparkle and understand nothing of its true value. Go on! Take it! Take it and leave me! I no longer have the will to fight you.'

Mezereon looked down at the bundle and then at the collapsed figure of the girl. Hexerne pressed her hot skin against the cool surface of the stone and waited for the sounds of the sorcerer tramping away through the undergrowth to reach her. Instead she felt a light touch on her shoulder. She raised herself from the rock and looked into a face filled with beneficence and admiration.

'Why don't you come with me?' Mezereon said softly. 'And we can cross the bridge together.'

The girl was stunned, and could only bring herself to say: 'The bridge?'

Mezereon smiled.

'The bridge that crosses the great chasm.'

Hexerne stared deeply into the sorcerer's eyes searching for the deception, her own face a picture of disbelief.

'You really mean it?' she said with an air of suspicion.

Mezereon took her by the hands and lifted her from the rock.

'To have come this far and fought so hard,' the sorcerer sighed, 'it would be too cruel to leave you behind. You have carried the Orb on a long road with the promise of no reward other than death at your journey's end. You have truly earned your right to cross the great chasm. Let us share the burden from here on, and we shall enter the North Spire together!'

Hexerne had to sit down again after Mezereon's words as if the weight of them was too much for her tired limbs to bear. She stared up at him open mouthed as though mesmerised by this uncharacteristic flood of kindness from a character from whom she had formerly only known spite and scorn. This new Mezereon was clearly bewildering to the girl.

A sprig of evergreen was carefully pulled down to allow a pair of bright green eyes a better look at the two figures at the rock. The observer was also very interested in the crumpled form of the knapsack which lay very close to the thicket of bushes in which he was concealed. In fact it was almost within arm's length, although the would-be thief doubted if he would be able to drag it into the undergrowth without attracting the attention of the two figures within the circle.

The crouched figure turned to gaze into the sparkling eyes of a tiny dragon, and in a whisper barely audible shared the details of a hastily hatched plot.

'Why?' Hexerne asked of the tall figure standing before her. 'You have never shown me kindness in the past. Why do you do so now when you are free to do as you please?'

Mezereon lifted his foot on to the rock and folded his arms on to his knee.

'Do you remember asking me of your parentage, before the battle?' he said to the girl. 'I spoke only of your mother.'

Hexerne's eyes suddenly filled with apprehension, and she hardly dared voice what thoughts suddenly appeared in her mind.

'And my father?' she asked tentatively.

Mezereon met her anxious gaze and held a long moment of silence between them.

'He is before you!' he said at last.

The girl's eyes slowly dropped to the floor and a long pause passed between them before she could bring herself to speak.

'You - and Tuatara!' she exclaimed without raising her head.

'It was His will,' the sorcerer told her. 'The Ice Witch did not give her consent. The memory of it was stolen from her.'

Mezereon lifted the girl's chin and looked into her glassy eyes.

'She does not know, Hexerne,' he said finally.

The girl swallowed hard and rose shakily to her feet, as if the truth was a strong potion that had taken a heavy toll upon her tired body.

'You *loved* her!' she said to the sorcerer, his eyes smarting at her words. 'You love her still!'

Mezereon turned away from the girl, staring into the distance. He offered no denial to her blunt declaration.

Suddenly a violent chattering from just beyond the open circle shattered the mood of intimacy, and served as a bold reminder to the both of them that they were still inside the forest of the elves, and a long way from their goal. They turned to investigate the strange commotion, and the sight of a small pale creature dangling upside down from a low branch squawking for all it was worth, did little to allay their reawakened fears. Then a cold shiver touched the girl and she turned to look back at the Orb. To her horror she saw only the loop of one of its straps disappearing into the bushy thicket. With a scream of anguish she flew across the circle and charged into the undergrowth; but the thief had already gone. The girl stopped and listened and heard his noisy descent down the tree-lined slope. She searched for signs of the thief and at first saw only the movement of brush and foliage in his wake. Hexerne launched herself in pursuit, almost losing her feet to the slope in her eagerness to catch the perpetrator. She grasped at limbs and roots on her way down always just out of sight of the figure ahead. Her focus on recapturing the Orb was so complete that she had forgotten all about Mezereon and did not even hear his frantic calls after her from the head of the slope. Addax was continuing to prove something of a distraction for the Dark Sorcerer. The brave dragonet doing everything in his power to stop

Mezereon from following the girl in the chase for the Orb.

At the foot of the long slope just before dashing along the narrow channel that ran between the two great flanks of trees, the agile thief paused to look back at his pursuer. Hexerne burst through a thick growth of tall ferns, a little way up the slope, seizing large handfuls of the tough plants to slow herself, when she caught sight of him.

For the briefest moment the two stared at each other, their panting breath the only sound to pass between them. Then Hexerne recognised the face of her thief, and her eyes glared with hate.

'You!' she screamed.

Jonquil gave her a wry shrug of the shoulders and then hared along the course of the trench. Hexerne shuffled down to the narrow strip of flat ground and sprinted after him, filling the space between them with a string of murderous profanities. Her mind unable to accommodate any thought other than recovering the Orb.

Jonquil's fresher legs carried him swiftly along the channel and before long he had outpaced the furious pursuit of the girl. As the failing light of evening darkened the wide sky above the banf lost sight of Hexerne altogether. He decided that it might be prudent to climb out of the narrow trench through which he was currently moving, and see what manner of terrain might be found beyond the icy ridge to the east. The banf repeated this exhausting manoeuvre a number of times; sensible that he was leaving a not inconsiderable trail in the snow and ice behind him, but hopeful that the succession of steep climbs would take such a toll upon the strength of his pursuer that she would be forced to take a rest, and so allow him to increase his lead and find a good hiding place. Jonquil was confident that it was only a matter of time before Throstle would come to find him on Gracewing, and that all he had to do was keep the Orb from those who craved it until he was rescued.

Night fell swiftly over the mountains and Jonquil suddenly felt a terrific weariness strike him as he rose over yet another high ridge. Below him, the banf could just make out a snowy vale that was populated by a few solitary trees. One of these tall sentinels had the height and bearing of a tower pine; the northern equivalent of a green oak, in that like its southern counterpart it offered an exposed rootcage in which a stranded traveller might take shelter. Jonquil descended the powdery slope and carefully approached the large tree. The fatigue in his legs and shoulders screamed for relief, and with a sigh of gratitude the banf eased the knapsack from his back, pushed it before him and dragged himself inside the tangled cave of roots.

The Guardian of the Path

Jonquil slowly became aware of a vast open space. The impenetrable darkness denied him sight, but his keen ears could hear the soft echoes of a huge chamber. The still air seemed almost to scream with silence, its only competition the dull thumping of his heart. Before the banf's eyes a faint light began to grow; horizontal lines gradually appearing one above the other, rising into the blackness in a tapering, vertical column.

Jonquil approached the first step of the stairway, and as he lifted his eyes the light grew until all the contours of the ice platform were revealed soaring high above him into the void. Each step glowed with a pale bluish light as his feet trod upon them. The light, building from within the structure, spread outwards across a wide, empty floor until by the time the banf had climbed half the stairway, the walls of an immense mansion of ice had been drawn upon the blackness. Ahead of him, Jonquil saw a large throne rising from the summit of the high platform. The wide fan of ice spears spreading outwards from its back was reminiscent of another throne the banf had seen long before in the Throne Citadel's chamber of mirrors. When he reached the top Jonquil saw that like the other ice throne, the regal seat before him had a half-spherical depression set into one of its long angular arms. The throne began to fill with a gentle light as the banf moved towards it, threads of bright sapphire creeping along the edges of its glassy geometry to converge finally as a fringe of glowing points. The hole in its right arm burned with an insistent brightness, and the banf suddenly realised that he was holding a large, cold ball of crystal in his hands; the Orb of Winter. Deep inside its black heart there flickered a plume of blue fire. The flames grew rapidly as he watched them until they had swallowed up all of the blackness inside the globe, and began to lick hungrily at his exposed palms. The freezing pain shot up his arms like darts of ice, and before Jonquil could stop himself he hastily dropped the Orb into the gleaming depression on the throne.

Immediately he did so, light poured into the great chamber from the high space above. Thick swathes of white and blue that sliced through the darkness to spill onto the massive glistening floor in bright pools. The banf slowly turned to gaze upon the wondrous spectacle surrounding him: an incredible palace of ice. Towering columns like the wrinkled trunks of a frozen forest rose into great sweeping arches overhead. Beards of icicles hung from the vaulted ceiling, and any ledge or protuberance, in profuse, spiny clusters. The whole glorious scene was ablaze with light, and when Jonquil turned back to the throne and seated himself upon it, the wall of mist that floated before him began to clear.

The scene that gradually appeared before Jonquil was like a dragon's eye view of the lands of Enchantica. Sun-drenched valleys and plains rolled past carpeted with lush grass and vegetation; it was the Commonlands of Enchantica bathing in the full glory of Summer. For as far as the observer's roving eye could see, the land was green and bountiful. Then the billowing grey clouds of a storm rose into view, clouds heavy with snow herded by raging winds towards the shining splendour below. At once Jonquil knew what was about to happen and he cried out, 'No!' Then the tumult descended. Hail storms as thick as fog slanted down from the sky to tear the bright petals from the flowers and the tender leaves from the trees. Vast blankets of snow crept over the grass and meadows smothering the verdure, freezing the life sap in the delicate stems. The innocent form of a rose was focused upon, its tissue thin petals shrinking away beneath a glistening crust of ice crystals, until its blackened head shrivelled and died. The emerald skin of the land turned pale and then white with snow, and before his very eyes, the green paradise that had been Enchantica was swiftly transformed into a barren desert of snow and ice.

The viewpoint of the watcher now moved to regard the skies above, bruised with snow clouds, raked by searing ice winds. The leaden sky was zig-zagged by close formations of snowdragons; thousands of winking forms, wave upon wave, crossing under the dark heavens to do battle with the dying rays of the sun.

Jonquil leapt to his feet, his heart heavy with guilt, as if he was in some way responsible for this final victory for Winter. For somehow the banf knew that what he had just witnessed was an act of conquest from which Enchantica could never recover.

The banf sensed rather than saw the tall shadow rise at his back. Then freezing hands with a grip like iron closed around his neck, steely fingers digging into his throat. The strangler pulled back Jonquil's head so that the banf could see the inverted face of his attacker before he died. Even upside down, the piercing, pale eyes and snarling grin of Vrorst were unmistakable.

Jonquil suddenly awoke. His eyes slowly focused on the pale stain of dawn that was just brightening the sky beyond the blackness of the nest of roots and branches above him. The tightness around his throat, however, had not remained in his nightmare, it had returned with him to consciousness. The banf tried to raise himself. As soon as his shoulders lifted from the ground the pressure around his neck increased. It felt like a thick, rough rope, hairy and very strong. His hands instinctively reached for the coarse bond to loosen it, and one of them was immediately snatched away by a strong strap-like loop. Another noose flew at the other hand but Jonquil managed to grip it in his fist before it could slip over his fingers and fasten him by the wrist. Even so, the noose tightened severely about his palm, and tried to pull the hand away from his neck. The banf kicked violently with his legs as he felt similarly dreadful cords curling about his ankles. Thick tendrils snaked across his rigid body and then slipped beneath him to re-emerge in a constricting coil. In the shortest time the banf was held fast by a nest of writhing cords. For an instant, Jonquil thought that perhaps he was still in his nightmare, and that with the mere opening of his eyes the struggle would end; but then he realised that his eyes were open and the struggle was real. The cord about the banf's throat began its final squeeze. He could feel his veins standing out from his skin turgid with blood. His eyeballs felt as though they were about to pop from his skull with the pressure in his head. An awful high pitched scratching noise whined in Jonquil's ears, and with horror he realised that it was his own breath being steadily choked from his body. Clouds of stars sparkled before his eyes, and refused to be blinked away; and the noose at his throat tightened yet further. Jonquil had received the last breath his attacker was going to allow him. He had to act. The banf pulled his fist, which still wrestled against its tugging bond, with all his remaining might towards his chest. As his knuckles pressed into the spongy material of his coat, his fingers flew open to search for the shards of crystal which hung from the leather thong about his neck. As if the cords sensed his plan they all exerted a terrible pressure on his racked body, raising him from the ground with their strength. Jonquil found the pendant, and his fingers shaking with the strain slowly closed around its cool facets. The sound which emerged from his swollen lips was so faint that even his own sensitive ears failed to hear it; but he had invoked the name of the Three Wizards never-theless, and with the sharp crackle of Old Magic the banf's fist suddenly glowed with light. Golden rapiers stabbed through the slits between Jonquil's fingers, slicing through several vital bonds like flashing sword strokes. As soon as the banf felt the pressure give at his throat, and his body fall to the ground, he scrambled on to his knees and fought furiously with the cords which still held him until he was free of the rootcage. Jonquil did not stop pushing at the ground with his hands and feet until he was well out of reach of the coiling tendrils, which still snatched at him; and then he collapsed into the snow heaving drafts of cold air into his burning throat.

When Jonquil's breathing had recovered slightly and the feeling started to return to his tortured body, the deep furrows left in his flesh by the root cords began to sing in painful harmony all over his limbs and trunk. To his horror Jonquil realised that he had no feeling in his left hand. He suddenly remembered the first vicious loop which had snared it and kept him from freeing himself from the cord at his throat. He slowly lifted himself on to one elbow and discovered that the offending bond was still tightly wrapped around his flesh. A slither of fear stabbed through him when he saw that it was not a root from the tree which grimly held on to him, but a tightly wound length of strap from the Orb's knapsack. A chilling understanding of what had just happened crept over him; and the banf suddenly appreciated the dreadful power of the object that he had stolen from the two enchanters. Throstle had warned him of its evil might, and had it not been for the

Dragonmaster's pendant, Jonquil would have fallen prey to the Orb's malevolent power. The tree roots were still once again. The dark enchantment had evidently returned to the great crystal.

The banf frantically unravelled the tight strap from his wrist and pushed the bundle away, not wishing it close to him. He then flopped back into the snow and lay there exhausted. Jonquil stared up at the dark towering plume of the tree under which he had sought shelter; hardly able to comprehend that such a tall, noble being could be employed by the Orb to commit its wicked desires. Even the terrible fatigue that had crept upon him so suddenly the night before now seemed suspicious. Could that also have been the work of the Orb: its malicious intelligence knowing that the travel weary banf would choose to seek shelter within the welcoming nest of roots?

Jonquil closed his eyes and tried to rest. He was too tired to move, and the Winter clothing that Indlewick had included in Gracewing's baggage for him, kept him perfectly dry in the snow. Sleep must have taken him for a while despite his exposed situation, for when he awoke the light beyond his eyelids seemed much stronger. Jonquil suddenly felt a stab of panic. How long had he been asleep? Then the light beyond his closed eyes darkened a little as if a shadow had crept over him. His eyes flew open and met with the hostile stare of Hexerne who was standing right over him. Both her hands were balled into fists; her left holding the straps of the knapsack, her right closed about the curved blade of a dagger.

'You!' she hissed. 'Will we ever be rid of you!'

These words might just as easily have come from the lips of Vrorst, and the fiery light in the girl's eyes was filled with his insanity.

Hexerne fell upon him, her right knee landing on his chest, pinning him to the ground. The dagger arced down through the air hungry for Jonquil's throat. Somehow he managed to glance the blow aside so that the blade struck wide. Hexerne had unwisely burdened herself with the knapsack, allowing her eagerness to possess it again rule her wits. The weight of the bundle disabled her left hand, and she was unable to grapple with the banf to full effect. Jonquil seized her knee with both hands and heaved upwards. Despite his residual weakness from his ordeal with the tree roots, he succeeded in throwing the girl off balance. She tumbled on to her back, giving the banf time to stagger to his feet. Hexerne, despite her significant height advantage over Jonquil, looked fearful and uncertain. Anyone could see that the banf was in no condition to pose a threat, but merely the sight of him on his feet filled the girl with doubt. After all, this was the puny creature who had defeated her beloved master. Like the rest of his enemies, Hexerne had learned that Jonquil's benign appearance was deceptive. He was mightier than he seemed.

At that moment, Jonquil felt anything but mighty. It was all he could do to stay on his feet; and if the girl was to rush him in a determined charge, she would have finished him off for certain. However, Hexerne did not charge. She just stood there looking troubled, clutching the knapsack to her chest as if it was a small child or animal that she had to protect. Then she turned and ran from the banf, still hugging her precious bundle to her.

The banf gave chase as best he could, but the strength was slow to return to his legs, and his breathing was still difficult. The girl ran on through the narrow valley as it wound its way in a northerly direction. Jonquil tried to keep her in view but eventually her lead on him grew until she disappeared into the distant bend of the snowy vale. The banf stumbled after in dogged pursuit, his tired feet dragging a weaving scar in the shallow coverlet of snow.

So the chase continued for a long while until the fatigue numbed senses of the banf were shocked into life by a shrill scream which rang out from beyond a sharp curve in the valley up ahead. The cry of alarm injected new vigour into the banf's legs and he sprinted after the noise, quickly rounding the bend. The sight which greeted him, caused him to check his speed to a slow step. Thrusting out into what had become a rugged channel of snow-dusted rocks, were huge spikes of ice. On both sides of the new landscape long, cruel points grew at every angle into the narrow space; creating a precarious, meandering pathway through bristling ranks of vicious spears. A short distance ahead through the crystalline barricade, Jonquil could see the girl standing motionless. At first, the banf thought that Hexerne, in her blind haste, must have run herself on to one of the spikes, and that was the scream he heard. As he gingerly approached, he discovered the truth of the matter. The girl was standing frozen with fear, her eyes fixed on one of the long spears that had pushed its way through a slim gap in the rock. Impaled on its end, hanging above her like a discarded marionette, was the frozen remains of a corpse.

It was the body of a tall warrior, still clad in its handsome gold chased armour. The unfortunate soul looked as if he might have perished only the day before, so well preserved was the flesh in the freezing climate. His face was a mask of pain and terror, and it took a greater steadfastness of spirit than the banf possessed to look long into its staring eyes, swollen with horror. Perhaps the only thing more chilling than the sight of this wretched figure was the thought of the foe that had inflicted such a terrible end upon him.

Hexerne suddenly sensed the banf close behind her and she turned to face him. Their eyes locked on to one another as the girl warily retreated. She froze again as she backed into a rigid point. Her first thought was that she had retreated against the sharp end of one of the spikes but on turning she discovered it to be the index finger of a fighting elf. This victim had been petrified in a more animated pose than the first corpse, and looked as if he was caught in mid leap pointing excitedly at some terrible enemy, his sword drawn in readiness in his other hand. It was hard to believe that these petrified figures were not alive. Moreover, if it had not been for the skewer of ice protruding from his ruptured chest plate, one might almost have believed that the elf could land on the ground and charge forward at any moment. Like the first fallen hero, the slain elf also retained his wealth about him, including his sword (a beautiful blade drawn from a golden scabbard sparkling with jewels). He had clearly brandished the princely weapon as his last futile gesture against the monster that had assailed him; its pristine, untainted blade testament to the blow that was never struck. Jonquil tried not to look too closely at the figures of the dead, but could not help but notice the remnants of a curious glaze of ice encrusting parts of their bodies. The icicles, which trailed in a frosted fringe from certain limbs did so at an unnatural angle, as if the warrior had been caught in a sudden slanting jet of freezing water.

The banf had to wonder at the motive behind such vicious acts. Theft was clearly not the inducement. If goblins or trolls had been the perpetrators the victims would have been stripped of every valuable item. It occurred to Jonquil that these individuals had been displayed in such a dreadful manner as a warning. A warning to proceed no further lest the same fate should befall the beholder. Jonquil smiled wryly to himself: what use are warnings to those who are driven by a force beyond their control? The same thoughts must have occurred to the girl, but Jonquil saw that Hexerne showed no signs of turning back.

Further along they encountered more skewered bodies. Hexerne and Jonquil wove their way through a gruesome gallery of ice demons, goblins, more northern elves, assorted warriors from the races of men, and various fierce looking creatures some of which were entirely new to Jonquil. Most of them bore traces of the same coats of blasted ice. It was impossible, with the lack of corruption, to age the bodies; but because of the number and variety of the victims, the banf had to reason that the grisly collection lining their path was the dark work of many years. The greater proportion of the bodies seemed to belong to the fighting classes, as they were heavily beweaponed. Quite why so many warriors had all attempted this path the banf could only wonder; but it seemed likely that the rumour of some great prize must be connected to this fearsome path. Jonquil could not believe that the hope of finding Vrorst's secret well of dark power had been their goal, as surely that was the one place in the whole of Enchantica that every sentient being would want to avoid; unless like him they had no choice. The banf had to admit that there was an avaricious quality to the faces of some of the dead, and that could mean only one thing: the pursuit of treasure. Could it be then that a desire for wealth had drawn a large part of this multifarious army to their deaths? It was strange then, the banf thought, that Throstle had never spoken of a great treasure hoard secreted in these parts. Jonquil mulled these thoughts over in his mind as he slowly followed the girl's careful progression through the rocky trench. Then it came to him; there was treasure here, he had seen it with his own eyes. It was worn by the dead themselves. The mighty collection of richly adorned corpses were the attraction; and every doomed adventurer that came to steal from the dead, ended up adding his own personal wealth to the great collection.

The banf and the girl moved through the forest of spines with a slow dream-like step. They were both transfixed by a dread fascination, the girl keeping about ten paces ahead but in no mood to run. Unlike before, she was now holding the Orb as if it might afford some protection to her, lest she should suddenly come across the author of this barbarism.

Eventually the spear-filled channel wound its way towards a wide gap, which opened on to a broad, half moon shelf of open ground surrounded by a bay of rugged cliffs. Ahead of them, beyond the wide expanse of flat, snow covered rock the world fell away into a steep fathomless void: a great chasm, whose far walls soared from the hazy depths as sheer cliffs of ice, craggy and splintered with great age. Palls of mist like diaphanous serpents rose out of the general soup of vapour, drifting as slow as clouds in the icy air. Above, the tips of the peaks were swallowed by a thick canopy of billowing white, dragging itself across the mountain tops, dividing land and sky like the foam on a vat of ale, impenetrable and eternal.

The foot of the jagged rock face which fenced in the half circle of open ground was also furnished with a deadly fringe of ice spears; and as Hexerne and then Jonquil entered through the gap in the cliff wall, they saw that many of these too bore a grisly cargo. The banf noticed with dismay that even hefty ice trolls were amongst the slain. The being that could overpower the likes of those giants and hoist them to their deaths, had to be a creature of formidable stature.

Hexerne tentatively moved out into the open space, clearly torn between the fear of venturing forward alone, and not wanting Jonquil too near to the Orb. She kept throwing fearful glances back at him, whether to make sure that he was following, or in the hope that he wasn't, the banf wasn't sure. He decided it was probably a little of both. Jonquil threw a few nervous glances of his own at the sweeping faces of rock on either side. He expected the hideous spectre of the killer to leap out from one of the large ruptures in the cliffs at any moment. The banf could not dismiss the thought that the spread of open ground before them had the feel of an arena; complete with macabre audience looking on.

The girl was almost halfway to the brink of the chasm, still moving with her hesitant, little-child-lost walk. Suddenly she turned to face Jonquil. Hexerne's countenance spoke volumes. Her enchanter's senses were clearly alive to the terrible atmosphere that lingered over that place of death. It was like an axe hovering over their heads, choosing its own moment to fall. The only question was which of them would it strike first? The girl and the banf stood facing each other across the bed of flat rock. Hexerne looked lost. The flat curved shelf was hemmed in by the cliffs on all sides. There was no path leading away along the edge of the cliff, and no bridge spanning the chasm. They had reached a dead end. The girl hadn't chosen this path for herself, her every step had been guided by the Orb. The Orb had wanted her to come to this place; but why, when there was no further path to take? Vrorst's globe had clearly fallen silent now, for the girl looked hopeless.

The banf broke away from the girl's stare and scrutinised their surroundings once more. He had the same feeling about the wide shelf that he had about the winding channel. That it was somehow 'intentional', its shape a little too regular, the ground a little too free of debris. Yet if this was true, and the place had been created by Vrorst servants in the ancient days, for what purpose if there was no way forward from here? Had there once been a bridge, its long neglect condemning it to the elements? If so, there were no signs of a thoroughfare on the far side, or any trace of construction to be seen anywhere.

'Mezereon spoke of a guardian,' the voice was frail and tremulous and hardly seemed to belong to the girl. Nevertheless it carried easily in the still air, too easily, across the distance between them. It was all Jonquil could do to stop himself from hushing Hexerne with a raised finger. Her voice was practically a whisper, but in that unnaturally silent place that even a breeze would not enter, it seemed to have the intensity of a roar.

'We must be near its lair,' she said.

Jonquil nodded. He could not bring himself to add his voice to the girl's. To his mind, silence was a friend that he did not wish to break faith with. He longed to ask Hexerne what she was going to do now. He wanted to persuade her to accept defeat and hand the Orb over to his keeping. Throstle couldn't be too far away, and once the Orb was in the possession of the High Wizard surely its fate was assured? Hexerne turned from him to regard the cliffs.

'He said that the path to His sanctuary would be guarded by dark enchantment,' Hexerne said almost to herself. 'It is strong here. I can feel it.' The girl began to wander in an aimless manner as if waiting for instruction. Her meandering taking her ever nearer to the edge of the chasm.

'But I have the Orb,' Hexerne muttered. 'I should be safe!'

The banf decided that he had better follow at a cautious pace, and was just about to do so when he thought he heard the faintest trace of a flute coming from the direction in which they had just travelled. His thoughts immediately flew to Throstle and Rattajack. The wizard must have been trying to tell him that they were on his trail and following close behind. This comforting thought lightened Jonquil's heart and put an extra spring in his step when he turned again to pursue Hexerne.

The roar almost knocked Jonquil off his feet, such was its sudden intensity. Hexerne was struck with terror, the Orb bundle almost tumbling from her hands as they jolted with shock. Hardly noticed by either of them, almost at the point where the curve of the rock wall met the chasm, a large, dark hole was situated half way up the scarred cliff face. It was from this jagged aperture that the terrible noise had emitted. The owner of the voice followed it into the light.

Xedrethor erupted from the rock face like a dark torrent, throwing wide his great black sails and clawing at the air to pull himself aloft. He rose as a living silhouette, huge membranous wings swallowing up the light to climb powerfully into the pale ceiling of cloud. The bone-jarring roar blasted down upon the two lonely figures once again, the terrible noise rooting them to the ground. Then the monster began a slow descending spiral, his wings parting the freezing air like a vast wheeling scythe, his long horned tail snaking through the air behind him. Jonquil recovered first from the shock of the dragon's emergence, and sprinted for the girl. Before she knew what was happening, the banf had grabbed her by the wrist and was pulling her towards the cliffs. Eventually, Hexerne was herself again and snatched her arm away from the banf. Jonquil screamed at her to go with him, but the girl refused his company.

'It will kill us both' Jonquil cried. 'We have to seek shelter!'

'No!' the girl bawled. 'I do not need your help! The Orb will protect me!'

Jonquil grabbed her wrist once again.

'Do you want to end up on one of those spikes? Come on!'

Hexerne pulled back her arm a second time.

'I will seek my own shelter!' she screamed, and with that she pulled the knapsack on to her shoulders and ran off in a different direction.

The monster was swooping in to land, its hooked claws splayed wide to seize the ground. A storm of snow powder was thrown up by the giant thrashing wings, the enveloping surge of freezing crystals stinging the ears of the banf as he fled for cover.

The snow trembled on the rock floor as the great beast thundered after its prey. Jonquil spotted a modest crevice in the base of the cliff up ahead, and ran with all his might towards it. Suddenly a sound like the roar of an avalanche tore through the air above the banf's head, and a jet of something which glistened like silver overtook him and smote the bolt hole he was heading for. To Jonquil's horror the splash immediately crystallised into solid ice forming an impenetrable seal over the crevice. The banf skidded to a halt and spun around to face his attacker. The Guardian of the Secret Path had turned his attention to the girl who was still running for her life over the flat snow; but to Jonquil's amazement she had ignored the shortest route to the cliffs to veer in a long curve back towards the chasm. The malevolent beast eyed her progress with a cruel fascination, eventually sauntering casually after her to bring her within range of its breath. The monster belched forth a shimmering stream of silver which splattered in a deadly pool a few yards ahead of Hexerne. The girl quickly checked her flight, and, just as Jonquil had done, turned to face the beast. Hexerne, of course, had the mighty Orb of Winter at her fingertips, Vrorst's globe of power. She pulled the bundle from her back and tore open its wrappings. Still holding the powerful ball through the thick fabric she showed its naked form to Xedrethor. Just as the jaws of the great beast were about to lunge for the girl, the Orb suddenly ignited into a burning star of blue light, its intensity so bright that Jonquil had to avert his eyes, even though he was some distance from the great globe. The monster immediately twisted its face away from the painful glare, and began to retreat. It then lowered its head as if in obeisance to the Orb and remained in the same submissive attitude for a few long moments. When the beast finally turned its face back to the banf, its features were contorted with new malice, as if its greatest enemy had just been revealed to it.

The creature moved between Jonquil and the girl, his monstrous black form extinguishing the astonishing brilliance of the Orb. Jonquil gazed up in stupefied horror at Xedrethor: a terrifying dragon, the colour of midnight. His body, hunched between two great sickles of folded wing, was as black as jet; the pale, cloud-diffused daylight registering upon his layered scales in waves of shimmering colour, like the glancing hues of a raven's wing. His long, sleek head swept back into a fork of steely rapiers. His narrow eyes glowed with an evil red fire. As the dragon slowly eased himself forward on his crumpled wings like a giant black bat, the banf saw that his talons and spines gleamed like silver. When the dragon's malicious grin drew nearer Jonquil could see that his teeth were a similar colour, shining in the light thrown up from the snow like rows of polished blades. Xedrethor had been created by the darkest sorcery centuries before, to guard the hidden ways to his master's secret refuge. He was a proud and diligent servant. Vrorst had made him fierce and cruel, a worthy sentinel to defend the forbidden path. No warrior had ever bested him or found a way past him. Nor had any ever returned from the attempt. For once they dared to enter the dragon's domain their fate was sealed, and like flies on thorns they were added to the monster's morbid collection. It was a strong testament to the lasting influence of Vrorst's power that Xedrethor remained loyal to his bidding; and the physical embodiment of that power, the Orb, still held sway over the dragon's will.

Jonquil looked about him franticly. He was too far from any decent shelter; and to flee would only provoke the dragon's freezing flame. There was no choice open to the banf. He was beaten. He could only stand there and await his doom.

Xedrethor towered above Jonquil, his head rising arrogantly as he tilted his huge frame to sit on his back legs. He unfurled the vastly elongated fingers which were the bones of his wings, and two immense walls of rippling skin unfolded to blot out the world, until all the banf could see before him was a mountain of black. The dragon's eyes never left their mark for a second, his glaring beads of scarlet watching intently for any last minute dash for freedom. The dragon reached down for the banf. His small hooked claws rising from the wrists of his great wings closed tightly around Jonquil's waist and lifted him steadily into the air. The dragon held up the banf for scrutiny, his terrible head coming very close to eye him thoroughly. Jonquil was rigid with terror as the long, glittering jaws swayed menacingly before him. A distant movement caught the banf's eye, and to his further dismay, he saw Hexerne climbing up the steep slope of the cliff towards the dark opening from whence the mighty Xedrethor had emerged. She was coolly leaving him to his fate. The Orb had finally broken its silence. She had found her way forward at last. It was clear that the path to the Spire led right through the lair of the black monster. Not that this revelation would profit Jonquil much, his part in the quest looked about to be concluded.

The dragon reared up on to his strong back legs, transferred the banf into one wing, and strode purposefully across the open space, his long, barbed tail swishing a weaving trail through the snow. He was heading for the crescent of the cliffs and the spikes that grew out of them. Jonquil looked on in horror as the glistening fence of ice spears, and the wretched souls they bore, drew nearer. Xedrethor halted at the foot of the rugged wall, still holding the banf aloft, the long spear-like spines of his free wing idly playing up and down the glassy shafts that protruded from the rock before them. Jonquil stared in dread at the array of glistening points, horrified at the thought that the dragon was casually choosing which death spike was to be his. The evil head turned to him, his two fiery coals boring into Jonquil's eyes. Then he extended a short claw towards the banf. Jonquil braced himself for what he thought to be a killing thrust; but the hooked digit approached slowly and gently raised Throstle's crystal pendant from the banf's breast. The dragon studied it with interest as it sparkled against the curve of his long talon. Eventually he tired of it and let it fall back on to Jonquil's chest. He then turned his attention to the spikes, and the monster's terrible grin exposed his shining jaws once again. Jonquil gasped in terror as he was lifted high over a cluster of deadly spikes, the longest of them ringed with frozen waves and needle sharp at its end. With an evil grunt, Xedrethor flicked a claw across the tip of the ice spear dulling its point. The dragon had clearly been instructed by the Orb not to make the banf's death too easy. The force that inhabited Vrorst's globe wanted Jonquil to suffer.

The banf then heard a voice cry out, too far off to make out the words, but the tone was strong and commanding. The dragon immediately stiffened at the sound, his eyes searching angrily along the line of the cliffs for its source. Suddenly there was a loud crack, and a bolt of golden lightning streaked out of the pallid sky striking the dragon in the chest. The force of the heavenly blow knocked the monster back a few paces, a bellow of pain erupting from his throat. His head craned upwards, his burning eyes scanning the skies for the shape of his assailant. A thunderous growl rumbled into the air as the dragon caught sight of another dragon, pale and graceful, falling swiftly from the blanket of cloud, its rider's staff thrust aloft, poised to strike again. Xedrethor's grip tightened about Jonquil's waist as the dragon sucked in a huge breath of air. The banf tried to shout a warning to the wizard but the monster's grip stifled his voice. The black dragon let forth a glistening jet that surged into the other's path. With incredible agility Throstle's mount flipped itself upside down and rolled over the deadly spout of freezing flame, righting itself in time to let the wizard send another shrieking fire bolt against Xedrethor. The blow thudded into the evil one's forearm, just below his wrist, the burning thread of power exploding against his inky hide, and causing the claws which held the banf to fly open in shock. Jonquil dropped into the curled canopy of the dragon's wing and slid down the chute of springy membrane to the ground. The dragon's wings swept open and he furiously searched about his feet for the banf. Throstle urged Gracewing into another close pass, and rent a small, sizzling hole in one of the dark creature's splayed wings. The great dragon screamed its fury, and belched another blast of silver fire after them.

Jonquil was already scrambling amongst the boulders and spikes at the foot of the cliff seeking shelter, but the monster saw him and lunged forward. The banf cowered in a small crevice as the dragon tore into the skirt of boulders. He wrenched the crop of thick ice spears asunder in his rage, hurling the broken debris into the air behind him, or smashing it violently into the rocks in the hope that the resulting storm of flying shards would flush the banf out. Eventually the dragon found Jonquil, curled up into a tight ball to protect himself from the savage hail. He roared the banf's death knell, and then began to fill his chest with air to seal Jonquil in his tiny hiding place for eternity.

Suddenly a green blur swept past the black dragon's head, he twisted to follow it and on its return it spat a spark of golden fire directly into one of his glowing red eyes. The dragon bawled in agony and thrashed with furious wing and claw about the rocks. Rattajack, who had previously been observing all from the cliff top, fluttered to the ground, skirted the mad flailing of the dragon and pulled his beloved companion from the crevice.

Gracewing also landed, and Throstle leapt from the smaller dragon's back and ran to confront the dark monster. Xedrethor angled his head to fix the wizard with his good eye, and then rotated it to locate the banf and the terragon who were slowly backing away through the rocks on the other side of him. The great dragon breathed deeply, and both Throstle and the two companions braced themselves for the freezing torrent that was sure to follow. None of them knowing which side the dragon would choose to attack. Suddenly with a twist like a whiplash, Xedrethor spun around and shot a streak of silver flame at the two companions. Their agile reflexes just saved them as they both ducked behind a jutting slab of rock, the volley of freezing fire exploded against their makeshift shield in a huge starburst of ice. The black dragon roared his displeasure and turned quickly back to the wizard before Throstle could fire another lightning bolt from his staff.

Jonquil and Rattajack darted from behind the sparkling star and sprinted to Throstle's side. The wizard immediately pushed them behind him to shield them with his body, and as the evil dragon sucked in yet another large volume of breath, hastily uttered a string of enchanted words. As soon as the incantation was complete, Throstle held his staff before him, the crystal in the jaws of the carved dragon glowing with a golden light. Without taking his eyes from the dragon, who had now thrown back his wings as a preliminary to emptying his great lungs, the wizard spoke in a low voice from the corner of his mouth.

'Jonquil,' he said in a hoarse whisper, 'give me the crystal pendant from around your neck!'

As the wizard reached back with his upturned hand, the banf quickly lifted the leather cord over his head and laid the cluster of small shards in Throstle's palm.

With a terrible din the inevitable onslaught was projected from the dragon's jaws. Suddenly a bright disc of light was thrown out from the glowing crystal on Throstle's staff, and with a mighty hiss as Old Magic clashed with Dark, Xedrethor's evil fire was extinguished by the staff; a thick cloud of billowing steam lifting into the air. Then the wizard raised his fist containing the pendant, and with a few swiftly spoken words, drew back his arm and hurled the crystal cluster at the raging jaws of the dragon. A trail of gold was left in the air as the pendant flew upwards, and disappeared between the monster's silvery snarl. The pendant, propelled by Throstle's enchantment, struck home with such force at the back of the dragon's throat, that in his surprise the great beast swallowed it.

Xedrethor took two powerful steps forward towards the group, and then faltered. A strange fire began to glimmer in his ruby eyes, the glow of uncertainty. The dragon's body began to convulse, and his long scimitar talons screeched against the rocky ground beneath the snow, as his feet clenched into shuddering fists. He suddenly wrapped his vast, wrinkled wings about his rearing black form, rocked back against his squirming tail and trumpeted his agony to the skies.

Jonquil gripped Throstle's arm.

'What's happening?' he cried.

There was a look of real sadness and regret in the wizard's eye as he gave his reply.

'It is the Old Magic in the crystals,' he sighed. 'It is poison to him.'

The dragon suddenly threw down his head and charged forward at the group, a roar fuelled by rage and pain blasting in their ears. The wizard and the two companions hurled themselves aside from his path, and the accelerating beast stormed past them on pounding legs, to fling open his great spans of skin and heave himself into the air.

Like a pulsating shadow the dragon spiralled upwards in a frenzied flight. The wizard, the banf and the terragon picked themselves up out of the snow and watched in wonder as their evil foe embarked upon a mesmeric display of violent aerobatics. Whether driven to such gymnastics by the maelstrom of pain within him, or as a desire to make a last defiant show against his enemies, Xedrethor's observers would never know; but after a wild, rolling swoop, the climax of which brought him screaming low over the heads of the threesome, his wings spinning like seed propellers, the end finally came. The black dragon rose again using the accumulated speed of his dive, but before he could employ his wings to take him higher, he was suddenly gripped by a paroxysm of pain. A plume of red fire burst from his chest, and his fearsome body crumpled and dropped. Throstle pulled his hat from his head as the plummeting shape of Xedrethor crashed at the foot of the crescent cliff. His once proud form impaled and broken upon the bed of spears below the wall.

Throstle bowed his head in respect for the passing of the great Guardian of the Path. His deep love of all dragons prevented him from rejoicing at this death, even though the creature had been the spawn of Vrorst.

'A magnificent creature,' he said at last. 'Even though his heart was as black as the power that drove him.'

'But your power was stronger,' said Jonquil, touched by the wizard's compassion for the dragon.

'Not mine alone,' Throstle answered with a smile. 'My power would have soon faded against the dark forces that inhabit this place had it not been for your pretty necklace. That crystal pendant was sent to me with the Lord Yelver by the Three Wizards themselves. It was made of shards chipped from the three Fire Orbs of Spring, Summer and Autumn; fragments of their own great power.'

The banf was astonished, and an eerie feeling crept over him when he thought of how long he had worn the pendant, blissfully ignorant of its great potency. A pretty necklace indeed for a simple banf to wear. However, its purpose had been fulfilled, and the quest still remained. There could be no time for resting, that would have to come later, if at all.

Jonquil courteously thanked Throstle for saving his life, and then told him of Hexerne's departure from the scene via the black dragon's lair. The wizard told the banf that finding him alive and well was payment enough for his aid, and congratulated Jonquil for managing to keep track of the girl, over so long and difficult a trail. The banf then asked Throstle of his encounter with Rhazgor. The wizard smiled patiently, only too aware of the danger of being waylaid by the two companions insatiable appetite for storytelling.

'I will give you the full rendition of that momentous meeting when time is not so precious,' Throstle told them. 'Suffice to say that I made Rhazgor sorry that he ever dared to venture beyond the sanctuary of his ice refuge. His power was strong, but mine was stronger. I broke his staff; and then the elves took him with their enchanted webs. As for Juvula, he escaped during our fiery duel, and I could not linger to find him. I must hope that the elves captured him also in the end.'

Throstle called Gracewing to him, and the graceful white dragon trotted over to the threesome. With an ecstatic trill the diminutive form of Addax lifted from his perch on the dragon's saddle, and flitted over to Jonquil, alighting on the banf's shoulder. The miniature dragon purred contentedly at his reunion with the banf, and gave Jonquil's earlobe an affectionate peck.

'Jonquil,' the wizard said, still smiling at the little creature's antics, 'you and Rattajack must take the black dragon's lair. Follow in the girl's footsteps and see where they lead. Gracewing will carry me over the cliff to see if there is a bridge further along spanning the chasm. For by the music of my flute I'll warrant our goal lies on the far side. If fortune is with us, we'll trap her between us. Be vigilant, my friends. Hexerne takes the Orb ever nearer to the Spire, and its strength and guile grows with every step!'

The wizard called Addax to his shoulder and mounted the pale dragon once again. Jonquil took a last look at the broken black mass that had once been a proud dragon, and then ran with Rattajack to Xedrethor's cave. As they walked they watched the sleek form of Gracewing rise from the open ground and then glide effortlessly out of sight beyond the curve of cliffs.

The Final Chapter

Jonquil and Rattajack scrambled up the steep slope leading to the dark portal of Xedrethor's lair. After stealing a couple of moments to catch their breath, they tentatively stepped inside. The air inhabiting the large space that had housed the dragon was spiced with the strong smell of musk. At its heart the odour was so intense that it caught in Jonquil's still tender throat making breathing uncomfortable. With the little daylight that managed to filter through from outside, the two companions saw that not all Xedrethor's victims had ended up on spikes. The floor of the cavern was littered with ancient, gnawed bones and the accumulated debris of countless warriors' apparel. Buckled breastplates, shields and other mangled remnants of armour still lay where they had been thrown down by the dragon. A discarded armoury of swords, scimitars and lances, now all redundant, kept company with the piles of assorted ironware, and a great stash of gold and jewels. The banf and the terragon could only wonder at how many brave and reckless souls had lost their lives to the black dragon over the centuries, their only monument a petrified corpse or a few scattered bones. Jonquil shivered when he thought that without Throstle's timely intervention he too would have joined the long, butchered procession of the dead.

Rattajack became suddenly agitated, his scaly hand reaching out for the banf's arm. Jonquil assumed that it was the heavy atmosphere of death haunting the cavern that was upsetting his friend, and seeing a dim circle of light at the rear of the chamber that he took to be the mouth of an egress, he led the terragon towards it. A sharp scraping sound stopped them both in their tracks, and as one they turned to face the direction of the noise; a large curtain of blackness in a far corner of the cavern. They froze with fear, both of them wondering if the black dragon had not been alone, and they were now to face the wrath of his widowed mate.

Suddenly, a harsh, disembodied whisper sounded in the dark chamber, its rasping, hollow tones accusing and spiteful.

'I knew you would follow,' it said. 'I knew you would hound us to the end!'

There was more scraping. It seemed to the sensitive ears of the banf and the terragon like the sound of metal dragging against rock. The blackness of the far corner was quite impenetrable, only sound could betray the movements of the being who shared the enclosed space with them.

'The wizard thinks I have passed through the cliff and entered the deep wood on the other side. I have even laid a trail of footprints down the slope to the edge of the trees, as I was told, to make my escape look more convincing. Then I came back here to wait for you. And now the wizard is gone, and there is no-one here to help you!'

Jonquil took a small step forward, his eyes searching the black veil for shape or form.

He spoke to the girl, a twinge of fear tightening his throat. 'Why didn't you use the time to get away?' the banf asked the darkness.

'Get away where?' came the hissing reply. 'This is the end of the path! For the Orb and for you!'

Hexerne's final word grew into a piercing scream that shook the confined air of the dark chamber, a startling sound that seemed barely human. With the scream came the scrabble of movement, and suddenly a sharp triangle of reflected daylight emerged from the blackness followed swiftly by the snarling face of the girl. The head of the deadly spear lunged at the banf, and with every ounce of strength she could muster Hexerne charged forward. Jonquil was caught completely unawares, the girl's savage scream dulling his reflexes. Suddenly Rattajack leapt at his surprised friend knocking the banf sideways with his weight. The terragon just managed to bend his torso to stop the advancing spearhead piercing his body, but could not prevent the iron blade from pinning his wing to the rock wall. Rattajack squealed in pain, and Jonquil threw himself on to the spear to deny the girl a second thrust. Fearful of an attempt on the Orb at her back Hexerne relinquished the shaft of the weapon and fled towards the mouth of the cavern. Jonquil threw aside the spear that had torn a deep rent in his companion's wing, and was about to offer comfort to the terragon when Rattajack pushed him towards the cave entrance, urging the banf with insistent cries to pursue the girl. Jonquil could see by the fear burning in the terragon's large eyes, that his friend was more afraid of Hexerne's escape than the wound from the spear. The banf could only conclude that Hexerne had been telling the truth, and that the half-moon of flat rock really was the end of the path. Rattajack could somehow sense that the Orb was close to home.

Hexerne practically tumbled down the slope leading back to the wide plateau. She had to pull the knapsack from her shoulders and hold it in front of her, for fear of the Orb's weight causing her to overbalance. As soon as her feet were reunited with the flat ground she raced towards the edge of the chasm. Even though there was no bridge for her to cross, and no sign of a palace or construction of any kind on the far side, she obeyed the voice in her head and ran blindly onwards. All that faced her across the huge divide was a sheer wall of ancient, crumbling ice.

Suddenly a grip of iron enveloped her legs, and the girl crashed to the floor. Jonquil's flying tackle arrested her progress with such force that the large globe of crystal in her arms burst from its wrappings and rolled out over the flat rock towards the lip of the mighty drop. Both Jonquil and Hexerne watched in horror as the glistening ball trundled away from them towards disaster. They were lying almost side by side, their enmity momentarily suspended as all of their attention focused on the moving sphere. The Orb, propelled by the momentum of the girl's fall, began to slow as it neared the jagged brink. The banf and the girl held their breath, powerless to save the crystal from the void; their eyes, like saucers, glued to its shiny skin.

The Orb stopped barely a thumb's length from the edge of the cliff.

For a moment, neither Hexerne nor Jonquil moved. They could hardly believe that the Orb had not rolled off the ledge. Then Hexerne was on her feet, a sharp sideways kick knocking the rising banf back to the ground. The girl reached out for the crystal globe like a frantic mother reaching for an endangered child. Such was her concern for the safety of her charge that she forgot the precaution that Mezereon had drummed into her a thousand times. Forgot? Or perhaps the remembrance of it was smothered in her mind by some insidious power. Whichever it was, before Hexerne had time to consider the significance of her actions, her bare fingers closed around the cold, polished form of the Orb, and she lifted it to her chest.

The sudden realisation of what she had done washed over the girl in a cold wave, and she stared transfixed with apprehension into the endless depths of the crystal. The heart of the globe was as black as night, but as Hexerne's eyes were drawn into it, a tiny spark of blue fire ignited and began to grow rapidly against the darkness. Suddenly a bolt of energy surged into the girl's slender body, filling her veins with a searing, shrieking power. Her whole being convulsed with pain, and had she not been holding the Orb tight against her, it might have flown from her hands and been lost to the void. With the shock of power came a sudden upsurge of wind that roared from the depths of the chasm loaded with snow and ice. The onslaught rushed over the lip of the cliff and stormed across the open shelf. It seized the banf who had just risen to his feet and bowled him over like a leaf before an Autumn gale. The air about the girl became a swirling maelstrom of white flakes, billowing and writhing in furious twisting patterns. Her robes and hair were thrown up in rolling waves by the whipping gusts, but her body remained still, unmoved by the tempest, planted to the rock like a statue.

If Jonquil had been in a position to observe Hexerne's eyes, he would have seen them burning with blue fire; just as Tuatara had once appeared to Meadolarne. Hexerne herself, however, was looking out through eyes that could now see a whole different world.

Ancient ramparts crowned with natural points and spires glowed with an ethereal brilliance behind the now transparent shield of ice that for Jonquil still appeared as the solid far wall of the chasm. The frontage of the spectral palace was arranged into two clusters of towers, divided by a narrow corridor of space that led away into darkness. Below an arch of ice fronting the corridor, a thin bridge reached across the void in curved ghostly lines to the edge of the cliff only a few paces from where the girl was standing.

Hexerne began to move slowly towards the foot of the bridge, the barrage of snow stinging her eyes making it difficult to look ahead. Jonquil

managed to fight back against the storm somewhat, and gradually made his way back towards the edge of the chasm. Shielding his eyes from the bite of the driven snowflakes he watched incredulously as (to his eyes) the girl stepped out from the ledge on to thin air. By the time he staggered to the place where Hexerne had performed this amazing feat, she was already a third of the way across the span of the invisible bridge. Jonquil's mouth fell open in awe at the sight of the girl standing in mid-air between the wide jaws of the bottomless gorge, the raging clouds of snow swirling all about her, seemingly nothing to support her or prevent her dropping like a stone into the endless depths. The banf watched Hexerne carefully edge forward in space with the tiniest steps, cautiously feeling her way along some unseen platform; and guessing that this incredible act was the work of enchantment, either that of the Orb or the place that awaited it, he decided to see if it might allow him to cross also.

The banf drew a straight line with his eyes from the girl to the ledge, and positioned himself at the point where he thought the invisible bridge must join the cliff. Leaning as far back from the edge as he could manage, Jonquil tentatively extended his foot from the lip of rock, and to his amazement felt the sole of his boot connect with a firm structure. He gently transferred his weight on to his leading foot, and gingerly took another step. The banf's heart thumped in his chest as his disbelieving eyes stared down between his feet at the sheer wall of the cliff plummeting into the milky haze below. He had to keep reassuring himself that there was a solid platform beneath his feet, and that he would not fall, even though every sense he possessed was screaming at him to go back to solid ground. Squinting through assaulted eyes, he peered ahead at the girl. Hexerne was now almost halfway across the chasm and seemed to have stopped. Jonquil made sure that he kept himself in as straight a line behind the girl as he could guess. He did not wish to investigate the width of the bridge, for something about the cautiousness of Hexerne's progress suggested that it was narrow and precarious. The gusts of wind and snow that hurled themselves against the two figures did their best to topple them, but the banf kept his centre of gravity as low to the bridge as he could, and the girl, holding tightly to the Orb, seemed as immovable as a statue. Jonquil knew he had to try and stop Hexerne from delivering the Orb to the far side of the chasm. Due to their current perilous situation, making a dash for the girl was out of the question, so, with no other option, the banf decided to try reasoning with her. He called out to Hexerne, his voice dulled by the howl of the violent snowstorm. When she turned around to regard him, Jonquil gasped, for he saw that her eyes were two ovals of flickering blue fire. The banf collected himself and called to the girl again.

'Hexerne,' he cried. 'Come back! Don't go on into that dark and evil place. Come back with me and give the Orb to the Wizards, where it will be safe. They will take good care of it. Please Hexerne, don't go any further!'

The girl stood motionless staring at the banf with her burning eyes.

215

Her face betrayed not the slightest emotion, and the banf began to wonder if she was even able to hear him.

Hexerne could hear the banf but she was so filled with a cold fear that she was unable to respond. Then a new voice sounded in her head. A strong, clear, commanding voice that called to her from the far side. The voice was reminiscent of the one that she believed came from the Orb, but somehow different; different and yet very familiar.

'Little Sorceress,' it softly called.

Hexerne slowly turned about to look in the direction of the voice, and as her eyes traced the contours of the shimmering bridge continuing before her to the far cliff, they focused upon the hem of a white, ermine-trimmed robe. Her eyes rose steadily upwards, and a tall figure was revealed, clad in a long wizard's robe of white, black and purple hues, glittering crystals fastened into its exquisitely embroidered decorations. Finally the girl's eyes met those of the other, and the shock of recognition made her almost faint away.

'Come to me, Little Sorceress,' the figure called again.

Hexerne's eyes, already stinging with snow now began to smart with tears, and a cry, choked with a sudden rush of emotion, struggled from her throat into the howling wind.

'Master!' she wailed.

Hexerne's eyes had not looked upon his form for many years, but he appeared to her exactly as she remembered him. He was adorned in his imperial robes, a high crown of ice glistening on his head, a large blackheart crystal, like a hungry pool of darkness, set in silver on his breast. Vrorst's eyes sparkled with blue stars, and his mouth was drawn into a benevolent smile. He held out a hand to the girl, and told her to trust in him. Her destiny awaited her on the far side, and all she had to do was walk on across the bridge and embrace it.

Jonquil tried to look around the girl's form to try and see what it was that held her attention so completely. He could just about see to the far side of the gorge through the dizzy haze of snow, but his eyes could see nothing there. He called out again to the girl. She turned to him but was quickly distracted back to the far side, as if the other voice had called her once more. Then she began to move again, but not with small, timid steps. This time Hexerne took bold strides as if she had been suddenly filled with a new confidence and purpose. Jonquil called out once more but his cries were ignored, the girl was fiercely focused on the remaining downward slope of the bridge.

The banf had no choice he had to follow and was just about to quicken his own pace to try and reach Hexerne before it was too late, when a gut-wrenching scream sliced through the already noisy air. Jonquil squinted at the blurry form of the girl, initially assuming it had come from her, but then with a sickening rush came the realisation that the noise had originated from beneath their feet, from the bridge itself. A stomach-churning shiver vibrated the banf's legs, and ahead of him he saw Hexerne start to waver. In an attempt to steady herself she had shifted the precious crystal globe into the cradle of one arm and was using the other to try and balance. The bridge began to tremble violently, and it was then that Jonquil realised that the invisible structure was not formed by sorcery, only concealed by it. Under his feet there was a real bridge, a real bridge that was in the throes of disintegration.

Hexerne threw a desperate glance at the figure of her Lord. She implored the image of Vrorst to help her, to save his most loyal servant and the Orb; but Vrorst just looked at the quaking figure of the girl with cruel, pitiless eyes and began to laugh. He had lured Hexerne past the apex of the bridge to the part that was riddled with cracks and ready to crumble. A light, careful step, especially that of a slender female might have crossed the ancient ruptures without mishap, but a girl made heavy by the weight of the Orb and the confidence instilled in her by the lies of Him to whom she had dedicated her young life, were more than the delicate platform could bear. With a final shriek of splintering ice the section of bridge beneath Hexerne's feet crazed into a glaring mosaic of blue lines and fell away into the misty void. Hexerne wailed in terror as she dropped from the banf's sight. Jonquil instinctively fell on to all fours and crawled cautiously forward. The girl was dangling above the great bottomless yawn of the chasm by her fingertips, clinging to nothing it looked to the banf. To his unenchanted eyes, Hexerne was hanging desperately from an invisible broken edge, her body, still clasping the Orb with one arm, swaying dangerously with the force of the surging tumult.

Again she cried out for aid.

'Master! Help me! Please help me!'

Jonquil continued to crawl forward, now on his belly. The bridge began to shake once more as he neared the broken end, the ice structure groaning with the weight of the dangling girl, and the might of the storm pushing against her swinging body. The banf heard Hexerne's desperate voice again.

'I can't hold it!' she screamed. 'It's slipping! It's slipping! Nooooooo!'

Hexerne could feel the mass of the crystal globe grow heavier and begin to push its way through the crook of her arm. Her utter despair poured into her voice as she realised that the Orb was falling and she was powerless to prevent it. Inside her head, Vrorst's laughter still rang out in evil, jarring tones. Hexerne was hysterical with confusion, she could not understand why her lord and master had forsaken her, and why the imminent destruction of his great tool of sorcery should please him so. She continued to call out in the vain hope that her heartfelt pleas might solicit a show of mercy from Vrorst's presence, but as the heavy weight suddenly dropped from her arm, the misery of failure and rejection began to rack her twisting body with painful sobs.

Jonquil watched aghast as the shiny sphere plummeted towards the pale sea of mist that floated in the distant depths of the mighty trench. His eyes followed the globe until it was a tiny speck of black against the milky sea of vapour. A wail of grief rose from the girl and she looked as if, at any moment, she might follow the Orb on its endless dive. The banf scrambled onward ignoring the protests of the splintering bridge and reached for Hexerne's hand. When her head lifted to him, Jonquil saw that she was still possessed with the blue fire.

Hexerne's face was contorted with grief, trails of tears glistening on her cheeks. When she saw the face of the banf above her, a low moan rose from her lips.

'You've won!' she sobbed. 'You've won!'

With her last word she dropped her head and calmly relinquished her fingertip grip on the ruined edge of the bridge. Jonquil, whose fingers had just reached the girl's wrist, suddenly grabbed hold as he sensed Hexerne begin to fall. The dead weight of the girl jarred against the banf's shoulder, slamming him hard against the cold platform of the unseen bridge. Jonquil hastily tried to gain some purchase where he lay, but to his horror felt Hexerne's weight dragging him bodily towards the jagged edge. Then his sliding was firmly arrested by a strong grip on his ankle. The banf looked back over his shoulder, and out of the corner of his eye he could just see the crouched form of Rattajack, holding on tight to his friend with his two hands. Neither of them able to see the structure which supported them. She that could see the bridge seemed to have drifted into an hysterical delirium, and was deaf to Jonquil's calling. He was trying to get Hexerne to hold on to the bridge again, to ease the strain on his arm, but she showed no interest whatsoever in saving herself. The banf gritted his teeth and tried to ignore the burning pain at his shoulder. He did not have the strength to haul the girl up to the bridge by himself, and Rattajack could not help because he was fully occupied holding on to the banf. All Jonquil could do was close his eyes against the swarms of snowflakes that busied themselves in the air, and try to hold on until help arrived; whoever and whenever that might be.

Jutting out from the cliff of ice on the north wall of the great chasm, far below the surface of the lingering fog, was a formidable buttress of rock. Submerged in the ocean of mist that permanently inhabited this depth of the gorge, it rose to a blunt pinnacle and then fell away to continue the unfathomable plunge to the distant floor. The Orb of Winter parted the vaporous air with a muffled roar, its plummeting speed increasing the further it fell. Perhaps it was more than chance that in a space as large as the great chasm of ice the plunging Orb should meet with the protruding anvil of rock, striking its hard crown like a hammer blow of the gods.

Vrorst's power globe exploded into a thousand radiating fragments, the noise of its demise cracking the air like thunder. The shards of crystal hurtled through the air, each of them trailing a wake of blue fire, showering into the vast emptiness as a burning sapphire rain. A faint afterglow lingered in the air about the outcrop of rock, slowly spreading through the sea of pale mist like a shimmering stain. It began to build into a churning cloud, pulsating with washes of colour and sparkling with blue stars. Soon it was a glowing mass expanding into the space of the chasm, devouring the floating mist, and growing like the gathering leaden clouds of a titanic storm.

Two servants parted the drapes to allow Waxifrade, Lord of Autumn, to enter the Orb Chamber followed by his closest attendants. The Lords Orolan and Fantazar were already standing within the circle from which rose three empty pedestals. The Autumn Wizard gave each of his brothers a solemn greeting and then took his place within the circle. None of the three lords had been summoned to this place, they had all come because of a sudden sense of dread which had invaded their peace. They had all simultaneously experienced an urgent need to be close to their great crystals.

A low moan of mourning and despair emanated from the circle of attendants that lined the small chamber. The faces of the three great lords were black with grief. The three tall pedestals and the patches of floor upon which they stood were drenched in shattered crystal. Lazy wisps of golden vapour spiralled into the air from where the great globes had once sat, and the air within the circle was alive with swirling clouds of multicoloured stars.

'Brothers,' Orolan spoke forth, 'the thing we feared the most has come to pass. The Orb of Winter has been destroyed.'

There was a low murmur of agreement from the other two wizards, and a spreading sigh of dismay from the ring of attendants who surrounded the circle of enchantment.

'It may be some time,' Orolan continued sombrely, 'before we know the circumstances of the Winter Orb's destruction. Whether it came about by accident or design. Also, we cannot know how near to the North Spire the Orb was broken; for our eyes have long been blind to its progress. There can be no doubt, however, that, as we had foreseen, the power that dwelled within that mighty crystal has now been freed. To what end we cannot tell.'

The Three Wizards then bowed their heads to combine their wills into one potent force. They had done this many times before in an attempt to break through the impenetrable veil the Orb had drawn around itself. All of their previous attempts had been unsuccessful, the power of Vrorst's crystal had been too great; but with the Orb now destroyed, the Three Lords believed there was a chance for them to finally lift their blindness.

A hum of curious voices began to build amongst the group of lesser beings collected within the silk walls of the Orb Chamber. The Three Wizards reached out and pressed their palms against those of their brothers. A collective gasp rose from the Wizards' attendants, their excitement caused by the glinting mass of released power within the circle being drawn into a large globe of golden light that slowly appeared above the heads of the Three Wizards.

An image slowly grew within the shimmering sphere, and the

enthralled audience realised that they were seeing the thoughts of the three lords made visible. A thin, white, spindly bridge spanning a wide chasm slowly took shape within the floating globe of golden light, its fragile arc breached by a large gap in its northward slope. The open space was filled with a fury of snow, and as they watched the crowd thought they could see tiny figures on the frail structure, one of them dangling like a windblown rag from one broken edge.

Jonquil felt before he heard the mighty rumble rising from the depths below. The bridge began to shake, forcing new cracks in its already fractured form. At least the narrow strip of ice was visible to him now, a change which had occurred following the sharp volley of sound that had reverberated up through the chasm from somewhere within its hidden depths a little while before; although Jonquil was not altogether sure that seeing the bridge beneath him was an advantage, as he could now observe with his own eyes its truly perilous condition. He thought about ordering Rattajack back to the cliff, but knew it was hopeless to ask his beloved friend to desert him and just leave him to his fate; at least there was always the slight comfort of knowing that the terragon could fly (if only weakly), and therefore save himself. There had been a time, of course when Jonquil also enjoyed the power of flight, but his wings were still tightly bound in their orchin dressings, awaiting the day when they would emerge from their chrysalis wrappings, healed and whole. That is if he survived to see that day. Jonquil sighed inwardly. Never had he had need of his wings more than at that moment, and they were useless to him. It would be ironic indeed if he were to fall to his death with his wings still bound and dressed at his back.

Another change to follow the loud report from below had been in Hexerne. At precisely the same moment that the thin contours of the bridge had materialised, the girl had suddenly awoken from her dazed stupor. It was as if she saw her precarious situation for the first time and was thrown into panic. The banf had little difficulty persuading her to try to save herself by lending him her other hand, which up to now had hung uselessly at her side. Only now she was struggling so much to improve her grip on the bridge that she was placing more stress on the ice structure and endangering them all. Jonquil found himself trying to calm a very different character to the one he had shared a significant part of this adventure with. This Hexerne had none of the hatred or bile that had so possessed the soul of the former. She did not snarl or curse or try to do him injury, but rather she cried out in terror like any other natural creature in fear for its life, and begged the banf to save her. Her eyes no longer burned with the blue fire, but were themselves again; urgent pools of fear as bright as sapphires.

Jonquil still held fast to the girl's wrist, but now grabbed hold of her other arm as the girl raised her free hand. Her fingers clamped on to the crumbling edge of ice, and at last the banf felt a degree of relief in his tortured shoulder. Then Jonquil's eyes grew wide as he saw the sea of mist below them swallowed up by a rising inferno of blue flame.

The chasm was soon filled with a surging torrent of blue fire, flowing up towards the quaking arc of ice like a mushroom of burning energy. It swept past the dying bridge, the dancing tongues of brilliant flame snaking upward until they had climbed the full height of the ice cliffs and threatened to challenge the mighty peaks themselves for majesty. The intensity of the flame seemed to repel the thick canopy of cloud lying across the valley, creating an oasis of clarity. Then, as the two companions and the still dangling Hexerne looked on in terror, the vast pall of energy began to form into a shape. It was the shape of a figure. A giant who stood with arms thrown wide, an immense cape hanging in glimmering folds from his hands. The points of a high collar rose either side of his proud head, an imperious face capped by the tall peak of a sorcerer's crown. The rolling sapphire flames slowly took on colours, showing patches of pinks and purples. The great cloak became as white as the snowy cliffs and the face, so high above the chasm, was framed with a black beard. The mighty apparition rippled with great waves of transparent flame, the sheer walls of ice still visible behind it.

'Vrorst!' the word emerged as barely a whisper from the banf's lips, but the monstrous form of the giant looking down at his minuscule foe began to shake with laughter.

'You fools!' came a voice like an earthquake. 'You pitiful fools! Did you really think you could stop me?'

Vrorst's words might have been directed as much to the Three Wizards who now observed this incredible scene as to those struggling on the bridge. Great slithers of ice began to tumble from the ancient face of the far wall with the force of the giant's voice, the rumble of his laughter threatening to bring the whole unstable landscape crashing down. Sizeable chunks of the bridge also fell away with the increased vibration, and Jonquil knew that the thin platform had finally lost its battle to hold together. The mighty image of Vrorst seemed to take note of the destruction he was causing, and with an evil grin threw back his shoulders and roared. The terrible sound tore through the frozen gorge, hammering against the walls of the chasm with a deafening cacophony of echoes; and was immediately followed by another more ominous sound. Like thunder it came; the shrieking, tearing, pulverising sound of destruction. Vast slabs of cliff sheared off and tipped into the void. Wriggling cracks ran like demented snakes across the ancient ice veneers delivering huge crumbling ramparts to the hungry jaws of the gorge. The north section of the ice bridge shattered and dropped into the churning clouds of debris and dust. The southern expanse looked as if it might follow its other half imminently.

Hexerne cried out, her voice barely audible above the din of ruin. She was staring at what had once been the sheer north wall of the chasm. The facade of crumbling ice was gone, and revealed in its stead was the soaring columns and towers of an ice palace. Two wings of crystalline architecture reached out to the brink of the chasm, their stout ramparts protecting a central corridor that retreated far into the heart of the structure, ending in a jagged mouth. Rising above this single portal, reaching into the sky, flanked by several lesser points, was a mighty needle of ice. The legend was finally unmasked, Vrorst's secret sanctuary revealed; it was the Spire of the North.

Abruptly the giant's roaring ceased and the great sheet of flame that had become the dreaded shape of the Ice Sorcerer now returned to its former substance. Tendrils of fire began to be drawn into the long corridor of the ice palace, the fingers of blue light eventually disappearing into the dark mouth of the portal beneath the great spire. The vast burning plume diminished and shrank, surging into the tiny mouth with increasing speed. Soon the last flickering tongues licked at the thundering turmoil filling the chasm and disappeared between the twin clusters of towers. The whole of the fiery giant had been sucked into the enchanted palace by some titanic force.

The ruin however did not cease with the disappearing of the blue fire. With a huge effort on both their parts Jonquil and Rattajack heaved Hexerne up on to the disintegrating platform of the bridge, but the strain of remaining whole whilst its surroundings were dissolving into chaos was too much and the bridge began to bow in defeat. The banf and the girl started to run as they felt the structure fail beneath their feet, but the destruction was too swift and they were both caught up by its ravenous progress. Their cries were added to the general melee in the chasm, arms and legs flailing to grasp any firm hold to save themselves as half of the bridge's length collapsed.

Suddenly a sleek, white shape plunged into the valley through the great hole in the cloud canopy. A fleet dragon with half-closed rapier wings that sliced through the turmoil like a gleaming arrow. Tuatara urged Starblade into a steep spiral, and the white dragon carried the Ice Witch and Meadolarne past the newly revealed towers of Vrorst's sanctuary, and on in a wide sweep to approach the desolated ice bridge.

It had been the banfina who had first spotted the gaping breach in the cloud cover, when she and Tuatara had been soaring aimlessly over the endless sea of white. They had searched tirelessly through that frozen terrain, beneath the blanket of fog; league after league of anonymous, snow-lagged mountains and their empty, featureless valleys. The witch had known that they were close to the Spire, she could feel its power clawing at her soul, drawing her to it; but it would not reveal itself to her. She did not have the Orb, and Tuatara knew that only the Orb could find the secret portal. Despite her frustration the witch had a sense that something was about to happen. There had been a tension building within her that she knew would soon reach its climax; and so she had commanded Starblade to ride the updraughts until they had broken through the lid of cloud, and wait for signs of the momentous happening that would lead them to the hidden place.

Ahead of them, Tuatara and Meadolarne saw the wreckage of the bridge, and the frantic figures which dangled in a precarious chain from its jagged stub. Hexerne was hanging from Jonquil's ankle, who himself was suspended from Rattajack's jaws by the collar of his coat. The terragon had secured himself by jamming his tail spear into a crevice at the base of the ice structure. By the way the pendulous figures were being jolted and shaken it was clear that the bridge's destruction was not yet over. Starblade sped towards the splintered platform, and as she did so a scream rang out, and the girl dropped from Jonquil's stretched leg. With arms and legs flailing Hexerne began a swift descent, the dragon responded immediately with a stomach lurching dive to overtake Hexerne's plunging body. A long scream trailed into the air behind the girl as the dragon drove herself downwards with rapid, snatching wing beats. Eventually Starblade dove past the girl and then spread wide her wings to level out. Hexerne fell perfectly into the path of the dragon's swoop, striking Starblade's back a short distance behind Meadolarne; but such was the speed of her landing that the girl bounced awkwardly against the dragon's scales and was deflected into the taut membrane of her wing. The white beast dipped suddenly with the girl's weight sending them into a violent curve which threatened to dash them all against the rugged face of the chasm. Starblade somehow managed to veer sharply at the last moment and squeeze the tightest turn to skim past the wall of towering rock.

Meadolarne realised that it was up to her to save this dangerous situation. One of them had to slide down the wing to Hexerne who had managed to grab hold of the raised ridge of the dragon's nearest fingerbone, and help her to climb up to white beast's back. Tuatara was too large for the task. Her weight on Starblade's wing as well as the girl's would finish them all. Meadolarne was the only one light enough to achieve it. With the deepest breath of her life, the banfina unbuckled her slight frame from the flight harnesses and secured one of the straps around her wrist. As the snowdragon continued her long downward spiral, Meadolarne edged herself on to the springy sheet of skin that reached across to the bony strut to which Hexerne was clinging. The banfina's hair was lifted high by the fierce draughts that surged across the dragon's wing. The strength of the gale threatened to drag her to oblivion also, so Meadolarne kept as low to the wrinkled membrane as she could, gripping the long, scaly arm that powered the wing to steady herself. She finally reached Hexerne's terror-struck form, and grasped one of her wrists. The girl had her eyes tightly closed, her own long black mane whipped up furiously by the wind. The banfina called Hexerne's name, and she slowly opened her eyes. For a few moments the banfina and the young sorceress just stared at each other. Hexerne's initial countenance was one of uncertainty. She recognised Meadolarne, and for a moment must have wondered at the banfina's intentions. Had the banf female, she had once enslaved with her juvenile power, come for revenge? Did she intend to prise off Hexerne's strained fingers, and fling her to the void? Or was it possible that Meadolarne was risking her own life, just as Jonquil (her mate) had done earlier, to try and save hers?

Despite the severity of her situation, Hexerne could not help flushing with shame at the thought of her past deeds, albeit they were committed under the powerful influence of the Ice Sorcerer. With the smashing of the Orb, Vrorst's control over the girl had been finally broken. Eighteen years of slavery to a force that had infiltrated her every thought and whim, departed in a split second of time. Hexerne was free of her winter shackles; but as Tuatara could also testify, liberation did not necessarily bring on a state of euphoria, but rather left them feeling exposed and a little fearful. As if a deep layer of protection had been stripped away, laying them bare to a world that had no reason to show them friendship.

Meadolarne smiled at Hexerne, and the girl saw at once that the banfina had forgiven her for what had passed between them. Her heart was warmed by such a generous show of kindness. She took the banfina's offered hand and carefully manoeuvred herself up the slanting wing. Meadolarne allowed the girl to use her body as a makeshift ladder, to climb back up the wing to the dragon's spine. With a little adjustment and imagination, Hexerne and Meadolarne were able to share the banfina's flying harness, and when all was secure, Starblade, who had now recovered full use of her wings, was able to carry them all to the cliff top and safety.

Jonquil and Rattajack were already waiting for Meadolarne and the others at the edge of the half-moon shelf. With Hexerne no longer a burden on his leg, Jonquil had surrendered himself to the strength of the terragon, and Rattajack had spread his wings and leapt from the crumbling bridge. With a good deal of frantic flapping and panting, the terragon had managed to ride the violent winds that still blustered through the chasm, and deliver them both to firm ground, the banf clasped firmly in his jaws.

The reunion was made complete by the arrival of Throstle on Gracewing; Addax giving his own inimitable greeting to the group, and this time choosing Meadolarne's shoulder as an eventual perch. The wizard was most upset to learn from Jonquil and Rattajack that he had been duped by the Orb's trickery, and consequently had missed out on all the action. His disappointment was short lived though, such was his great pleasure at seeing all safe and well; and to further illustrate his joy at this happy meeting, he plucked his flute from his hat and charmed the air with a merry reel.

Throstle's face darkened a little, however, when sometime later Hexerne told him of the giant figure of Vrorst that had risen from the depths, and how it had been drawn into the portal of the Spire like a mighty intake of breath. The wizard looked thoughtfully across to the tiny, dark aperture nestled beneath the mountainous rise of the ice palace, and as if reading his thoughts, Tuatara approached him and placed a friendly hand upon his shoulder.

'You will achieve nothing by entering that evil place, Horcust Rothgilian,' she told him. 'Apart from offering yourself as an instrument of

its malice.'

Throstle turned to the witch. Tuatara's eyes were fixed upon the glassy columns of the great structure on the far side of the vast divide.

'The shadow that inhabited the Orb,' she continued, 'is now without form or focus. Unless one such as yourself should foolishly enter that place........' Tuatara looked back at the wizard. 'Do you really believe you have the strength to resist its power? In its own well of Dark Magic?'

Throstle shrugged and cast his eyes down into the swirling depths of the chasm. He did not answer for a long time, but then with a heavy sigh he said, 'It is most frustrating to leave things so..... unfinished! We failed in our quest, Tuatara! We were supposed to capture the dark power, not release it!' The wizard struck the rocky cliff top with the finial of his staff, his knuckles white with the intensity of his grip. 'And now it's in there,' he growled. 'Festering, growing, healing itself! Waiting for the day when it can once again cast its shadow upon the world.'

'We should count ourselves lucky,' said Tuatara, 'that we were both far away from this place when the crystal shattered. For if it had been you or I on the bridge when the power rose the ending might have been much worse. As high enchanters we would have been vulnerable to its force; consumed... possessed! Let us be thankful that it was these simple, honest creatures that were here at the end.'

'End?' Throstle cried. 'This is no ending! How can there be an end when Vrorst's shade is still free to threaten the world?'

'But it is greatly diminished,' Tuatara reasoned.

'Aye, until it finds another form, and a new vessel for its power.'

'Even then it will be many years before it has the strength to show its face beyond that portal.'

Throstle was not convinced. 'From tiny acorns do mighty oak trees grow!' he argued.

'Not if they are cut down before their time!' the witch countered, and with that she turned and strode away from the wizard into the thickening veil of evening.

Throstle fell silent for a few moments, his eyes staring hard into the translucent structure of the glistening fortress, which was caught in a fading beam of sunlight slanting into the chasm from the shrinking hole in the cloud cover. Eventually he spoke out loud to himself in a quiet, thoughtful tone. 'Better yet, to crush it before it has time to germinate!' The wizard felt distinctly uneasy about turning his back on the Spire of the North now it had been finally revealed to them. He could not believe that they were meant to simply turn tail and run from the power that dwelt within; a power that now had the enchantment from the Winter Orb to nurture and develop like a new born child. Throstle simply could not understand Tuatara's unwillingness to finish the job. Together the two of them could do it, surely? The witch had said herself that the power of Vrorst's crystal was greatly diminished.

Throstle continued to stare at the ice palace, which seemed to glimmer and sparkle before his eyes with increasing fascination. The more he gazed into its enticing depths, the more he became convinced that there was nothing to fear. He alone could master the force which occupied the dark sanctuary, and bring it to its final defeat. Suddenly he could see it all with amazing clarity; Throstle the Victorious, Horcust the Hero : Destroyer of the Freezing Fire! The wizard's head began to swim with thoughts of an Enchantica free from the menace of Vrorst for all time. A world that no longer had need to fear the coming of Winter.

There was a nudge at Throstle's shoulder. It was Gracewing, come to keep the wizard company on the edge of the great bottomless divide. Throstle turned and stroked the dragon's head, his eyes wild with sudden speculation.

Tuatara returned to the rest of the party to find that they had organised a fire and some food from the two dragons' store pouches. The four adventurers, five including Addax, were tucking into quite a hearty meal. Jonquil, Meadolarne and Hexerne were heavily engrossed in swapping tales and reminiscences, whilst the terragon and the miniature dragon exchanged unspoken stories of their own. The group gradually became silent as the witch entered the circle of firelight and extended her white palms to the orange glow of the flame.

'Strange,' she said to them, 'I never used to feel the cold before; but now......' She finished her statement with a shrug.

'I know,' said Hexerne. 'It is the same for me.'

The witch looked across to the girl she had once so passionately despised, but now knew to be her daughter. How could she have looked upon that face for all those years and not recognised her. It was powerful enchantment indeed that could blind a mother to her child.

Tuatara spoke softly into the warming flames: 'It was like a piece of my soul being torn out when.......,'

'The Orb died,' Hexerne softly concluded.

'Yes,' her mother sighed.

The two of them stared into each other's eyes for a few long moments, knowing that the empty space that had been left inside them was ready to be refilled with each other's love.

Jonquil's cheerful voice broke the mood. 'Where's Throstle?' he inquired.

The witch turned to him her mind still occupied with other thoughts.

'Er.... he will join us shortly,' she said at last.

No sooner had the words left her lips than Addax immediately stiffened on his perch of Meadolarne's shoulder. His sparkling eyes staring sharply into the growing darkness. Suddenly with a shrill call of alarm he burst into flight, skimming the tops of the flames, and disappeared into the gloom, his fading trill the only clue to his direction. The whole group tensed with apprehension, five anxious pairs of eyes staring out into the inky veil.

Addax's nerve-jarring voice grew louder again as the frantic reptile flew back towards the fire. Tuatara suddenly felt a sinking feeling deep within her, and she knew that something was terribly wrong. The small, pale dragon entered the pool of firelight and fluttered over the heads of the company like a demented giant butterfly, never for a moment ceasing its piercing cry.

'Throstle!' shouted the banf, jumping to his feet. 'He's in trouble!'

Jonquil was about to sprint into the darkness when Tuatara caught him by the shoulder.

'No, Jonquil,' she said firmly. 'I alone can help him now!'

The banf was about to protest, but the severity of the witch's countenance told him that this battle was far beyond his mortal powers. He reluctantly bowed his head in compliance.

'Hexerne!' Tuatara spoke commandingly to the girl. 'Make sure you all stay within the light of the fire! Addax too!'

The girl nodded fearfully, and ushered Jonquil to sit back down with the rest of them. There was nothing the four of them could do now but await the return of the two enchanters, and pray that such an event would come to pass. As for the small dragon, Addax did not seem too reluctant to stay within the warm protection of the fire, having now raised the alarm on behalf of his beloved master. He was clearly distressed for the wizard, but was equally fearful of something he had encountered beyond the light of the flames. His little body was agitated and tense, as if he expected the dread shape of an enemy to emerge from the wall of darkness leading to the cliff edge at any moment.

As Tuatara summoned Starblade to follow her, and they both hurried towards the edge of the chasm, the witch tried to focus her thoughts. Her prowess as a sorceress had not just been an invention of the Ice Lord, she did have power of her own. Vrorst may have encouraged and increased it, but beneath the veneer of his might and authority there had been an enchantment that was entirely hers; after all, she was the daughter of an elf prince. It was this inner reservoir of power that Tuatara now had to try and reach. She knew that she would need every ounce of her strength for the trial ahead, she could only pray that it was enough. Across the divide, only the soaring point of the ice steeple itself, silhouetted against a violet landscape, betrayed the existence of the frozen fortress within the towering blackness of the far wall. Tuatara needed no sight of the malignant palace to know of its presence. She could feel its malevolence flowing through the darkness towards her like an evil tide. Icy fingers of Dark Magic writhed unseen through the air, probing at her mind, her soul, searching for a weakness, longing to enter inside and claim her once more. Tuatara was confident that the warmth of the camp fire would keep Hexerne and the others safe from this insidious enchantment for the time being. She wondered if Throstle had been aware of the dark power's influence reaching out into the growing gloom to test him, working its deceit into his reason and thoughts. She also wondered if he had crossed the chasm on Gracewing believing himself to be in control of his actions. The witch was afraid that Throstle's fiery mood would have made him vulnerable to suggestion; his blood had been so hot when Tuatara had left him, that it would have taken little provocation to tempt him to try his hand against the power in the frozen fortress.

The witch climbed into the snowdragon's saddle, and the white beast unfurled her great sails of skin and charged into the wide river of blackness that was the chasm.

Throstle stood just inside the entrance to the ice palace, facing a narrow, roughly hewn corridor that gradually faded into darkness beyond the gentle glow of his staff crystal. The relatively small portal was hung with a lethal curtain of ice spears that gave it the forbidding appearance of ferocious, snarling jaws; and it had taken a considerable force of will to dismiss the sensation that he was walking into the deadly gape of a sleeping monster. He had not lingered beneath the row of glistening fangs, unable to conquer the fear that they might snap down upon him at any moment. Throstle was alarmed to see how quickly his inflamed bravado had deflated now that he had landed on the north side of the chasm within the boundaries of his enemy's refuge. The anger and the eagerness that had so gripped him on the safe vantage of the southern cliff had faded somewhat now he was faced with the prospect of exploring this terrible place. The oppressive, clinging cloaks of darkness that were draped so heavily over his surroundings sapped his vigour, charged his imagination, and left him chilled and uncertain.

The wizard looked back towards the gorge and could just make out the profile of his faithful steed waiting nervously at the mouth of the long gap between the two extending arms of the structure; the dragon marginally paler than his inky background. A moment's hesitation seized Throstle, and the urge to rush back to the friendly figure of Gracewing, leap into his saddle and flee from that dreadful place became almost overwhelming. However, the wizard might have been abandoned by his courage, but he still had his resolve, and with a heavy heart he turned away from the path to freedom, and started along the rugged ice passage.

The soft glow from the crystal held in the wooden jaws of the carved dragon's head cast a modest pool of illumination into the sea of blackness about him. Throstle could have conjured forth a brighter light if he had wished, but he feared angering the darkness with too great a show of energy; not to mention the power that dwelt within the darkness!

Eventually, the wizard found himself faced with the choice of three passages: North, East or West. The side passages felt innocuous enough but the black arch that stood opposite him reeked with the stench of evil. There could be no doubt in Throstle's mind that the path to the power of the ice palace lay northward. The wizard swallowed hard and passed through to the north corridor. Before long, the confined space of the passageway abruptly gave way to an immeasurable void. Throstle was just about to cross the threshold of what seemed to be a vast chamber, when, shifting the projection of his staff's glow, he noticed a single thread of blue light drawn across the darkness of the narrow entrance at about waist height to him. He studied it closely for a few moments unable to recognise what manner of phenomenon it was. It might have been placed there as a single strand of a glowing spider's web such was its taut delicacy, but rather than reflect the light of the crystal, it seemed to generate its own luminescence. The wizard decided that he did not like the idea of breaking this fragile thread, and so entered the great chamber by stooping beneath it. When he looked back to see if it was still intact, he had to look so closely that he nearly touched the thin shining strand with his nose. Then a thought struck him which he found somewhat disturbing. What if this was not the first near invisible thread he had encountered? He had only just noticed this one. He might have walked through a dozen similar, needle-thin sapphire beams without knowing during the course of his exploration. Throstle cast his eyes over his robes, there were no limp threads attached to his sleeves or body as would be the case if these were the product of some light spinning spider; but then there was no evidence to suggest that these mysterious beams would leave such a residue. Throstle moved away from the entrance and tried to cast some light on the immense hall that lay before him. He froze suddenly as his eyes focused on the massive interior. The giant chamber was not a great void of blackness as he had first thought, its every contour was visible to him, illuminated by an incredible net of light threads covering every inch of the vast space; sweeping across wide plains of wall, hanging between pillars and across arches and openings like one gargantuan cocoon. The wizard stepped into this mesmeric space, staring all about him like a child at a carnival. Such was his fascination that he failed to notice that there were threads reaching through the chamber as well as across its surfaces; and Throstle's body soon gathered a collection of bright strands about itself.

In the centre of the vast, vaulted ceiling, which bristled with giant icicles, the wizard saw that the light web formed an intense, thick tunnel of strands rising upwards into an unseen space. Directly underneath this luminous shaft there rose a mighty platform like a blunted pyramid. The shape appeared black beneath its sheath of woven light, a fan-shaped silhouette similarly draped with glowing strands rising from its peak. The walls of the great chamber were draped in deep shadow, and so their detail was lost to the wizard; but he had the impression of a multitude of informal arches and pillars rising up either side of him, opening out to yet more sweeping apertures, that extended far into the deep fabric of the fortress.

As Throstle slowly stepped forward, unheeding the weave of fibres that tangled around his feet, he thought he saw a movement at the top of the high platform; the web of gleaming filaments drawn over the dark fan bending into the profile of a body rising against them. The tall figure was invisible save for the form it made in the clinging blue gossamer; but when it stood at the edge of the high summit, a beam of brilliant cold light, originating from the central shaft, struck the platform invading it with a brightness that steadily filtered down through its frozen, triangulate fabric. At the same time, the light poured into the network of lines that radiated outwards from the high structure, making them burn with a bright blue intensity.

The tall figure standing erect at the head of a long stairway that swept down towards Throstle was also suddenly bathed in full illumination. The wizard stood transfixed as a shock wave of recognition washed over him. His eyes had last looked upon the figure which now stood aloft on the high platform, in the Canvas City, when Throstle had attended the Great Council of the Wizards. Only then the figure had been reclining with full funeral honours upon a silken catafalque; his dead body, imperious and serene, robed in his finest sorcerer's attire.

The spectre of Vrorst began to descend the glowing rampart of ice; the stairway slowly illuminating before its feet. Throstle made to back away from the approaching entity, barely able to believe his eyes, but the cords of enchantment fastened to his feet began to grow taut. The hair-like beams which he had snagged with his body pulled against his arms and trunk as the wizard tried harder to retreat. Too late he realised his carelessness with the light strands and their true nature, and like a fly in a web he began to struggle against his bonds. The majestic character drew ever nearer to the ensnared Throstle. Like a patient spider Vrorst's shade made sweeping gestures in the air, conjuring new gleaming threads which streaked through the shadows in bright lines and seized the wizard's flailing limbs, securing him with yet more unbreakable bonds. Soon Throstle's struggle was all but spent, his arms and legs splayed and held by a hundred shining cords. The wizard still held his staff tightly in his hand but was unable open his mouth to utter a single counter spell. He could only gaze in restrained terror at the ghostly image of his former foe whose eyes glared at him as blind orbs of blue fire. Then the wizard began to feel pinpricks of icy pain where the fiery strands touched him, as if tiny streams of freezing fire were slowly entering his body. The veins and blood vessels of his arms and legs screamed with the burning progress of the invading force. Cold claws scratched and stabbed at his brain sending jolting sparks across his already blurring vision. The figure of Vrorst began to grow hazy in his sight, its outstretched arms triumphantly conducting the rampant possession of Throstle's being.

Suddenly, a bolt of lightning, many branched like a searing tree of white fire, shrieked into the glowing chamber shearing most of the burning blue lines holding the tortured body of the wizard. Throstle crashed to the floor, a scream of agony bursting from his mouth with the shock of his deliverance. Strong hands dug under his armpits and dragged him backwards towards the small opening from whence he had entered. Tuatara stooped over the limp form of the wizard and screamed his name. Throstle's eyes were glazed and lifeless, there was no response to the witch's cries. A roar of anger drew Tuatara's attention back to the figure of Vrorst. With hands held aloft he summoned a great downfall of threads which flew towards the two enchanters in converging streaks of power. The witch immediately conjured a sphere of protection which enveloped the two of them causing the attacking strands to deflect or shrivel from its kaleidoscopic skin of elvish enchantment. More in an attempt to confuse than injure, Tuatara sent forth a surge of her own power at the shimmering image of her once liege lord. The fiery missile split the air with its speed and intensity, but for all its potency passed unhindered through the imperious apparition causing scarcely a ripple in its ethereal fabric. Vrorst began to laugh at the feeble efforts of his opponents, and then a voice issued forth from his ghostly shape, a voice of such measure that it seemed to fill the entire space of the great chamber.

'Fools!' it boomed. 'You cannot fight me! Not in this place! I have a bottomless well of the blackest power to draw upon! Now, I will have both your souls!'

The figure of Vrorst threw wide his arms and summoned all of the burning threads to himself. A thousand shining strands were drawn down from the walls and the ceiling, each of them pulsating their dazzling power into the diaphanous body of the sorcerer. Throstle was slowly released from his stupor as the enchantment left him to gather with the rest. The image of Vrorst began to glow with the building energy until he too became incandescent, burning with a light so intense that the witch and the wizard had to avert their eyes. Then an explosive roar assaulted the walls of the great ice cavern, and the dazzling figure of the Ice Sorcerer shattered into a mighty starburst of blue fire. As if born from this violent eruption of power, like an azure phoenix rising from the rolling flames, a brilliant dragon snaked into the air. Its whole being was a soaring inferno, a twisting, flickering column that eventually curled over into an arched neck and terrifying head; bright tongues of flame rising as horns and a dancing crest. Great sheets of blue fire swept out into the darkness on either side to form awesome, blazing wings; their infernal span seeming to fill the entire chamber. Aspects of the terrible creature were reflected in the myriad glassy surfaces of the walls and ceiling; an immense patchwork of glinting, flickering flames that made it seem as though the whole of the ice cavern was ablaze.

Tuatara gasped in horror, 'The Freezing Fire!' she cried to Throstle, who was now fully awake and sensible of the proceedings. It was a truly mesmeric sight, but the two cowering enchanters were reminded of their peril by a long plume of sapphire flame that streaked down at them from the dragon's fiery jaws. Tuatara once again conjured forth a sphere of protection against the deadly stream, but the strength of the blast was too much for her enchantment, and her elvish shield was blown away by the onslaught.

'Come on, Horcust,' Tuatara cried, hauling the wizard to his feet. 'We must run!'

She tried to drag Throstle towards the narrow opening which led back along the thin corridor to the outside, but the wizard stood unmoving, an attitude of stern resolution rooting him to the spot.

'It's no use,' he told the witch, with a calm determination that surprised her. 'We cannot outrun it.'

Throstle raised his wizard's staff and stared intently into the crystal held at its tip. He then quickly uttered an incantation in the old tongue of the Wizards. Tuatara was about to warn Throstle that the dragon's weaving form seemed to be preparing for another attack when the wizard cried aloud in a beseeching voice.

'Great Wizards!' he exclaimed. 'Lords of Light! If your eyes can look upon this scene! Grant us the means to destroy this spawn of the Dark Well! Let this humble rod be the channel of your power!'

A roar of outrage erupted from the fire dragon at the wizard's words, its bellowing response shaking the very fabric of the mighty hall, dislodging a volley of suspended ice spears which crashed on to the hard floor like thunder. Suddenly the staff crystal lit up like a golden star, bathing the two enchanters with a brilliance that felt warm like sunlight. The dragon lunged at Throstle and the witch, its burning jaws opening in readiness to belch forth a lethal torrent of flame. The wizard deftly tossed the staff into a javelin hold and hurled it with all his might at the giant's breast. With the furious hiss of white hot metal plunging into icy water, the gleaming projectile found its mark; the flying staff at once dissolving into golden flame as it punctured the swirling column of blue fire. The blazing profile of the dragon was suddenly veiled by a rising sheet of steam, the writhing white cloud pouring from the wound where the staff had entered. The monster swayed and squirmed as if trying to extract the source of its agony, its head blasting forth aimless jets of flame in torment; and then with a blinding flash its fiery form suddenly exploded into its frozen surroundings; the sculpted surfaces of the mighty hall trembling with the sudden charge of furious energy. For a few moments the walls and columns seemed to burn with an internal fire, the ice structures cracking and screaming with the strain of containing such a wild power. Tuatara regarded the structure above them with alarm; this was an ancient place, with the weight of centuries to bear, she had no reason to believe that it was immune to injury. The harsh sounds eventually died out until only a fading chain of echoes was left to remember them. Then all was quiet; and the great dimensions of the throne chamber slowly surrendered to the darkness.

'Did we destroy it?' Throstle cried aloud.

Tuatara's insistent grip was on his arm. 'Let's wonder about that at a safer distance,' she answered. 'If the power has been broken then this whole structure might fall. I don't intend to celebrate our victory beneath a tomb of ice! Come on!'

The witch pulled the preoccupied wizard towards the small archway and bundled him through. The rumble of destruction that Tuatara had

feared began to build around them, the narrow walls of the passage throbbing with the shock waves of ruin. Gracewing and Starblade had ventured into the long avenue that led to the main portal and were waiting for their respective enchanters as they flew from the snarling entrance. The witch and the wizard leapt on to their dragonsteeds and the determined beasts launched themselves into almost vertical flight to escape the enclosed space; tall columns of ice toppling all around as they thrust themselves aloft.

Eventually they found a friendly wind that lifted them out of danger and carried them to the southern lip of the great divide. The pale wings of the dragons glowed with moonlight, the sky above no longer obscured with a blanket of cloud. The icy tendrils of dark enchantment had vanished from the darkness, and Throstle and Tuatara were able to stand and observe the disintegration of the ice palace unmolested by evil power. They saw with a jolt of disquiet that the mighty spire no longer stood; it had crashed into the long space between the two arms of the fortress, that was to have been their path of escape had the dragons remained at the edge of the north cliff as they were told. The two enchanters found themselves offering thanks for their dragons' disobedience, an act which had certainly saved both their lives. By the time the chasm became quiet again much of Vrorst's final refuge had been levelled; the moon's gentle illumination revealing a desolate scene.

Throstle sighed with exhaustion.

'I......... should thank you,' he said awkwardly.

The sorceress smiled at him.

'There's no need.'

'Is it finally over, do you think? the wizard asked wearily.

Tuatara could not help a wry chuckle.

'That's the trouble with you wizards,' she told him. 'You insist on everything left neat and tidy. Concluded and complete!' Tuatara pulled the fur turban from her head and let the sharp, night breeze rifle through her long, black mane. 'Thankfully we witches are more philosophical,' she added. 'We accept that there must always be good and evil. They are two faces of the same coin. One cannot exist without the other.'

'Then was tonight's effort all in vain, Tuatara?'

The witch placed a hand on the wizard's shoulder.

'We did much good tonight, my friend,' she told him. 'But more than that we cannot claim! The prowess of the Three Wizards can never again be threatened now that the Winter Orb is destroyed. If the dark force that dwells in that place ever succeeds in sending itself again into the world ....we will have had time enough to be ready.'

Throstle searched into eyes that shone deep violet in the moon's glow, set like precious gems against the sorceress's snowy-pale skin.

'As long as we use that time wisely,' the wizard warned.

Tuatara nodded. 'We will.'

'For all our sakes,' Throstle said gravely. 'I pray you are right!'

The two enchanters turned from the chasm and made for the

welcoming glow of the campfire, and the friends old and new that awaited them there.

Epilogue

The powerful season of Winter had held Enchantica in a stranglehold for many years, but with the destruction of the Orb, its iron grip was finally broken. The vast, endless deserts of snow and ice slowly changed to rolling plains of green. Bright new shoots pushed their way through the melting crust of snow to herald the coming of a new Spring. The trees burst forth with fresh verdant coats, having held the precious jewel of life safe within them against the cruel reign of the dark season.

The Three Wizards commissioned the Lake People to find a new block of crystal from which their new Fire Orbs could be made. Fantazar, Orolan and Waxifrade then asked Tuatara, or Shoshonia as she now was, if she would sit in the fourth chair of their circle, and become the Lady of Winter.

The Wizards also requested from the Lake People a new staff for Horcust Rothgilian, Dragonmaster of Eyesand. In addition to his other titles, Horcust was named Custodian of Dragongorge; a title which greatly pleased Craagnagar, 'Old as Mountains', for this appointment meant that the dragon-loving High Wizard would oversee all the activities of men and wizards that took place in or around the kingdom of the great gorge.

Hexerne visited the elf kingdom with her mother, and despite an offer of marriage from Silfaladil, decided to leave the Northern Forest and go to Eddilee, where she would train to become a high enchanter like the Lady Shoshonia. After many years of hard study in the Vale of the Wizards, Hexerne eventually rose to the lofty position her mother had once occupied: High Witch of Winter. Ethva also did well under the watchful eye of her illustrious friend and mentor, finally succeeding in becoming a High Witch of Summer, under Vijian. Two of her contemporaries, Peermain and Ressina, followed her to high office, becoming High Witches of Spring and Autumn respectively, under the protection and guidance of Bruntian and Quillion.

With the season of Winter finally freed from the slavery of the dark power that Vrorst had embraced, the days following the demise of Autumn no longer struck fear into the hearts of the Commonlanders. The snows still fell, and the frosts still came; but the evil rampages of the fell creatures that had once accompanied the advent of Winter were not tolerated by the new power in the Throne Citadel.

Massazauga was removed by the Three Guardians from his place of guard at the mouth of the crystal mines, and the dwarfs were once again allowed to perform their age old tasks as miners. Dragonskeep was rebuilt to its former glory as a place for sorting and despatching the power crystals. The Three Wizards were eventually persuaded not to seek a home in the second

Well of Hope beneath the Marble Fortress, removed from the people of Enchantica, but to build the Throne Citadel anew, and the ancient practice of the Wizards marching from their secret kingdoms to take possession of the high tower began again. This time with Tuatara leading the march of Winter down from her new ice palace in Vrorst's old realm.

The great battle between the seven headed dragon and the Three Guardians is not told of in this tale; neither is the finding of Trea's lost family of silver terragons, and their eventual migration to the safe and plentiful kingdom of the banfs. A journey led by the incomparable Rattajack; whom the silver terragons, including Trea, looked upon as a veritable hero.

The conquest of the fruit forests is also not described here; when the valiant windsprites fought to win back their ancient realm from the dreaded Destroying Angels. Jonquil kept faith with his promise to Judruff, to join with his winged friends in their struggle against their supernatural foe. It was a sad day, however, when the time came for the banf to leave the comfort and safety of Dragonskeep to fly west with the falcons. His greatest heartache was having to leave Meadolarne behind, for although she had expressed a wish to accompany him on any further adventures he might have, being without wings, she could not go with him.

On a night two weeks before the windsprites departure, Halmarand held a great feast in their honour. The Lord Hoolock was special guest at the celebrations, and he brought the brave army of fliers the warmest salutations and best wishes for their venture from Waxifrade, Lord of Autumn; the Wizard who had always held the forests of Enchantica and those who dwelled in them dearest to his heart. Jonquil was curious to see Meadolarne receiving special attention from the High Wizard of Autumn and his attendants during the feast; and after wishing Jonquil goodnight, saw her leave the celebrations in the company of Fossfex, the Autumn fairy. The same cheerful sprite who had come to the aid of the windsprites all those years before when they needed the means to escape from their arboreal homes.

Jonquil did not lay eyes on the banfina again until the evening when he and his fellow fliers were to leave for the distant forests. For two weeks Meadolarne had refused to see him or speak to him. Jonquil had been heartbroken by her behaviour, and took little comfort from the solicitous commiseration of his friends.

As the fiery crucible of the sunset emptied on to the Western skyline, Jonquil made ready with his confederates to fly to the Fruit Forests. Meadolarne was nowhere to be seen, and the banf wondered if his banfina was still too upset with him to say farewell. Judruff called the falcon warriors to attention and led them up on to the strong breezes that were to carry them over the high wall of mountains that stood between them and their ancient home. Jonquil watched the long trail of winged figures lifting into the sky and knew that he could not wait long before he too would have to take to wing. Then a bustle of excitement drew the banf's attention away from the sky. A group of Autumnians were approaching, the fairy Fossfex at their head. They were all smiling furtively and giggling with each other as they neared him. Jonquil was most perplexed by the sudden appearance of this merry party until the crowd parted to reveal the smiling figure of the banfina standing within them. Meadolarne stepped forward from the crowd, and as she did so two beautiful wings swept out either side of her to reveal a breathtaking span of pale feathers.

Jonquil was at first dumbfounded, and then overjoyed. He hugged the banfina tightly and took a long look at her new acquisitions. Then he understood why she would not allow him to see her during the two weeks following her meeting with Fossfex. After taking the windsprite potion, Meadolarne had been using the two weeks to learn how to fly; and of course Jonquil would only have needed to look upon her to learn of her secret, and spoil his surprise.

Jonquil clasped Meadolarne's hand in his and they turned to face the dying glory of the sunset. As the last glowing spears pierced the scattered clouds of bronze, the two winged banfs leapt into the air together, and floated away towards the dazzling crust of gold blazing in the West.

A lone, dishevelled figure in a tattered cloak shuffled its way towards the edge of the mighty ice chasm. It was clearly exhausted, every step a great effort; and when it finally stopped to gaze across to what had once been the glory of Vrorst's secret haven, the figure fell to its knees and wept.

Mezereon lifted his head again and regarded dolefully the ruin of the ancient frozen palace. Before him a crazed, jagged stump was all that was left of the narrow bridge by which he had hoped to cross the great ravine.

A faint moaning sound from some distance behind him caused him to turn around. His dewy eyes fell upon another lone figure, crossing the deep shelf towards him. The figure staggered and stumbled with the effort of walking. He was barely half way from the gap in the cliff wall and looked as though he might not get much further. Even from this distance Mezereon could recognise the other, and he was in no mood to be charitable to lame dogs.

The black stain left upon the ground by the fire that Throstle's party had lit only two nights before, caught the Dark Sorcerer's eye, and for a brief moment he thought of Hexerne: his daughter. Now freed from the slavery of the Orb; free to forget him. Mezereon turned away from the long dead fire, and looked down into the yawning jaws of the chasm. He wondered how long it would take for a falling body to reach the bottom; if indeed it had one.

The sound of dragging feet and laboured breathing drew nearer, and Mezereon heard his name gasped aloud by a strangled voice. Juvula struggled up to him and finally crumpled to the ground. The Dark Sorcerer looked down at the pathetic remains of the Mage of Anconeus, and then gave an ironic laugh.

'Well, you're here, Juvula,' he sneered. 'What of your great destiny now?'

The minor wizard lifted his eyes to Mezereon and then looked across to the devastation of the North Spire. His face retained its blank, weary expression. Juvula simply did not have the strength for histrionics.

'What happened?' he rasped.

Mezereon kicked an ice fragment into the void.

'The Orb was broken,' he said.

A gasp came from Juvula.

'It was dropped from the bridge,' the Dark Sorcerer concluded.

Juvula struggled to his feet, his hand clamped tightly against his shoulder, and for the first time Mezereon noticed the deep red patch that coloured his robe. The minor wizard saw him looking, and gazed down himself at the bloody stain.

'Treachery!' he growled.

Mezereon nodded. 'Treachery!' he echoed. 'As slaves of the Orb what else should we expect?'

Juvula stared accusingly at the broken pile that was the former ice palace, his body trembling with an angry disbelief.

'The dreams!' he gasped. 'They were so real! The pictures! I believed! I believed!'

'I also had the dreams,' Mezereon told him. 'The vivid images; and for a lot longer than you!'

Juvula gave the Dark Sorcerer a long look of entreaty, his face racked with doubt and despair. 'What becomes of us now?' he said at last.

Mezereon turned to gaze once again into the vast drop of the chasm. The Pretender followed his eyes and immediately guessed the sorcerer's dark thoughts. Juvula shuffled forward until he was standing side by side with Mezereon. They looked together into the misty depths, the plunging cliffs drawing them closer to the edge. At last Mezereon looked into the fearful expression of the minor wizard, and smiled wryly at him.

'Well,' he said to Juvula, 'we have followed the Orb this far ....'

The minor sorcerer swallowed hard, and regarded the river of mist that floated in the great void below him. With one last wounded look at the ruined ice fortress, he turned back to the other wizard. When he spoke his voice was spiked with apprehension.

'Will you take my hand?' he said at last to Mezereon, offering his bloody palm to the Dark Sorcerer.

Mezereon watched him silently for a moment, and then slowly reached out to clasp the hand of the other. With a strong grip they edged forward until they could see the sheer face of the cliff beneath their feet falling away into oblivion.

Suddenly there was a great disturbance in the blanket of mist that filled the chasm, and the mighty sweep of a vast wingspan climbed out of the river of cloud. The two wizards cried out in surprise as a pale mountain of leathery wing and scale rose before them. Before the wizards had time to retreat, Grawlfang seized them both in his mighty claws and swept up and across the chasm to land on the far side of the divide, and the rubble of the North Spire.

The two sorcerers were still in shock when the Winter Guardian released them from his grasp, and they stared up dumbfounded at the magnificent spectacle of the massive dragon towering over them. Grawlfang regarded them both with a haughty air, his fiery orbs framed by the wide spread of his spiny collar. With a delicate step quite incongruous with such a huge body, the dragon stepped over Mezereon and Juvula and strode along the debris strewn corridor that led to the small portal. The hanging spears that had once graced the archway, had been mostly smashed by the falling rubble. The entrance itself was completely buried.

The two wizards obediently followed after the dragon, both of them still dazed and bewildered by their experience. Grawlfang clawed a passage through the layers of ruin for his two charges, and then heaved the pile of shattered pillars aside to reveal the dark doorway.

Without hesitation Mezereon and Juvula entered the portal, their movements stiff and trance-like, as if every last vestige of their will had been drained from them. Grawlfang watched them enter and then pushed the broken barricade back into place behind them. The great dragon then turned and strode back to the chasm.

Before returning to his secret den beneath the mighty river of mist, the Winter Guardian filled his great lungs with air and breathed his terrible flame over the ruined face of the frozen cliff. When he had finished, a new veneer of ice concealed the whereabouts of the former palace of his old master. Then Grawlfang arched his monstrous form and dived into the swirling mist, to await the day when his new master would call upon him to carry him forth into the world.

They had no light to guide them but somehow the two sorcerers found their way to the great hall in the heart of the frozen palace. The floor surrounding the high platform was littered with the remains of icicles dislodged from above by the recent trauma, but the main body of the chamber was mostly intact.

When the eyes of the two wizards finally came to rest upon the throne standing atop the long flight of translucent stairs, they suddenly felt a surge of energy, and an intense desire to claim it for themselves. As one they started for the stairs, jostling with each other to be the first up the frozen steps. The struggle continued as they climbed upwards, both of them holding on to the other trying to pull him back. Eventually they rose to the last step and tumbled over it, both falling heavily at the foot of the great seat of ice. Mezereon and Juvula were a frenzied tangle of arms and legs. The minor sorcerer ignored the pain that tore through him from the wound in his shoulder. The desire to keep Mezereon from climbing on to the throne ahead of him overpowered every other sensation.

In their furious conflict the two wizards failed to see a tide of light shards rising through the crystalline structure of the platform below them. Brilliant threads of azure creeping upwards along the lines and edges of the pyramidal form towards the two figures locked in desperate stalemate at the high summit.

Vrorst had built the triangulate tower to act as a giant crystal, channelling the power of the dark well below into the high throne. From there the Ice Lord would direct the dark energy up into the great needle of ice and out upon the world.

Suddenly the two grim combatants were distracted from their battle by a bright plume of sapphire flame that swirled and danced upon the seat of the ice throne, which now blazed with a furnace of blue light. The Freezing Fire burned in the eyes of the two wizards, who looked upon it in fear and wonder. Then a thin stream of flame poured down from the main blaze and started along the floor of the platform towards the two prone bodies. Mezereon and Juvula tried to disentangled themselves but found that their limbs would not respond. All they could do was lie together in a deadly embrace watching the trickle of flame creep nearer. No sooner had the leading tongue of flame licked against the first of the wizards than the tall fiery plume on the throne swept along the glowing trail and engulfed the entwined bodies.

The screams of the wizards rose with the roar of the inferno as their whole beings were consumed by the hungry blaze. Their combined forms were slowly obliterated by a brilliant shroud of fire, rising from the platform as a flickering wall of flames. After a while the screams of the wizards could be heard no more, and the blazing cocoon rose from the floor until it stood as a vertical pillar of fire. Within the blazing torch there were the glowing outlines of a figure, which began to move inside its sheath of flame towards the shining contours of the ice throne. The figure sat down upon the mighty seat and gradually the fire subsided. As the last flickering tongue shrank back into the body of the throne, a commanding beam of silver shone down from above and bathed the seated figure in a flood of light.

He was dressed in simple robes of pristine white, and upon his head he bore a crown of ice rising to an unadorned wizard's peak. His face looked familiar, and at the same time wholly new and unknown. His black beard and eyebrows might have belonged to any of those who had died in pursuit of the power of the Orb. The new being's hand found the empty depression in the arm of the throne, and knew what his first task was to be. Then he sat back against the great fan of ice spears and a slow smile grew on his lips; and deep in the heart of his black eyes danced tiny tongues of blue flame.

The adventure concludes..............................?

244

Roof of the W
The Elf Domain of The Great Forest
Zirobok
Anconeus
Glostomorg
Vrorst's Old Realm
Eddilee
The Vale of the Wizards
Jacquarondi
Marble Fortress
Gates of Frozen Kingdo
Dragonskeep
The Green Sky Forest